MEDUSA
A LOVE STORY

SASHA SUMMERS

Medusa, A Love Story
Sasha Summers

Copyright
Sasha Summers

Cover Art
Najla Qamber Designs

Interior Layout
Author's HQ

Editor
Candice U. Lindstrom/Sasha Summers

Re-release – Sasha Summers – August 2015

For the Believers in
Magic and Romance

Prologue

Perseus' heart pounded. Sweat ran down his forehead and into his eyes, but he ignored it. His hold tightened on the sword Zeus had given him as he pressed himself against the uneven outer stones of the temple ruins.

He peered inside cautiously, his eyes trained to the ground, searching for shadows – any trace of movement. He took a deep breath, readying himself. He was alone on his quest, but he had the Gods' favor. With their gifts of weaponry, surely he would prevail.

Time was his enemy, second only to the monster he'd come to kill.

He placed Hades' helmet upon his head, rendering him invisible to his foe. He raised the shield, a gift from Athena, and stepped inside the crumbling temple. A candle burned within, its flames casting shadows that jumped and fell.

It was silent...

A steady tapping, rhythmic upon the broken flagstones beneath his feet, pricked the hair along his neck. His heart accelerated, and he braced himself before turning a wary eye towards the sound's source.

It was the blood of the Gorgon's guard dripping from his sword, nothing more. He closed his eyes and tried to calm his nerves, swiping the sword along his cloak to cease the telling sound.

Steady, Perseus.

He must keep his wits about him. He must defeat the monster;

the fate of the woman he loved, his lady mother and all of Seriphos were in his hands. He could not fail.

He knew to be careful.

He knew what he must do.

And, just as important, he knew what he must not do.

To look upon Medusa was fatal. Not an easy end, but a painful transformation from life to death. One look from her serpent locks hardened the body, the blood, the skin, into brittle grey stone. What remained was but an effigy of the human form, a pathetic tribute seen only by the creature in her dim lair.

There was a rumor, one he would test this day, that Medusa's death would reverse this spell. Once she was dead, the horrid curse would be broken, and those poor souls trapped and punished by the witch set free. If...no, *when* he succeeded, he would have freed these people too, enabling them to leave this bleak place and return to their homes.

He moved stealthily, willing his steps to be silent. He needed the advantage if he was to cut off Medusa's head – a weapon, even after her death. A weapon he would use to turn the beast, Cetus, to stone, and free his captured love, Andromeda.

His toe dislodged a stone, sending it across the floor with a resounding racket.

"Perseus? Are you Perseus, then?" A woman's voice, lilting and melodic, echoed from within. "Are you the boy come to set me free?"

Perseus was startled. How did she know of him? Or of his quest?

He spoke boldly, "I am."

She laughed, a bittersweet sound. "What is it you want with my head? Gold? Power? Or do you wish to be a hero, celebrated by the Gods?"

"No." He stumbled, his agitation making him clumsy. The floor beneath his feet was covered in rubble and rocks. It was hard to navigate while keeping his back flat against the wall.

His hand clenched his sword. He was only slightly appeased by his invisibility – for Medusa was nowhere to be seen either.

"No?" She laughed again. "You've made me curious now, brave Perseus. What brings you to hunt such a dangerous trophy?"

"Something you know nothing of, Gorgon. I come in the name

of love. For the love of my lady." His voice rang out, echoing off the walls.

There was silence. No breath, no movement. Even the flickering candles seemed to still and wait.

He swallowed down the bile that threatened to choke him, fighting the urge to run – to hide. His very breath might expose him as her target.

"Love?" Her voice broke, surprising him. "Well, then, Perseus, you must heed my directions if you are to take my head without turning yourself into stone. I will have you succeed on your quest... for love." He'd never heard such anguish.

Perseus' heart pounded. What trick was this?

"And, if the Gods are finally done with me, I might at last find peace in Tartarus...or Hades before this day is through." She laughed sadly, then said, "Listen closely, boy."

Chapter One

One Year Earlier...

"**A**gain." Ariston smiled, encouraging his massive opponent.

But mighty Bion swayed where he stood. His broad chest rose and fell raggedly. He shook his head, visibly struggling to maintain his balance.

Ariston sighed. He felt no pity, only impatience. Each day the Persians sailed closer to the mainland. Each day he pushed these men, heedless of their fatigue. Their lives depended upon it.

These men were painters, scholars, philosophers, tradesmen, and servants, yes, but they were Greek. And Greece needed them now.

No. Greece needs skilled soldiers to defend her shores. But she must make do with these.

The men surrounding him offered little to be intimidated by, no matter how hard they drilled or practiced. He would pray to Athena and Ares. If the Gods heard his prayers, these men's bodies would become as fierce as the hearts in their chests. And then the Persians would know what fear was.

Ariston straightened his shoulders, smiled smugly at his exhausted sparring partner, and swung his sword once in challenge. Bion took the bait, surging forward on clumsy feet. His sword arm, as thick as Ariston's thigh, cleaved the air with a surprising whistle.

Ariston dodged the blade, pivoting on the ball of his foot to come behind Bion. He placed his foot at the base of the man's spine and shoved. Bion pitched forward, but caught himself.

"Good," Ariston called out. He narrowed his gaze, watching as Bion rallied.

The giant spun, his sword solid as it met Ariston's. Their blades slid, the metallic grate rivaling the sound of the waves pounding the beach before them.

Ariston moved suddenly, planting his foot in the larger man's chest and knocking him back. "Be mindful of more than your opponent's weapon."

Bion snarled, launching himself forward. Ariston stood his ground, side-stepping at the last moment and bringing his elbow forcefully into Bion's side. As his opponent groaned in pain and frustration, Ariston caught sight of the sun.

It was near sunset... A surge of energy rushed through him – anticipation tightened his chest.

But he lost sight of Bion. He did not realize he was beaten until he was sailing through the air to land solidly on his back.

A chorus of cheers went up, and he smiled in spite of his defeat. Bion held his arms high in victory, surrounded by those who'd watched the match. All shared in their comrade's triumph, for few had knocked a warrior of Ariston's skill from his feet.

"The savior of Laurium falls!" Someone cheered.

"He bears scars from Aeginian spears and Persian arrows, where is your mark, Bion?" another asked, laughing.

"Upon his pride," Bion answered with relish.

Ariston's smile grew as the men continued to congratulate Bion and clap his broad back.

It was good. If these men thought they might defeat him – a proven warrior, known and feared – they might believe they stood a chance against the Persians. And if they believed they might defeat their enemy, it might be so.

Ariston quickly waved a young attendant forward, shaking the sand from his hair as he did so. He plunged his hands into the basin the boy offered, splashing water on his face and chest. Once clean, he hurriedly laced his greaves onto his wrists and clasped his thick cloak about his shoulders. Only after he'd readied himself for the temple and collected his shield and spear did he call out, "Tomorrow

I won't go so easy on you, Bion."

Bion laughed. "Then I'd do well to enjoy the spoils of my victory tonight."

Ariston nodded, placed his helmet on his head, and sprinted from the hoplites' encampment towards the Acropolis. Each step took him farther from the art of war and closer to his duty to the Goddess. He welcomed the change, the quiet tranquility.

While his blood hungered for the thrill of the fight, his time at the Temple of Athena Polias had stirred him as nothing else...

Once he stood on the steps of the temple, he removed his helmet and turned his face towards the retreating rays of the evening sun. His eyes closed as a cool breeze lifted the cloak from his shoulders. It promised to be a fine evening and a chill night.

His gaze swept the horizon, studying the temple paths and making note of any activity in the courtyard.

All was quiet.

He heard her arranging the day's offerings within the temple. He turned, eyes narrowing as he searched the dim temple interior. Even in the flickering candlelight, she seemed to glide effortlessly.

She would leave with the sun, they both would. Duty required he escort her home. It was duty that brought him to Athens – to his country, his family, and his Goddess. And it was duty that required him to be graced by her loveliness each day.

Lovely or no, it mattered not. To think on her or grow distracted by her presence was foolish. He was not a foolish man.

He took a deep breath of the bracing air, clearing his head.

War would soon find them. The Persians' marauding and skirmishes left no room for doubt. And when it came, his time here would be over. These sunsets, this sacred place, the company he kept, would be but a memory. Memories he would hold dear.

He gazed upon the Temple of Athena with appreciation. In all of Greece, in all of his travels, he knew the Goddess of Wisdom must find this shrine the most pleasing. It perched almost precariously at the edge of the rock, providing a key defensive observation point for the Goddess and her city.

His eyes wandered again, sweeping the white-capped waves of the Aegean far beyond before returning to the etched stones of the temple frieze.

A stone Gorgon mask, carved into one of the pillars, startled him from his inspection. It never failed to disconcert him, giving rise to a mix of fear and disgust.

Truly such a warning would be heeded by even the most wicked of villains.

All who gazed upon the masks knew that this place and those here serving Athena were to be respected and treated with reverence. The Goddess Athena would tolerate nothing less.

Ariston paced, the dipping sun heightening his anticipation. Sunset had always been his favorite time of day. The last fortnight had made it even dearer to him. In that time, he'd been appointed guard to the Goddess Athena's priestess.

To serve Athena so directly was indeed an honor, but leaving his men without instruction had rankled him greatly. He knew he'd be better used schooling those who knew nothing about sword and doru. Being charged with the priestess' daily safety, her wellbeing, and her escort to and from Athena's temple had felt more an inconvenience than an honor.

But the council and statesman of Greece's capital had learned of a Persian plot. Their foe sought to capture or injure a servant from Athena's sacred temple. Such an act would give rise to outrage and fury prompting Athens to retaliate rashly – giving their enemy the advantage.

Greece could not afford such a misstep. The council's plan provided a simple but effective solution – Ariston. If the council had not demanded *he* protect the Goddess' priestess, he would have gladly deferred the post to another.

Then he had met her.

He walked back and forth, his spear and shield held rigidly. His eyes strayed to the interior of the temple. He tensed. It was dark, no candle flickered. Why was the lamp out? Where had she gone?

Her voice spilled over him with a mocking lilt. "I've slipped by you, soldier. Your thoughts must weigh heavily upon you."

Ariston's breath escaped tightly. All was well. He inclined his head. "My lady."

"Lady, I am, and mistress to those who serve me. But *your* lady?" she asked softly. "I belong to another, as you well know."

Ariston raised his eyes to her curiously, searching out her

meaning. She loved to speak in riddles.

Even with her features obscured by the gauzy white veils of her station, he could make out the curve of her smile. Above the brightly embroidered hem of her veils, eyes as vibrant as the cerulean sea watched him.

"Athena," she said, a hint of laughter in her voice. "I am *her* lady."

He inclined his head to acknowledge her words, unable to speak. He clenched his jaw, damning his response to this slip of a girl. Yet he could not tear his gaze from hers.

She blinked, her smooth brow furrowing before she turned away abruptly.

Had she sensed his...distraction? If his cursed newfound awareness was disconcerting to him, it would hardly reassure the one he was sworn to protect.

She is the priestess for your Goddess Athena, he reminded himself sternly.

The evening wind stirred the dust at their feet. Long skeins of her brilliant honey hair escaped her veils, floating about her and then falling against her hips as the breeze ebbed. Ariston's self-admonishments ceased as his eyes lit upon those tresses. How those creamy locks filled his dreams. It would not do to wonder how her hair might feel, sliding between his fingers or wrapped about him...

His hands clenched as he reprimanded himself. Where was his discipline? His self-control? He was not one to succumb to tenderness.

He must not falter now.

He had been warned. It was not only the Persians who threatened Athena's priestess. Her last guard had become so besotted with the young priestess that he'd planned to steal her from the temple and run, to hide from the Gods. Luckily, the plot had been discovered. The guard served Athena's temple on Crete at Gortys now, a lowly servant and eunuch.

No. He drew himself straight, his resolve strengthening. If she unwittingly bewitched her guards, he would not join them. He would enjoy the pleasure of her company, as his duties might require. But brooding over anything else was...dangerous.

With spirits high, she'd snuck out of the temple to tease him, emboldened by the brisk night air and fading sunlight. But his face, grave as he'd searched the empty temple, had filled her with shame.

As he'd turned his gaze towards her, her chest grew heavy, pressing the air from her lungs. His eyes were an almost-constant warmth upon her, steady and inscrutable. And while the presence of his hooded grey eyes afforded her much comfort, they'd begun to stir something within her.

He has such lovely eyes. She felt her cheeks grow hot and was happy for the veils.

She was startled by the way his eyes lingered upon her hair now. She wondered over the sudden tensing of his jaw, the way he pressed his eyes closed abruptly – almost angrily. He drew a deep breath, then glanced upon her. In his unguarded gaze she saw a flicker of...

But he looked away, breaking the spell that held her.

She took a hasty step back and turned to the city below. What were these strange sensations that coursed through her? Such an unfamiliar warmth and pleasure...

Her heart seemed to rise into her throat as she spoke breathlessly. "Have you finished your patrol, soldier? For my duties to the Goddess are done this day." She tried to resume her teasing tone, tried to ignore the tangle of emotions he stirred within her. "But I will wait, if you've need of more pacing."

Though she knew his duties did not include suffering her jests, she could not resist. It was no easy feat, drawing a smile from her guard. In fact, she'd found herself thinking of ways to do so the last few days. Eliciting his reluctant grin brought a satisfactory end to her day.

If he were indeed struggling with something, as she suspected, surely she should try to cheer him.

When she did not poke or tease at him, the silence hung heavily – the air seemed to thin and constrict. She did not know what it was, this pull between them, but she fought it, for both their sakes.

His eyes fell from hers, a small grin forming as he answered, "No, mistress. I only wait for you."

His smile caused warmth to spread within her.

Athena would not approve.

13

Her smile, her laughter, her body, all of her, belonged to Athena. She would be wise to remember that.

He waited for her, for the slight nod of her head, before turning to lead her on the long descent home.

She sighed, falling silent as they set off.

She'd had many guards while serving the Goddess, though she admitted she'd paid them little notice. Something about *this* man captured her interest. She spent far too much time lingering on his mood, the curve of his smile, his rugged jaw and welcoming grey eyes.

She followed several steps behind him, turning her attention – forcefully – to the journey before them.

The stone of the Acropolis dropped sharply away, jutting from the hillside as if Hades himself had thrust the peak from the Underworld – or so she thought. Athena believed that her priestesses should avoid the main road to the temple, keeping her servants from those with less restrained dispositions. Her priestesses and their protectors had to scale this slippery shale and sand path, barely fit for goats and ever precarious to those who used it.

But the Goddess' wisdom had led her to select the Acropolis for her temple. With its clean air and soothing sounds, one might watch over the city free from its noise and drudgery. No enemy could invade, by land or sea, without being immediately detected.

She admired the Goddess for such foresight, even if the climb was taxing. Her path was all the more unsteady as she was under layers of linen and wool.

Her guard turned back, ever watchful as she scaled down a steep drop. He did not meet her gaze, but stood waiting. He was gravely distracted, his displeasure evident by the furrow of his brow and the slight flair of his nostrils.

She could not bear it. She drew in a breath and asked, "Is Athens your home?"

"No, lady. My home is far across the sea on the shore of Rhodes."

"But that is leagues from Athens." She paused, surprised by his answer. "You traveled here for the Goddess?"

The path interrupted their conversation. He jumped down the sudden drop, sliding. Once steady, he nodded, a slight smile on his handsome face.

"Olympus will reward such fealty." She regarded him, momentarily distracted by the glint in his grey eyes. "You are loyal to Athena."

"I am." His voice sounded strained, she noted, but his smile did not falter.

He offered his arm, the leather greaves allowing such an action. He could never touch her, her skin must remain pure. But she might use his arm, covered, to help her scale such a sheer step.

She watched the muscles of his neck and shoulder flex as he offered her his arm and swallowed. Her heart thumped against her chest, further disconcerting her.

He glanced at her, waiting.

She cleared her throat and shook her head before leaping to the ground beside him. She met his wide eyes, a breathless laugh escaping her.

Her laughter stirs my blood. He drew a steadying breath.

Her eyes gazed into his, threatening his fragile control.

"I've heard of Rhodes' fair waters." Her curious blue gaze mesmerized him.

I am a cursed fool.

His voice was gruff, "I've never seen a lovelier shore."

"What a sadness." She sounded wistful. "To be so far from such beauty must leave an ache within."

He looked down at her, the corner of his mouth responding to her sympathy. "There are many beautiful things here, lady." *Though I suspect you are the loveliest by far.*

His breathing grew shallow as her gaze wandered to his mouth.

Deep lines formed between her brows and her cheeks colored, intriguing him.

"Lady?" What was she thinking?

She shook her head, turning to the city below. "I..." her words trailed off, and she drew a deep breath before continuing, "I've never been on the streets of Athens. Is it beautiful? My aunt and uncle tell me it's a place I must never go as a priestess."

"It has certain charms. But for you, I fear there would be too little beauty at too great a risk." He understood why Galenus would keep his niece from the city.

The rest of their journey led them away from Athens proper and towards the estate of her uncle. Their path cut across more gently rolling hills, broken only occasionally by a sudden rock outcrop. These hills were dotted with aromatic maquis bushes, poppies and cistus flowers, alive and in bloom. The cool evening breeze blew the scents about them, turning the evening fragrant.

He remained silent as they moved on, enjoying the sounds of the countryside. A black-headed bunting sang from its perch amongst prickly thistles. The bleating of a distant goat and the faint bark of a dog echoed from a neighboring hillside.

Galenus' home, their destination, lay before them. Only moments longer and they would arrive – she would no longer have need of him this night. Disappointment settled over him. He didn't like the feeling, or what it might imply.

She spoke suddenly. "In two days time I shall collect offerings for the Goddess, along the shore."

He nodded. "For the Festival of Anestheria?" Surely her uncle would expect her guard to escort the priestess and her companion, to ensure their safety. He ignored the anticipation he felt, saying, "I will accompany you."

She glanced at him, the corner of her eyes creased by a hidden smile. "I warn you now, soldier, on that day we depart before Selene's moon fades. I would greet the sun as it rises."

He nodded, pulling his gaze from hers. It should not please him so, to have more time with her.

In truth, such an added distraction should irk him. Readying his men for battle was far more valuable in a time such as this, surely.

And yet, he was not displeased.

"Anestheria is always an important time in the temple. More so this year, I think, as our enemies draw close. Athena's people need to be reminded of her protection and wisdom, and give thanks for her patronage. My offerings are small things, I know, but such ceremony provides encouragement to her city and its people." She spoke with care. "It is no great thing when compared to your soldier's work, but it is all I can give."

She is a wise priestess for the Goddess of Wisdom.

"You serve Athena well," he said.

A gust of wind tossed his cloak about him and caught in the dome of his round aspis, lifting the shield. He shifted easily, tightening his grip upon both shield and spear, and turned to find her staring at him with wide eyes. She swallowed, blinked rapidly, and set off along the path with renewed purpose.

They fell quiet as they passed through the gate.

When she spoke, he had to strain to hear her. "When I was a little girl, Uncle Galenus housed some of Athena's soldiers for a short time. We listened to stories about the fearsome Ekdromoi and the stalwart hoplites – of their courage and prowess. To the amusement of the soldiers and my uncle, my companion Elpis and I tried to heft a shield between us. I remember trembling under its weight. I feared the soldiers were descendants of the Giants. How else could they possess such strength?"

"They were but soldiers, mistress," he murmured. "A soldier's weapon is but an extension of his body. It must be, for him to survive."

Did his strength frighten her?

The Goddess had admired his form. She'd compared him to the beauty of her Acropolis, rugged and strong. When the Goddess had asked him to serve her with his aspis and spear, he'd been both proud and honored.

But Athena's priestess did not find his form pleasing, or so it seemed.

"I will bring my nets and fish for offerings for the Goddess," he offered gently. "If it pleases you?"

She nodded, peering at him from beneath the dark fringe of her lashes. "It will please the Goddess," she said softly.

"Goodnight then, my lady...mistress." He inclined his head. They'd reached their meeting place, three fig trees before Galenus' house.

This spot brought some of his brightest mornings and longest nights, sentiments the Goddess would hardly hold with.

She sighed loudly, but sounded amused as she said, "You may call me by name, soldier. There is no rule against *that*."

Ariston swallowed, taking a deep breath. His voice sounded strained, "Goodnight then...Medusa."

Chapter Two

He said her name, softly.

Not mistress or priestess or niece or daughter, just her name.

True, she'd goaded him into it – but it did not diminish the pleasure she felt upon hearing him. The deep cadence of his voice awakened the strangest sensations.

What was this warmth that filled her belly? What fire licked her skin? Indeed, even breathing in the cool night air seemed troubling.

"Goodnight, soldier," she murmured, refusing to look at him. "Blessings to you."

She moved down the smooth stone path towards her chambers, knowing he would wait until she was safely inside before retiring. She took several slow breaths, easing the tightness in her chest. How could he stir such strange feelings? It would be wise not to examine her reaction too closely.

She glanced up to find Elpis, her companion, watching her from the arched window of her bedchamber. Thea, her beloved owl, regarded her with huge yellow eyes.

She lifted a hand, smiling in greeting. Elpis waved back, saying something to Thea.

Medusa ran up the path, into the house and down the open walkway to her chamber. As she swept into her room, she greeted them. "Good eve, Elpis."

Elpis smiled. "And to you, my mistress."

Thea called out, a sweetly beseeching coo she made for Medusa alone.

She went to the owl. "And to you as well, my dear little friend. Have you kept Elpis company while I was away?"

Thea fluffed up her chest as Medusa stroked her head affectionately, clicking softly in answer.

"Mistress," Elpis' worried tone drew Medusa's attention. "It pains me to dim your bright smile, but your uncle seeks an audience."

"Now? Surely he can wait for our evening meal?"

Elpis shook her head. "Your parents have sent a letter."

The pleasure of the evening vanished. Medusa pulled the veils from her head and laid them gently upon her mat, anxiety pressing upon her sharply.

There were times when wisdom and reason failed her. Her parents were often the cause of these failings. Why had the Gods made her *their* daughter?

Such thoughts are not fitting for Athena's Priestess.

She closed her eyes and prayed for patience and generosity.

Thea hooted, seeking her attention. Medusa cooed back, watching the animal's eyes narrow into pleased slits.

Oh to feel such contentment, such peace and love.

Love had never been peaceful, not for Medusa. In truth, she'd seen very little to indicate love existed. Duty was her fate. Duty did not waver. It was constant. And she was content with her station – most of the time.

Duty was undoubtedly the reason for her parents' correspondence, though what new duty they might demand of her was a mystery.

"How was this message delivered, Elpis?"

Elpis' voice was unsteady. "Your sisters await you."

Medusa drew in a deep breath. "Help me change, then. The sooner I appease them, the sooner we may put any unpleasantness behind us." She attempted cheerfulness as she added, "I do hope they will behave this time."

Her sisters excelled at mischief. She had fond memories of them from her early childhood, teasing and goading one another to make her laugh. She'd been a favored toy, each trying to outdo the other to gain her giggling attention.

Things were different now.

She sighed and pulled her long hair over her shoulder. Elpis removed the white wool tunic that swept the floor and covered every inch of her skin.

Medusa wore her robes with pride, for they marked her as Athena's chosen within the temple. Every stitch and symbol was in celebration of the Goddess of Wisdom. Finely embroidered lavender orchids and white asphodel celebrated Greece. Copper and gold thread owls and serpents were symbols of wisdom. Green, black and brown olives were woven throughout, honoring Athena's gift of olives to the Athenians.

Away from the temple she could wear the simple peplos worn by other women. Her slender arms were free of fabric and her feet bare. Her neck delighted in the kiss of the air, the caress of the sun's warmth on her exposed skin. It was a kind of freedom, simple yet luxurious. And freedom was something she rarely enjoyed under the watchful gaze of her uncle, or someone he judged worthy.

Uncle Galenus believed as Athena, that men were easily tempted. He looked upon Medusa as too great a temptation for any man. As a result, only eunuchs, or those too aged to cause alarm, worked inside the house. The small contingent of troops that resided on his grounds was there because Athena demanded it.

Aunt Xenia had argued that, as Athena's soldiers, these men were able to set aside their manly passions in service to their Goddess.

"They are men, wife. And as such, they can be tempted," Uncle Galenus had replied. "I tolerate their presence, at a distance, for it is Athena's will. But if these soldiers do not abide by the order of Athena they will be punished. I will see to it myself."

Uncle Galenus preferred castration over death. He believed the loss of a whole servant was a far greater punishment to a slave's master than losing a small part. It was a relief to Medusa that neither punishment had ever been carried out. At least, not that she knew of.

Elpis used large bronze disks to clasp the lightweight, creamy peplos at each of her shoulders, draping the extra fabric in a becoming fashion. Medusa laced the leather cuff over her forearm to protect her skin from Thea's talons. Once secure, she sat so Elpis could dress her hair.

"There is no other maid in all of Greece with hair as thick or as soft. And such a beautiful color, like rich honey." Elpis laced a coil of bronze thread through Medusa's braid. "You're too lovely to stay in the temple, mistress," Elpis sighed, standing back to admire her.

"You begin to sound like my parents." Medusa smiled at her companion. "It is enough, I think, to live in Athena's good graces. If I am lovely, then surely that is pleasing for the Goddess."

"Then Athena is greatly pleased, mistress."

"You are a sweet soul." Medusa hugged Elpis.

Thea cooed at Medusa's tone, her fine feathered chest reverberating with the sound.

"Come then, Thea." Medusa held her arm out, offering it as perch. "You can protect me this night."

Elpis' face was distraught. "How can you jest? Knowing who waits for you and, likely, what news they bring?"

"Fear not, Elpis. Let me hear their wishes so that I may return to the peace of my chamber. I'll no doubt have need of your compliments and comfort then."

"You are brave, mistress."

"Before the moon is high this will be but an unpleasant memory." She squeezed Elpis' arm, hoping to reassure them both. She smiled at her companion again and swept from her room and down the hall.

A knot of dread formed in the pit of her stomach, but she would not burden Elpis. Athena would chide her for succumbing to distress, yet Medusa could not dismiss the churning anxiety. Her father was a temperamental sort, impatient and hot-headed. Word from him meant change. Or grief.

Perhaps this time would be different? She prayed so.

She let her gaze roam Galenus' house, her home since childhood. Built about an interior courtyard, she thought the house well appointed. Arched windows lined the entire exterior wall, affording a view of her uncle's vast property. The full moon illuminated carefully tended fields and a gated herb garden. Beyond lay Xenia's bountiful olive grove. Years of deliberate devotion to the land and the Gods had made Galenus a man of substantial wealth. And yet, Galenus valued his home, his oikos, and his position in Athens' society above all.

Thea cackled, ruffling her wings.

"Go on, Thea. It's a fine night for hunting." Medusa held her arm up, meeting the animal's eyes with a smile. "Come back to me when you're done."

Thea blinked at her once before releasing her hold and flying into the darkness.

Medusa lingered, enjoying the soothing peace of evening before it was taken from her.

At the gate old Nikolaos hummed hoarsely, the embers of his pipe flickering in the dark. He sank onto his mat, settling against the wall for the night. He refused to sleep indoors, a fact that frustrated her aunt and amused her uncle.

Medusa glanced up at the stars, sparkling brilliant in the night. Their presence would be a fine companion to happy dreams, she thought.

There was nickering from the stables and the bray of a mule. Thea called, hunting perhaps? Fainter, further from the house, the tinkling bell of Nikolaos' favorite nanny echoed as she led the herd to graze across the fields. These sounds of home comforted her.

A candle flickered in the guards' house beyond the stables, catching her eye. She wondered if Ariston was awake. On a night like this, he must miss his home...

No. You will not think of him.

She forced herself forward, banishing thoughts of her guard. She thought on him too often of late.

As she rounded the corner, she blinked. Brilliant candlelight overwhelmed the majesty of the full moon and stars. The light, more candles than Medusa had ever seen, chased away the uncertainty of the night and forced all within the courtyard from shadows, to be displayed clearly.

As clearly as one can be, shrouded in dark veils and thick shawls.

Her sisters had little choice in their attire, she knew. But cloaked as they were, encompassed by black and grey robes, only heightened the air of menace their towering stature and filmy veils stirred. She knew why Elpis was intimidated – even her uncle was discomfited by their presence. She also knew that her sisters without their veils would be far worse.

"Sister," Stheno and Euryale spoke as one.

"Good eve, sisters," Medusa answered, smiling.

Uncle Galenus moved to her side. "Niece, your sisters have come from Corfu." His loud voice echoed in the quiet of the courtyard.

Corfu was the westernmost isle of Greece, no slight journey. It did not bode well for her. Medusa said only, "You do me great honor."

"We simply do our parents' bidding," Stheno answered, the hint of a smile in her voice.

"As a good child should," Euryale added tartly.

Medusa waited, ignoring the barbed sting of Euryale's insult. She was a good daughter to their parents. She always had been, no matter what Euryale might imply.

Had she not come here, to Galenus and Xenia, upon her parents' bidding? Had she not entered Athena's temple to beg for *their* salvation? And when Athena had granted them favor in exchange for Medusa's service, had she not accepted without question?

But all her past deeds would be forgotten now. They had need of her once again. Why else were her sisters here?

"Have you eaten, child?" Aunt Xenia gestured towards the table. A small feast had been arranged to mask the underlying threat of this visit.

Medusa shook her head and made her way to the table, taking a fig and nibbling in silence.

Stheno moved forward, stooping to regard her from the depths of the black veils. Her sister towered over most mortals, yet Euryale was the taller of the two. As Stheno assessed her, two bright spots seemed to glow beneath the veils.

Medusa smiled at her sister, warmly. As a child, Stheno had loved her best.

"Our father believes he has given you time, Medusa, more than enough time to fulfill your obligations to Athena and to your..." Stheno paused over the tender terms Medusa had given her masters, "aunt and uncle." Stheno's voice softened as she added softly, "Come home, sister. We miss you."

"And I miss you." Medusa placed her hand on her sister's arm. "But I've little say so about when I might return...."

Euryale interrupted, her tone ever sharp, "The Anestheria. You have until then to tell the Goddess you're called home."

Dismay flooded Medusa's chest and stomach. How could she present Athena with such a decree? Athena was a Goddess – an Olympian. Athena might release *her*, when and if Athena chose to do so. If Medusa dared try such blasphemy, at her sire's bidding or not, the cost would be great. A cost she would be forced to pay, undoubtedly, as her father would not see reason.

She swallowed the bite of fig she'd been nibbling. It stuck, thick and uncomfortable, in her throat.

"Why now, nieces?" Uncle Galenus boomed, causing all to jump.

"She won't stay comely forever, dear Uncle. While the Gods thought to bless her with beauty and child-bearing, she suffers from mortality..." Stheno's explanation grew more troubling. "Father fears her loss and seeks the gift of immortality for her."

Euryale interrupted again, smugly this time. "Poseidon has offered –"

"Poseidon?" Medusa stared at her sister, surprised.

"Father has won the God's favor. He helped destroy a fleet of Persian ships. Poseidon was well pleased, so pleased that the Sea God will give you the Gift in thanks. By Anestheria," Stheno spoke with care.

Medusa chewed the remainder of her fig with a vengeance.

The Gift? Was immortality a gift? One life serving others was enough. As honored as she was to serve Athena, she knew the Goddess would eventually choose her replacement, for Athena had little use for the aged. And when Medusa was released, she would return to her parents to do their bidding, continuing her life of service. Once this earthly life was over, she imagined that life in Hades' realm might offer fewer restrictions. Or, at the very least, fewer demands.

If becoming immortal was a gift, she wanted none of it. But her wants would have no bearing, this she knew.

No matter how much she wanted to explain, to ask for their understanding and support, she said nothing. *I suppose that is the wisest course for now.*

"Athena has agreed to this.... arrangement?" Galenus' words were harsh.

Euryale shook her head. "Not yet. Poseidon will petition for her release, but Medusa might help it along by entreating Athena, as well."

"Do you know what you ask?" Galenus demanded, his face reddening.

"What will become of her?" Aunt Xenia's voice quavered. "Will the Goddess release her from her duties?"

"Athena is the daughter of Zeus," Uncle Galenus blustered. "To anger her –"

"Poseidon is his brother." Euryale shrugged. "Whose wrath is the greater?"

"Why must there be wrath? And against whom?" Xenia looked amongst them in panic. "If there is wrath, there will be punishment. So who is punished? Who? Medusa?" Xenia turned a sad eye on Medusa.

Medusa smiled at the woman, hoping to soothe her fragile nerves. She was the only child Xenia had ever seen live past the fourth year of life. It was a cruel trick of the Gods, to have her born from such monsters, Xenia oft told her. But it was her parents that had given her to Xenia and Galenus in trade. And for that, Medusa was grateful. She was truly fond of Xenia.

"Fret not, Aunt," Medusa said softly.

"No harm will come to our sister," Stethno's voice joined Medusa's.

"It is of little concern to you, Xenia. You can always find another girl to play your daughter or niece in her stead. Or is it the punishment that might befall her that vexes you so?" Euryale watched the older woman as she spoke. "If she is punished, mayhap she will be cursed to look as we do? So all will know we are sisters?" She turned, gliding soundlessly across the floor in her dark robes and veil. "Will you weep if her beauty is lost, *Aunt* Xenia?"

Stheno's tone was more entreating. "Beauty or no, she has a birthright. Medusa *is* a Gorgon and daughter to the most fearsome sea titans. She has been kept from her home these long years. You'd not abide such a separation, Xenia. No parent should."

"No." Xenia shook her head, visibly grieving for the children she'd lost. "I would not wish such misery on any parent."

A heavy silence filled the air.

Medusa felt despair churning in her stomach, but pushed such weakness aside. She was not alone. She would pray, she would find gifts, and hope her Goddess would grant her forgiveness and a solution to this dilemma.

Thea's screech filled the courtyard, the flapping of her wings signaling the owl's arrival. Medusa's offered her arm to her pet, seeking comfort in Thea's solid presence.

Stheno moved forward, cooing and clucking at the owl. The

owl stared back silently before she stretched her wings and yawned.

Medusa smiled slightly, impressed by Thea's bravery.

Uncle Galenus broke the silence. "Eat, rest. You must be weary from your travels?"

"We ate along the way. Goats are plentiful on the hillside," Stheno said, amusement in her voice.

"As well as young goat herders," Euryale added, her sudden shriek of laughter bouncing off the stone walls.

Medusa smiled in spite of herself. Her sisters still had a wicked sense of humor. It was said that the Gorgons would eat the flesh of one still alive, and use his bones to clean their teeth. But she knew them well. Stheno had little stomach for blood and neither was violent. They were indeed fractious, caustic and brutish – but nothing more.

"Tell me, did you cook them first?" she teased, aware that her aunt and uncle's faces grew more horrified.

"The goats?" Stheno asked, her voice merry.

"Or the goat herders?" Euryale finished, her shout of laughter filling the night air.

Ariston watched her run along the beach, her glorious hair swirling about her in the ocean breeze. Her blue-green eyes peered at him, and she laughed as she took his hand.

"My love?" she murmured.

He looked at their hands.

Medusa... She was his lady – a beloved and loyal wife. With each breath, the strength of their love filled him.

She ran into the waves, her hand slipping from his.

"Ariston?" she voice was soft, her tone desperate. Her face changed then, startling him. Her eyes widened and her smile faded.

The sun vanished. The sky grew dim, then black and grey.

When he reached for her, she was gone – swallowed by a dark mist. A sharp pain twisted his heart, his lungs gasped for air... He called to her, the sound echoing eerily through the fog. But there was no answer. And no matter how hard he searched, he could not find her.

Medusa screamed hoarsely. The sound, weighted with real

terror and despair, forced him upright.

He woke, heart pounding, dripping sweat. The images lingered, vividly. His hands trembled, rubbing over his face and through his hair. The sound of her cries echoed yet.

Need clawed his chest, followed by pain – such raw pain.

It felt real. He'd loved her... needed her so – body and soul. And he'd lost her to something or someone.

A dream, nothing more. Yet he felt no reassurance.

Sleep was lost to him. He would not revisit such things. Standing on unsteady legs, he breathed deeply of the chill morning air. *Just a dream.*

His eyes adjusted to the dim light, the moon glinting off the shaft of his spear. Clasping its solid weight within his fist offered him some sense of security. With shield in hand, he slipped from the long house.

His eyes narrowed, tracing the dim horizon. All was peaceful, yet he was not.

Damn the Persians for not making landfall, for he hungered for a fight. Restlessness seized him. He would run until he could think of her no more, run until the fear gripping him eased.

Sunrise found him still running, legs leaden. But the fatigue of his body did nothing for the ache in his chest.

It was as if all he'd dreamt was real. Never had he experienced such joy...or felt so unsettled, so troubled.

Once returned to the guards' house to wash, he splashed handfuls of icy water over his face. With a wince, he submerged his head and shoulders in its clear depths.

It helped.

But waiting for her, pacing the path between his home and hers, only resurrected his anxiety. He longed to see her, yet he dreaded it all the same. He would know that she was well and safe. But would seeing her force him to accept that the longing in his heart extended beyond the confines of his dream?

He busied himself, sharpening his spear until the tip of the doru was razor sharp, cleaning his helmet, and mending the seam of his cloak. When he had nothing left to occupy him, he paced.

The winds lifted, growing stronger with each passing moment.

At last he heard her approach and turned to greet her, too

eagerly. She headed towards him, blue eyes sparkling above her veils.

He nodded quickly and turned his gaze from her.

She was indeed well, easing his worry while tempting his soul. Her veils offered no buffer to his heart, the whisper of her smile was a shadow through its gossamer fall – enticing him all the more.

The wind was howling now, swirling sand about their legs.

"Take the mule," Galenus barked from the door. "And hold tight to the animal."

Ariston readied the animal, loading it with care while Nikolaos helped her mount.

They left the yard in silence. His jaw clenched. It would be better if they did not speak...

"Good morning," she said softly. "Or it was, until the winds came."

He shouldn't answer.

"Will it rain?" she asked.

He swallowed. "No."

She said nothing more.

He *would* remember his place and treat her as he would Athena, as was right. This was his vow, silently uttered; one he repeated as they made the climb to the temple.

A powerful gust of wind buffeted him. He turned quickly, fearful she'd been blown from the mule.

The wind lifted her veils for but a moment, revealing her vulnerability and weakening his resolve. He ripped his gaze from hers and swallowed the words he would offer to soothe her. His knuckles whitened about the mule's lead rope, pulling the stubborn animal with renewed determination.

He hesitated once they reached the steps of the temple, but knew there was no help for it. He turned to help her from the mule, offering his arm safely covered by his thick leather greaves.

But she was already moving, slipping from the saddle to loosen Athena's offerings before he could reach her.

"Allow me to help you, priestess." He watched her fingers fight the coarse rope knots.

She glanced at him, then stepped back. "My thanks, soldier."

He freed her parcels, hefting the lot into his arms with ease.

The wind gusted, prompting him to offer, "May I carry them for you? So none are lost to the wind?"

She nodded, moving towards the temple steps without a word or glance in his direction.

She did not meet his eyes as he pulled her offerings from the saddle. It would be her undoing, to find curiosity or sympathy in his grey eyes. Instead, she rushed up the steps and into the safety of her temple. She must pray, and put whatever tenderness she might feel for her guard from her mind... and her heart.

Once inside, she paused, feeling momentarily downtrodden. He entered the temple, cradling her offerings with surprising care.

She did not face him as she spoke, but moved to light the tapers surrounding the temple dais. "Thank you, soldier. You may place them there, by the altar. I know you've training to attend to. I'll not keep you."

She busied herself, waiting until he was gone before she glanced back.

It was a long trek to the camp Themistocles and the Athenian Council had constructed. But his responsibilities extended far beyond the care of a priestess. It was Ariston who trained new hoplites, led a troop of Ekdromoi soldiers, and offered strategies to the council. He served Athena, yes, but Athens as well. His skill with sword and shield were his tribute to both.

Elpis had learned much for her – never asking her mistress why she gathered such information. If Elpis had asked her, Medusa would not have had an answer.

She lit a long stick, sharpened and dipped in sweet incense, and carried the flame to the four unlit tapers that sat in each corner of the temple. The interior soon glowed warmly, easing some of her torment.

She had purpose to her life. It pleased her to serve the Goddess. And she must concentrate on her duties, cherish them – and them only. Surely then she would forget everything else.

"I did not expect my little one to come." Athena's voice was like the ringing of a bell. Not high and shrill, but deep and resonant, with a pleasing timbre.

The Goddess' voice, like her presence, demanded attention. From her elevated height to the luminescence of her skin, she exuded power.

Medusa fell to her knees, pure pleasure filling her. "Athena. I am here."

"As I see. Did the wind blow you here? Or did you walk?" Athena laughed, a mesmerizing sound. "Rise, little one, and show me what treasures you have for me."

Medusa smiled as she stood. Athena always made her smile. It was a delight when the Goddess came, each visit a rare and humbling gift. "I have many – all carried by a troublesome donkey that pulled against the wind and the efforts of my lady's soldier."

Athena laughed. "'Tis a shame that the sun chose to so abruptly hide itself, for it was a joyous morn. Apollo lit the sky with gold so brilliant it made many turn their eyes away." Athena sat in her chair, carved from pink marble and placed in the center of the dais behind her altar. "Did you turn your eyes away from its brilliance, Medusa?"

Medusa smiled and shook her head. "We rose to greet the sun, Thea and I, staring out the window at its beauty. Once it woke, I felt I had to keep it company."

Athena nodded. "But then it went away?"

Medusa paused, then whispered, "Did my company chase it away?"

"Why ever would you say such a thing? Have you done something to anger the Gods?" Athena regarded her with an affectionate smile. "I cannot imagine my little one capable of such a thing."

Medusa spoke softly, "I know not. But I would ask for your counsel, lady, as I am struggling so."

Athena sighed, her smile growing tolerant. "Speak, little one, so that you may show me what lovelies you have for me."

"My father, Phorcys –"

"Foolish monster that he is," Athena interjected.

"He would have me...home. He has procured the Gift for me from Poseidon, by Anestheria."

Athena rose, her finely arched brow rising. "What? And take the Priestess *I* have chosen to serve me?" Anger laced her every word. "What nonsense is this, child? You say my *uncle* aids your father in this move? Does Poseidon know who you serve?"

Medusa winced, startled by Athena's indignation. "I know not..."

"Phorcys thinks he has repaid me? That he, a mongering *Titan*, shall set the terms of your service?" Her face flushed and her voice echoed throughout the temple with unsuppressed fury. "Poseidon must know that championing this...this insult will lead to strife." Her eyes narrowed as she bitterly muttered, "A thought he relishes, of that much I am certain."

"I know only of my father's request, Goddess, nothing more." Medusa's words were a whisper.

"*I* will know the truth of it soon enough." Athena stood beside Medusa, staring down at her. The Goddess smiled slightly, sighing before she spoke again. "Now, do your duty and show me my tributes before I go, little one."

Medusa did as she was told. Athena praised the tarts and bread Medusa had made for her, sampling them as Medusa arranged the other offerings. She was pleased, and Medusa hoped that was enough.

"You shall train all of my priestesses, I think, as you please me so. I will have need of them in my new temple."

"New temple?" Medusa waited, surprised.

Athena pulled a scroll from the tuck of her robes, spreading the parchment on her dais with care. "My temple, the Parthenon. It will be the largest in Greece." Athena smiled broadly. "It will be a thing of beauty, a crown for my city of Athens."

Medusa marveled at the size and scope of the structure. "All who see it will be struck by its majesty," Medusa assured her.

"And know it is my house," Athena said. "Once the Persians are gone, building will commence."

"There is no hope, then? War will find Athens, Goddess?" she asked. And if there was, what did that mean for her guard? Though that question pressed on her as dearly as the first, she knew better than to ask it.

"It will." Athena nodded. "But Athens will not fall. It is too strong a city – as Greece is too great a country. You, gentle Medusa, need not let such events cause you fear. Bear such times, and strife, as they find you. Weather them as I would, with reason and wisdom." As she finished, she rolled up the plans and tucked them into her robes once more.

When Athena's brown eyes turned to regard her, Medusa smiled.

"As for this other matter, I will know the answer to this riddle soon enough. Phorcys is a fool of the worst kind, and you are blessed to be free of him. My uncle...my own uncle chafes when he must yield to me, in any way. I will have Zeus set all to rights." Athena sighed, regarding her tributes and offering as she continued, "You were wise to share this with me, little one. But do not let it weigh so heavily on you. Hold your head up and remember that you are mine."

Medusa straightened at Athena's words, wishing she might find comfort in them.

"You have no claim." Athena's brows furrowed and her cheeks blazed with fury.

Poseidon regarded his niece. Her eyes narrowed, and her nostrils flared at his unruffled calm. This *was* interesting. He schooled his face with care, portraying the picture of compromise, all the while relishing every twitch and shift of her discomfort.

"I need no claim," he spoke without heat.

She turned an alarming shade of burgundy. "To take her from my temple? From my service? She is *mine* until her parents' debt is repaid, Poseidon. And, I assure you, I will decide such matters. Not you."

"Cease!" Zeus thundered, holding his hands out. "Why *this* mortal? Why is she the cause of such discord on Olympus?" His angular face grew pinched, his thick arms rigid as he attempted to regain control.

Poseidon stifled a sigh. His elder brother meddled too often, stealing away his simple pleasures. As all eyes flitted between him and Athena he briefly wondered if Phorcys was worth the effort. One glance at Athena's florid complexion, her clenched fists and white knuckles, at the vein throbbing prominently from her forehead, and Poseidon had his answer. His mouth tightened, repressing a smile. *We will see how this plays out.*

"Medusa is *my priestess*, Father." Athena said simply.

Zeus scowled at Poseidon. "You would interfere in the care of Athens' temple?"

Poseidon rolled his eyes. "I would appease a Titan."

"And I would collect on that Titan's debt. A debt yet to be paid in full," Athena said.

Zeus regarded his daughter, then his brother. "I am weary of this bickering. Too many times the two of you have battled, hoping simply to best the other." His eyes narrowed. "Let us have peace, if we may? War is imminent for the Athenians, likely all of Greece. The mortals need our help to defeat the cursed Persians."

"Persian dogs," Ares snorted, lounging upon his throne in boredom. "It will be easy enough to cut them down."

"Ares, not all of Athens' soldiers are skilled. The cost of such a war – the loss of so many husbands, sons and fathers – is no slight thing," Hera chided him, turning her huge brown eyes upon the God of War.

"War is war, Hera. Death is part of the journey to glory," Ares countered.

"Not all are so eager to find glory," Hera bit back.

"Peace." Zeus lifted his hand, silencing them. "Brother, let the priestess stay with Athena. If Phorcys' debts to Athena aren't met, he can hardly ask for favors from you. Knowing Phorcys, whatever service he has performed cannot mean so much. Truly, has he done something of great import for you? "

Poseidon hesitated. He could back down and fight anew another day. But the haughty disdain his niece displayed spurred him on. "He has." His mind worked quickly, knowing the best way to play his weak hand. "But not just to me."

"We speak of Phorcys?" Apollo interjected in disbelief. "The same flotsam that delights in mayhem and serves none but himself?"

Poseidon nodded.

"How can this be?" Zeus shook his head, doubt and amusement on his regal face. "I've known Phorcys to do little but turn into foam to dally with sea nymphs or eat those who offend him in the guise of a shark."

"Phorcys did a service to all by swallowing three small Persian ships. He did so, without my request, in order to prevent the ships return to their waiting fleet – with reports on Athens' reinforcements.

He followed them, and when he had the gist of their mission, he acted." Poseidon looked at his niece. "Wisely, one might say."

Athena's eyes bulged, and her lips pressed to a tight line. A smile threatened, so Poseidon covered his mouth with a discreet cough. His brother, he noted, appeared duly impressed.

"Such a deed is worth reward," Aphrodite conceded. "Is there nothing else to be given?"

"He misses his daughter." Poseidon shrugged. Yet he knew his words had weight.

Hera cocked her head. "Indeed?" She cast her husband, Zeus, a beguiling glance.

Truly, a woman's power over man is maddening. Poseidon stroked his beard, his eyes flickering between his fellow Olympians with interest. Athena shifted in discomfort while Zeus paced, considering this interesting new development.

Poseidon envied his brother not a bit.

To side with him was to appease his wife and her service to home and hearth.

But siding against Athena would ensure peace was lost for all on Olympus. His niece was most insufferable when she lost.

And yet Poseidon had painted Phorcys as a noble creature, truly worthy of reward – something Zeus could hardly ignore entirely. If Zeus was taking his time to consider the matter, Poseidon did not blame him.

"I ask you, dear daughter, to credit this deed towards Phorcys' debt. Detract this favor from the girls' time in your service. Then you keep your precious servant for some time yet – a reasonable time, mind you. Poseidon, you have given Phorcys favor, albeit less than what he asked. When Athena releases this priestess, you may give her immortality. Phorcys should be well pleased and remain loyal to the Gods." Zeus shrugged, laughing. "If he is not then he may return to Hades in the Underworld. I think that would silence any of his protests."

General laughter filled the Council Chamber, but Poseidon cared little as he caught sight of his niece. Athena sat back with a smug smile. Her eyes narrowed as she regarded him with pleasure.

Poseidon shook his head. He had no quarrel with Athena, not really, not this time. But she gleefully poked at his pride. She loved nothing so much as to assert herself above him with Zeus – preferably in front of all who sat upon Olympus.

He could not bear it. It galled him further when she stooped, whispering to the women. She would lord this over him for some time yet.

Unless he managed to challenge this, she would needle him at every turn.

So he would steal the taste of victory from her and leave the flavor of bitter defeat instead. He pondered this while the others began to talk amongst themselves.

Once Zeus decided a matter, they were free to go. And, for those gathered, the matter was done. Talk of war, Sparta, and Athena's new temple continued about him.

Poseidon lingered, his mind at work, waiting until his brother was free from the others' ears.

"She has an iron will," Poseidon said when they were alone. He stood at his brother's side, a rueful smile set on his face.

Zeus shrugged. "A trait that runs in the family."

"If her will is wrong?" Poseidon asked with narrowed eyes. He took care, feigning a serious and concerned air.

Zeus regarded him closely. "This is more than a dispute between the two of you?"

No. Poseidon inclined his head, continuing with his pretext of concern. "Phorcys proved himself a fine warrior. None is more surprised than I. But the Persians threaten Athens by sea, and his actions show his fealty to us. Peace between the Gods and the Titans will help the mortals as this conflict with the Persians unfurls. They will need us, as you said, and peace on our part ensures aid when needed."

Zeus considered the words. "You think Phorcys would deny assistance?"

Poseidon did not. He knew Phorcys to be loyal, if selfish. In truth Phorcys was an exception among the titans for he lacked the cunning and strategy of his peers. The cause of this gripe had no bearing on the impending war. But Poseidon could not admit as much.

Phorcys' wife wanted her daughter home. True, it was not because she was distraught over being separated from her child –

Ceto wanted to marry their mortal daughter well and provide them with the grandchildren her other monstrous Gorgon children could not. It was a trivial thing, of no import to Olympus or Athens. But Poseidon knew such truths would hardly help his efforts to foil his niece's victory.

"I, for one, believe that we should make and keep our allies where we can. As this war will occupy the seas, Phorcys will be a mighty ally." Poseidon paused for effect, looking thoughtful as he met his older brother's eyes. "But perhaps Athena's temper is a greater threat? This mortal girl must be an uncommon priestess indeed for Athena to hold her so tightly, and on the eve of war."

Poseidon watched Zeus' face harden. Zeus paused, taking a deep breath. "Go, learn what you can. We've enough to occupy our time and attention without this Medusa upsetting the order on Olympus."

Poseidon nodded, repressing his triumphant smile until he left the Council Chamber. Athena would lose this challenge. He would make sure of it.

Chapter Three

The sky was still black. Only the faintest streaks of light glimmered along the distant horizon. Medusa slipped from the house with her cloak pulled tightly about her, a bundle in her hand. The morning was crisp without the sun to warm the air and color the sky.

But soon the day would begin – a day that promised distraction from her worries.

She wandered through her uncle's garden, absently rubbing the leaf of a fig tree between finger and thumb. A sleepy lark chirped in protest as her fingers released the limb, bouncing the lark's nest.

She smiled at the bird, whispering, "Forgive me for waking your brood."

The high-pitched squeaks of the larks fledglings split the morning. The bird cocked her head at Medusa in a contemplative manner.

Medusa laughed softly. "I'm not sure I'd forgive me either, little mother, for shattering your rest."

The bird turned her attention to her chicks, leaving Medusa to her thoughts once more. Her gaze wandered across the yard, lingering on the dark guards' house. He would not be awake yet, for all were abed at this hour.

But her mind had refused her rest. Uneasy thoughts plagued her, spiraling about until she was more exhausted than before she'd lain upon her mat. There seemed little point in staying within the walls of her room when her mind might be better occupied without.

Yet, now that she'd ventured out into the relative tranquility of the morning, she felt no relief from her inner tempest.

While she contemplated a long hike, she knew wandering off on her own would cause distress to her aunt and uncle. She'd caused enough turmoil without adding to it.

She slid down the base of a fig tree to sit, resting her elbows on her knees. Thoughts of her father, her sisters, Athena, and her unknown future tormented her.

Athena's anger was most unsettling. In all Medusa's years with her Goddess, she'd never encountered Athena's wrath. In some small way she pitied Poseidon.

The knowledge that she had no control, no say, in this matter burned like a hot coal in her stomach. What she would give for a moment's freedom, to do as she wished. It was folly to imagine what could have been if she were not a priestess or the daughter of a Sea Titan.

But, for a brief moment, she did.

To be a woman from a family of no import, with little or no responsibility beyond that of daily life to carry out...to just *be*, sounded as close to Elysium as could be found outside the Underworld. She tried to imagine such a life. To love and be loved, to dance together, to touch a man's hand or be drawn into his strong, warm arms...

Her eyes shifted to the guards' house for but a moment.

She held her hand out, regarding its delicate bones and pale skin in the waning moonlight.

She'd never touched a man. Yet she wanted to. She longed to be held tightly, with no hesitance. She craved affection, comfort – and someone to share it with. Not just any man. She could no longer deny the truth in her heart.

"Lady?" Ariston's voice was a whisper, but he startled her anyway.

She stared up at him in shock, blushing even though she knew he could not know her thoughts were of him. Thoughts of being in his arms... Her heart thundered, then seemed to stop altogether as she took in his ruffled appearance, still wrinkled from slumber. He looked young, tousled and only slightly fearsome without his soldier garb. He looked...beautiful to her eyes, but no less a man.

She could scarcely breathe as his eyes found hers.

His gaze was warm upon her, so warm she could almost feel his touch. Her stomach tightened and her longing sharpened.

She forced her gaze beyond him to the golden border widening along the horizon.

She said softly, "Tis too early, I know, soldier." She did not look at him as she added, "And yet I'm awake."

He remained silent, making her shift uncomfortably. Why did he say nothing?

"Mayhap the moon, or her Goddess Selene, was calling to me?" she tried to tease.

She looked at him and instantly regretted it. Standing amongst the silver strands of waning moonlight, he seemed to call to her – her mind and body. And it took all of her strength not to answer.

He'd stumbled from his bed to relieve himself, eager to return to the warmth of his blankets. Her silhouette had caught his eye and beckoned him to her side.

Seeing her without her veils brought him up short. While he'd been rewarded with a teasing glimpse now and then, he'd never had the opportunity to soak her in. He could not have anticipated how it would feel to look upon her.

In the pale cast of the moon, she appeared as an ethereal nymph. Her honey tresses spilled over her shoulders. The long line of her ivory neck arched as she looked up at him. Her face was…

He swallowed. There was nothing more lovely on this earth. He knew it.

"Mayhap the moon, or her Goddess Selene, was calling to me?" Her question, tinged with a hint of sadness, roused him. And when she turned her huge blue eyes upon him, he swallowed the knot in his throat to answer.

"Perhaps. It is not yet dawn." He could find nothing else to say.

Her face softened as a small smile formed. But her gaze wandered from his and her brow furrowed.

If only he knew how to cheer her.

Master Galenus' herder, old Nikolaos, had regaled the guards with quite a tale. Galenus' home had an unexpected visit from two witches,

witches known to this house. They had come with a dire message for the master and his niece, traveling from Corfu to deliver it. While Nikolaos only alluded to the contents of the message, he made it clear that its portent had been most upsetting.

Ariston had no means to learn the rest of it. If he'd sought the whole of it from Nikolaos, the old man might have grown suspicious. He knew no one else in Galenus' household, as Galenus refused to acknowledge their presence on his property.

It was not his place to ask his mistress. No matter how much he wanted to help her, he'd hold his tongue.

Athena decreed him her protector. He must hold to that, honor his station. Whatever else she might stir within him was a temptation to resist.

But now, in the shadows of first light, his carefully crafted armor of indifference began to crumble.

She rose to her feet, sighing with barely repressed impatience. The look on her face revealed her longing. Was she anxious to escape the walls of her uncle's homestead – to escape whatever burdens may have found her? He would gladly go with her.

"I fear I'll miss the sunrise." She lifted her head and spoke clearly, brooking no opposition. "Join me when you are ready."

She took a few steps towards the gate.

He couldn't let her leave, with no guard and uncovered. "It's not safe, lady. Give me but a moment."

She glanced at him, one finely arched brow rising high. "I am Athena's priestess, soldier. No one would risk Athena's anger."

"Yet not all who reside in Athens serve the Goddess. Not all would honor your service to Athena," he said softly, imploring her.

Her shoulders fell, exposing the dejection she felt. The urge to pull her into his arms, to comfort her, rose within him. He took a steadying breath, holding himself in check.

"You are right." Her voice dropped. "Even those professing fealty to Olympus dismiss duty and loyalty when it serves their purpose."

Ariston again ached from the pain in her words. He spoke quickly, seeking to cheer her. "But they are not here now. They will not ruin this fine morning, will they?"

"No." She gazed upon him. "But, I would ask you something, soldier. Today, I am free of the temple, my veil and my robes. So let us pretend that I'm only Medusa." She started towards the gate. "Then you've no need to worry over me and I've no need of guarding—"

He stepped into her path.

"You need my protection, with or without your priestess garb," he insisted. "It is not safe for any woman to venture out alone. I pray, mistress, be patient and stay but a moment longer."

"I have little patience this morning." She made to move around him.

He raised a hand to grasp her shoulder, desperate to stop her. As his hand descended, he remembered himself. It froze a hair's breadth from her shoulder.

She gasped and took a quick step back. Her huge eyes stared at his outstretched hand in complete shock. When her gaze found his, he swallowed against the depths of her distress. He had been kicked by his father's mule once, knocking the air from him. He felt more startled now.

His hand dropped and his body tensed. What had he almost done? He swallowed, fighting the anger and self-loathing twisting his stomach.

Yet these emotions warred with such pleasure, such awareness, that he could only stare at her. In the depths of her Aegean blue eyes, something shifted and changed. Whatever it was affected her as well – so much that she turned from him, breathing rapidly.

He suspected the punishment might be worth it if he were able to touch her for even the briefest moment.

Her heart raced, her lungs gasped desperately for air. He'd reached for her. She'd wanted him to...

What had almost happened could never happen. He must never touch her. The Goddess would punish him, most severely.

Her chest tightened, a sharp, physical pain. Medusa could not abide such a thought.

He bowed awkwardly, his voice hoarse, "Lady, I beg for your forgiveness."

Medusa stared down at him. Worry over losing him was troubling. If Ariston's actions were witnessed her forgiveness would carry no weight.

She searched the grounds in the dim morning light, her gaze seeking out each shadow and movement. She could see no one present in the courtyard. It appeared they were alone. She prayed it was so. He would be safe. She would not lose him.

Her thoughts jarred her, and she corrected them. Athena would not lose a worthy soldier.

Her eyes settled upon him again. What had he done, really? Nothing.

His hand, so close that she'd felt his warmth upon her shoulder, had not reached her. It was her doing. She had forced him, pushed him without the wisdom or reason she should take care to use. She would not have him punished for her failings.

A gust of wind stirred the air about them, setting his wheaten curls dancing in the wind. Her fingers were intrigued by them. She wondered what they would feel like, slipping between her fingers...

She clenched her hand, trembling where she stood. "There is nothing to forgive. It is my fault – my doing."

He stood straight, staring at the ground between them. "Allow me to gather my weapons, mistress, so that I may carry out my duty."

Her heart pounded on. "I will wait for you," her voice wavered.

He ran without a backward glance, tearing into the guards' house. He returned quickly, carrying his spear, shield and a tangle of nets.

She smiled. He would fish for the Goddess in offering.

They made their way to the shore in silence. She used the time to calm herself, a greater challenge than she expected. But the peaceful sounds of the morning helped ease her strain. Birdsong, the whistle of the wind through the olive trees and the whisper of the waves bid them good morning. As they neared the shoreline the hill dropped, falling away to soft sand and rolling white-tipped surf.

She dropped her cloak and parcel onto the beach and ran to the water's edge. Wriggling her toes into the warm sand, she relaxed. The muted waves roared, washing against the beach to froth around her ankles.

Pleasure erased all else. She loved the sea, and the peace it afforded her.

Ariston watched her sprint into the shallow water, her glorious hair moving with the ocean breeze, the smile on her lips pulling one from his own. He walked slowly, desperately trying to rein his wayward thoughts.

Why must this woman wreak havoc on him, when there was no hope for them? He dropped his things with hers before coming to stand at her side.

Having viewed her beauty through the veils, he explored the features of her face in the rising sun. Her skin was alabaster, without freckles or imperfections. Her eyes, he knew all too well. Her nose was slight and straight. Her cheeks were high and soft, making his hand itch to touch her.

He could do nothing but stare, memorizing her as she was.

She seemed unaware of his fascination, lost in the pleasures of the morning. Her brilliant blue gaze was trained on the sun breaking over the water, watching its gilded fingers streak across the water to reach them. She smiled and closed her eyes, tilting her face towards the sun's light.

If there had been any hesitation about his feelings, they vanished. He'd vowed to serve as her protector, he'd promised to look upon her as a handmaid for their Goddess.

But now he loved her, as a woman.

He stared out at the sun, Apollo's orb, grappling with this realization.

He would not deny the truth of it; he could not. Nor could he ignore the dread that filled his chest.

The Persians offered no threat, for his body was prepared for the challenge they brought with them.

But his heart... His heart offered him his most daunting battle.

He would fight against his love. He must. If he was found out, the wrath of Athena and Olympus would fall heavily upon him – and likely Medusa too.

He took a steadying breath, willing such thoughts from his mind. It would not come to that. He would make certain of it.

Two fish jumped from the water's depths. Medusa laughed, pulling his gaze back to her.

She glanced at him, grinning. "Are you hungry, soldier?"

He nodded, rendered speechless by her beauty.

She ran back to their things, left on the edge of the rocky shore. She sat gracefully on the soft sand and waved him to her. Within her bundle she'd packed a fine breakfast for them – cheese, fruit and crusty bread that she ripped into equal portions with nimble white fingers.

He watched her fingers, her hands... He took a steadying breath.

"You should have a larger share. You need your strength more than I." She held a larger piece of bread to him.

He took it, carefully avoiding her fingers. "I need no more than you, lady."

She nibbled her bread, watching him curiously. "I suppose mistress or lady is better than my lady. But it is still more than my name." She looked displeased as she offered him cheese.

I cannot speak your name, for it will reveal my affections for you. He regarded her silently, before asking, "What will you find here? To take to the Goddess in offering?"

She turned her attention to the beach. "Shells of white and lavender and pink I shall string as a necklace or bracelet. Athena has a most discerning eye, so only those fine and delicate and whole are acceptable." She ate a grape, silencing the conversation briefly. "I once found a pearl. After swimming for hours, that is. Athena was very pleased."

Ariston imagined her, her tunic tucked up to allow her to swim, emerging from the sea with a triumphant smile and a pearl. Her long hair would have dangled about her thighs, her face alight over her treasure – beautiful and tempting. He shifted, his arousal immediate.

"A pearl?" His voice revealed nothing.

"It was a gift from my parents, I think." She mused, her face closing. "They dearly loved to surprise me."

His brow furrowed at her sudden change in disposition. "Should we try to find another?" He would cheer her – that much he could do.

She shook her head. "There will be no gifts now."

"I will look." He stood, seeking her approval. He would stay close and protect her, but do his best to make her happy as well.

Her face lightened and she smiled up at him, blue eyes sparkling. His heart ached anew. "You may try."

He tossed his cloak on top of his shield and ran to the water's edge. The water was warm, inviting him into the crystal clear depths. He turned to see her, tucking her skirts up around her legs and wading into the shallows behind him. The flash of her thigh, white, amidst the fall of her thick honey hair, gave him pause.

Sucking air into his lungs, he dove deep. Knife in hand, he began to chip away at the larger oysters at the base of the oldest rocks. If there was a pearl on this shore, he would find it for her.

For the Goddess.

The pale morning sunshine turned bright and hot, and still Ariston continued to dive and cut loose oysters from their rocky anchors. Each one he removed brought a twinge of hope. Only to have it dashed once he'd pried the shell apart to find it empty. This news had not surprised his lady, but he'd seen the sheen of tears fill her eyes. It pained him to see her sadness.

After collecting a pile of empty oysters, he collapsed on the beach with a sigh. He could not bear to further disappoint her. His arms ached and his lungs protested any further dives, anyway.

He whistled, echoing the call of a gull as it swooped closer to the scraps of the breakfast. The gull answered, settling close to the blanket. He threw it the last bits of crust.

He felt her kneel beside him in the sand. "Can you teach me?" she asked as the gull lifted, riding the sea breeze higher into the midday sky.

"Possibly – it's no easy trick." He arched an eyebrow at her, knowing she would accept his challenge.

"It is said that a student's only as good as her teacher, soldier," she returned, smiling.

He laughed and she joined him. It was a glorious sound.

He taught her how to make the call of the gull. And when she mastered the call, she laughed with such delight that his pulse quickened.

"I fear I'll not have enough for Athena, soldier, if you keep distracting me." She stood and made her way back to the shore to wade into the water once more.

She trawled the shoreline, scooping bits of loveliness from the water and assessing their worth. If she was pleased with her find, she dropped it into the pocket the tuck of her tunic provided. If she deemed something unworthy, she tossed it over her shoulder to fall back into the water.

Normally, the bright sun and roaring waves reminded him of his tiny home of Rhodes, making him homesick. But today, watching her in the morning sun, he felt only happiness. She was a tribute to Athena, taking time to find only the best for her Goddess. It served as a reminder to him...

She glanced up, smiling at him.

He smiled back. He had no choice.

"Mistress?" a woman's voice called from the hill above.

Ariston rose quickly, standing at the ready. But the young sprite of a girl who bounded down the rocky hill to the beach posed no threat, so Ariston returned to his resting place. He wrestled with a sense of disappointment. The fragile intimacy they'd built would be gone now. He would simply be Medusa's guard once more.

"I'm here, Elpis," Medusa called back.

The young woman – Elpis -- leapt onto the beach, a basket in her arms. She caught sight of Ariston and held the basket to him. "Here, hoplite, for you and your mistress."

Ariston rose, taking the basket from the girl before she bounded into the water. She giggled as Medusa splashed her. They splashed and laughed until they were both squealing and dripping wet.

He turned away, suddenly wishing this adventure was behind him.

Though he was loyal to Athena, he was a man, young and virile. The sight of his lady, wet and lush, would be too much for even the most indifferent of men. The Gods were surely laughing down at him as he tried again to deny the hunger raging in his blood.

The air by his ear stirred suddenly, causing him to turn – alert once more. He was greeted by two yellow eyes. A regal owl sat on the rim of his shield.

It stared at him, clicked, and bobbed its head.

"Hello." He grinned, amused by the animal's behavior.

The owl cooed, its gaze narrowing to slits. It clicked again, then turned its attention to the women in the water. It made a series of small coos, as if pleased by the sight.

Ariston looked too. It was a lovely sight to behold. His blood warmed as he watched Medusa. The finely spun linen of her peplos clung to her curves. He turned, looking desperately for distraction.

"You were up with the sun," Elpis spoke, still gasping from their antics.

"I slept not at all," Medusa said.

"How could you? I've been haunted by their visit and I have yet to see them."

Ariston shifted closer to hear them. Whatever troubled his lady, he would find it out.

"Tis a shame such terror is caused by those I call kin," Medusa teased.

"What will you do?"

Ariston watched as his lady's features changed, her earlier sadness returning. He felt the desire to go to her. Instead he leaned forward, fetching the water skin and shifting to better hear their conversation.

"There's nothing I can do, Elpis."

Elpis nodded. "Either choice has grievous consequences. My heart breaks for you, mistress." The girl sounded close to tears.

Ariston watched as Medusa drew her companion to her, hugging her. "I have asked Athena. Surely the Goddess of Wisdom and Reason will know my path."

"But to go against your parents?" Elpis gasped. "Against Poseidon? Or against Athena? Is the gravity of such decisions lost upon your good parents? If so, do they love you well enough? It is cruel, to leave such weighty matters on your delicate shoulders."

Ariston sat frozen, the water skin gripped in his white-knuckled fists. What matter would place her at odds with not one, but two Olympians?

"Poseidon cares not. Why would he? But my father and mother..." Medusa sighed. "Titans are fearsome creatures. Their wrath is something I know, Elpis. And I fear for Athens, for her people, if my father is too displeased. I could not bear being the cause of such a disaster." Medusa's hands swirled in the water as she continued, "I will trust Athena's guidance."

Ariston stared at her, a knot of anxiety hardening his stomach.

Medusa splashed Elpis then, a gay smile chasing her gloom away. "I will swim, Elpis. Join me?"

Elpis splashed Medusa, making her mistress laugh with delight.

The owl at Ariston's back cooed when Medusa laughed, making

him smile up at the small bird. "It is the sound of joy, is it not, little one?" he whispered.

The bird's eyes narrowed again and it clicked at him, softly, in reply.

"I may splash, but I do not swim. It's your delight, not mine," Elpis said.

"Will you stay and eat with us?" Medusa glanced at Ariston, her eyes growing wide as she saw the owl. "Be careful, soldier. My Thea is a fickle friend. She will woo you with her bright eyes and soft sounds, and bite you when you'd stroke her."

Ariston assessed the delicate owl with a dubious frown. "She'll not bite me." He cleared his throat when his gaze settled upon Medusa, her wet form undeniably woman. But his voice belied none of his agitation as he asked, "*Your* Thea?"

Elpis nodded. "Thea was Medusa's gift from Athena. And Thea is Medusa's most loyal companion."

"She rivals even you in her fierce protection of me." Medusa smiled, teasing him again.

He did not still his smile, for his pleasure at her happiness was swift. "She is a fine specimen indeed." *As is my Lady – my love. May the Gods forgive me.*

He lifted the water skin, drinking deeply.

Medusa nodded. Her eyes flashed in the bright sunlight as she added, "She is."

The water skin paused on its way back to the sand. The curve of her smile, the impish merriment of her eyes rendered him immobile. She would be the end of him, with only a smile.

Elpis splashed her mistress then, breaking the spell that held him so transfixed. She cast a wide-eyed expression upon her mistress and said, "Swim, then, mistress, so that we may eat."

Medusa nodded, took a deep breath and disappeared beneath the waves.

Ariston braced himself as Elpis sloshed out of the water and went to the basket. She spread the linen sheet upon the sand and regarded him steadily.

"If you care for our mistress, you must be more careful," Elpis said softly, peering over her shoulder. Medusa's feet disappeared as she dove under the water, leaving him at the mercy of Elpis' scolding.

A scolding he knew was founded.

Ariston arched an eyebrow and took an apple, but said nothing.

Elpis returned the look, shaking her head. "I saw you this morning. And if I saw you then someone else might have, too. She'll need you now. She needs someone to watch over her, to care for her, as they're pulling her every which way."

Ariston sat forward, eyes narrowing. Finally he might have his questions answered. "What is it that grieves the lady so?"

"You know who she is?" Elpis asked incredulously, kneeling on the blanket by the basket.

Thea cackled, displeased by the brittle tone of Elpis' question.

Ariston regarded the owl with a slight smile before turning to Elpis. "She is Athena's high priestess."

Elpis assessed him with care. "You have much to learn about our mistress. For our lady is also the daughter of sea titans, Ceto and Phorcys. She is sister to those monstrous creatures, the Gorgons."

Elpis' words briefly silenced him. "How can that be? Phorcys is a...a monster, not a man." Ariston's voice was sharp.

Thea cackled again, ruffling her feathers.

"He is. A monster that does not deserve his sweet daughter," Elpis choked out. Thea hooted, causing Elpis to glare at the owl. The young woman clasped her hands in her lap and lowered her voice. "Phorcys was steadfast to Zeus and the Olympians during the war with Cronus and the Titans. As reward, he kept his powers *and* Medusa was born. A mortal child, she is all that is most valued among man – loyal, gentle, and beautiful."

"But what use can such a creature have for such a daughter?"

Elpis shook her head, her eyes drifting to the water where Medusa swam. "Phorcys has found his uses. She was bartered to Galenus as a child, offered to Athena as a youth, and she will marry now – if her father has his way. Master Galenus believes she will wed someone of value and stature. I have heard him speak of Phorcys' hunger for more power or wealth – that he's shameful and selfish. Our mistress is simply another means to achieve his goals."

"I did not know," he murmured. His head was spinning.

"And yes, she is also Athena's priestess."

Ariston turned towards the water. Medusa lay back, floating on the vibrant blue waves, seemingly at ease. Her hair surrounded her, as if she wore her veil. "She cannot..." He could scarce speak the words, and his mind rebelled against such thoughts.

"She will do as she is told. That is her way." Elpis followed his eyes. "She prizes duty."

His heart twisted sharply, both frightening and angering him. "She is suffering." His words were the softest whisper – too soft, he hoped, for Elpis' hearing.

He would protect her, from Poseidon himself if need be.

Thea called out then, a strange keening that drew Ariston's attention. He stiffened as the owl flew to him, settling on his shoulder with a flurry of feathers. The owl cooed, nuzzling his ear with her delicate beak. She did not bite him, but gently sorted his curls, clicking and cooing all the while.

Ariston relaxed, his hand settling briefly on the owl's head as it continued its ministrations.

Elpis gasped, becoming as still as a statue. "Thea does not give her affection without cause, soldier. She must sense some worth in you."

"I've never been judged by the affections of an animal before. But I assume I should be flattered by Thea's acceptance?"

"You should." Elpis nodded. "She is an excellent judge."

He regarded the owl, the keenness of its stare. Could this creature sense his devotion to their mistress? If so, Thea must approve. He smiled, rubbing the animal's head again. He wondered what Medusa would say to this alliance?

"I've found a conch shell," Medusa called out to them, delighted.

He tore his gaze from her before it could linger, knowing Elpis watched his every move. He saw Medusa wave from the corner of his eye, saw her excited smile.

"Remember your place, Ariston of Rhodes. You are a soldier, a soldier serving *Athena*." Elpis' tone was low, almost apologetic. "If Medusa's father wants her home, far west of the sea, for a beneficial marriage..."

"Athena has agreed?" the urgency of his tone was inescapable.

Elpis shook her head. "No. But somehow Phorcys has found a champion in Poseidon. The Sea God has pledged to make her immortal. To what end seems yet to be determined, but make no mistake, her father means to have her back. What or...or who

Medusa might want matters not."

Ariston felt sick. What would become of her? Would immortality make her into a true Gorgon, as hideous as one of the masks scowling from the temple pillars? Would she become a warning to those with a wavering heart? He shuddered.

"Surely Phorcys knows of Athena's temper. How can Phorcys ask his daughter to refuse the Goddess?" Ariston asked, spinning the apple in his restless hand.

"That is our mistress' dilemma. Either choice is...damned. If Medusa goes with her father, as a dutiful daughter, Athena may punish her for breaking faith. If Medusa goes with the Goddess, the lady's father will punish her for her disobedience. Phorcys, it is said, also has a temper to be feared. Medusa worries he might punish Athens, and risk Olympus' ire, to bring her to heel." She rubbed a hand over her face, her final words a whisper, "And if Poseidon cares beyond the oath he gave to the lady's parents, a battle between two such gods the likes of Zeus' favorite daughter and beloved brother cannot bring—"

"Any peace." Medusa's voice startled them both.

Ariston looked up, devouring the sight of such perfection with hungry eyes. He did not deny himself her beauty. He looked upon her with such need and admiration that his mouth grew dry. But his desire was tempered by this new knowledge. She was in danger – and he would protect her.

"I'm sorry, mistress." Elpis rose and wrapped Medusa in a dry cloak. "I'd not meant to go on so. Your soldier—"

"No, no, Elpis. It would serve him well to know the truth, for he might try to protect me from my sisters and end up ripped apart for his noble efforts." Her amusement was forced. Her face revealed the truth. She needed peace and laughter this day.

And he would give it to her.

Elpis shook her head. "Your soldier would know them, mistress, and think before he used his spear."

Ariston took a deep breath, steadying himself before asking, "Are they so fearsome?"

Medusa smiled slightly, wrinkling her nose as she considered his question. "No worse than the temple masks. But never worry over seeing their faces. For they are both two heads taller than you and cover their features with veils and cloaks, to startle their... victims even more, should they feel the need."

"Victims?" he asked.

"It's rumored that they've a fancy for children..." Elpis began nervously.

"Oh, and goats as well." Medusa's smile grew.

"Truly?" He felt a smile pulling at the corner of his mouth.

Medusa shook her head. "No. They are but nasty rumors – likely born and spread by my sisters to keep fear foremost in the minds of those that might cross them."

"If they were true, you shouldn't worry. You're too big a meal for them, hoplite. You should be safe from their appetites." Elpis giggled.

He laughed as Elpis made a frightful face. His lady laughed, too. It soothed him, the sound of her happiness. He cast a furtive glance at her, and met her fathomless blue gaze.

How he wished he could speak to her – to reassure her that all would be well. The way she looked upon him, her eyes clear and searching, made him ache to comfort her.

Then she noticed Thea and her eyes grew rounder. "She's never..." she trailed off, shaking her head. "She fancies you."

Ariston shrugged, unsettling the bird and making her fly to Medusa.

Thea landed in her mistress' lap, burrowing against Medusa's chest and cooing like a pleased infant.

"Not so much as you." He chuckled, his brow lifting at the bird's display.

"She knows that I love her dearly." Medusa stroked the owl's head, running her hand down the bird's body in long fluid strokes.

Ariston watched, mesmerized.

Elpis shook her head. "She tried to tear my finger off when I offered her a treat. Count your blessings that she finds you more favorable."

Once Elpis had shared her story, he was pleased Thea had found him an acceptable companion. And that her story had distracted Medusa, for Elpis was a gifted storyteller. She started with Thea's bite, moved on to Xenia's fear of the animal and eventually made her way back to Medusa's sisters while they ate their meal. He laughed, enjoying the way Elpis carried on about the Gorgons' treacherous habits.

When Medusa laughed, warmth spread throughout his entire being.

All the while he felt Medusa's every move and sound. He was attuned to her, anticipating her reactions. How he would love to know her thoughts.

As Elpis continued, he shifted, reaching for a slice of lamb.

He felt her gaze upon him, and turned to meet it. But she stared upon his body, his chest, and then the length of his arm. She blinked, turning her attention upon his face. She explored each feature, focused yet hesitant, as her eyes fell to his lips, then the rapid pulse in his throat. She blinked again, glancing at his face once more.

His chest was tight and heavy, yet his gaze met hers. He could not help the heat that coursed through him as she flushed in obvious confusion. His jaw clenched, as did his body, as he fought for control. And still she did not look away.

He took what she offered, letting his eyes travel slowly over her face as she had him. He traced the line of her brow and the sweep of her lashes. Her cheeks were high and her lips... He drew in a deep breath, returning her openly curious stare.

Her breath hitched and she swallowed. In the slim column of her neck her pulse was visible. It raced, in time with his. Pleasure flowed through him, sweet and pure, as he smiled at her.

She blinked, turning to the sea, giving him time to slow the racing of his own heart.

"What think you, mistress?" Elpis asked.

Medusa did not respond. Had she not heard the question? It had barely reached him.

Elpis glanced at him, then at Medusa. He saw the fear on their companion's face and felt the gravity of it settle heavy and hard in his stomach. His fear had little to do with the punishment he might endure for loving Medusa. He would never act upon it, for she would suffer too. No, his fear was born from the knowledge that – for the first time in his life – something mattered more to him than duty and honor. And he was willing to do anything to keep her safe.

Chapter Four

"A letter for you, girl." Uncle Galenus handed the folded parchment to Medusa and watched her expectantly.

"I believe it's from your father." Aunt Xenia smiled at her, attempting comfort.

Medusa scanned the bold script, recognizing it. "So it is." While she would have preferred to pour over the missive in the quiet of her room, she knew her adopted aunt and uncle were waiting most anxiously.

Her eyes were burning by the letter's end.

"Well?" Uncle Galenus thundered, his brow descending low onto his forehead.

She handed him the letter. "It is as you anticipated, Uncle. Father is angered, greatly, by Athena's interference."

"Phorcys is angry? With Athena?" Aunt Xenia was astonished, clasping a hand over her bosom. "He must see reason."

"He will carry on as he wishes – as is his way. But even a Sea Titan bows to the will of the Gods." Uncle Galenus studied the note.

"What grounds does he have for his anger?" Xenia persisted.

"He insists I've repaid his debt to the Goddess," Medusa explained. "And he has need of me at home." She moved towards Xenia, smiling at the woman she'd thought of as her mother for most of her life. She placed a hand on the older woman's arm, squeezing gently. "But all will be set right, Aunt. I have faith in Athena."

"Phorcys is an ass, petulant and careless." Uncle Galenus

regarded Medusa before skimming the note again. He scowled. "He thinks only of himself."

"What did he say? What has upset you so?" Xenia's hands fluttered at the note, her lips pinched tight as she waited.

"Phorcys now argues that Athena is abusing the girl... That Athena is keeping his child from him out of spite." Galenus' face turned an alarming shade of red as he blustered, "And that is what he will present when next he speaks to Poseidon. Or Zeus, so he claims."

"What?" Xenia cried, her face blanching.

"He is determined to have Medusa home." Galenus slapped the letter emphatically.

"Why?" Xenia asked.

Medusa swallowed. Why indeed. If her father had declared he was missing her she could not have been more surprised.

"To marry," Galenus grumbled.

"Surely Phorcys is not willing to challenge Athena over marriage? Medusa is young yet, there is no need to force such an event." Xenia blinked back tears as she regarded them both.

"If he would have her marry, she will. But not when Athena says otherwise. Is there some reason he forces this now? And who does he woo for his daughter? Who is worthy of her?"

"Someone of great import, certainly. Phorcys is nothing if not ambitious. The suitor himself may be unaware... Or may not yet exist." He shook his head. "But the matter has become less about Medusa and more about this perceived challenge by Athena. A challenge he cannot win."

"My uncle is wise, sweet Aunt. I am of little use to my father here. Some scheme has availed itself to him that makes him have need of me now." Medusa attempted nonchalance, to mask her dread. Her father was scheming, and she would be the one to pay the price for it. She had since she was a child.

First she'd been given as a servant, to repay her father's debt. He had come upon Galenus' ship long ago, when Galenus was more warrior than politician, and almost sunk the vessel. If not for Galenus' booming voice and determined manner, Phorcys may not have paused to learn the truth. Galenus had been on a mission for Athens, a mission for Athena. Galenus had threatened Phorcys boldly, for he had done no wrong and deserved no torment. And Phorcys knew this too. Knowing the Olympians' temper, Phorcys devised a bargain. As Galenus and Xenia had no living children, he'd offered up Medusa in reparation for the ship's damage and delay – and Athena would never know of it. Galenus had happily accepted.

Several years later Phorcys had caused a storm upon Athens, washing away the new foundation for Athena's temple. Athena had been greatly displeased. Quick to make amends, Phorcys offered Medusa to Athena as an arrephoroi. Athena had agreed, honoring the eleven-year-old while ensuring Phorcys' transgressions settled.

In the years she'd served as Athena's priestess and Galenus' servant she'd found comfort and peace. That Galenus and Xenia loved her dearly was a blessing, that she loved Athena a gift.

"Whatever he's thinking, child, I fear you will bear the brunt of it." Galenus regarded her with true sympathy.

Medusa felt the prick of tears in her eyes, but smiled at him. "It will be bearable. He may be strong-willed and, on occasion, self-important, but he's not without heart, I think."

Galenus snorted, shaking his head.

Xenia took a deep breath. "He is foiled, for now. We must not think on it, child. Anestheria is soon upon us and there are preparations to be made."

Medusa watched her aunt, quick to dismiss any unpleasantness. It wasn't that Xenia cared little. She cared a great deal. So much so that even the threat of harm towards Medusa quite unnerved her. Medusa was her only child. The five she'd birthed had not lived long on this earth, a devastating loss for any woman. She prayed that whatever drama her father had begun would not be too much for her sweet aunt.

"It is a glorious eve. Take Elpis and find some night-blooming jasmine for me?" Xenia smiled, cupping Medusa's cheek with a soft hand.

Medusa nodded and went to find Elpis. Her companion was lighting the lamps in Medusa's chamber.

"You have news?" Elpis took Medusa's hands in her own.

Medusa smiled. "I have, a bit. Athena has rejected his plea, for now. And my father cannot abide it. He is determined to get his way."

Elpis' eyebrow arched. "Phorcys will yield, in time, mistress."

Medusa wanted to believe Elpis and her aunt, but she knew better. Her father was rarely distracted when his mind was set. Perhaps he had changed. Perhaps he would accept Athena's decree in time. She dearly hoped so.

As she and Elpis found cloaks and baskets for the jasmine, her heart lightened.

Ariston would accompany them.

The shell necklace she'd threaded and braided lay in the jewelry box on her table. Her fingers traced the smooth curve of the white shells, remembering the warmth of the sun and the merriment in his eyes. It had been a glorious day. She'd wanted to give him some token of appreciation. That he would have something from her to keep with him pleased her greatly.

But such a gift was unacceptable. He was doing his duty to Athena. After all, the shells had been meant for Athena.

She placed the necklace back in the box on her desk and pushed the box away. She must stop this nonsense. She must. Whatever had passed between them...

"Ready?" Elpis asked.

Anticipation tightened her stomach as she headed towards the gate. But it was old Nikolaos who greeted them at the gate with distressing news.

"It's too late to wander far, mistress. I'm not so young as your guard," the older man rasped. "Suppose that's why he was called this eve to fight the Persians, while I stay with the women and goats." His laughter was creaky, bursting from his chest in short wheezing breaths.

Coldness seep into her bones. He had left – to war.

"He's gone?" Elpis asked.

"All soldiers have been summoned to prepare the city for invasion, the runner told me. The Persians bring their black ships ever closer, bobbing about to stir panic. Worry not, Ariston and his soldiers have gone to make sure Athens will be ready." Nikolaos continued, "It would be a good time be young – to feel the call of the blade and the glory of battle."

Elpis took Medusa's hand in hers, saying nothing.

Medusa heard bits and pieces of what the old man said. "The Persians are unforgiving warriors, they say..."

Ariston. She stopped the dread that crept into her heart. He would not thank her for it. He was a soldier. Fear was a sign of doubt. If she feared for him, it meant she doubted his skills and prowess.

She did not doubt him.

"Master Themistocles' ships are ready, though," he continued. "The Persians have seen nothing like Athens' Ekdromoi. When they sail out to greet them—"

"Will the Ekdromoi sail with the rest of the hoplites?" Elpis asked.

Nikolaos nodded. "They'll lead Athens' ships..."

Mighty Ares, hear my prayer. A warrior goes to battle, to lead Athens' men. Fill him with your spirit, guide his sword with your strength, and see him victorious for you... Let him stand and defend Athens another day. Over and over she prayed, halfheartedly collecting sprigs of jasmine. Her stomach roiled as Nikolaos carried on, excited that the siege might finally be underway.

Elpis, bless her, set to work collecting more than enough for Xenia. Medusa followed, too dazed to do little more than nod occasionally. She'd known this would happen – but she'd hoped it might be resolved without him.

The moon seemed uncommonly cold as they finished. Elpis offered to take the jasmine to Xenia, pressing a good-night kiss on Medusa's head. Medusa smiled her thanks and hurried inside, seeking the privacy of her chamber.

Thea greeted her with a coo and she smiled slightly in answer.

Her eyes wandered to her jewelry box and the necklace inside. Would he have worn it if she'd given it to him? Would it please him to have it? How she wished...

The owl hooted plaintively, seeking Medusa's attention.

"Thea." Medusa felt tears spilling onto her cheeks. "He's gone. He might be sent to sea, to danger. I may... He may never return to us, little one." Her voice wavered as more tears flowed. Her heart twisted, flooding her with such pain.

Thea hooted softly, clicking and bobbing in agitation.

Medusa stroked the owl with a trembling hand. "I'm sorry. I've no case for tears. It's shameful of me. He is a soldier, gone to do what he is trained to do." Her voice faded.

Thea was silent, her yellow gaze riveted upon Medusa.

She turned from her owl and knelt by the window. Her whispered prayers were for peace and Athens' safety...and the safety of the soldiers who would defend them all.

A fortnight had passed since Ariston was called to duty.

Medusa was thankful for Anestheria. Without the many festival preparations, she'd have nothing to distract her. She felt his absence nonetheless.

A temple guard had little chance for glory while serving Athena's priestess, she knew that. And glory was a soldier's greatest reward. She hoped he would find it, and come back to her.

His absence, coupled with the constant correspondence from her parents, plucked at the edges of her patience. Yet she prayed, knowing the Gods would hear her and champion her as they saw fit. Her faith was strong.

Anestheria came upon the city and surrounding countryside with noise, drink, and people. As Athens filled with revelers, Medusa watched from the safety and distance of the temple. She would stay at the temple through the festivities. Anestheria was not one of Athena's celebrations. The three-day festival celebrated Dionysus, The Lord of the Vine in this, the Festival of the Vine Flowers. And while reason and wisdom had little to do with drink, Athena received numerous offerings and tributes just the same.

On this, the first day, Pithoigia, spirits were high. On Pithoigia, jugs of new wine were opened and shared between servants and their masters. All was done in leisurely fashion, encouraging camaraderie.

On the morrow, drinking the wine became sport. Drunken crowds grew unruly and the festivities less restrained. Every maiden in Athens was locked away or carefully guarded. Innocence, a revered virtue, might be stolen by those lost to the drink.

Medusa lit her lamp and knelt to arrange Athena's gifts so that more could be added in the morning. Athena was certain to be pleased.

Her arms trembled as she hefted a large basket of apples. She'd felt weakness more than once recently, but she had no appetite and sleep would not find her. She ran a shaky hand over her face, thankful she was kneeling as dizziness swept through her.

"Mistress," Elpis said softly.

Medusa attempted a smile. "I'm fine," she reassured her companion. "Help me up?"

Elpis rushed to her side, slipping her arm around Medusa for support.

"You must eat," Elpis chided her.

"I will later," Medusa promised.

Someone stood, waiting in the shadows beyond the antechamber. Medusa turned, her eyes narrowing as she tried to make out who was there.

"Lady," Ariston's deep voice reverberated off the temple walls.

Medusa froze, her heart and lungs convulsing with pleasure.

He'd come back.

It struck her, almost physically, how her mind and body were buoyed by his presence. She clung to Elpis, her hands tightening upon her companion as she sought to stand her ground.

He stepped forward, bowing low before her. Then he stood, staring. How she'd missed his face, his steady eyes upon her...as they were now. How she'd missed the sound of his voice, calling her 'Lady'.

She stilled the smile that threatened to spread across her face, meeting his gaze with barely suppressed delight.

Elpis squeezed her hands in warning. Medusa stiffened, but understood.

"Your soldier returned to watch over you through the Festival," Elpis said lightly, "in time for Choes on the morrow when we will need him most. A wise gift from your Goddess, I think?"

Medusa inclined her head in acknowledgement, releasing Elpis as she did so. "Indeed. Welcome." She said no more, but turned back to the altar before her pleasure revealed itself.

She clenched her trembling hands, pressing them against her sides. She would need to be strong, to fight the pleading of her overflowing heart.

Ariston watched her. He suspected his helmet did little to disguise the longing and pleasure on his face, but he cared not.

His lungs burned, still shuddering from the pace he'd set to reach the temple. Once he'd been free to return to her, he'd run. He'd raced from the shore to Galenus' home. But she was not there, having already stationed herself in the temple for Anestheria. Shifting his doru and shield, he'd set off again, sprinting up the hill to find her.

He'd not known Elpis watched him as he scaled the hill, for he ran as if his life depended on it. She had greeted him with a disapproving frown and a deep sigh.

"You betray too much, soldier," she'd chided him.

His eyes closed at the young woman's words. He shuttered his face, but could not control his excitement. He'd followed Elpis beyond the antechamber and into the white walls of Athena's temple.

His breathing slowed as he watched his lady from beneath his helmet. After two long weeks of readying Athens' ships, two weeks of training hoplites with doru and shield, knife and sword, he should have been exhausted. Yet seeing her soothed the soreness of his muscles and the fatigue of his soul. And for the first time in a fortnight, his heart didn't ache.

When Elpis had helped her stand, he'd fought the desire to do the same.

Her gaze met his for the briefest of moments, and his heart was whole. He swam in the blue depths of her eyes before she'd turned from him to her duties.

He could not be certain, but he thought she was pleased by his return. He hoped so.

She seemed fragile, more so than when he'd left. Had something happened with her father? Had her sisters visited again? Was there news from Athena? Had a decision been made?

In his time away, Ariston had prayed. Not for favor with the Goddess, or glory in battle – for none seemed to matter.

Only his lady... He prayed for her. He prayed that she might be released, that her father, the Gorgons, the Goddess, all who had some claim on Medusa, would let her go. He prayed for her freedom, that she might choose her life. And, if his prayers were heard, he would help her have whatever she wanted.

His will was no longer his own. Even his service to the Goddess did not compare to the devotion he felt for Medusa.

Before he stationed himself at the top of the temple steps, he glanced at her again. She knelt before the temple dais, her head bent in prayer.

But if she was not released, he would watch over her and love her silently – for as long as the Gods allowed it.

"You are staying at the temple?" he asked Elpis softly.

"Yes. We stay in the robes room."

He nodded, his eyes traveling back to Medusa. On this night, he would sleep outside and keep watch. He was satisfied.

He straightened his cloak and stepped out onto the temple steps, scanning the empty walls of the temple. How odd that, on the verge of war, he felt such peace.

Medusa's heart raced on. She heard him on the temple steps, heard Elpis' whispered good night, but did not turn from the dais. She could not risk it.

Joy overwhelmed her, unknotting the muscles of her back and the ache in her head.

How she'd feared for his safety.

While no Persian army had landed at Athens, skirmishes had been reported. Several Athenians had lost their life at the hands of traitors and spies… She'd barely controlled her agitation as Galenus had shared the names of those who had fallen under a Persian sword. She could hardly contain her relief when Ariston's name had not been among them.

She'd tried not to let her worries color her every waking moment, but Uncle Galenus railed against the Persians' vicious nature nightly. And while Nikolaos accompanied her to temple, he worried aloud over their enemies' cunning and brutality at length.

War was men's work, and they seemed eager for it.

She had missed him.

But he was safe.

Having him here… She drew in a steadying breath. She would savor every second.

And yet, she must steel herself against her heart. She would not yield to sentimentality. She could not. No more jests or teasing, no more days in the golden sun on the shore. It was wrong, for them both. He was Athena's, as was she, and there could be nothing between the two of them except that.

She would be satisfied with that, she must be.

As the candles burned down, Medusa glanced about the temple. She was thankful to Athena, pleased that she served such a worthy goddess. It was no hardship to serve her.

The piled offerings were a testament to her favor. Beautiful carved owls, finely woven linens, shells, carafes of wine and oil, woven baskets of olives, painted jugs, and grapes and figs. All had been given for the Goddess' pleasure. And tomorrow, more gifts would come.

But tonight, she could sleep easily. For the rest was manageable now that she knew he was safe. She smiled, shifting a listing basket so it would not spill.

She was aware of nothing amiss. The sudden dimming of the candles must be a trick of her tired eyes. But a queer chill crept up her spine, lifting the hair along the nape of her neck and the length of her forearms. She shivered, rubbing her arms to warm herself. But there was more, something else... She stood, peering into the shadows of the temple. Wariness replaced her exhaustion.

A fog rolled in, pouring quickly across the marble floor. A gust of wind tossed the candles flame, lifting her veils from her face and casting them into the dense vapor now rising about her knees. She stooped to search for them, but the fog was so thick she could no longer see the marble floor beneath her, let alone her sheer veils. The wind rose again, swirling the fog around the pillars and chilling the air with an unsettling whisper.

Her stomach tightened as the thick grey mist filled the temple, swallowing everything – except her.

She shifted, tending to the flickering candles before they sputtered out. She had no desire to be swallowed by this fog and the blanket of night. She pulled the heavy ceremonial robes tightly about her, and yet she felt strangely exposed to a new presence – one she sensed but had yet to see. She shivered as she spun about, searching out the cause of her discomfort.

"You are Medusa?" a deep voice spoke, a voice she did not know.

She had not seen anyone enter the temple, nor did she hear any footsteps on the marble floor. Yet there was someone here, with her.

"I am." Her voice wavered.

A soft chuckle bounced off the walls as a man stepped from the fog. He looked at her, intently. "Of course you are."

Medusa stepped back as he approached.

He was handsome – more handsome than any man she'd ever seen. Laughing eyes, the palest blue, widened as they inspected her. He sounded amused when he asked, "You are her priestess?" He chuckled again. "No wonder Athena would keep you."

"Do I know you, sir?" No. She would have remembered such a face, angular and fierce, demanding of attention. From the breadth of his chest and the confident air of his stance, he was not a man to trifle with or forget.

His eyes traveled over her again. "No, lady, you do not." He paused, adding, "Not yet."

She stiffened under the heat of his gaze, speaking coolly. "Have you brought a tribute for the Goddess?"

One side of the man's mouth elevated. "I come with no offering."

No matter his odd manner, this man was in Athena's house and she must welcome him. "Your prayers are offering enough. On a night such as this, with the feasts of Anestheria, you are most loyal to the Goddess."

"I am not a pilgrim and I have no prayers for Athena." He did not move, and yet he was suddenly before her. So close that she could feel his breath upon her face. "I come for you."

Medusa stepped back, unsettled all the more. Alarm gripped her. But here, protected within Athena's temple, she had no reason to fear. Did she?

He smiled, his voice cajoling, "You've been loyal to Athena, to Athens, these many years?"

"I have." She fought the urge to shiver.

"And you're happy to serve as a priestess?" His voice was husky, mocking. "Serving your Goddess?"

The fog grew, rising high and encircling them. It clung to him, she noted, swirling about his shoulders like a vaporous cloak. His eyes narrowed as he waited for her answer.

She nodded, unease flooding her. Yes, she should fear this man.

His lips curved into a dazzling smile. "Have you not wanted

more?"

Her voice trembled. "What more is there? To serve the Goddess is enough, sir."

"There is more – much more. And I would give it to you."

Medusa stepped back again, knowing the temple wall was close behind her.

"I would give you your heart's desire, sweet Medusa." His voice was entreating.

She looked at him, wary. Was this a test? "I am the Goddess Athena's until she releases me. It is my heart's desire to serve her."

The man looked at the temple altar, his eyes narrowing further. "Arranging treats? Discarding those Athena casts off? Hiding yourself from the eyes of those who would feast upon your beauty? This is your heart's desire?" His voice coaxed, tempting her.

No, her heart cried out. *No.* She did want more. She wanted Ariston. By the Gods, she wanted to be his. She wanted to love him, and have him love her. Her heart twisted and her cheeks colored.

This was not the time for such realizations – surely. She could not lie. But she dared not speak the truth. So she said only, "It is an honor to serve Athena."

"Yet you do not answer my question." A slow smile pulled up the corner of his mouth, his gaze seeming to beckon her. "You do want more. I see it on your face. Come with me. Leave this place and come away, woman."

His words horrified her. She had no desire to go anywhere with this man. And she knew better than to consider breaking faith with Athena. That he dared to suggest such things... "You speak blasphemy," she whispered.

She glanced towards the temple's entrance in panic. The fog was too thick, hiding all.

He could take her if he chose to.

His breath stirred the hair at her ear. "I cannot speak blasphemy, Medusa." His voice was soft, silky. He moved effortlessly around her, the space that separated them so slight that a single step would compromise her. He was smiling as he came to stand before her again. "I am Poseidon."

Looking upon him, she knew it was true. He was Poseidon.

She stared at him with wide eyes, her throat tightening

painfully. She dropped to her knees.

But why was he here? What was his purpose in coming to her?

"Do not kneel before me, woman," he commanded, waiting for her to stand before he continued. His voice was at her ear again, making her shiver uncontrollably, but he stood an arm's length from her. "I could give you freedom, Medusa. Freedom to return home – if you wish. Or freedom from your parents, if you prefer, to do as you please." His voice was husky, tickling her ear. "But I would have you come with me now."

She could make no sense of this. "My parents? Are you here on their behalf? Athena told me that I was…"

His hands hovered over her shoulder, but he did not touch her. "Your lady can find another priestess. She uses you now to gain favor with Zeus and cause strife with me. 'Tis more of our…game, no more. A game I shall end, as victor." He leaned forward, his eyes darkening. "And you will be my reward, Medusa."

She looked up at him. "I don't understand."

His eyes bore into hers, palest blue. "You will come with me. You will be my wife."

Medusa stared at him, her heart thumping desperately inside her chest. This was no test. Athena would not test her so.

Then he… he wanted her? To marry? A God? Poseidon's bride?

She would have no say in these matters. Why would she? It was more than her father could dream of. It would be her duty, if her father wished it – he would most assuredly agree to such a match. Her duty to marry a God…this God. She cast a nervous glance at his magnificent face.

There was no gold in his eyes, or wheaten curls on his brow. His skin would not glow in the sun, and his laugh would not make her heart swell. He was not warm. He was not her love.

Her stomach twisted. She took a deep breath, her voice a strangled whisper. "You do me great honor, but I am Athena's. I cannot leave my lady." Would Athena fight for her? She did not know.

He laughed, as if she had surprised him. "You cannot? Or you will not?" His voice dropped, the sound rumbling. "You would say no to me? To Poseidon?"

She trembled. "I belong to Athena."

He rose high above her, elevated by the fog, to peer down at her. "You will belong to her no more. I will come back for you."

"Lady?" Ariston's voice filled the temple.

The sound of his voice sent terror coursing through her. This was Poseidon, a God. With a word he could end Ariston's life. She felt the hot prick of tears burning her eyes.

Poseidon watched her. "I will have you."

She felt the wetness of tears on her cheek, but she said nothing. There was nothing for her to say.

But she saw Ariston then. And, as the cloud parted, he saw her. His anger was evident as he came towards them – his face twisted and his body grew taut and ready.

Poseidon watched Ariston with an amused smile. Her fear mounted.

Ariston charged, his sword drawn.

Medusa drew breath to cry out. But Poseidon rose high into the air, buoyed by the fog, and vanished.

The grey cloud thickened. It swirled around her, a vaporous serpent, before it gusted from the temple. As it left, it lifted Ariston and threw him against the wall with uncontrolled power. Ariston's body fell to the floor, his head striking a column with a resounding thud.

Medusa cried out, horrified at the sight of his still form. She ran towards his crumpled body and knelt beside him with her heart in her throat. But his chest rose and fell. He lived. Her tears spilled over at her relief.

"Heal his wounds, Hera, for he is a son of Greece. Give him strength, Ares, for he is a warrior for Olympus..." she whispered prayers as she leaned over him, calling on each God.

Finally his eyes fluttered open, causing her prayers to stick in her throat. He stared about him, blinking rapidly. His gaze found hers, widening in surprise.

She sat back, silently offering up prayers of thanks.

He rose onto his elbow, holding his head and speaking softly, "Who was that villain, lady?"

Medusa shook her head. Words would not come. She must gather herself. Ariston was well. Poseidon was gone.

But the God's words filled her ears anew.

No, not words, not idle conversation. He'd promised her,

a pledge she knew he'd keep. Coldness found her, causing her to tremble.

"Are you injured, mistress?"

"No." She was shivering. Why couldn't she stop shivering?

Ariston unhooked the gold disk that secured his robe and slid it from his shoulders. He moved closer to her, carefully, draping the softly worn fabric about her shoulders. He pulled the fabric together then slipped the clasp home, ever mindful of his closeness.

"He touched you?" Ariston's voice wavered.

She shook her head, staring at him with unspoken need. Heat radiated from him, clinging to his cloak, offering comfort and safety. She ached for him, for his arms about her.

"No one saw, lady. No one will know." His voice was firm, entreating.

"He did not touch me." Medusa's voice hitched.

His face, his beautiful face, twisted. Medusa saw the anger he fought to repress. "What happened?"

"It... He was Poseidon... He came for me." She stood, bracing herself against the pillar.

He watched her face. "He came for you?" He stood slowly, moving closer to her. "For your father? But Athena..."

She shook her head, leaning against the pillar as she whispered, "For his wife... He would have me as wife..." She could not stop the panic that colored her words. She regarded him through fresh tears, her voice hitching uncontrollably as she tried to go on. "I could not..."

He bit out the words, "You cannot. You are Athena's. And she will protect you." He paused, his chest rising and falling harshly as his eyes traveled over her. His next words were strong and clear. "If Athena does not protect you, I will. I swear it to you." The muscle in his jaw tightened – inviting her touch.

They were the sweetest words she'd ever heard. She knew he meant them. With every fiber of his being, he would protect her.

She searched his face, drawing upon his strength. Whatever her fate was, knowing he was alive and well would bring her happiness. "No." She would not risk him. "You must do your duty, soldier, as I must do mine." She pulled her gaze from his, pushing herself from the pillar and moving to the robes room.

But his troubled face, the raw anguish she felt, kept sleep at bay.

❖

"This is your solution?" Zeus looked astounded.

"It will make peace with Phorcys *and* Athena. It will honor them both. Surely you see this, brother?" Poseidon asked. He would need his brother to succeed.

Zeus stared at him from under thick brows, amused. "You think Athena will be honored to have her priestess taken as your wife?"

Poseidon's irritation with Athena was all but forgotten. "I will give my niece a statue for her new temple. It shall be larger than any other of her likeness, as grand as she desires. I will give her whatever tribute she asks." His voice grew rough. "But I will have Medusa as wife." He burned with a new fire – to possess Medusa.

Zeus watched him with growing understanding. "I see."

Poseidon saw Zeus' look and shook his head. Poseidon was known for his conquests. He'd sired more children than any other God, by women willing or taken by force. Hera had often chided him, comparing his temperament to that of his kingdom, the sea.

He preened under such comparisons.

Truly, was there a more glorious thing than the untamed sea? His affection ebbed and flowed, he took what he wanted – regardless of the destruction it might cause. He was a selfish deity, but he felt no shame for it. Why should he? He was a God.

"You will *marry* her?" Zeus asked again.

"Yes." His passion drove him. He had no doubt that his lust was evident on the flush of his cheeks and the dew of his brow. But if marriage was the only way to have her, this untried prize amongst women, he would happily wed her.

"Can not a nymph…" Zeus began.

"You have not seen her," Poseidon countered, shaking his head.

"Should I? Should I see this creature that's bewitched you so?" Zeus asked, only half in jest.

Poseidon glared at his brother, his anger rising. "You have a wife. You need not another consort. You worry over Athena? Your daughter would hardly be pleased by such an arrangement. At least I might attempt an honorable offer." He spoke urgently. "I will wed Medusa… I must have her."

"And Phorcys?" Zeus asked.

"Will have his daughter wed to a God. I will give her immortality. His grandchildren will be demi-gods. How could he not be pleased?" Poseidon cared nothing about Phorcys or the Titan's wishes.

"Mayhap you are right, but this is a delicate matter that will take time..."

"Soon." His blood would not cool. She'd bewitched him.

Zeus regarded him closely. "You question me?" His words were hard, the edge a threat his brother was quick to recognize.

Poseidon was wise enough to avert his eyes, staring at the floor while he wrestled with his fury. "No, brother." To challenge Zeus was to lose Medusa. He would endure his brother's decree until she was safely his.

Zeus sighed, taking his time before pronouncing, "It is Anestheria. On the final eve, two nights thus, Athena will select her new handmaiden. This is when Athena will release your bride."

Poseidon relaxed. "Two nights...."

"Hold, brother," Zeus cautioned, "Let her find some rest before she is summoned back to Athena's temple. Two days more and she will be yours. You will have your bride, for I see the fever in your blood."

Poseidon held his tongue, his frustration trapped inside.

Zeus grasped his shoulders. "You must have patience. Go, gain Phorcys' blessing." He paused. "I will deal with Athena. When I do, you should be far from Olympus."

Poseidon's irritation eased then. His hunger for Medusa had wiped his original intent from his mind. And yet he'd won. He'd bested his insolent niece – and he would have Medusa, too.

Chapter Five

Medusa leaned against the temple column in the fading sunlight, vaguely aware of the goings on about her. The distant sounds of Athens reached her, lifted by a crisp breeze. Someone was singing, accompanied by a lyre, on a distant hill. It was a pleasant tune – especially when compared to the sounds of her aunt and uncles' quarreling. She could hear them inside the temple, placing their offerings on Athena's dais.

Elpis was at her side, waiting anxiously. She knew Elpis worried over her, more so since Poseidon had visited. In truth the one thing Medusa wanted was something Elpis wouldn't give her – a moment's solitude.

Thea circled overhead, searching the temple grounds for any sign of food. Medusa watched the owl, relishing the animal's grace and freedom.

Tonight she envied even the sun's rays. Spread across the horizon, streaks of orange, pink and red faded far to the east overhead. Medusa's gaze traced a bright magenta streak, wishing she might slip away with the sun. Far, far away.

As she turned, she was careful to keep her gaze from Ariston. She could imagine his curls dancing in the evening breeze, flaxen as the sun shone on him. She knew that he, too, stood close enough to protect her, yet far enough to see any advancing danger. Yet she could not look upon him – had not since Poseidon came.

"Look, there, Thea has her prey," Elpis said, capturing Medusa's attention.

Medusa looked where Elpis pointed. "A mouse?"

"Or a small rabbit?" Elpis suggested.

Thea ate quickly and flew to Medusa, settling onto the leather brace over her mistress' arm with a satisfied coo.

"You are a mighty huntress, my Thea." Medusa praised the bird.

A shout went up from the city, followed by much laughter. Medusa looked at Elpis, who smiled and shrugged.

Choes had been uneventful, Medusa was thankful for that. She'd been weary enough, with troubled thoughts and dreams, without worrying over the dangers of a drunken city. In a few hours, Athena would meet the Chytroi's procession here at the temple. The procession marked the end of the Sacred Marriage, Hieros Gamos. It was a great celebration, honoring the city's Goddess and her birth.

Once the Hieros Gamos ended, Athena would visit her temple for her naming ceremony. While it was a simple ceremony, Athena's rituals did not include the citizens of Athens. Citizens did not know which maid hid beneath Athena's veils for the first year in her position. Whoever was chosen would simply be called "Priestess". Those maidens Athena did not select for Athens, she might send on to another of her temples. The others returned home, to marry or care for their family.

Medusa remembered her first ceremony. She'd barely reached her twelfth year, having served as an arrephoroi, acolyte to Athena, for three years prior. Athena had known Medusa, loved her, called her "Little One" since she'd been a small child.

When Athena had called her name, Medusa had never felt such joy. Through that act, Athena had guaranteed Medusa a home, peace, and purpose.

Medusa's name had been called for the last five years. Each time Athena would smile and say simply, "My little one."

But Poseidon may have pled his case by now. If Athena called her name this night, would it be to place her hand in Poseidon's?

Her aunt and uncle had arrived at the temple earlier, laden with offerings for the evening's ceremony, as was their tradition. But their presence served to stretch the limits of Medusa's endurance. Galenus complained loudly, disgruntled by the festival, their travels, and all.

Thea seemed to share in Medusa's restlessness, flitting between the branches of the olive tree and the roof of the temple. When she'd tried to soothe Thea, the bird had flown to Ariston, settling upon his shoulder and leaning into his caress.

Oh, how she envied Thea.

"That is done," Galenus said, leading Xenia from the temple. "Let us eat before Athena arrives, shall we?"

Sitting upon a thick rug beneath the shade of a large olive tree, Xenia shared their adventures in Athens with Medusa and Elpis. Xenia was absorbed in her storytelling, finding nothing amiss. Galenus, however, stared at Medusa. From the corner of her eye she saw her uncle's gaze narrow, peering at her with ever increasing impatience.

"What ails you, niece?" Galenus asked, effectively ending Xenia's praise for their earlier meal of tender braised pheasant and roast lamb. "Are you ill?"

There was no reason to keep Poseidon's visit from them, yet she suspected sharing such events might only add to her burdens. "My heart is heavy, Uncle. And I've slept little of late." Yet she knew to proceed with caution.

"Are you sickly, child?" Xenia repeated, her voice growing anxious.

Medusa shook her head. "No... I'm fine."

"You are plainly not fine," Galenus asserted.

Medusa's eyes traveled up, into the branches of the olive tree that gave them shade. Thea regarded her with round yellow eyes. The bird, sensing her mistress' nerves, cooed to Medusa softly in encouragement.

Medusa smiled slightly at Thea, then said, "I was visited... by the Sea God."

"Visited? By Poseidon?" Galenus scowl deepened. "Speak plainly, girl."

Xenia gasped, covering her face with her hands. "He... he has compromised you?"

"Has he... What?" Galenus voice rose, leaping to his feet.

Medusa rose too, shaking her head. "Peace, Uncle..."

"Where was your soldier?" Galenus roared. His face grew mottled, reddening as he turned in search of Ariston.

Ariston stepped forward, ready to answer to her uncle. She knew he'd stayed, with ever more diligence, constantly in her shadow since Poseidon had left. His devotion knew no bounds – sleeping outside the robes room, standing in the temple door, and following her every step.

And her heart was both full and heavier for it.

Medusa dared to meet Ariston's gaze briefly, struck by the agony in his silver-grey eyes. It saddened her to see such suffering at her hands. As if he, her beloved Ariston, could have protected her from Poseidon.

He could not.

"He did not touch me, Uncle." Medusa said quickly.

Her aunt and uncle regarded her in confusion.

"I have no patience for this, Medusa," Galenus warned.

"Poseidon would have me as wife," Medusa said softly. Beyond her uncle's shoulder, she saw Ariston's face turn ashen.

"His wife?" Xenia stared at her in shock. "He said those words, Medusa? He would have you as his wife?"

"He did," Medusa admitted.

"His *wife*?" Her uncle's delighted shout of laughter was undoubtedly loud enough to reach those celebrating in Athens below. "Wife? Indeed."

Medusa understood her uncle's pleasure. Medusa's marriage to a God, to mother his children, would bring honor beyond anything Galenus had ever hoped for his family. His niece's marriage would elevate him, his household, into Athens' most elite ruling class.

Medusa cautioned, "I fear Athena may not find favor with his proposal."

Galenus was silent, mulling the matter before he voiced his opinion. "Fear not. Your Goddess will see the wisdom in this choice, as Poseidon surely has. By taking you to wife, he strengthens his ties with your parents and ensures allies for all of Greece – and Athena's city." Galenus assessed his niece with an appraising eye. He nodded, clearly pleased.

Medusa sighed, casting a tired eye upon Xenia. Her aunt was regarding her with a thoughtful expression, apparently discerning the worry Galenus was too delighted to notice. Was it possible that Xenia would see more than the benefits of marrying a deity like

Poseidon?

It didn't matter, Medusa knew. Even if Xenia did object, she would never say so or go against the decision of her husband.

"Walk with me, niece?" Xenia asked, leading the way from the temple.

"For a moment, wife. Our niece must ready herself for her Goddess and whatever news Athena may bring." Galenus smiled, his enthusiasm obvious.

Xenia nodded and tucked Medusa's arm through hers, leading her away from her uncle and up the stairs of the temple. They walked along the top step of Athena's temple, staying well within the candlelight and under Ariston's watchful eyes.

Thea followed, swooping to settle on Medusa's arm. Medusa suspected her pet sensed her mood and sought to comfort her. And that the bird had little love for her uncle. It was understandable, as Thea had sensitive ears and Galenus could only speak loudly – or very loudly. Whatever the animals' motivation, Medusa was thankful for her solid comfort.

Thea inspected Xenia, her round yellow eyes sliding over Xenia before yawning. Medusa smiled. Apparently her aunt warranted little interest for her pet. But when Thea's yellow eyes settled upon Medusa, the owl's gaze grew heavy-lidded. Her pleasure was evident through light whirs and clicks that bubbled up from her chest.

Xenia glanced at the owl, then moved to Medusa's other side. Her aunt clucked over Elpis' deep scar regularly and took great pains to stay far from Thea's reach.

Once assured that she was out of harm's way, Xenia spoke carefully. "Your uncle is right, child. You will give your family honor, beyond imagining." She paused. "While Poseidon's favor will bring with it challenges, you will learn how to please him. Remember what Athena has taught you: loyalty, reason, and patience. For your new master – your husband – will expect no less from you. Now you must accept him, celebrate his offer as a blessing." She regarded Medusa with sympathy. "I fear you have no choice."

Medusa stared at the ground as her heart twisted and her lungs screamed for air. She drew in breath slowly and nodded.

"If this is the Gods' will, child, be merry. Welcome this with an open heart and give Poseidon the pleasure you've blessed Athena with these many years. I beseech you." Xenia patted her hand. "Only you can make this burden into something joyful. And truly, this is no burden at all. For you shall want for nothing and live forever. Such tidings fill my heart with joy."

Medusa accepted her aunt's words with a stiff nod.

"Enough of your talk, wife, I'd be in my own bed before the moon is high." Galenus met them, tucking his wife's arm in his. "You will send word, Medusa, as soon as you have it."

"Rushing home will not hurry Athena's arrival or news of Medusa's future." Xenia smiled at her husband.

They were interrupted by the arrival of a young soldier. He ran up the temple steps and froze, obviously uncertain how to proceed. Medusa waited, giving him time to collect himself.

His cheeks flushed, and his eyes flitted amongst them, discomfited by the small group regarding him with intense interest.

Catching sight of her priestess robes, he hurried towards Medusa and knelt. His words rushed as he caught his breath. "Mistress, I seek your Ekdromos soldier."

Thea screeched, spreading her wings and flapping at the cloud of dust the soldier's hasty arrival had stirred into the air. Medusa ran a hand over the owl's back, steadying herself as she did so. Medusa stared down at the young man, her fear nearly choking her.

She knew why this soldier was here. She'd seen the distant ships on the horizon. Each day they sailed closer to Athens, bringing a mortal foe like none Athens – nay, Greece – had ever faced. She knew it would not be long before Ariston left her, and she would be alone.

Ariston was her soldier, yes, but only in times of peace. His first duty was to Athena and her city. He was a mighty Ekdromos.

Galenus had said so himself, and he rarely praised another. "It appears your soldier is somewhat of a hero, Medusa. I've heard the generals praise him. Why even Themistocles knows of him. He is known for being fleet of foot and lethal with his doru, wielding the nine-foot-long spear with lethal accuracy."

Ariston was an asset to Athens, her hoplites and allied soldiers. And Athens needed him now. She would not stand in the way of his honor or his duty.

She found her voice, soft and wavering. "He is here, soldier.

Calm yourself."

The young soldier looked up at her, his eyes growing wide and his mouth falling open. He said nothing, but nodded.

"What news have you?" Galenus moved to his niece's side, his tone demanding.

"None, sir. I was been sent to replace Ariston while the Ekdromoi have council." The young soldier seemed unable to tear his gaze from Medusa.

"*You* will replace him?" Galenus stepped in front of Medusa, his brows furrowed in ill-disguised displeasure. "Do you serve Athena, boy? Have you vowed to uphold her order?"

Thea screeched again and stared at Galenus, snapping her beak in irritation. Medusa stroked her back, hoping to soothe them both.

The soldier swallowed, intimidated by the older man's anger. He nodded, his skin draining of color.

"Peace, husband. Medusa's soldier will not be gone long. He will return to her as soon as he is able. This youth will serve. For Thea is here, as well – even if she is only an owl." Xenia placed a hand on her husband's arm, speaking in a soft, placating tone. "And the Goddess Athena will soon arrive. She will provide Medusa with the greatest protection. What say you?"

Galenus grunted at his wife, but continued to stare pointedly at the young soldier. The soldier swallowed again and looked down, seemingly entranced by Medusa's feet.

"Come to us when you are able, niece. Or send word to us, by and by. I would have your news as soon as able." Galenus glared once more at the young soldier before turning and leading his wife toward the gates of Athena's temple.

Medusa watched them go. They seemed fragile in the fading light, almost as if they were fading with it. She wanted to call out to them... but for what purpose?

A desperate foreboding closed her throat and held her silent. She drew in a deep breath, gasping as her lungs relaxed.

Thea bobbed her head, hooting sweetly, until Medusa smiled at her.

"I'm sorry, little friend. You are with me still and I am thankful for you."

She must be brave now and send him away with Athena's blessing – as was her duty.

❖

Ariston stepped forward, pleased to see Galenus and Xenia leave. Their ideas of honor and duty were tainted by the knowledge that they would profit from such a marriage.

A marriage to *Poseidon*.

This was Poseidon, who knew nothing of loyalty. He was a God, yes, so he demanded fealty. But he was not known for displaying such a trait, as much as he expected it from his subjugates. His code of honor was dictated by his mood – a mortal trait most of the Olympians shared. She should not be bartered to the likes of Poseidon, no matter who he might be.

And now Ariston had been summoned.

Mayhap it was best if he were gone. But if he left, who would keep her safe? His hands fisted before he stepped forward to address the waiting youth.

Standing beside his lady, he did not resist a glance from the corner of his eyes. Her sadness twisted his stomach, for he could do nothing to aid her.

The young soldier cleared his throat, attempting to gain control of his wandering gaze. Ariston felt for him. "You are Ektor?" he asked. He knew the boy, he was familiar. Ektor was nephew to one of the commanders, Nereus of Athens. He was a lively youth, full of wit and easy banter. And, Ariston thought, he would one day be a fine man and Ekdromoi.

The young man nodded.

"You may stand, Ektor. The priestess does not require you to grovel at her feet." Ariston spoke brusquely, growing irritated by the youth's fawning manner.

Ektor stood. Tearing his attention from Medusa took obvious effort. Thea cocked her head, cawed loudly at the young man, and flew into the dusk. Ariston smiled. Her owl was his only ally, it seemed.

"The council will meet at dusk, Ariston. Your presence is requested immediately." Ektor's gaze strayed to Medusa once more.

"Go with Elpis, soldier. She will find you drink," Ariston barked, drawing Ektor's attention back. "Then you must prepare for Athena's arrival."

Ariston gave him brief instructions about the Naming Ceremony. Ektor listened carefully, asking few questions. When Ariston finished, Ektor nodded and ran to Elpis, following the companion into the temple.

Ariston stood in silence, aware only of Medusa. There were words he would say, if he could only find them. He could not leave knowing what the evening might bring with it.

"I would stay," he murmured.

Her eyes closed and she shook her head. "No. You must go. It is your duty."

He waited, and when she glanced up at him he let his eyes bore into hers without restraint.

She looked away, but not before he'd seen the sparkling sheen of tears.

He hesitated before he moved, standing as close to her as he could. His voice was soft, meant for her ears alone. "I care not for your aunt's counsel, though I know it's of great import to you. Know this. Your life has been lived for their honor. You *have* done your duty by them – all of them." His voice softened, causing her to lean closer. "It is your honor, your loyalty…your gentle heart that makes you my lady."

Her startled gaze flew to his. He heard the sharp intake of breath that stirred her veil. But she said nothing.

He drew in a harsh breath before he whispered, "The love I have for you gives me breath and strength. You will always hold my heart. Let it give you the strength to do what must be done. For you will be *my* lady, forever."

He was gone.

And she'd said nothing.

Not because she had nothing to say, but because his sweetly spoken words had surprised her so.

He'd smiled, boyish and full of promise, before he'd left the Temple.

He'd said, "You will always hold my heart."

But her words had come too late, after he'd gone. How she wished she'd told him, "As you hold mine."

She wasted no time seeking out Ektor, and found him enjoying a modest meal at Elpis' hand.

"Ektor," Medusa addressed the young soldier. "What news have you? Tell me all what you know, I beseech you. I will pray to Athena, but I would know what to pray for."

It was true, she would pray to Athena. More than that, though, she had to know. Was his summons to the council for talk and strategy? Or was he leaving, sailing out to battle?

The young man, scarce more than a boy, blushed. He swallowed the large mouthful of food he was chewing and wiped his face with a cloth. He stood. "The Persians will land before the next full moon. If Athens' ships do not stop them, that is."

Medusa nodded.

Elpis nodded, too. She'd expected as much and told Medusa. "And the priestess? Who will guard Athena's servants?"

Medusa watched as the young man grappled with Elpis' unintended insult.

"I will, with a troop of hoplites. We will protect Athena's priestess and her temple. We may be young, but we are able, mistress," his voice betrayed only a hint of irritation. "We've been trained by Ariston and his Ekdromoi."

"The Persians – they are great in number?" Elpis continued.

He nodded, taking the bread she offered him. "They are. But our ships are faster and we've the favor of the Gods. Have no fear, we will be victorious."

Medusa considered his words. "I pray it is so."

As Elpis handed the young soldier the rest of the bread, she shook her head. "The sight of you might lose Athens favor with the Gods. Hurry, Ektor, prepare yourself. The Goddess Athena will arrive shortly."

Medusa smiled, leaving Elpis to sort out their new guard. She returned to the altar, lighting more candles and kneeling on the stone floor. She prayed until the procession was about to arrive. Only then did her thoughts turn to the festival at hand.

This evening brought more than a visit from the Goddess. Tonight was a rite of passage. Some would receive the greatest honor, others would return home without.

Living so much of her life at the temple, Medusa would know none of the virtuous daughters of Athens who would soon join her at the altar. But she knew Athena would choose well from amongst them. Two priestesses, four acolytes and two young arrephoroi would be selected.

Would she be one of them? She knew not.

Medusa heard Elpis readying the chamber for their visitors. Athena would soon be with her. Her fate was to be decided, her life's course set. And still she thought of Ariston. His words filled her heart with strength and hope. He'd told her to be strong. She would be.

It was easy to lose herself to the ritual of preparation. Athena was precise in her ceremonies. Eight long candles were arranged, four on either side of the temple's altar. Athena's throne sat between them and before the dais. A meal was carried up by the Goddess' servants and a long table was set under the olive tree for the great feast that would follow the Naming Ceremony.

Medusa set the table with care. Athena would sit in the middle, her priestesses and arrephoroi across from her, her acolytes on either side. She favored her acolytes, ever patient in their tutelage. When the time came, those who showed promise became her favored priestesses. After all, Athena loved and knew them already.

It was a trait Athena valued, loyalty. And loyalty was built over time.

The procession of candidates climbed the hill, illuminated by the slim torches they carried. They filed slowly into the temple to the sound of whispering linen, for twenty skirts, veils and robes stood awaiting the Goddess' arrival.

The youngest, no more than seven years of age, peeked from her hood. Her huge brown eyes stared around the temple in wonder, making Medusa smile.

The atmosphere was that of excitement, of anticipation. They looked upon the Goddess with hope and longing, as was right. As she once had.

"My, what a crowd I'm given." Athena's voice was playful.

Athena presented a fine figure. With the moonlight at her back, the Goddess was illuminated by its white rays and framed between the ionic columns that held her temple straight and tall.

Thea arrived amidst a flurry of flapping wings and sing-song calls. She circled once before perching on Medusa's shoulder. The bird called out to the Goddess with a loving coo. Athena's gaze swept the room.

Medusa smiled as Athena's eyes met hers, amused by Thea's preening.

But then Athena did something she'd never done before. The Goddess walked, fluid grace, across the marble floor to stand before her. She touched Medusa's cheek, sighing as her brown eyes examined her priestess with an unsettling intensity. Then her touch was gone and the Goddess moved back to inspect the rest of the maidens offered as her servants.

Medusa touched her cheek, the sense of foreboding returning to race up her spine and prick up the hair along her neck.

Thea cooed at Medusa, leaning into her mistress's shoulder. Medusa stroked her repeatedly while waiting, hoping her unease was naught but nerves.

Athena addressed them, "I am pleased by such devotion from the families of Athens, even when the city itself faces siege. Rest easy, for you will be well protected if you're selected. I am pleased to have Ektor, nephew of Nereus, as guardian to the priestess, and a full troop of hoplite guards to protect the temple from threat." The ceremony was simple, witnessed only by Athena's guards and Ektor. They would be responsible for the well-being of those Athena selected.

It took no time, for Athena knew who to choose. Eight names were called, each pronounced by their Goddess with a reverence they would cherish long into their memories – Medusa knew.

"Korinna, daughter of Theodoros..." Athena began, calling out name after name until only one remained.

"Elaini, daughter of Kallitratos," the Goddess finished.

Medusa drew in a deep breath. Her name was not one of them. "Little one," did not ring out. Athena had not chosen her.

Had Poseidon prevailed? Did she belong to Poseidon now?

She felt dizzy. Her fate had been decided then...

She straightened. She would not falter, no matter what Athena told her.

As the new priestesses gathered – for Athena would instruct them of their duties – the Goddess called to her, moving away from the rest inside her temple. Athena smiled warmly at Medusa, watching her as she came closer.

The Goddess removed the veil from Medusa's face, shaking her head as she did so. "So lovely, more so than when you came to me. Nine years is but a blink of an eye to me, but a lifetime for some mortals. You have pleased me greatly, little one. I set you free now. Spend two days hence with your loved ones, then return to the temple. I have one more gift for you, to honor your service to me."

Medusa blinked. What was this? "I need no other gift from you, Goddess," she whispered. Athena's words spun about in her head, filling her with hope and longing. "I have sweet Thea."

Thea seemed to know she was being praised, for she ruffled her neck feathers and regarded the two women with extreme satisfaction.

It was only when Medusa's attention returned to Athena that she noticed something amiss. Athena's face was pinched, her arched brows knitted. Her veil, clasped tightly in Athena's hold, trembled ever so slightly.

Was the Goddess moved, too, to part with her? It pleased her to think so. She watched the Goddess brush her hand down the animal's feathered back. Thea's head turned to watch Athena's hand, but she made no move to displace it.

"It is nothing. Nonetheless, you shall have this gift." Athena's eyes narrowed as she patted Medusa's cheek. "Return at sunset, two days hence."

Medusa nodded, uncertain of how to proceed. She took a hesitant step toward the dais.

Athena smiled. "Go, Medusa, you are free. Go now."

She glanced uncertainly at Athena before she walked, slowly, making her way to the temples entrance.

Athena's laugh echoed off the temple walls. "Go. Enjoy your freedom, little one."

Thea startled at the sound of Athena's laughter and flew from the temple without a backward glance.

Free?

Medusa's mind raced. Surely any moment Poseidon would arrive and demand she go with him.

But mayhap her Goddess had defended her? She must have. Athena must have pleaded her case with Zeus and, somehow, challenged Poseidon's proposal.

Medusa's heart filled with such love, such joy.

Athena had given her freedom, from the Gods, from Poseidon. She cared not about the gift Athena would bestow upon her. The greatest gift Athena could ever give her was this.

Medusa's eyes traveled over the temple, alighting on each of the new priestesses and servants, on Ektor's entranced face, and Elpis' clear astonishment.

She was free?

She made it to the steps before she turned again. Elpis followed her.

"My uncle will not be pleased," Medusa whispered, smiling. Her joy did not wane.

Elpis smiled in return. "He will carry on. But your aunt will appease him."

Medusa looked at Elpis, her eyes bright. Her smile grew wider and she hugged Elpis to her.

"You're free, mistress. The Goddess decreed it so – I heard it," Elpis whispered in her ear.

Medusa nodded as she released Elpis. Had there ever been a more lovely night? The moon hung low, illuminating the path to Athens, to the shore and the encampment of the Ekdromoi.

To Ariston.

The thundering of her heart filled her ears.

Thea screeched, regarding Medusa with wide yellow eyes before flying towards the shoreline. She cooed, calling to her mistress as she flew.

I'm coming. Medusa's heart swelled.

"I implore you, sweet Elpis, for assistance?"

Elpis nodded quickly.

"I need clothes, food…and a witness. Will you serve as my witness?" Medusa's eyes lingered on the road to Athens.

Medusa ran.

Her skirts blew about her ankles in her haste. She slipped often, the shale disturbed beneath her flying feet. But she did not fall or slow. Her excitement carried her.

She did not pause to admire the orchids that bloomed, fragrant and purple, along the hillside. She did not linger over the shepherd's dog that ran along with her, barking in greeting. Even the stars, glistening like dewy pearls in the fading velvet sky of night, held no fascination for her.

She ran, with her lungs bursting and her heart racing.

She skirted the city, following the trails Ektor had told Elpis to follow. She had no desire to be waylaid there. Time was a precious gift she would not take for granted.

She ran on, her side aching and her breathing labored.

As she crested the last hill, her destination was in sight. Athens' ships, a hundred or more, rested their bows on the bone-colored sand of the beach. Tents clustered together, the makeshift homes to this legion of Athens' brave hoplites.

All too soon their tents would be traded for the ships. They would depart, to protect their city from invasion. Hours, days – even Ektor was uncertain.

Her heart leapt into her throat, fear clawing at the sweet bliss she'd felt since leaving the temple. She placed her hand upon her chest, steadying herself with care.

She would not burden him with her fear. There had been enough of that between them. Whatever time they had now would be about joy and love. She would wave and watch him sail from Athens' shores, holding herself straight and proud for him, until he could be seen no more. She gasped for breath.

She would not think on that now.

Now she was here. And she must find him.

The council convened in a large tent, Ektor had told Elpis. It was larger than the others, red, with a tall flag pole, hailing all who could bear arms, all who were Greek, or her allies, to come and fight. The tent would have to be large enough to accommodate the commanders of the Athenian hoplites, the trained Ekdromoi, and even the less skilled psiloi and peltast soldiers – all gathered together against one great enemy.

Medusa scanned the beach with narrowed eyes. Ektor was right. This tent, larger than the others, sat on the edge of the shore, removed from the rest of the camp. This was a place for strategy and discussion, to plan for war.

She ran along the steep hill peaks, climbing up onto the flat face of a rock. She sat, breathing hard, and leaned forward to search for him. The tent was open, allowing the cool night air entrance, and the flaps lifted and fell in the sea breeze.

More than a hundred men were gathered inside, she was sure. While most stood back, pressed against the tent sides to form a human wall, a handful stood around a table.

Ariston was not one of them.

The men were gesturing, pointing and slapping a chart spread before them. Though she could not make out their words, their agitation was visible.

One man, with a thick thatch of long black hair, gestured wildly. He stopped, scowling, and straightened. He stepped back so that the other, a bald and weary looking giant, spoke. The giant's finger jabbed at another spot of the map with fervor, ending his speech by slapping the table with one large open hand.

Medusa wondered what they argued over. Where the enemy waited or the best route to intercept, perhaps? Ektor had said the Persians were coming, but they must stop them from a land invasion if Athens was to survive.

Tonight she would not think of war, but these men could think of nothing else.

Her gaze searched eagerly amongst the men, knowing she'd find him.

And then, she did.

Ariston stood, with his head tilted forward, listening, it seemed, to the two men. His helmet rested under one arm, his fingers drumming impatiently on the metal dome. His other hand came up to rub the back of his neck.

She shifted, pulling her knees up and drawing the heavy brown cloak around her peplos as she watched him. Everything about him pleased her so. It was no burden to rest her chin on her knees and watch him.

He shifted from one foot to the other, revealing his restlessness to her. His face was hard. His eyes moved, she noticed, glancing through the tent opening. He was distracted. Worrying over the coming battle?

A shout went up from the bald man, startling her. The bald man's arm flew up and his cloak billowed about him. He stood, towering over the other man, who yelled back without flinching.

Medusa looked at Ariston, concern mounting. His eyebrow rose, his frustration plain to see. She knew how tiresome it was, to be at the mercy of others' dictates. While it was an honor to be trusted by those of great import, there were times when that honor meant enduring a vast exercise in patience. She suspected this was one of those times for Ariston.

If only he could see her.

Thea appeared then, cooing. Medusa held her arm out to the owl, but Thea flew toward the tent. The owl flitted past the opening once, then twice, the night filled with her endearing call.

She watched as Ariston's eyes traveled to the tent's opening, piercing the dark with their silver-grey warmth.

Thea flew again, swooping past the tent opening, hovering briefly.

Did he see Thea?

His features were fluid, displaying his heart with no words spoken. His gaze narrowed then widened. His jaw tightened and his chest rose sharply. She tensed, waiting, as his eyes peered into the darkness.

He found her.

Her heart leapt into her throat as she waited. He would come to her, she knew it.

Ariston had cursed his summons, cursed the Persians and cursed the Gods. The trek from the Temple of Athena Polias had been unbearable, each step a cut upon his heart.

He did not know if he would see her again.

If she was called by Athena, nothing would change. A gift, he supposed.

But the alternative, his lady claimed by Poseidon, was beyond bearing. His hands tightened as images of her laughter, her smile, filled his mind.

Would she laugh with Poseidon?

No, no good could come from such thoughts.

A heated curse filled the air, forcing him back to the matter at hand. Why did the council continue to debate? The Persians were coming. The Athenians and their allies were ready, as ready as they would ever be for such barbarians. Action was needed now. The time for words had passed. He could hardly wait for battle. Those who fell beneath his sword and spear would find no mercy. It was there, upon the battlefield, that he could release the anger and pain he'd held at bay.

His lady's fate was unknown, pressing upon him. His eyes continued to stray to Athena's temple, a pale shadow in the moonlight. He should be there, with her.

She'd chided him to do his duty. She'd accept nothing less, for duty ruled all of her.

But *his* duty was of little import to him.

And now the bickering of Athens' great commanders was more infuriating than a swarm of gnats. He knew his Ekdromoi would lead the Athenians into battle. They were far superior in close combat than the others. Yet the two commanders roared on, delaying this verdict.

The night dragged on as they argued over the formation of their fleet, the worries over Thermopylae's fate, and the massing hordes of Persians at Sardis. He knew things were grave, but his restlessness could not be soothed. His gaze wandered again to the temple, the hillside, the rocks... A flicker of movement caught his eye.

Thea fluttered by, her coo confirming her very real presence.

He narrowed his eyes, unable to accept what he saw. Yet the owl flew past once more, calling to him – surely.

But what he saw, sitting upon the rocks, could not be. The Gods were playing a most cruel trick on him. Medusa was not here, she could not be.

Yet his eyes found her, knew her, and his body reacted.

She is here.

His comrades were lost in the throes of debate. They had no need of him now.

This war, these soldiers, even the Persians sitting upon the sea's edge, could not stop him from going to her.

He slipped from the tent undetected. Circling behind the tent, he moved past the guards at watch without hesitation. He jumped on the back of his horse and nudged the animal forward, onto the thin path that cut sharply up the hill, towards her.

It took him moments.

As he crested the hill, she rose to meet him. In the pale light of the moon, he stared at her in wonder.

Chapter Six

He slid from his horse, running to stop before her. Her face, white and luminous in the moonlight, tilted toward him. Her veils were gone, freeing him to explore every curve and line of her face.

"Lady?"

"Soldier." Her voice was soft.

"You come alone?"

She nodded, a hesitant smile gracing her lips.

He smiled in return, unable to refuse his instant response.

Though questions swirled in his mind, none found their way from his lips. She was here.

Her mouth opened, then closed, and she shifted on her feet. She was uncertain – was the news so grave then? Had she crept away to ask for his help? He swallowed against the tightening of his throat.

She took a deep breath and spoke quickly, her voice quavering, "I am released from Athena's temple."

Ariston froze, his chest leaden as he waited for the rest of it. His gaze traveled over her, taking in her peplos and chlamys, the garb of a woman – no longer a priestess.

Did she wear the robes of a wife now? If she was in fact Poseidon's wife, or was to become his bride, he should celebrate her honor. And keep his searing agony hidden from her brilliant eyes.

He spoke the name, forcing it from him though it pained him to do so. "Poseidon?"

Her eyes were as fathomless as the sea as she shook her head. Her voice trembled as she whispered hoarsely, "I'm free."

His brow furrowed. "Free? To marry Poseidon?"

"No. Athena has given me my freedom." She watched him closely.

Free?

He wavered, pulling air into his lungs with great gasping breaths. Athena had given her freedom? His relief was a physical thing.

And she'd come to him.

The roaring thrum of his blood filled his ears, unbalancing him as he absorbed this turn of events. Joy followed swiftly, buoying his love and spirit beyond measure. He did not catch himself but kneeled before her.

She had come to him.

He reached for her with wavering hands, tentatively clasping her skirts. Comforted by the feel of her within his reach, he drew in a deep breath. She was here. His hands fisted and grasped the fabric, pulling her gently against him. His arms twined about her knees and he burrowed his face against her stomach.

He closed his eyes to everything but her lush feel, the smell of her, firmly – finally – in his arms.

Medusa's chest tightened. Indeed, it was hard to breathe.

She had not expected his reaction. She could not have imagined her own.

She had thought of nothing but coming to him.

Seeing him trembling on his knees, reaching for her – drawing her to him without pretense or reservation – unlocked something inside of her.

She felt his hands tighten in her skirts, felt his hands draw her close. And she wanted more.

She was spellbound in his hold, enraptured by the feel of his arms about her knees. His hard chest was flush against her, the strong beat of his heart thumped rhythmically against her thighs. His head pressed beneath her bosom, fitting against her. Fitting perfectly, she thought.

His ragged breath caressed her skin through the soft linen of her peplos. His breath, a hot whisper, brushed across her stomach and the curve of her breasts – stealing the remaining air from her lungs with its intimacy.

She had no will to stay upright, her senses were so overcome. Yet his arms encircled her, holding her tenderly against him. She looked down at the top of his head.

She could touch him...if she dared.

Her hand rose, pausing before she gave in to the temptation. The downy softness of his curls was a feather light caress against her fingertips, teasing her. She watched her fingers as they slipped into his curls. She sifted through his silken locks, exploring and reveling in their feel.

Her breath caught and her hands cupped his head, pulling him tightly against her. Such new sensations filled her, tumbling about and making her light-headed. She clung to joy, she clung to him, overcome.

She loved this man. The power of it rolled over her.

His arms tightened about her, unwilling or unable to release her, she knew not. Nor did it matter, as long as she was in his arms. Her hands tangled in his hair, savoring the way his curls twisted about her fingertips, as if they were embracing her too. She smiled at the thought.

Her hand slid to the nape of his neck, startling her anew.

His skin... his skin, against hers... He radiated heat. Her fingertips felt afire, as if his touch had ignited her body and soul. Not with pain but with an exquisite pleasure, unknown but most welcome. His heat flowed into her hand, connecting her with him.

It was too much.

She drew her hand away from his flesh and placed it on his shoulder, safely covered by his cloak. Still, her hand tingled and she felt unsteady on her feet.

His hold loosened gradually, as if this was a most difficult feat. As he stood, releasing her, she met the intensity of his blazing eyes. His face, the steadiness of his gaze, was heavy with something more, something heady.

The silence pressed her, stirring her uncertainty. But he seemed satisfied.

She must speak...she must breathe. "You are warm," she murmured.

His eyes, silver in the moonlight, moved with leisurely contentment over her face before he spoke. "And you are my lady." His words were a promise.

"I am," she whispered.

He smiled, staring at her with a look of uninhibited pleasure. Her words, spoken without hesitation, seemed to echo in the air about them.

She returned his smile, joyfully.

He swallowed then, regarding her so closely that she felt her face burning from the heat of it. But she could not look away. She watched as his jaw tightened and he drew a deep breath.

"Shall I walk with you to your uncle's?" he asked.

Her courage mustn't falter now. "No."

"No?"

"No." She held her hand out to him, ignoring its telltale tremble.

His words were unsteady as he stared at her hand. "I would give him my pledge, Medusa. I would have an exchange of vows – a promise made that cannot be broken, by anyone or anything."

She understood him, his worries. But she would not share one second of their time together.

"*I* have your pledge, I hold it dear." She stepped closer to him, her hand wavering before she placed it on the chiton covering his chest. His warmth reached her through the linen. She stared fixedly at her hand upon his chest. "I would have *you* for what little time is left us."

How was it that no flames licked at her skin where her flesh met his? The heat which unfurled inside of her was as strong as a living, burning flame. Unbidden, her body swayed towards him. "Please," she whispered, meeting his gaze.

Ariston's hand clasped hers. Her hand, so small and delicate, lay in his hold. He hadn't anticipated the sense of wholeness her touch afforded. But he welcomed it, letting his fingers wrap about hers. He was defenseless against her touch, but empowered beyond measure.

He would give her whatever she wanted to keep her here, with him.

"I give you all of my time, Medusa. But there must be a witness. You've lived too long under the mantle of honor. A witness to our vows will give me peace of mind when...when I must leave you for battle." His hand tightened about hers.

She seemed to consider his words. "Will Elpis serve? And Ektor? As witness to such vows?"

He nodded. "Yes, they would do quite well."

"I hoped so." She blushed. "They wait for us at the Seat of Poseidon, in the cove."

He smiled down at her, astounded. She had taken pains to make sure no obstacles stood in their way. She would have him as her husband. She wanted him to be her husband. His laughter rang out. "Then let us make haste."

He moved back to the horse, leapt astride and urged the animal forward.

She stared up at him, eyeing the horse with undisguised apprehension. Her voice wavered, "I've never ridden. Nikolaos' donkey hardly counts."

"I'll keep you safe," he promised.

Her smile, her faith in him, warmed him through. He reached down, offering his hand to her. She took it, clinging to his arm as he swung her up behind him.

"Hold tightly, my lady," he said over his shoulder.

He heard her gasp as his knees tightened about the horse and the animal jerked forward. His stomach constricted beneath her touch. Her arms wrapped tightly about him. Her cheek and chest pressed against his back, swaying against him with the gait of the horse. He knew she would hear his heart – beating as if it would break free from his chest.

His hand covered hers, holding her soft palm against the hard plane of his stomach. His thumb brushed across her knuckles before he clasped her hand in his, squeezing it gently. She returned the squeeze, her body softening against his back.

They moved quickly, traversing the country and avoiding the main roads. No doubt Galenus would make this marriage wait, to consult Medusa's father and gain his permission. But he would make certain Phorcys was well pleased with the bride price he would provide for Medusa. If Phorcys was not satisfied, he would give more. He was willing to give all he had for her, without quarrel. None here knew that, in Rhodes, he was a man of substantial wealth, rank, and property.

He was only Ariston the warrior in Athens, he'd preferred it. The legacy of his father and uncle cast too great a shadow to give him prospects for one of his own. He'd set out to prove himself, without the use of his family name, and had done so, remaining simply Ariston.

Still, Ariston would not risk Galenus' interference this night. He would deal with whatever consequences their secret union might have once the deed was done. He would not risk losing Medusa to anyone.

He glanced at his waist, following the line of her arm wrapped about him. Exposed from elbow to wrist in the white light of the moon, he could scarce believe that they were bound as they were. Yet they were. Her arm seemed to disappear at the wrist, clasped warmly in his hand. This was how it should be, this bond between them. Having her with him now left no doubt.

He did not think of Persia or strategy, he did not worry over retribution for deserting the meeting or the lack of his weapons or helmet. All would be forgiven. They would need him too greatly.

She would be his, through witnessed vows. She would be his wife, his love and his lady, for all time.

It was slow going, for Ariston's impatience mounted with every bend in their path. Yet they forged ahead, the stars the only light as they ventured far from the city and surrounding farms. He turned the mount, steering them closer to the sandy beach and the cove at Poseidon's Seat. When they rounded the final outcrop, Ariston slowed their horse and stared in amazement.

Beneath an olive tree set far from the shore, Elpis was arranging a make-shift altar. She was pointing, speaking to Ektor in hushed tones. The young man stood back, adjusting one of the two tall tapers set beside a flat rock. The rock was covered with flowers, fruit and nuts, as was customary for a vow ceremony. How he wished theirs would be such a ceremony, attended by all who loved them. That would wait, when there was time for such festivities to be savored.

This was not that time. And though it had yet to begin, he longed for the time when this war was ended.

He would take her home, to Rhodes. The sun was brighter there, warmer. She would be even more radiant from its rays. They would run through the hop fields, eat the grapes from his family's vines and dive for pearls and shells before having a feast on the beach, just the two of them ...or with their children. He would enjoy showing her his boyhood home and sharing it with her. He could see it, their future, and knew the rightness of it.

He nudged the horse onto the beach, slowing it to a walk.

Thea sat in the tree, watching them with wide yellow eyes. She did not join Medusa, but emitted little purrs and clicks. He smiled at the owl, fond of her presence and the attentions she provided her mistress.

"She approves," Medusa said.

He slipped from the horse and reached up for Medusa, his words for her ears alone. "She knows I am yours. We are alike, she and I."

She shivered as his hands grasped her about her waist. As he lifted her, her eyes searched his. The shadows on her face could not hide her smile. Even after he'd placed her on the ground, his hold lingered. It had little to do with ensuring she find solid footing on the soft sand.

"Tis a good thing," Elpis said. "If Thea did not approve, you might lose a finger, or your nose."

Ektor eyed the owl warily at the words.

Ariston searched through the sack hanging from the horse's flat wooden saddle. Inside he found the supplies he needed. The others waited while he scribbled two notes. He sanded them, rolled them and tucked them into his belt.

Ariston led Medusa to the rock, stopping before the makeshift altar. He glanced at Elpis and Ektor, and they joined them.

His voice was steady, strong and sure as he said, "I, Ariston of Rhodes, take Medusa of Athens, daughter of Phorcys and Ceto, as my wife. In her honor, I give Phorcys gifts of thanks. To Galenus of Athens, her guardian, I have made provisions for her loss to his household. Ektor, you will deliver these to Galenus." Ariston handed Ektor the two rolls of parchment. "It is a fair agreement, binding according to the laws of Athens and Greece. Medusa is now my property and my family."

Ektor stared at them, clearly uncomfortable with the role he was to play. Elpis sniffed, tears rolling down her cheeks.

His gaze did not linger on them. Medusa was looking up at him, waiting for something.

Medusa whispered, "Have I nothing to say?"

Ariston smiled. "If Galenus or your father were present they would speak the words."

"What would they say?" she asked.

"I give you, Ariston of Rhodes, my daughter to sow for the purpose of providing legitimate children and increasing your oikos." Ariston waited.

Medusa glanced up at him, her brows rising and her face thoughtful.

Ariston knew them to be cold vows. He'd thought so when his father had said them at his sister's marriage. But they were binding, they were the law.

"I give myself to you, Ariston of Rhodes, for the purpose of providing legitimate children and increasing your oikos." Medusa's voice did not waver.

Gazing upon her, he knew she meant them. And smiled broadly at her, his wife.

Medusa was lost in his eyes.

He was her husband now, he was hers. There was comfort in the knowledge. And she could look into his soulful grey eyes without censure, speak his name…or take his hand. She smiled.

"We shall leave you then, mistress," Elpis said.

Medusa turned to her friend, "I thank you, Elpis." She hugged her companion to her, whispering, "Thank you," again.

"I am pleased for you, lady. You've all you wanted now. Let your heart be peaceful and happy." Elpis whispered into her ear, "He is a fine man. Being his wife will be no hardship."

"I've never known such happiness. The Gods have given me all," Medusa murmured.

A spark of apprehension found her, making her cling to her

companion a bit longer. She knew what it was to be married, what was expected of a wedding night. She'd heard her aunt speak of it in less than pleasing tones. But she was a wife, and her husband would expect such things.

"Fret not," Elpis squeezed her hands as they drew apart. "He is a gentle man, for all his strength."

Medusa nodded in agreement. She must not forget how precious this time with Ariston was. And she would endure whatever needed to make their marriage contract binding – even if she did not enjoy it much.

"You've been generous? The hedna provided will please her family, sir? The lady – your wife – is a great prize." She turned, surprised to hear Ektor question Ariston. "I fear protestations of the match..."

Ariston nodded, smiling at the younger man. "She is. And I have been. But if there is any question, I will double what I've promised. Make that known to Galenus."

Medusa cast a curious glance at Ariston.

A hoplite soldier would not have the means to be 'generous' with men like Galenus or her father. His pay would be drachmas, and whatever spoils his battles might provide him. He might have a small kleros on Rhodes, such farming plots were passed down from father to son. But, even combined, these gifts would hardly be considered generous.

"I will make sure Master Galenus knows this," Ektor nodded.

"When do we tell them?" Elpis asked.

For but a moment, Medusa wished they'd never have to tell them. She knew it was unreasonable, but they had such little time – too little to share.

Surely they could wait.

"I go to the temple at sunset in two days' time, Elpis. Athena has a gift for me, as you know. Let this news wait until then. Whatever her gift is, it may make news of my...marriage more pleasing to my uncle and father." Medusa turned to Ariston questioningly.

Ariston nodded.

"And if your uncle asks where you've gone, I will tell him the Goddess sent you away until that time," Elpis said. "But I will assure him you are safe, well guarded. It is all true, Mistress. She did tell you to go – to be free. And your guard is with you. Galenus can hardly argue with Athena."

Medusa smiled.

"You are a good friend to my lady, Elpis. Should you tire of Athens, I would have you go with her to Rhodes," Ariston chuckled.

Elpis said, "I go where my lady goes, Master Ariston."

Medusa watched as Ektor helped Elpis onto the horse.

Ektor and Ariston clasped forearms. "I give you my thanks, Ektor."

"It is an honor to serve as witness for you, Ariston of Rhodes." Ektor smiled. "It is something I might share with my children in the years to come."

Medusa's eyes traveled over Ariston. He was smiling as he stood back, allowing Ektor room to swing up behind Elpis. He glanced at her, his smile growing as their eyes met.

She looked away, watching her dearest friend depart. Little was said, though she waved when they reached the hilltop. As they disappeared, Medusa regarded Ariston with renewed nervousness.

He turned toward her. His jaw grew taut and his smile faded slightly.

They stood, regarding each other in the flickering light of the tapers.

He was so beautiful to her, just his presence teased flames of heat to life under her skin. His smiled brightened, fanning the flames higher.

Thea clicked, resting on Ariston's shoulder.

"Thank you, little one," Medusa heard him say, "for bringing me to my lady."

Thea cooed, a soft bubbling call.

Medusa stepped closer, stroking Thea's head. "She knew, Ariston."

Ariston's eyes widened. "Not soldier? Or hoplite?" She suspected he was trying to tease her, his words were hoarse.

"No. Though husband, mayhap."

His hand came up, hesitantly resting against her cheek. "What did Thea know?"

His fingers were warm, his thumb a light caress. Breathless, she whispered, "That I would come to you."

Thea fluffed up her feathers and flew back to her perch in the tree.

Ariston's hand lifted from her, a small smile on his lips as he glanced at the bird. "She is wise. Like her mistress."

The sound of a lyre floated down the hilltop, wrapping them in its sweet song. Medusa turned toward the hill, searching for the player. But there was no one to be seen. A voice rang out then, a man singing to the rapid beat of a drum.

She ached to reach out to Ariston, to have his hands upon her.

He watched her, but made no move to touch her.

This would not do.

After all this night had brought, could she ask him for more? She walked to him, so close she could feel him, the tension within him.

"Do I not please you?" she whispered.

His eyes grew wide.

"I..." she faltered.

"You please me," he spoke softly. "You please me greatly, lady."

She placed her hand on his chest, "Too long I've wondered how it would feel, to have your arms about me..."

"Wonder no more." His arms came around her, pressing her to him.

His strength and scent assailed her. She closed her eyes, resting her cheek against his chest. His arms, thick and solid, cradled her. She felt his breath stir her ear, his cheek resting against her head, and pressed herself closer.

Her arms slipped about his waist, her hands pressed flat against his back. And still it wasn't enough. Her grip tightened, pressing him closer still.

His breath hitched and the rise and fall of his chest quickened against her.

With a sigh, she turned her face into his chest and breathed deep.

"Is it satisfactory?" he whispered.

She glanced up at him. "What?"

He laughed. "Being held so?"

She shook her head, teasing him with relish. "It is too soon to say, husband. Sit with me a while longer so I might better decide."

She sat on the sand, pulling his hand.

He laughed again, sitting at her side, his arm wrapping about her.

She leaned against him, but found too much space separated them. "Mayhap I prefer standing."

The look in his eyes silenced her, the pull of him sweeping through her. She rested her head on his shoulder, calming the fire in her belly.

The music played on, though the rhythm changed and a new voice rang out. She strained to hear, but the words seemed slurred. "Do you know this song?" Medusa asked.

Ariston cleared his throat, smiling down at her. "I do."

She closed her eyes, leaning towards the singer. "I'm not familiar with the story." Her eyebrows arched as the singers proclaimed the many virtues of the nymph's form and features.

"No, it would not be sung for a priestess." He seemed greatly amused.

Medusa opened her eyes. "But I'm a wife now."

He nodded, his gaze lingering on her mouth.

Medusa was vaguely aware of the rapid pounding on the drum. How could he look at her and inspire such feelings within her? How had she never known such feelings existed?

A cry went up, jarring her. Shouts and laughter joined and the music began again, fast and spritely as it teased its listeners into movement.

Medusa smiled at Ariston. She dearly loved to dance. If Elpis were here, she would dance with her. She felt his eyes upon her as she stood.

"Is dancing permitted for soldiers?" her voice wavered, uncertain.

He nodded once.

She could hardly speak the words. "Do you dance?"

"I can, mistress." He smiled up at her, a lop-sided grin.

She pulled her cloak from her shoulders and placed it on the sand. Standing, vulnerable, she held her hand out to him. "Show me?"

She could not know how beautiful she was to him.

His heart thundered in his ears as he stood and captured her hand in his. He removed his cloak and cast it upon the sand with hers.

This contact was so new, so raw with his passion that he loosened his grip on her. His touch affected her too, he saw it. He must be careful of her innocence. Each touch brought new sensations – and worries that he would frighten her away.

Each touch made him ache for more.

He came to stand inches before her, and she froze. She tilted her head, staring up at him as he reached for her. He placed his right hand slowly, deliberately, cupping her left side. She gasped, sucking in her breath sharply.

His hand tingled, aching to pull her against him, aching to love her.

He waited but she said nothing.

"Raise your hand," he said. He demonstrated, raising his left hand and arching it over his head. When she lifted hers, he grasped her hand. Her skin was smooth and soft in his. He took a steadying breath. "Now place your other hand as mine."

Ariston's stomach clenched as her soft hand slid across his skin, curling around his side. His muscles contracted as her fingers tightened, forcing him to draw in another steadying breath.

"Now, hang on." He smiled and held her, turning them both rapidly. Round and around they flew.

Her laughter surrounded them, drawing a smile from him.

When he expected her to pull away, she grasped the front of his exomie, the other hand sliding up from his stomach to rest on his bare shoulder. She did not know that her hands had moved over him so, for her eyes were shut. She did not see the hunger he felt for her.

She clung to him so she would not fall. He would never let her fall.

His arms came around her, holding her in a loose embrace. She weaved on her feet and leaned into him.

Medusa felt his arms about her and knew she was clinging to him. He held her in his steady arms, securely – carefully. And yet she felt a new ache that troubled her. Was there something wrong with her that his gentle embrace made her want something more? She had no idea what was missing, yet she felt it all the same.

She looked up at him then, wondering if he felt this strange reaction.

His eyes were heavy, waiting for hers.

The ache tightened, making her glad he held her upright.

His skin was warm. His heart beat, rapidly, under her right hand.

Her gaze fell to her hand, glowing white against his shoulder. She saw the convulsive swallow of his thick neck and the unsteady breath he took. His scent – sun, earth, and something more – filled her nostrils. Instead of loosening her grip, she found it tightening upon him.

Her heart. Her heart was beating... pounding. Her breath quickened as their eyes met.

She knew what this was, what she could now admit. Beyond the stirring caress of his hand upon the base of her back or the rippling strength of his arm about her waist, she wanted his hands upon her. She wanted him to touch her as a man touched a woman.

Still he watched her. She knew her wants, her thoughts, were visible upon her face. As hard as it was for her to breathe, to speak, she wondered at his silence.

"Ariston," she spoke softly, unsure of how to go on.

His eyes were steady on her, his mouth tight and his nostrils flared.

He felt the same?

Medusa shook her head. She leaned forward and rested her forehead against his chest. She took a shaky breath and turned her head, pressing her cheek tightly against his chest and wrapping her arms about him. Her hands clung to his back, twisting in his tunic. "Oh."

His arms tightened instantly, his breath caressing the top of her head.

"Ariston," she whispered against him, her tone betraying her nervousness, "I would have you show me...what it is to be a woman... loved by a man."

She felt his arms tighten about her.

"You have my heart," his words were hoarse, whispered against her forehead. "I fear my body is not as tender."

"I know only that there is something more I crave from you." She pulled back, looking up at him. "Show me, please. Love me."

His hands moved up her back quickly, as if he'd been waiting. One hand caught her hair, the other cupped her cheek. She leaned into his touch, reveling in the fluid heat he unleashed. As he bent his head to her, she closed her eyes. She was lost to the feel of his hand on her cheek, his breath mingling with hers.

His lips lightly pressed to hers. Once – soft and lingering. His lips were firm, but yielding. The heat of that touch seared her, melting her against him.

There was more, she knew it.

She did not open her eyes, but slipped her hands about his neck. She was rewarded immediately.

His lips were soft, surprisingly so, as they settled upon her again. Her mouth responded, fitting against him as his became more firm upon her. His hand turned, and his thumb grazed her lip, startling her so that her lips parted.

His mouth kissed her lower lip, pulling lightly upon it.

Surely the ground had fallen away beneath her feet.

She gasped again, and felt his mouth test and pull upon hers. Their breath became one, their lips clung. Her knees buckled as his tongue touched hers and a small sound escaped her. But his arms caught her, steadying her against him.

She'd never imagined such a thing, that a kiss could be so intimate.

Yet this kiss went on, stoking the fire inside of her to a feverish burn. And his mouth fed the flame, enticing it ever higher. His lips, his tongue, moved on her, within her mouth, until she was breathless.

When his lips tore from hers, his breath was ragged in her ear. He pulled her against him, and she burrowed closer. It was only then that she realized they were kneeling on the sand, tangled in each other's arms.

"My lady," he whispered in her ear.

She could not speak.

He pulled back, cupping her cheek again. "You set me afire. I'd hoped—" His words ended abruptly, forcing him to swallow before he drew in a deep breath and said, "How could I know how it would be between us?"

His words flowed over her. She, too, was on fire. And she ached for him with a fierce desperation. Her body, alive in a way she'd never known, was calling for him.

Words would not find her. But the caress of his thumb across her lower lip elicited a most telling shiver.

He stood slowly, reaching out to her. "Let us find our bed, wife."

Medusa took his hand, letting him pull her up and lead her down the beach. A light shone from the window of the watchman's cabin, welcoming them.

Chapter Seven

It was a fine morning, hot and brilliant. Ariston glanced up, admiring the beauty of this new day. He stretched his arms and shoulders, soaking in the balmy heat of the rising sun. His bare chest warmed under its rays, tensing as he cast the net that would catch their breakfast.

As tired and hungry as he was, he was complete. Never had he known such happiness.

He pulled in the net, waded further into the sea and cast it out again. The net held the sunlight for only a moment, but the weave shifted, resembling honey strands of silken hair. His mind would not focus. Images of his lady wife would not be held at bay.

His hands tightened on the net.

Her mouth, her sigh, her hands upon him had shown him pleasure like no other. And yet they'd been awkward at best, hesitant and unschooled beneath one another's touch. The freedom of their love was a new gift, one that would take time to grow accustomed to.

The hunger she stirred... He swallowed. His body throbbed in response to his memories. His need for her had been immediate, leaving little room for tenderness on their wedding night. He'd tried to go gently with her, to bring her pleasure. Instead he'd trembled with his need, held her tightly to him and lost control. The smell of her, her sighs, the quiver of her skin beneath him, the slight catch in her breath when she'd moaned softly against his throat... She had

Medusa, A Love Story

been his undoing.

She'd fallen asleep in his arms. And he'd watched her.

In the candle's glow, her cheeks had been flushed, her skin dew-kissed from their lovemaking. His eyes had pored over every inch of her, etching her form into his mind.

Her hair twined about her, wrapping about her waist. He smoothed it back, letting the silken strands slip through his fingers. She sighed and rolled onto her stomach, one hand pillowed under her cheek. Her shoulder, bleached white in the moonlight, begged to be kissed. He leaned forward and did so, inhaling the smell of her sweet scent.

His fingers lightly traced the curve of her shoulder, sliding along the dip at the base of her spine. His fingers were a whisper on her skin, trailing down her back and the curve of her buttock.

She stirred. "Ariston?"

He kissed her shoulder again, whispering, "Sleep, love, sleep."

She sighed, searched out his arm, and burrowed under it. It pleased him greatly that she sought him out. He pressed closer to her, draping his arm across her in return. Though he tried to sleep, his eyes would not close. She was too recently won to part with. So he watched her until the sun rose.

He would sleep later.

As the sun had woken he'd slipped from the cottage with his net, to fetch them breakfast.

He glanced back at the beach. It was early yet, she likely slept still.

But she sat, wrapped in his cloak on the shore, watching him. His heart thundered as he lifted a hand in greeting. The morning grew sweeter yet when she smiled and waved back. He dove into the water and swam to the shore, pulling the net behind him.

As he waded from the sea, Medusa met him. She stared up at him, her welcoming smile unguarded. Her eyes slid over his face, resting on his mouth. His wife blushed.

There is no sight lovelier. "My lady..." his voice was soft.

"Husband." She stepped closer to him. Her hand hesitated before she placed it on his arm.

Ariston's heart tightened in his chest, pleased that she would touch him. He closed his eyes as her hand slid from his wrist to his

107

elbow. Her arms slid around his waist and her cheek rested upon his chest with a sigh.

He dropped the net, shivering at the feel of her. Even now, this simple touch captured him.

"How are you this fine morning?" her words were said against his chest.

The clouds shifted, hiding the sun. The wind stirred her cloak about them, sending a shiver along his spine.

It was a fleeting sensation, this fear that robbed him of his breath. He knew not where it came from, but a coldness gripped him so deeply he was frozen. Her hold on him seemed to lessen, as if she was moving away from him – beyond his reach and his help. The pain was blinding, and terrifying. Ariston's arms came around her with a suddenness that surely startled her. But he feared she'd slip away if he let her go.

He shook his head.

Yet she still stood with her arms about him, calling him, "Husband?"

He could not relax his hold on her, for the feel of her chased away his terror. His anguish, which he knew was unfounded, was too real – too severe. So he held her to him until he grew calm, if not quite peaceful.

"Had I known this was a riddling question, I might have started with another." Medusa leaned back in his arms. Her face was alight with a mischievous grin, one that soothed him almost instantly.

The clouds shifted once more, and the sun broke free, restoring the day's glory and peace once more. 'Twas fatigue that played upon him, nothing more.

"I've never seen a brighter morn. Nor felt as blessed by the Gods as I am this day." His eyes met hers before he pressed a kiss to her forehead. "Are you hungry, wife?" he whispered into her hair, soft and silken against his lips.

"I am, yes."

Ariston stared down at her. She looked up at him, her smile dimming the morning sun. He sighed deeply, at ease once more.

His hands explored her face. He seemed unable to stop touching her. His thumbs caressed her brows, her lashes and cheekbones as his eyes traversed the plains of her face. She leaned into his touch, making it easy for him to tilt her face to his. Their kiss was soft, lingering and sweet as her mouth opened for him.

Before her wedding night, she'd never had lips upon her own. But his fit against hers as if his mouth had been made to meld with her own...as her body had held his. They were made to be one.

Her hands covered his, holding them to her cheeks as she kissed him back. She leaned into him, pressing herself to him and absorbing his heat.

"There is food in the cabin. Elpis brought enough for your army," she whispered against his mouth.

Ariston peered down at her. "I've fish as well."

She nodded, her eyes resting on his mouth. His lovely lips turned up at the corners as beneath her gaze.

"Shall I start a fire?" she asked.

She saw him nod and tore her attention from his mouth. She held the hand that clasped hers and let him lead her back to the cabin, unsettled by how he affected her.

She busied herself with preparing their meal. He made quick work of the fish, while she stoked the fire. Figs and berries would join their fish, a hearty breakfast after such a vigorous evening. She blushed at such a thought.

"Is your father a soldier?" she asked.

He shook his head. "He, like most Greeks, has fought when called upon. But he is a statesman."

She froze, surprised. "I know little of your family."

"What would you know?" He smiled.

"Everything." She shrugged. "If he is a statesman, you must have other brothers..."

"No, I'm his only son. I will inherit my family's basileus and all the responsibilities that come with it."

She was astounded, staring at him openly. "But why would you leave if you're the eldest son?" Medusa watched as he pushed the rocks further from the fire, keeping the fish from charring.

"My father and I quarreled." He stared into the fire, his face shuttered.

She moved closer, taking his hand in hers. His touch made

her heart stumble, before its beat grew steady once more. "Was he unfair to you?" Her words were soft.

He looked at their joined hands, momentarily silent. "No. He was a fine father. I was a poor son."

His words surprised her. "You? You are a man of duty and respect—"

"Because he sent me away." His eyes moved over her face as he continued, "I was disrespectful to him and to the elders of our village. I scorned their need for ceremony and religion, calling their patient deliberations and debate a useless waste of time. I baited them, tested him. I was not worthy to take on my family's basileus, my father's title and property. Father told me to leave."

Medusa wrapped her arms about him, saddened. "Ariston," she murmured as she pressed a kiss to his cheek.

His hand caught her cheek. "He was right, love. And I went. At first I had no purpose, no thought for anything but the wrong my father had done me. I sailed, riding the waves with no care where I'd come ashore. I hid from him and my duties for more than a year. And while I was away I began to see my crassness through the eyes of others. I was naught but a boy, privileged at that. I had no knowledge of the world beyond the peaceful boundaries of my island. The world...it is a different place when one has no home, no family."

Medusa took his hand in hers. "You made amends with him?"

"Yes." He smiled. "I went back, though I was hungry, beaten and bruised. And my anger was more fearsome than when I'd left. But my father took me in and asked nothing of me. I ate and slept, spent time with my mother and sisters."

"They must have been pleased to have you home?"

"My mother and sisters? Yes. But my father... He went about his work, spoke at council, and worshipped Athena most loyally. He valued Athena's altar most, wisdom and reason are noble aspirations for a man, you see. I watched him in wonder for, he did his duty tirelessly. And still he said nothing to me. The very things I'd shunned or ridiculed he did with pride. The longer he held himself from me while giving me everything I had need of, the more I wanted to hear him speak to me. The more I understood what it was to be a man and not a boy playing at being a man. Honor, duty, loyalty – I wanted those things. And I wanted to give those things to my father, my family." He paused, pulling the stone from the fire and serving them both some fish.

"What happened?" Medusa couldn't eat, she could only stare and wait.

"I asked him for forgiveness." He shook his head. "I begged him for it."

Her heart tightened as she said, "And he gave it."

"He did. But it wasn't enough for me. I needed to prove myself worthy. I needed to know I could be strong and capable enough to lead and defend. These are things that cannot just be said. They must be shown. When Athena called, I answered."

"But what of your home? Who holds your family's basileus and protects them in your stead?" Medusa was stunned.

"My father is hearty," Ariston laughed. "It is likely I will not carry the family mantle until I am old and grey. Which is good, for you will have years to know and love them as I have."

Medusa smiled, warmed by his words. "Will they mind that you've wed?"

Ariston's hand slipped to her neck, pulling her towards him and pressing his lips to hers. "No. They will rejoice. And they will love you almost as dearly as I do."

Medusa felt herself soften. Heat, warm and fluid, rushed through her.

Ariston set her away from him, but not before she felt his response. It pleased her to feel him tremble as she did.

His voice was gentle as he said, "Eat, wife. So I will not worry over you."

Medusa ate the fish in five bites, swallowing it hot. She knew he watched her, heard him laugh as she swallowed the last of it. He handed her the water skin and she drank thirstily. Once he'd finished his breakfast, she stood and held her hand towards him.

"Swim with me?" she asked.

He took her hand, nodding.

They ran from the cabin to the water. Thea cooed to them, cackling briefly before she took flight. Medusa called out, "Good morning, little one. Hunt well."

Once they reached the surf, Medusa took a deep breath and

dove, kicking as she pushed herself under the water.

The water was warm and glorious. In its clear depths, tufts of sea grass swayed in the undulating rhythm of the waves above. She swam down, looking back to see Ariston behind her.

He smiled at her and pointed. Her eyes followed, making out the thin blackish grey snout of a great pipefish. It was but a shadow next to one of the large boulders that protected this small cove. She moved closer to the rock to investigate and brushed the sea grass, upsetting a sea horse from its hiding place. She kicked, aligning herself with the grass to find more of the animals. Their tails were wrapped tightly about the blades of grass, to keep them safely attached to their home in the shallows.

Ariston joined her watching the little creatures. His finger touched the animal's small head and it recoiled, startling. He smiled.

Medusa could not tear her eyes from her husband. His curls danced in the water, moving as the sea grass. He was unlike any man she'd seen, and he was hers. He was her husband. Her heart full, she reached for him.

His jaw tightened as he regarded her. His arms caught her around the waist as he kicked, jetting them out of the water.

As they broke the surface, Medusa drew in breath and wrapped her arms around his neck. She kissed him deeply. His lips, open and wet, clung to hers with gratifying urgency. His hands clasped her back, leaving no room between them.

She was mindless of their labored breathing or the waves that washed them back towards the beach. She wrapped herself around him and held tight, her legs encircling his waist and her arms anchored about his neck. She was vaguely aware of the sand beneath her, aware that the waves washed over them, but no longer moved them.

His mouth lifted from her lips and she opened her eyes.

He was staring at her, his curls dripping on her face and neck. His fingers came up to trace her lips. She watched him, mesmerized by his fascination. Her mouth parted beneath his fingers, making his breath catch. She reached for him, tangling her hands in his hair and pulling his head to her.

She shivered as his tongue caressed hers, stroking her and making her weak with need. She wanted more. She wanted all of him.

Her hands slid down the wet expanse of his chest. She smiled against his mouth, reveling in the subtle spasm of his stomach under her touch, the hot burst of his breath on her lips.

A soft moan slipped from her as his mouth moved down her throat, his hands lifting the soaking wrap of her peplos. His fingers traced her collarbone, his lips followed. She closed her eyes, her head falling back, as his hand cupped her breast.

Ariston slipped the peplos from her.

Wet as it was, its sheerness served to provoke the fire in his blood. Removing the wrap bared all of her to him, golden in the sunlight. She was a feast for his senses. She was beauty. Her hair floated in the gentle lap of the waves about them, her eyes were closed and her chin tilted. Her face was tight, yearning. For him.

His gaze explored, and his hands followed.

Her skin was velvet, white as the richest cream. The swell of her rounded breast drew his hand, while his lips eagerly captured the puckered pink tip. She quivered under him, moaning softly and inflaming him all the more.

His hands continued, moving to her side, tracing the curve of her waist and the swell of her hip.

It was sudden, but he stilled, his breath catching as his awareness sharpened.

He felt a presence – someone watching them. He glanced up, searching the cliffs that sheltered their cove. They were alone. Or so it seemed.

Thea called overhead, a loud grating caw.

I feel it too, Thea.

The sun seemed to be prying, the water grasping, the open air exposing them. He grew chilled, wary, and drew Medusa close against him.

"Come with me, wife." He continued to search their surroundings as he stood, drawing her up before him. He draped the sodden fabric of her peplos over her and took the hand she offered freely.

He glanced at her hand, softening to smile at her.

He led them from the beach, away from the prying eyes he could not find. Once inside the cool shadows of the cabin, he turned towards her and saw the question in her blue eyes.

"What is the matter?" she asked as he pulled her against him.

Ariston glanced outside. Once again he studied the brilliant sea and the sharp relief of the shoreline. He saw nothing to warrant his suspicion. And yet, he knew better than to question his instincts. Or Thea's warning.

Here, in the cool of their cabin, his anxiety disappeared. It was likely a passing goat herder or farmer, mayhap even a scout – nothing more. He gazed down at her, stroking her face and smiling at her.

His eyes fell to her lips, stirring the hunger that was only momentarily dampened. He laughed softly, saying, "I would not share you with the rays of Apollo's sun or gentle waves of Poseidon's ocean. I would keep you for myself."

His hand caught the base of her head, pulling her against him. She stood on her tiptoes to kiss him. He caught her to him, sweeping her off her feet to lay her back upon their mat.

He pulled the wet fabric from her, pressing her to him. As their skin touched, a hoarse gasp caught in her throat. The sound pleased him.

"I would hear you, wife, and know that I bring you pleasure." He regarded her face as her eyes found his.

"There are no words..." her voice trembled, the faintest of whispers.

He clasped her face and kissed her, losing himself to the feel of her.

His hand grasped her hip while his body tightened. Her legs parted in invitation and he moved between them. She moaned as he joined her body, making them one. Once again, his attempt at a gentle union was lost.

He pushed into her, sliding deep. Her cry caused him a moment's hesitation.

But the look on her face showed him the truth of it. Pleasure was teasing his lady. And he would help her find it.

Her hands clung to his back as he lifted her hips and fit her more firmly against him. He moved, watching her tremble and flush beneath him. Her breathing tore from her, her breasts shuddering as her chest rose and fell with her rampant breathing.

When her eyes opened and met his, a cry tore from her lips. Her body tightened and convulsed, and still she cried out.

He felt each quiver, each spasm, buried as he was deep within her. And her release forced him over the edge. He moaned as his body stiffened – one long heated contraction of ecstasy – as he filled his wife.

His passion left him trembling upon her. He lifted himself, to lessen her burden, but her leg tightened about his hips.

"I'll crush you, love," he whispered in her ear.

"I won't mind," she assured him, breathing heavily still.

He looked down at her with a smile on his face. "I would mind. I would keep you safe and happy."

"Keep me here as I am…joined with you," her voice was husky as her eyes met his.

Her love for him sparkled in her huge blue eyes, dazzling him with its simple truth. His voice was raw, "I am favored by the Gods, my lady, to have you."

"As am I, to have you as my lord and husband." Her fingers traced his jaw.

"I please you, then?" he teased softly. He shifted, sliding from her to lie at her side.

She frowned at him, making him laugh.

He could not tear his eyes from her, but watched as she tilted her face towards him and let her leg slip down, as if exhausted. "You do… I did not know such pleasure existed."

His hand found hers and he lifted it. He kissed the tip of each of her fine white fingers before pressing another to her palm. "What would my lady wife want of this day?"

She smiled at him. "This. Only this."

Poseidon was pleased.

He had expected nothing less from Phorcys. The Titan was humbled and honored, groveling over Poseidon's choice. But then he was offering marriage to Medusa, whom Phorcys had described as 'his lowly mortal daughter'.

"You've no need to marry her," Phorcys had smiled. "Get a son on her. Let her bear you a child if you will. To take her as wife is more generous than I could ever have prayed for."

Poseidon had laughed. "You would have me sully your daughter, Phorcys?"

Phorcys' incredulous look had amused the God, but the Titan's words were wise.

"My wife is a help to me. She is a Titan, strong and fearsome in battle. She bore me strong, immortal children – except Medusa. My daughter is beautiful to be sure, but the wife of the great Poseidon? What does she have to offer the likes of you? She cannot serve as your partner, as my Ceto is to me."

Poseidon watched his ally. "But she will be my wife. As such I will see that she becomes immortal. And that she gives me many sons. It is a good match, Phorcys, one that suits all."

Phorcys bowed deeply, "You do my family great honor."

Poseidon did not argue. He did indeed do Phorcys a great honor. But his marriage had nothing to do with honor or finding a partner. It had nothing to do with Athena or pleasing Olympus.

He wanted Medusa.

His lust robbed him of sleep and wit. His temper was quick for his blood still boiled.

Thoughts of her coming to him, beckoning him to their bed... Images of her silken locks tangled about them haunted him. He could almost taste the sweet softness of her lips, smell the fragrant bloom of her scent, and his body ached with it.

This longing for Medusa, a lowly mortal, had become an affliction for which there was only one cure.

If his brother had not warned him against it, he would have her already. It was not an easy choice, for he rarely heeded Zeus. But he would not jeopardize his prize or have his ownership of the girl forfeit to Athena's prattling or Zeus' spite.

Medusa would be his until he tired of her.

Once he left Phorcys, he set out on the waves, riding on their very tips as foam. He moved quickly, skimming along the shores of the sea. Mortals did many things along his shores, from fishing to bathing. He watched them with indulgent interest or played with them at will.

And then he found a more interesting sight.

Poseidon unfurled himself, letting his frothy fingers float and pull him towards the couple on the beach. This was a past-time he enjoyed mightily, for young lovers often found passion on the sand. They would be unknowingly wrapped in his form as he became the waves that coursed over them.

He saw no point in depriving himself this slight pleasure, for the sea was his domain. As he was also the God of Fertility, he would appease both his duties. He would make sure that those who loved here would have evidence of their passion in due course.

Whether or not the resulting babe was sired by him, as sea foam, or the mortal involved depended on the woman. If she was beautiful or passionate, if there was something that drew him to her beyond the need to free his seed, then the babe would be his, of that he was sure.

Poseidon was generous when it came to women. He had many sons.

This couple was so absorbed in one another that he wondered. If he transformed into his human form, would they be aware of his presence?

He would not risk disturbing such a coupling. Their passion was great. Poseidon could see it, feel the current of it in the water about them. This man, whose back rippled and tightened as he knelt over his lover, was a virile sort. Yet he felt such tenderness towards the woman beneath him.

A tenderness Poseidon could not fathom.

He could also feel the man's barely repressed passion.

Poseidon felt himself tighten, wishing he was that man. He would not hold himself from this woman. He would unleash the full extent of his hunger upon her. And she, Poseidon suspected, would take it eagerly.

For the woman's body was both beautiful and passionate. She was writhing, naked in the sun, and so lovely that Poseidon wished his hands might reach out and stroke her. Instead he slipped forward on a wave, and washed over them.

The sudden sharpness in his chest startled him.

It was beyond his understanding.

But this was more than lust. This was not mindless desire, but a joining of two people beyond their physical being. There was a giving of self here, of the heart.

He was a God. The affections of mortals could not affect him. And yet, did they? His heart shuddered, pulled painfully tight.

Lust he knew well, it was his constant companion. He took what he wanted, with no remorse. But this was different. He washed over them again, feeling the woman tighten and rise beneath her lover's touch.

And he wanted this.

The man froze. He grew taut, expectant, and turned to search out the source of his unease. Poseidon smiled to himself. The man, handsome in the prime of his youth, had sharp senses.

But his smile faded as the man drew the woman from the water.

Poseidon reached for her, the tightening of his chest suffocating. His watery countenance pooled about her ankle, attempting to pull her back into the water, to him.

He wanted this woman. He wanted to feel the release of this couple's passion. He wanted to be this man.

The man led his lover from the water, shielding her face from Poseidon's sight. The man draped the wet cloth over his woman, covering her beauty. It was a shame. He might have searched her out when next she visited the shore. But she entered the cabin with the man, lost to the shadows within.

Poseidon hurt, aching sharply – which he did not take kindly to.

Frustration stole his breath, forcing him back, forcing the water from the warmth of the sunbaked sand.

How dare they inspire such feelings within him. He was Poseidon. He had no reason to envy *mortals.*

And he was deprived again. Once knowingly, for Zeus knew the toll this time was taking upon his brother, and again by these... selfish mortals playing at love upon his beach.

The waves reflected his irritation, rising high and growing cold.

He turned loathing eyes upon the sun. It was barely midday. Another day stretched out before him, before he could claim his wife, his Medusa. He would have to bide his time.

With his anger rising, he considered drowning these lovers.

He cared not that his temper was petty, that their death might be sorrowful to those who loved them. They had taunted him with their bodies, so lost in one another – in the shallows of *his* ocean.

A wave could crush their small cabin about them...

It was a pity he'd not pulled them into the ocean. Watching as their lungs filled, as their faces turned blue and they thrashed about in a useless effort to rise from the depths of his ocean. He could see to it that they'd never rise... Imagining it made him smile.

Mayhap it would appease the burning Medusa had infected him with.

"Patience, brother," Zeus had cautioned.

Poseidon turned his gaze towards the cabin. The lovers were inside, no doubt wrapped about one another.

No. To die in a lover's arms was no punishment at all. They were not worth his time or his thoughts.

Poseidon moved deeper into the sea. It would do to find some way to lessen the fire that consumed him, but only fleeting. For while he might lessen this painful hunger briefly, his appetite for Medusa would not be dampened for long.

"Teach me," she kissed him, laughing when the net had slipped from his fingers so he might pull her against him. "I'm hungry," she teased, pulling away from him and retrieving the floating net.

He sighed, taking the nets from her and pulling her against him again. He kissed her until her knees trembled. Only then did he set her away from him, smiling triumphantly. "Watch me."

She watched him gather in his nets closely, then cast it wide. He was a patient tutor, and she wanted to learn everything he would teach her.

"Now pull it in quickly," he said, moving forward to help her draw in the net.

"Like this?" Medusa stood, her skirts tucked up and her hair braided from her face. She lifted the net, preparing to cast it into the rising tide.

She glanced his way, waiting for his answer. He was smiling, a smile that almost made her lose her grip on the net. But she did not want to disappoint him, so she clung to the net's edge and waited.

When he nodded, she let the net fly into the deeper waters.

"A good cast, my lady." How his praise warmed her.

They worked together, catching their dinner. She lost the net once and he tossed her into the water, diving after her. They swam together, laughing, until they reached one another.

His hands cupped her cheek, his lips found hers and fishing was forgotten. Her limbs grew heavy, desire and fatigue warring within her. He swam, setting her upon the rocks with care.

"The net," he murmured with a smile, swimming after it.

She sat, catching her breath, watching the raw power of his back and shoulders. A warrior's body, his strength was tireless. He grasped the net and dove deep.

When he resurfaced, there was a smile on his dripping face. He shook his head wildly, dousing her with water and causing her to shriek. Still smiling, he pulled himself onto the rock beside her and handed her an oyster shell.

She looked at him, wiping the water from her eyes. "What's this?"

He shrugged. "A gift."

Medusa opened the shell, smiling in pleasure at the gift inside. A finely carved owl hung from a leather thread. Medusa stared at the necklace, then at her husband.

"It's lovely," she whispered. "Is it Thea?"

She would treasure his gift. Though he'd given her so much in the brief time they'd shared.

His smile dimmed Apollo's sun. "I know she watches over you, my lady. As I watch over you."

She couldn't help returning his smile. "When will we go home, Ariston?"

"Home?"

"To Rhodes? Once you leave on Athens' triremes—"

He shook his head. "I shall not. They've little need of me."

Medusa took his hand in both of hers, gazing up at him with solemn eyes. While his declaration thrilled her, she knew it was selfish. If he took her to Rhodes, he would be turning away from all he'd fought for. Pride, honor, respect – things he valued. Things his family, his father, valued. She would never ask him to make such sacrifices.

She spoke earnestly, "You are an honorable man, Ariston. A man I love because of your honor and duty."

Medusa saw his face change, growing unsettled by her words.

He turned, staring over the open sea in silence. She squeezed his hand, holding it tightly.

"I fear I may not be able to leave you," he whispered. He looked at her then, his eyes haunted.

She smiled, stifling her grief, and leaned forward to kiss him. He caught her cheek, holding her to him.

"Then I shall leave you," she murmured.

He drew back, his brow furrowed. "What?"

"Elpis will come on the morrow and take me to Athena. The Goddess has a gift for me." Medusa smiled at the necklace, tying it about her neck. "I fear any gift will pale in comparison."

"And then?" His hands tightened the knot, then claimed her hands once more.

"I may wait for you here, at my uncle's house?" she asked. "Or I may sail, with Elpis, to Rhodes and wait for you there?"

His hand smoothed the hair from her face. "Would you stay here?"

Medusa's eyes settled on the small cabin, built into the side of the rocky hillside. "Is this yours?"

Ariston pointed to the large house set high above them on the cliff-top. "That is my Uncle Themistocles' home..."

"Themistocles? Athens' statesman?" She gasped, stunned. "He is your *uncle*?"

"He is. And a good man, as well." Ariston smiled. "This is his cabin – one that will be occupied by a sentry shortly, no doubt. Themistocles has long since moved into the city, to live in her walls until this siege is finished."

"He has no family?" Medusa asked.

"No." Ariston's eyes traveled over the length of her braid. He lifted a finger to smooth back the loose curls from her brow. "His work sustained him. I suspect now that he's older, he regrets such loneliness."

Medusa nodded. It would be a lonely life indeed, with no one to share it with.

"So where will you go, lady? I shall follow you when I am able."

His words were hoarse, betraying his emotion.

She could not look at him, she would reveal too much. Her grief, like his, was sharp.

Instead, Medusa's eyes traced the shoreline. It was beautiful here. The sandy beach veered sharply up, transforming into rocky hills then higher still to become steep cliff faces. A rebellious tassel hyacinth peeked here and there, providing vibrant splashes of color between rocks otherwise sparse in vegetation. Overhead a golden eagle left its rocky nest and flew higher, its shadow sweeping across sea and sand.

Medusa narrowed her eyes, peering into the shadows on their beach. There, head burrowed under her wing, slept Thea. Ever present, ever watchful...though today her pet had trusted Ariston to do the watching.

She turned, settling herself closely against his side on their rocky seat. "I would be where I can feel you with me."

"I am always with you, Medusa." He sighed, hesitating before he offered, "Shall I arrange for a ship to take you to Rhodes? Elpis will go with you." He pressed a kiss to her forehead. "My family will welcome you. And I will come back to you quickly."

She nodded, letting herself go soft against him.

She would not betray the pain his words brought. She would not beg him to stay or plead with him to go with her. She could not. She would be strong. Her love demanded it.

"When will you leave?" Her voice was soft but calm.

Ariston shook his head. "Soon."

She looked up at him, her hand on his cheek. Her heart was in her throat, but she swallowed the lump that settled there. "We have this day, and this night. Our memories must bind us together until you find your way back to me."

She watched as his eyes closed. His jaw grew rigid, his nostrils flared, but he said nothing. She was not alone in this suffering. He felt it too.

She reached for him, welcoming the weight of his arms as they pulled her to him.

Chapter Eight

Ariston's heart grew heavier the higher the sun rose. Elpis would arrive soon, if Ektor did not arrive first.

The time for farewells had found them too quickly.

He placed his hand over her heart and prayed that their separation would be brief. He would come back to her a greater hero, but a warrior no more.

Medusa lay against him, her softness pressed close along the hard angles of his body. His hand cupped her breast, savoring the feel of her.

He prayed she was with child. His hand splayed her stomach, thumb and pinkie resting on the bridge of her hip bones. A babe would be irrefutable proof of their union.

He dismissed the knowledge that this war might tarry too long and he might miss seeing her grow round with his babe. She would give him many children.

She stirred slightly, a soft sigh escaping her. He smiled down at her.

A child. What a joy that would be.

A child would add weight to this marriage. Galenus was an honorable man. He'd be offended by the secrecy of their marriage, of that Ariston had little doubt. But Galenus would be appeased with the gifts he received. He would be pleased to know that Ariston was not just an Ekdromoi leader and servant to Athena, but heir to his oikos and his family basileus. These would serve Medusa's family well.

Since Poseidon was not her intended and Athena had released her, Galenus and Phorcys should find him a mighty addition to their family.

His worries could wait. Time with her was slipping away.

His eyes drifted over her form, soft and limp in a deep sleep. He lifted a finger to smooth a single curl from her face. She shifted in her sleep, her arm slipping across his chest as she stretched. She pressed herself against him as she did so, stirring him again.

He kissed her, lingering over her lips until they parted for him. And his tongue slipped in, teasing her until she moaned in the back of her throat. His hands and mouth slid over her, kneading and cupping, kissing and licking the planes of her. Her hands tangled in his hair, pulling him closer.

When would he next make love to her? When would he next hold her in his arms or gaze upon the curve of her face? Urgency gripped him. His chest seemed to press against itself, collapsing upon him and his heart and lungs with a leaden pain.

He stilled, letting his eyes look their fill.

"You're staring at me," she whispered as her hand settled on his cheek.

"I am." He held her hand to his cheek. "I cannot stop."

"I see the love in your eyes, Ariston."

He would hold this moment dear, to warm him on nights when they were far from one another.

"I love you." His voice reverberated in the quiet. He wanted his declaration to be heard. He needed her to hear him say, "More than my life."

She rolled onto her side and gazed at him, eyes bright, cheeks flushed. "My husband," she whispered.

His hand cupped her cheek. "My lady."

He rolled, sliding her beneath him. He wrapped his arms about her, pressing kisses to her throat, her breasts. He drove into her, his groan echoing within the small cabin. He would remember the smell of her, the taste of her, the feel of her, on those nights they were apart.

He felt her hands tangle in his curls, felt her pull his lips to hers. She gasped, her body tightening around him, and yet he pushed on.

The cries of their release, guttural and ragged, were caught in their kiss.

He held her to him, listening to each breath and beat of her heart.

"Oh how I love you, husband," she whispered, holding his head to her heart.

His arms tightened, pressing her into the shelter of his arms.

The gentle roar of the ocean, the call of the gulls and Thea's coo, even the wind through the sparse trees rooted to the hillside could not ease the ache threatening his peace. He knew that time would separate them, if only for a while.

Fear rose, shooting up his spine. It grew, stealing his breath and churning his stomach. He was loath to release her, to let her leave the safety of his arms. He held her close, and breathed her in.

He'd never known such fear. But then, he'd never had something he was fearful of losing.

She looked up at him, kissing him on the lips. "Come." She slipped from his arms and stood on unsteady legs. "Swim with me. Elpis will be here shortly."

Ariston took her hand, grabbed their clothes, and followed her to the water, determined to reveal none of his apprehension to her. They had enough to endure. This unnatural panic would lend nothing good. He must be strong, for them both.

She distracted him, pulling him into the water with a bright smile. Her nakedness was a dazzling sight, beauty amidst the blue waters and the warm sun. She stooped, collecting handfuls of sand to rub him, cleansing him.

He closed his eyes, allowing her touch to soothe his troubles. And then he washed her, gently scrubbing her with handfuls of sand until her skin seemed to glow.

"You are more beautiful than..." he paused. "You are beauty."

"If I am, it is because you make me so." For the first time her smile wavered. She bit her lip, blinking furiously. "I'm sorry." A single tear slipped from her eye.

His heart was breaking. He caught her in his arms and pulled her against him. He kissed her tenderly.

"I *am* proud of you, husband. Proud of your loyalty to Athens and the Goddess, and I would have you do your duty," she assured him, her voice unsteady. "But I will miss you."

"And I you, Medusa." He took a fortifying breath and smiled at her. All the while he felt a desperate pain filling his heart. "I promise you," he said against her lips. "I will come back to you."

Elpis found them this way, walking from the water. Her mistress was naked, lovely and damp. Ariston was, too, but she tore her eyes from his figure. He was Medusa's. She'd no right or desire to look upon him in such a state of undress.

She was glad she'd made Ektor wait behind the rocks, for he'd doubtless be overcome by such a sight.

Thea cackled, drawing all eyes.

"Good afternoon, Thea," Elpis returned the bird's greeting.

"Good afternoon to you, sweet Elpis," Medusa stooped to retrieve her peplos from the sand.

Elpis moved forward, helping Medusa dress. "And to you, mistress."

Medusa hugged Elpis to her. Her lady trembled in her arms. So Medusa's smile was for Ariston. She squeezed Medusa, proud of her bravery.

"Are you well, Elpis?" Ariston asked, safely draped in his chiton.

"I am well. And ready for our travels to Rhodes. My lady's things are ready to be packed and carried to our ship upon my lord's bidding." Elpis released her mistress. She glanced back and forth between the two, both pleased and saddened by what was to come.

"You are a gift to my lady." Ariston dropped a kiss on the top of his wife's head. "Look for a messenger shortly. He will have the name of your ship as well as the means to take your things with him."

Thea cooed and flew to Ariston, landing on his shoulder with the slightest ruffling of feathers. "And you will watch over my lady while I'm away, mighty Thea. I charge you with her safe keeping." Ariston's voice was soft. But he met the owl's yellow eyes with such conviction that Elpis wondered at it.

Did he believe Thea would hear him – understand him?

"If she has need of me, come and find me, Thea," the last was the faintest of whispers.

Thea clicked and cooed.

Mayhap she does, Elpis wondered. "Ektor awaits my lord. We met on the way…"

Elpis saw Medusa's hands tighten about her husband's. Soon they would be parted for who knew how long. It hurt her, this sadness that tinged their blissful union. But surely the Gods would find favor with such a match and preserve it.

Ariston turned to Medusa, his eyes fierce upon her. "I will return to you as soon as I can. I give you my word."

Medusa nodded, then wrapped her arms around him.

In those few moments, Elpis could not look at them. Sorrow replaced whatever joy they'd shared. And Elpis understood it. After so long having been denied love, being parted would be a terrible blow. In fact, Elpis could imagine nothing more painful for either of them.

"Ariston!" Ektor's voice traveled down the hill to them.

Elpis turned, catching sight of Ariston's handsome face contorting. He pressed his face into his lady's hair and whispered something. His arms tightened.

Medusa buried her face against his neck, her hands fisting in his robe to hold him to her.

"Ariston?" Ektor called again. "It is time. Nereus demands your presence immediately. The ships leave at first light."

In the fading sun Elpis watched as Ariston grabbed his wife to him, kissing her with more tenderness, more ferocity, than Elpis had imagined. She stared, amazed at the way they swayed together before he tore himself from her arms and ran. He did not look back when he crested the hill or as he pulled himself onto his horse.

But, as Ektor's mount leapt forward, Ariston looked back and raised a hand to them.

Medusa's hand gripped hers, crushing her hand. "Hold me, Elpis, so I will not beg him to stay. Help me not shame myself," her voice trembled.

Elpis saw her lady smile, waving after the fading form of her husband.

Once he was gone, she pulled her mistress close and let her sob until she had no more tears.

Medusa sat behind Elpis on Ariston's horse. In one hand she clutched the missive Ariston had sent to them on their slow trek back to the Temple of Athena Polias. He had not tarried, but immediately made the arrangements needed to send her and her companion to his home on the far isle of Rhodes. A messenger had delivered the note, along with Ariston's horse, to them. Elpis was to give this missive to the courier who would come to fetch their belongings. Once they'd departed, Galenus would have Ariston's mount as part of the bride price.

Thea circled overhead, hooting in the darkening sky.

Galenus would have word by now. Elpis had delivered it before she'd left to collect Medusa from the cabin.

Her uncle would bluster and rail, but then he would see reason. She prayed he would. Ariston was a good man. Her new husband's gifts had been more than generous. Surely Galenus, a practical man, would see that. If Poseidon would not have her and Athena was finished with her, then her marriage was a very good match – even if it did take her to Rhodes.

Rhodes.

A tiny island leagues across the sea. To a family that she knew nothing of – though Ariston assured her they would love her dearly. He'd sent a dispatch to them so they would know of his marriage and her arrival.

Sunset was upon them as the horse stopped at the base of the temple steps. Medusa looked up, admiring its loveliness.

Her gaze swept the top step. A half dozen well-armed guards stood ready to defend Athena's temple if the Persians reached Athens' soil.

She slipped from the saddle. "Hurry back, Elpis," she whispered. Elpis' hand squeezed hers.

"May Athena's gift give you some solace, mistress," Elpis said.

Thea hooted and Medusa held her arm out, smiling as the owl landed gracefully on her leather cuff. Her little pet was mindful of her mistress' well-being, and her slight presence lifted Medusa's spirits.

She touched the charm at her neck.

She hurried up the steps, thankful for the soft chlamys Elpis had brought for her. The wind on the Acropolis blew cold compared to the warmer breeze of the beach.

Once of the soldiers appraised her through narrowed eyes. He smiled slightly, his gaze lingering on her face. She did not like the way the man looked at her. She missed the cover of her robes, the shield of her veils.

Medusa pulled the hood of the chlamys up, shielding her face from his prying eyes as she entered the temple.

Something was not right. Why were no tapers lit? Where was Athena's priestess? Her unease grew stronger.

Athena stood, staring out over the sea. Her posture was rigid as she held her golden shield at the ready. Perhaps Athena had sent her priestess away? This war troubled the Goddess, too, then.

"Athena?"

Athena turned to her. "You've come, little one."

Medusa knelt before her Goddess. "I have."

Athena's voice was soft, "You have never failed me. You are a dutiful sort."

A queer anxiousness ran down the length of Medusa's spine.

Athena studied her, open curiosity in her round brown eyes. "Do you know what gift has been bestowed upon you?"

"I do not, Goddess." She tried to smile again, but could not quite manage it.

Athena arched an eyebrow. "No, I thought not. You are most blessed, little one, for your gift is more than a mere mortal could dare to hope for." But Athena's voice was laced with bitterness. What was this?

Had the Persians found entry to her city? Was the siege already underway? Whatever had happened, the Goddess was not pleased, Medusa could tell.

"Enough, Athena, let us be done with this. I will take her." The voice was low, alluring and seductive in its cadence.

Thea cackled, ruffling her feathers in agitation.

Medusa knew that voice, though she'd hoped never to hear it again. A terrible premonition began to unfurl within her.

In the shadows of the temple, her eyes sought and found Poseidon.

She could not speak, could not move. She felt only terror, cold and heavy, settle in her chest.

"He has pled his case, little one. The great Poseidon has humbled himself, for the want of you. And now you are honored among women. This is your gift. You will wed my uncle and be wife of a God. What say you?" Athena watched her carefully.

Medusa struggled to breathe. Her heart convulsed as she heard Athena continue gently, "It is the will of Olympus, of Zeus, and your father."

Medusa tried not to cringe as Poseidon came to her side.

Thea hissed, shifting from talon to talon as she attempted a defensive posture.

His pale blue eyes peered past the owl and into hers, assessing her hesitancy. "You are displeased?" Poseidon knelt beside her, his blue eyes narrowing to slits. "How is it that our marriage, the honor I bestow upon you, could displease you?"

How could this be? Athena had released her, given her freedom. If she'd known, if she'd suspected what this was her gift – but how could she have known? Never had she entertained such a thought.

As her eyes met his, she knew she must be cautious now.

She drew a breath and whispered, "It is a surprise..." Her voice wavered as she added, "You do me a great honor." She murmured the next words, knowing they were dangerous indeed. "One I am unworthy of... One I am unable to accept."

But what choice did she have?

Athena gasped.

Poseidon smiled, his voice edged with laughter. "Do you think to toy with me, girl?"

"Medusa, think before you speak, I implore you." Athena moved forward, her face astonished.

Thea cackled and flew away, leaving Medusa alone. She didn't fault Thea – she would escape as well, if she could. But she couldn't. She could only plead her case, and pray for understanding from the Gods.

Medusa glanced at the Goddess. There was concern in Athena's eyes, it was clear.

She knew the words she should speak. She should accept Poseidon and bow to the will of the Gods. But she would not dishonor her husband or her marriage. She could not.

She drew a shaky breath and spoke softly, "I have married."

"What?" Athena gasped.

"In two days' time?" Poseidon laughed – a grating sound that unnerved Medusa.

"You've married?" Athena repeated.

"You were released to marry me, Medusa. Because I would have you," Poseidon's voice grew louder, each word rising as his irritation mounted. "I would secure peace between the Titans, the Olympians, and the mortals. Persia is waiting to destroy Athens, all of Greece. Our marriage would have secured such a treaty. But now…" he sighed and brushed a single finger down her cheek.

And then Poseidon froze. His eyes narrowed as he stared at his finger, resting upon her.

"Married two days past?" he growled. His hand fisted and his face filled with such anger that Medusa drew back. Touching her seemed to unleash his fury. Real fear gripped her. She'd never seen such a look of unconcealed rage.

His heart, if Poseidon had one, could not be so attached to her? Surely not. Athena had railed against Poseidon often enough. She thought him incapable of affection or attachment. Athena had compared her uncle's selfish nature and blind ambition to that of her father on more than one occasion. Neither would rest until they had what they wanted…

He must want her, greatly. Medusa repressed a shudder, her mind filling with unbidden images.

His unyielding gaze pierced her calm exterior to clutch at her heart, terrifying her beyond reason. She could barely breathe. Something had changed within him. Gone was the playful yet selfish God. The Poseidon before her was one of vengeance and retribution. Scorn lined the planes of his face. And yet desire blazed from the paleness of his eyes.

One moment he was before her, the next he was leaning insolently against the dais. She drew in a deep breath before casting a tentative glance his way. He seemed amused suddenly, his rage gone.

He looked at Athena then, as did Medusa.

"You give me little choice, Medusa." Athena began, her voice echoing off the temple pillars as thunder.

"Peace, niece, I will take her." Poseidon spoke with contempt.

"Her father offered her to me as a mistress long before I offered my suit. It will suffice, and appease."

Medusa was shaking. His hand cupped the side of her throat, startling her. The coldness of his skin pressed against hers, making her shiver all the more.

She saw his face darken instantly. His gaze, so fixed upon the hand that touched her, blazed once more. He pulled his hand from her, as if burned, and stared at her. There was no mistaking the fury he fought. "I will take the place of her husband. She will come with me. Until I tire of her, that is."

"I cannot," Medusa gasped, reeling from Poseidon's words. "I cannot betray him."

Athena's eyes narrowed. "You are wise to declare such fidelity to your husband, little one. If indeed the vows spoken are valid and binding. Did you marry with the blessing of your father or your guardian? I thought not." Athena's brown eyes looked between the two of them. "A bargain has been struck with your father – a bargain with Poseidon. My uncle is being most generous."

Medusa felt as if she was tied beneath the crushing waves of high tide. She could see those things beyond the water, make out their shape and presence – but could not breathe or blink clarity into her eyes.

Athena was resolved as she continued, "This is a matter which impacts all of Athens, girl. You will be forgiven your selfishness. Poseidon has given you the means to repair the damage done. Take it."

Ariston's words echoed in her head and her heart. *You will always hold my heart. Let it give you the strength to do what must be done. For you will be my lady, forever.*

How could she endure the hands of another upon her? How could she lie with this...this God while married to one fighting for her protection – no, the protection of all of Athens? How could she contemplate dishonoring Ariston in such a way? His love gave her the strength to whisper, "I cannot."

Athena turned from her. "Leave this temple. Now. You've lost favor with me and Olympus. I will look on you no more."

Medusa felt tears slipping from her eyes. She was truly alone now. "Please, Athena."

"Go!" Athena roared. "You speak honeyed words of loyalty and duty then turn your back on them. You would risk Athens? For what? A virtue you no longer possess? How dare you. Do not desecrate this holy place any longer. Go. Now!" Her words rolled throughout the temple, a force to be obeyed.

Medusa rose on trembling legs. She stumbled as she carried herself from the temple, but knew better than to stop. Her steps were halting, yet she pushed on. She collapsed as she came to Athena's olive tree. She closed her eyes, to pray...

But who would she pray to?

What should she do? What could she do now? Her heart was throbbing, each beat sending pain throughout her.

She shook her head, a sob catching in her throat.

This was her making. Her naiveté had brought this about. She should have known she'd never be free, not really. Loving Ariston, tasting the promise of a real life had blinded her to the truth.

She'd served Athena with such joyous devotion because she believed in the Goddess, in her wisdom. She'd rejoiced in the knowledge that she served Olympus' will. That she was of use to them, as she was to her father, was understood.

For the first time Medusa questioned this. Requiting Poseidon's lust seemed a less than noble goal for Olympus, when the Gods themselves revered marriage. How, then, could Olympus ask such a thing of her? Nay, demand it?

But Poseidon had offered marriage first... It was her father, her own flesh and blood, who had offered her up for Poseidon's pleasure. Her father.

"Are you angry?" Poseidon asked, at her side.

She started, turning round eyes on him. A surprised smile appeared on his devilishly handsome face.

He circled her with interest, stopping to look into her face. "Your attempt at honor is admirable, but misplaced." His eyes settled on her lips.

She continued to stare at him, his words barely reaching her.

He assessed her before turning his gaze to the sea below. "Ask yourself, Medusa. Would your husband cross the Gods for you?"

Medusa considered his question, all the while wary of his presence. Would Ariston cross him? To protect her?

A small smile formed on her lips as she knew. Ariston would take on all of Olympus for her, even knowing he would fail. "He would."

Poseidon was thoughtful, his gaze searching her face. "Perhaps. But an honorable man understands the importance of sacrifice. Your man would acknowledge its very necessity – if he's as honorable as you think him." His smile grew. "Surely he would never want you to risk his life? No, if he's so noble his life would mean little... He would never want you to risk the lives of others? The lives of his men? What honor could be found then?"

A prick of apprehension shot up her spine. She stared apprehensively at him, while dreading the meaning behind his words.

"Where is your sure response, Medusa?" he asked softly.

"But how... It would not come to that..." Watching his face, she understood. He was warning her. Bile choked her as she realized the depths of his selfishness.

"Will it not? You were the cost of a mighty treaty. I know not what will happen now."

"Do you not?" her voice broke as her eyes locked with his.

He moved closer, his hands cupping her face and his thumb running across her lips. "There will come a time when you'll need my help. You will understand the gravity of what you've done. And when you come to me, know what is expected in return. You will welcome me, with open arms, and give your body freely to me." His pale eyes held hers. "Without tears or weeping."

She shook her head, trying to dislodge his hold. "Athena will protect her city and those who champion it." His hands tightened and she could not.

"You have affronted my niece and offended Olympus—"

"My offense will not prevent Olympus from rallying behind Athens. The Gods are merciful to those who are loyal." She spoke with conviction, praying it was true.

His brows rose at her words. "There will be consequences for your actions, no matter how costly. I wonder, is it that you can't stand what I require of you, or that you think your noble husband will cast you aside after I'm done with you?" He paused. "Hear me now. I will aid you when no one else will. But know what I expect from you in return." He stepped back, a cool fog building about him.

His words churned her stomach and she clutched Athena's tree for support.

Though his voice remained strong, his figure began to bend and fade, transforming into a dense cloud. "You will call for me soon. The fate of your beloved husband and Athens' trireme fleet may depend upon you and your precious honor." He laughed, softly.

The fog rose, sweeping about him and engulfing his figure. The fog moved away, spilling over the cliff and taking him with it.

She followed the vapor to the cliff's edge. Such coldness gripped her, leaving her numb. Her eyes followed the writhing cloud as it slipped across the hills and floated over the sea. It, he, vanished there.

Elpis hurried, navigating the treacherous slope up the hill to the temple. She'd left her master's house in an uproar. Ariston's note had been met with thunderous anger, though reluctant acceptance was quick to follow.

While Galenus was disappointed that Poseidon had overlooked his niece, Ariston's gifts and pledges were more generous than any marriage contract he knew of. Ariston was, after all, a better match than expected. And Galenus grew more pleased each time he reviewed the bride's price Ariston had paid.

He knew Phorcys would as well.

The news that Ariston's uncle was Themistocles, a man of great power in Athens, was a pleasant surprise. Themistocles was a man who appreciated the importance of the seas in battle, and Galenus had praised his vision. If not for his skills as an orator, Galenus had told all who would listen, Athens would not have the largest fleet of trireme ships in the world. And now Themistocles was part of Galenus' oikos – an honor indeed.

As Elpis watched their things depart for their ship, another note arrived in the hands of the Gorgons. Elpis was filled with such a terrible foreboding that she'd listened from the shadows of her master's courtyard.

"What is the meaning of this?" Galenus asked after reading the note.

"Our father states it plainly, does he not?" Euryale snapped.

"We've come to help our sister, to bring her things to Poseidon's house," Stheno said.

Elpis felt the words as if they'd been a physical blow.

"But she's gone..." Galenus was dismayed, greatly so.

"To the temple, to collect her gift?" Euryale laughed. "The Gods have a cruel sense of humor. Do they not, *Uncle* Galenus? Who would find marriage to such a faithless immortal a gift?"

Galenus said nothing. Elpis understood. What could he say? He was as stunned as she was, but he had no shadows to hide in.

"It is an honor to be chosen, by any God," Stheno said. "And she will see the good in this marriage, if not in her husband. Which way to our sister's chamber?"

"You'll find it empty," Galenus voice was soft.

Stheno and Euryale turned to regard him, waiting from their lofty height for some further explanation to his peculiar statement.

"Has she learned of her betrothal?" Stheno asked.

"In a manner of speaking..." Galenus sat in his chair. He was not threatened by the Gorgons he was so lost in thought. "She's married. But not to Poseidon."

Elpis did not stop to think. She ran from Galenus' home, moving more swiftly than she thought possible. She knew her mistress needed her. And she would help Medusa...somehow. She had to stop twice, for fear her lungs would burst. She waited only long enough to catch her breath before running on.

As she flew up the temple's steps she heard Poseidon speak, and her blood grew icy. "I will take the place of her husband. She will come with me. Until I tire of her, that is."

Elpis knew her mistress would never willingly enter into such a bargain. Just as she knew the Gods would never take Medusa's rejection lightly.

She was startled when Thea circled lower, clicking and calling. "What shall we do, Thea?"

Thea cooed, hovering briefly before she flew towards the coast. Elpis wondered about the wisdom of including Ariston, but knew she had no choice. Her mistress was in danger. She followed Thea, praying Ariston would know how to handle this dreadful situation.

The sun was rising. Ariston could feel the warm whisper of its rays caressing his cheek as he woke. The gentle sway of the ship lulled him into a lingering doze.

Dreams of his lady wife were so real that he felt the silk of her skin beneath his fingers and the scent of her, clean and salty, filled his nostrils. Her image teased him, reaching for him while staying beyond his reach. He could not rise until he held her, once more. The pull of such dreams kept him sprawled upon the deck longer than his crew, but he could not bear to part with her again.

"Sir," someone dared to wake him. "Ariston? They're waiting for us."

Medusa faded, running into the waves with a happy laugh and a flash of her blue eyes... And Ariston forced his eyes open, ignoring the sharp ache in his chest.

The sun was bright, too bright.

"When?" Ariston's voice was brusque. He forced himself onto his feet, the rolling deck beneath his feet giving him no pause.

"They must have seen us coming." His second, Pamphilos, stared over the water at the fleet on the horizon. "They've come to meet us."

Ariston stretched, his night on the deck affording little comfort. He'd left his tent to sleep under the stars in the hopes that he'd find peace. Instead his dreams had taunted him, flooding him with longing.

He stooped, shaking out his well-worn cloak – his makeshift pillow – and pulled it around his shoulders.

A swarm of ships with black flags stretched as far as the eye could see. The horizon was thick with them, this loathsome enemy. Peace would not find him this day.

Welcome, Persians. At last he would meet these dreaded invaders. His blood pounded and the taste of the hunt flooded his mouth.

"We lead?" Ariston asked, glancing behind them. Athens' triremes trailed their ship.

Pamphilos laughed.

Ariston nodded.

It was tradition. His men led for glory – they had little patience for Athens' newly trained forces. Only the best and most skilled served on his ship. While his uncle's maneuvering had provided Athens with their ships, Themistocles could not build troops to man them. Ariston could only pray those he'd trained would earn the name soldier. Hoplites and citizens alike, any man strong enough to lift an oar now rowed out to their destiny.

He regarded the ships with pride. Not all were as skilled as his Ekdromoi, but what these men lacked in skill they made up for in determination.

The swell of bloodlust, the rush of anticipation, would soon wash over Athens' impatient fleet and bid them fight. It was known that the Persians' cavalry and infantry were to be avoided at all costs. But these ships offered a chance at victory and true glory.

Victory.

Glory.

These had been his goals as well, until Medusa. Now glory, victory, paled next to the peace and pleasure he found in her arms. This would be his last battle. He would be victorious so he might return to her.

Pamphilos' eyes narrowed as he pointed to the sky. "A storm is coming, one that will tip their heavy loads and buoy us over them."

"Let it come. If Poseidon seeks tributes, we shall help them on their way." Ariston's eyes narrowed as his eyes scanned the sky, then the water.

There was a storm coming. Grey and black streaked across the sky, spreading across the blue sky and darkening the sun itself. Ariston watched and felt his senses sharpen. This was not the advantage he'd hoped for. Nor was this storm a comfort – there was something more...

The clouds rose, then split sharply as if the sky were being cut in two.

The wind fell flat, the air silent and still.

Just as suddenly, the sky roared. Thunder rolled over the waves, deafening Ariston and all upon the sea. With a staggering gust, the wind pulled sharply at their sails. The ships surged, carried ever closer to the Persians.

"A strange storm," Pamphilos noted.

Ariston nodded. "Anchor the oars. We cannot afford to lose our speed."

Pamphilos hurried towards the galley opening, bellowing Ariston's orders through the hatch to the oarsmen below.

Ariston reached for his linothorax, slipping it on and lacing the sides of his leather and bronze chest plate in preparation for the day to come.

When he returned, Pamphilos held a letter. "Ektor gave this to one of the men last night. It's for you." Pamphilos was smiling, a knowing kind of smile. "The girl, Elpis, left it for you. She's from Master Galenus' household? Your lady wife's house?"

He took the note from Pamphilos, opening it even as his second watched him closely. "She is," Ariston said, already reading the words.

Master,

Your lady wife knows nothing of my plea. She would not thank me for interfering. Athena's gift was no gift at all. The Olympians demand a union between our lady and Poseidon. Medusa refused. Poseidon then bid her be his mistress. She refused that too. But I fear he will not rest until his will is done.

I know you leave to serve Athens when our city needs you most. But I beg for your aid. Guide me, help me to help our lady, I implore you.

I await your good word. Your humble servant – Elpis

The parchment crumpled in his hold, crushing the words that cleaved his heart. Ariston stared back towards Athens, beyond his reach.

The wind continued to howl about him. But his ears throbbed and his blood roared.

She was alone. In danger. Had his dreams not warned him of such? Had they not tainted his sleep and robbed him of any pleasure he might find with her?

With hands tight upon the rail of his ship he held himself in check.

"Pamphilos," his voice trembled with rage, masking the fear that twisted his stomach. He could not leave her unprotected. He knew he must reach her. "Turn the ship about. We return to Athens."

Chapter Nine

There were no ships for Rhodes – there were no ships leaving Athens.

Medusa could not return to her uncle's house. She would have no hand in the suffering of Galenus or Xenia. She feared her actions would bring them misfortune as well, but prayed staying well away might spare them.

She pleaded with Elpis, urging her to return to Galenus' home or her own father's house. But Elpis would not leave her, even though they had no place to go.

The storm had been so sudden, they'd been forced to find shelter. Since its beginning, intermittent sheets of rain and spears of ice had pelted Athens. They'd been relieved with the herder's shelter they'd found, uncaring that it was little more than a cave. Huddled together about their small fire, they waited. The rain had poured steadily since noontime the day before, the sky shaking with thunder. Surely this storm would not last forever.

While the fire offered her little warmth, its glow helped disperse some of the gloom that threatened to overwhelm her.

Since they'd found their shelter, she'd done nothing but pray. Surely one of the Gods would hear her and have mercy upon her.

She prayed to Hera for her husband, for all of the husbands.

She prayed to Aphrodite for her love.

She prayed to Ares for prowess and skill – for Ariston, for all those fighting.

She prayed to Apollo, entreating him to shine.

She prayed to Athena for wisdom, to guide her troops to a victory.

For hours she pleaded and prayed.

But they would not hear her.

The sky cracked, shot through with spindly lightening fingers, chased by mighty bursts of thunder. The sky, this storm, was rife with threat.

And there was no one to blame but herself.

Thunder shook the hill, jarring her from her useless musings.

Thea slept, her head buried beneath her wing. How she could stay so unaffected by such a tempest, Medusa couldn't fathom. But she knew her little friend, like Elpis, worried over their uncertain circumstances. Circumstances she'd caused.

Only one solution offered hope. She must go to Athena and entreat her to listen. Surely the Goddess would see Poseidon's pettiness and prevent any harm to the soldiers who fought to protect her city. Athena would save her soldiers to save her city, Medusa prayed.

She stood, draping her chiton over her head as a hood and pulling it tightly about her shoulders. "I can bear it no longer, Elpis. I must go to the temple and beg for her mercy. For her soldiers, for their lives..."

Thea roused, cawing loudly and flapping her wings in alarm.

"You cannot," Elpis protested. "Even Thea sees that. Athena will not hear you. She will not. In truth, you risk her wrath – a fearful prospect to be sure."

Medusa refused to give in to tears. "I cannot sit by and do nothing. This is my fault!"

"I will go." Elpis stood as she spoke, gathering her robes about her.

"It's my burden to bear..."

"You're wrong, mistress. Whatever the cause, Athens suffers. Tis my burden, as well as yours." Elpis' tone was soothing, her brown eyes regarding her earnestly.

"I... You shouldn't..." she began, but Elpis held up a hand to silence her.

"I want to."

"Thank you, Elpis."

Elpis kissed her cheek and hurried from the cave.

Medusa knelt to pray, but words stuck in her throat. It was not enough. She had to do something, for the storm most certainly hindered any progress Athens' soldiers might make against the Persians.

She waited only moments longer before following her companion, ignoring the plaintive coos from Thea.

Though it was midday, the sky was inky black. She could see the sun, but it could not reach the shore. There was no break in the massive thunderheads surrounding Athens to provide its rays entry. The sky had been torn apart, two separate halves atop the sea.

The sea... She moved to the edge of the cliff.

Below her, the sea rolled. Gone was its clear green and blue depths, a thing of beauty. The sea that greeted her was black and grey, its waves twisting and tossing angrily, striking out at the ships that tried to stay afloat.

What sun was visible shone brilliantly over only part of the Aegean, the other roiled with the destruction of the storm.

It was the Persians who sailed waters untouched by the ravages of this storm. They sailed beneath the rays of the sun, on gentle seas. While Greece's sons were tossed about on waves that threw their ships from trough to peak, a force greater than the mortal foes they battled.

It was a message for her.

Was Athena so angry that she could turn a blind eye to this? Would the Goddess take the lives of so many soldiers to punish her? Could she punish Medusa for a deed born of love?

She felt her heart drop with the ships as they slid into a trough from the top of a wave, towering twenty feet over them. One ship could not right itself, listing so far its sailors were thrown into the sea. She cried out, but it was lost to the angry call of the raging storm.

The sea was not controlled by Athena. The Goddess would not sacrifice these men; she loved her city too well. Nor would she willfully endanger those loyal to her.

This was Poseidon's doing.

Her love had brought this about. And her fidelity to a mortal man would be the end of these Greek soldiers. The Gods, it seemed, would not intercede.

Her heart, her love, would die with them.

Ariston, tender and loyal, filled her senses. She could not lose him.

If she went to the temple...but there was no time. And Poseidon would not stop.

She had no time for sadness. He needed her help, her protection. She would do what she must to ensure he came back to her. She would fight for him the only way she could.

Forgive me, husband. She cried, a sob choking her.

A scream tore from her – carried on the wind – taking all of the air in her lungs. It was a wordless, sorrowful sound, tearing at her throat and staunching her tears.

She must cling to her resolve. For no matter how much she feared Poseidon, or the deed she must endure, she must bend to his will. There was no other way.

She closed her eyes, pulling an image of Ariston to mind. He was smiling as she cast the net into the water. His hair lifted in the breeze off the waves, his eyes sparkled in the sunshine. It steadied her, to think of him so.

She drew air deep into her lungs. "Poseidon!"

He was there before her instantly. His near colorless eyes regarded her with mocking amusement, while the muscle in his jaw tightened. "Did you call me, fair Medusa?"

She met his eyes, met his undisguised lust with only the slightest flinch. Her panic rose, choking her, so she nodded silently.

"Very well." He reached for her, offering his hand.

She stared at his hand, at his long fingers and well-formed arm. To have the power he controlled. What would she do with such power? Would she grow jaded and use it to suit her purposes?

She turned her eyes towards the ships churning below, dismissing her fear – and her fury.

She placed her hand in his.

His hand was hard and cold. His grasp unbreakable, she suspected, though she did not try. His fingers seemed to undulate about her, free flowing yet molding to her. His touch was alive, rippling as the winter seas upon her skin. To the eye, he simply held her hand. But his coldness leached all warmth from her and chilled her to the bone.

He looked at their hands, joined, and smiled.

In that instant the wind calmed. Her cloak no longer whipped about her. The rain lessened, then stopped. The waves settled, falling flat and lifeless.

They churned anew, shifting against the Persians without mercy. Those waves that had toppled Athens' triremes now towered over the Persian vessels with a mighty vengeance. Eight Persian ships were swallowed, two more driven to collide. So quickly he'd turned the tide on Athens' enemies, with terrifying and immediate finality.

Poseidon had played with her.

As the sun broke through the grey clouds, Medusa thought she heard a cheer from the ships below.

Medusa took a steadying breath. Her heart would survive, if Ariston did. "You will protect them? Promise me you will keep my husband safe."

He inclined his head, his cold hand tightened about hers. "And you will carry out your part of our bargain."

She nodded once. She would not beg. She would not cower or tremble. She would be strong now.

"This is your fate." His voice wasn't harsh or angry. He spoke to her with the same cajoling tones one might use with a child. "Come with me now."

Medusa turned to him, meeting his eyes. "I will honor our bargain, Poseidon. But I ask you a kindness."

"You ask for more?" His eyebrow arched higher, but he waited.

"Let this be done in darkness... so that I might bear it more easily."

Poseidon's smile twisted, the muscle of his jaw tightening. "I could take on his form, Medusa, for you."

"No, no. I beg of you." She feared she would cry then.

His eyes narrowed as he lifted his hand and covered her eyes. Darkness found her, though she no longer felt his hand upon her. She blinked, for her vision was dark and cloudy. She jumped as his breath stirred the hair at her ear.

He whispered, "Then I will close your eyes, and keep them closed until I am done."

Ariston felt the thrust of the sword, piercing his skin to bury itself in his chest. The blade was cold, slicing cleanly. The spurt of heat that followed, running down his chest, was his own blood. He grabbed for the sword's hilt, but his combatant was faster. He pulled back, tearing the wound wide as the serrated edges came free. White-hot pain blinded him, but he fought through it.

His strength must hold.

He shook his head, narrowing his eyes. He must focus. His attacker would lift his blade again, Ariston was certain. And before he could wield his vile sword again, Ariston must overcome him and end this. He steadied himself.

His foes black eyes widened.

Ariston sneered, goading the man. "It will take more than your blade to kill me."

As the Persian raised his sword arm, Ariston reached for him.

He grabbed the man about the waist and ran, slamming his opponent into the mast with the last of his waning strength. His attacker's head bounced off the mast, the rewarding thunk jarring his bones. Ariston slid his short sword into the man, relaxing his hold only when the Persian went limp against him.

He waited, too weak to stand. No new sword bit into him, no fist gouged, or spear pierced. With no one left to fight, he felt the depth of his injuries. The wound on his arm was deep, bleeding freely. His chest wound made breathing difficult, but he did not linger over it.

He fought upright, swaying as he propped himself against the mast for support. He stared at the man he'd killed, and then shifted slowly to assess the rest on the ship. What he saw amazed him.

The rain, the thick sheets of freezing rain stopped, the wind died. The sun attempted to break through grey clouds, its rays shooting shafts of light onto the calming waters and the pitching deck of his ship.

The sight that greeted him, bathed in pools of white hot sunlight, was grim. The deck was littered with the dead and wounded. Some were Ekdromoi, but most were Persians. He shifted, but could not find the strength to push himself from the mast supporting him.

His lungs seemed to constrict and he drew a shallow breath. It did little to help, and he gasped.

A cry went up, catching his attention. He was not alone as he watched the sky. The grey-black cloud towering over them parted to the blue sky beyond. The tossing waves that had made defense secondary to staying afloat now rolled steadily beneath the ship.

The Persians lost the wind.

The closest Persian ship, whose men had swung aboard his own, dropped suddenly. The sea seemed to yawn, opening wide to ensnare the Persian vessel, before the water rose over the ship, pulling it beneath the water's surface and out of sight.

He heard the cheers of his men.

"Poseidon is merciful," one said.

"He's come to our aid," another declared.

The pain of his wounds paled in comparison to the anguish he felt. He knew what had saved him and his men. She had saved them... she had... His hands fisted and he bit back the cry as his mind and heart fought the truth.

For two days he'd tried to break through the ships that had circled him. For two days he'd pleaded with the Gods, begged for mercy, threatened his men and exhausted those at the oars.

But fate was against him. A Persian ship had caught them. And he'd had to fight.

Now the sun burst from behind the clouds, casting the blood-soaked deck in brilliant light. The sun's rays poured over his skin and chased the chill from the air, but he began to shiver uncontrollably.

She'd sacrificed too much – for him. For the Gods. His lungs constricted.

His agony was unbearable. He'd failed her, leaving her alone with no protection.

Forgive me, lady.

Poseidon was not merciful. He deserved no tributes. He deserved nothing but the wrath of these men, earned by the God's selfishness.

Anger surged through him. He stood tall, bracing himself on the ships rail as his fury stoked strength he thought he'd exhausted.

"Ariston?" Pamphilos said hesitantly, regarding him with unconcealed concern. "You fought more fiercely than any I've ever seen. I am honored to be at your side."

Ariston stared at his second in confusion. Pamphilos could do little but stare at him, his chest. Ariston glanced down. His chest was grave indeed. The skin was flayed from his collar bone, his muscles split wide from the jagged teeth of the Persian's blade. Blood seeped, sluggish and red.

He closed his eyes and cursed the Gods anew.

"I will not die, Pamphilos." His face was resolved as he regarded his second. "There is too much left to be done." His words were rough and unsteady, taxing him with the simple effort of speaking.

He would not die. The battle was far from over. He must make it back to his lady. He'd given his word.

A queer coldness flowed over him, lessening his pain. He gazed over the ships, relieved to see the Persians had turned away from Athens' shore.

"Send me Chariton. He will stitch me up." He could not bear the feel of Pamphilos' hand upon his arm, offering support. He blinked, his sight blurring momentarily. "Take us back to Athens, Pamphilos."

Pamphilos nodded, staring at his wounds. "Find your bed, for you can barely stand. I will send Chariton to you."

Ariston nodded, moving slowly toward his sleeping quarters on the ship. He was shivering in earnest when he reached it. His hand, cold and numb, found his chlamys by his mat. He lay slowly, feeling heavy and oddly numb. He covered the wound on his chest, pressing against it with weakening limbs.

Though the words were garbled and his eyes fell closed, he heard his second speak. Pamphilos' words reached him, a familiar soldier's farewell. "May you find glory in Elysium, Ariston."

Elysium must wait, Ariston thought before his eyes closed.

Medusa searched the ground, fighting tears. She was freezing, even covered as she was. But that mattered little. Her necklace was gone.

He'd pulled it from her neck.

The crescent moon was high, but its slight light did nothing to aid in her search. Instead, it cast long shadows across the ground –as if even Selene was scorning her.

She could not stop shivering, or catch the soft moan that slipped from her throat as her search became frantic. Every part of her throbbed, her body and soul ached.

"Medusa?" Stheno stood, a wraith-like visage illuminated by the glow of the lamp she held aloft. "We've searched these two days, to bring you home."

She couldn't speak, so she nodded.

"What ails you, sister?" Euryale moved closer, holding her lantern high above them.

The two stood, regarding her from the depths of their veils.

Medusa stared back, swallowing convulsively as she sought the words to explain. None came. Even if she had the words, she would never speak them.

"What has he done to you?" Stheno asked in a voice so full of despair that Medusa closed her eyes.

"What Poseidon always does, I fear." Even Euryale spoke gently. "He is a beast."

Their pity chafed her, forcing her to stand straight. But the effort cost her, making her sway on unsteady feet.

"Come with us, sister. Come home," Stheno implored. "It is done. Father will welcome you back."

"Life will go on," Euryale added, not unkindly. "And you may... heal at home."

Medusa shook her head. "I will wait for my husband." She would not leave.

"Will he want you now?" Stheno spoke so softly that Medusa wondered if her sister had said the words or if she'd asked herself such a question.

"If he is alive," Euryale said. "Many lives were lost to the storm and the battle..."

"He is alive." Medusa's voice rasped from her throat.

"Will he still want you?" Stheno repeated. She moved closer and draped her arm carefully about Medusa's shoulders. "Come away. Let us find you a bed. Galenus has been searching for you, worried and fearful."

Medusa shook her head. "Look at me. Will seeing me make all right for them once more?" Her voice hitched as she held tightly to what little control she still had.

"You look as you always do." Stheno hugged her.

"Whatever injury Poseidon has inflicted, it is visible only to you.

Galenus and Xenia will be pleased, in their own way." Euryale shook her head, making the long veils sway. "Your suffering has brought joy to all else, sweet sister. You have fulfilled the will of Olympus."

Medusa stared at her sister.

"Poseidon is appeased. Father will be appeased. An alliance will be forged. It is done," Euryale shrugged.

"Come, Medusa, let us go..."

Medusa wrenched from Stheno's grasp, horrified by the truth of her sister's words. She'd done her duty once more. And, in betraying her husband, she'd likely once more earned favor with her father, her family and the Gods. It galled her, making a knot tighten and twist in her stomach.

None of them mattered.

Ariston was all now.

And she would wait for him.

Until he came home, she would have his gift. "I must find my necklace." She stumbled once, but continued to peer into the darkness. "I will not go until I have it."

"We will help." Stheno moved forward, holding the lantern high for Medusa.

Zeus leveled a hard look upon Poseidon. "You are satisfied?"

Poseidon nodded. His brother need never know the truth.

Zeus sat back in his throne, a smile upon his face. "And was the bedding worthy of such a hunger?"

"She was lovely." His words were curt.

More lovely than he'd expected. When she'd taken his hand, his delight knew no bounds. Yet she'd refused to look on him, refused to move beneath him – as she'd done on the beach with her man. No matter how soft his lips or how gentle his touch, she was unmoved. And his delight vanished.

Zeus laughed. "Would you still have her as wife?"

Poseidon felt anger rise within him.

Her body was undeniably soft and inviting. And his need had consumed him as he'd touched her. But the memory of her gasping and mewling beneath her husband had twisted his desire, had mocked him. His lust had turned to anger – an anger that overwhelmed him. No matter what caresses or strokes he bestowed upon her, she'd refused pleasure at his hand.

And if she would not sigh with pleasure, he would have her cry out for mercy. He had used her badly. But her tears, when they came, had been silent. She'd robbed him of satisfaction even then.

The things he'd done, he could never take back.

He should have killed her beloved husband. He should have drowned them both in their cove, and wiped away his longing. Instead she'd stirred his heart and made him want.

Not her. He knew the truth of that now. Such love, to know the depth of real love for another and have it returned, was beyond his understanding. And yet, someday, he might deign to consider such a partnership. Someday.

"Would you, brother?" Zeus interrupted his musing.

Poseidon regarded his brother, noting the impatience on Zeus' face. "No. Medusa belongs with the man she calls husband. Her heart is true and there is no room for another." Though he thought her husband was a foolish man, leaving her behind to fight Athena's battle.

"Then peace," Zeus sighed. "Your lustful nature is most worrisome. Let us hope you will find a partner to calm the fire in your blood." Zeus led him into the Council Chamber.

"You believe such a woman exists for me?" Poseidon laughed. He doubted one woman would be able to love him, and he her, with such true devotion.

Zeus regarded him with amused eyes, shrugging. "And Athena? Have you made peace with her?"

"Was there need to make peace?" Exasperation tinged his voice. "I cannot bed a woman, raise a storm or send an earthquake without needing to apologize to your daughter." And yet, he would be forced to apologize to Athena if she discovered his latest exploit. Athena, chaste virgin Goddess that she was, would likely turn her spear on him if she learned that he'd found his pleasure with Medusa on the dais of her temple.

It was more than an insult, but his fury had been beyond control. He'd dragged her to the temple, intending to throw her at Athena, to expose her as a trollop. But watching her shiver upon the cold marble had stirred his blood again.

"Find a way to end this feud between you. It is unseemly." Zeus spoke with authority, scowling at him in subtle warning. "She is a Goddess and worthy of your respect."

"I will try, brother. I will." He resented his brother's superiority at times such as this. If he, Hera, and Athena had been successful in their attempt to overthrow Zeus – would Poseidon himself have become so insufferable and self-righteous?

But then he wouldn't enjoy haranguing his niece. Controlling her was a chore he would never attempt. If their conquest had been successful, he would have been forced to kill Athena for the right to rule Olympus.

He grudgingly admitted that Zeus managed her with a calm he would never own.

Zeus clapped him on the shoulder. "I will hold you to that. We are Gods, yes, but we are family as well. I would have you remember that." And then his brother went to join his wife.

Poseidon's eyes swept the chamber, a familiar sense of discontent settling over him.

"Is she awake?" Medusa heard her uncle's voice, but did not acknowledge it. If they thought she slept, she would be left in peace. She'd earned that.

"She is not," Stheno snapped.

"When she wakes tell her Elpis has arrived. She brings news," Galenus spoke softly.

Medusa stirred. News – from Elpis? Had she brought word of Ariston? Perhaps he'd come back or was on his way... or injured. She took a deep breath and waited.

"What news?" Stheno's voice was a whisper.

"I dare not speak the words twice," Galenus said.

Medusa did not move, though she grew rigid with apprehension. "Send Elpis to me."

"Are you well, niece?" Galenus asked.

"No, Uncle. I am not." She made no attempt at pleasantries. "Please send Elpis to me."

She heard the door shut and knew her sister had sent him away.

She lay, listening to the sounds of the early morning spilling into her bedroom. Such sounds would normally give her ease, lulling her back to sleep. But there would be no sleep, not yet.

"Has Euryale returned?"

"Not yet." Stheno brushed a long lock from Medusa's cheek. "She will not give up. You know that."

Euryale had offered to stay, to search for Medusa's missing necklace on the rocks of the cliff. Medusa had fought to stay as well, but the Gorgons would hear none of her arguments. Her mind was able but her body was not. Stheno had helped her home with the promise that Euryale would find the carved owl Ariston had made for her.

"Mistress?" Elpis' voice was unsteady.

Medusa sat up, turning towards her companion with arms outstretched. "Elpis."

"Oh, lady," Elpis cried, hugging Medusa to her. "Are you ill?"

"It is plain to see that she is," Stheno said, startling Elpis into silence.

"Stheno, be kind to my beloved Elpis. She has been a sister to me in my time with Galenus and Xenia. I ask that you treat her as such." Medusa glanced at her sister, all the while holding Elpis to her.

Stheno straightened. "If she pleases you, then I will try."

"And you," Medusa smoothed the soft brown hair on Elpis' head. "Where did you spend the night?"

"Under the dock." Elpis shook her head. "I was too afraid to make the journey after dark."

"That was wise," Medusa soothed her.

"I am sorry, mistress. I went to the temple..."

"Was Athena there?" Medusa asked.

Elpis shook her head.

"She would not have listened," Stheno assured, "if she had been there. Her mind was set. Elpis was on a fool's errand."

"Mayhap you are right," Medusa whispered.

"I lost my way coming back to the cave. I could see the docks and went in hopes of hearing news." Elpis was shaking as she spoke.

"And what have you learned?" Stheno asked.

"The storm was a grave...danger," Elpis voice wavered. "Ektor said fifteen triremes were lost to the storm alone. And more were taken in battle. Two returned to Athens while the rest went on to Salamis."

Medusa searched Elpis' face. "But Ariston is safe and well, is he not?"

Elpis regarded her with troubled brown eyes. "He... he was gravely injured, mistress, though his ship went on to Salamis."

"He is well," Medusa whispered fiercely. "He must be."

"One of the injured soldiers that returned spoke of his bravery. He said your husband fought valiantly." Elpis' words were hoarse. "His sword and spear killed more men than any other on his vessel."

Medusa grasped Elpis' hands. "Please, please tell me everything you know."

"He was struck many times. But he did not stop fighting... The storm bore his ship into the path of a Persian vessel and his ship was overrun. The storm tossed them, knocking more than half of their crew into the seas. But Ariston fought on."

Medusa's heart swelled. She was proud of him, even as she ached at the thought of his suffering. Sharing Ariston's battles – his victories – gave him glory.

"A sword struck his chest, a fatal blow. And still, Ariston defeated his foe... He fought until no Persian stood on his decks... Only then did he fall."

Medusa shook her head, stunned. "No."

Elpis whispered, "I am sorry, mistress... Pamphilos was in command as they set sail for Salamis."

"No, no." Medusa's voice rose, a high, agitated cry. "He was to be protected. It was part of our bargain. He promised... He promised me Ariston would be safe."

Elpis' brow furrowed. And then understanding dawned. "Oh, my lady," she sobbed anew.

She shook her head, unable to accept Elpis' words. It was not true. He lived. He must live...

"It is no matter for a God to break their word, sister. They've no need to answer to us," Stheno said. "We will go home tomorrow. It will do you good to be gone from this place and all that has happened here." She opened the door. "I will tell Galenus that we leave at first light."

Medusa heard the door shut as Stheno left the room.

"I'm so sorry, mistress." Elpis clasped her hand, offering support.

Medusa longed to shake off her touch, but she could not move.

"He loved you dearly," Elpis whispered. "Ektor said he'd turned his ship towards shore to return to you..."

Medusa startled. "What?"

Elpis blushed. "I...I sent him a note. Once I'd learned what your...gift was to be, I ran to the temple. I heard Poseidon's offer and your answer...and feared the repercussions. I asked for his guidance."

The air drained from Medusa's lungs.

"I ask for your forgiveness, mistress. I meant no harm..."

Her heart shattered, pulsing shards of agony through every part of her. He had died knowing her plight. He'd tried to return... She was to blame for his death, then. Such a burden would have clouded his focus, shaken his control...

A sob choked her.

"Elpis," she gasped, clinging to her companion's hand in desperation. She had no words, only anguish.

Had she not done everything asked of her? Had she not given everything she had, or was, in her service to Olympus? And still, they had made him suffer. Their soldier had been shown no mercy – or respect.

A peculiar numbness licked at the soles of her feet. Her toes curled as the slow rush of frost moved, traveling up the length of her legs and pricking frigid needles across her stomach. It lodged itself in her chest, turning her heart and lung to ice. She felt heavy and slow, but the pain was less. It was there, screaming at the edge of her consciousness, but she would not yield to it – not yet.

She could not stand Elpis' touch upon her.

She could not bear to sit in this room.

She would not accept this... this punishment when she had done their will.

"Help me dress." Medusa's words were clipped.

"Where are you...?"

"Do not ask me questions, Elpis. Do what I ask." Medusa did not look at Elpis as she spoke.

"Mistress?"

"Once I'm gone, find Stheno. Tell her we will depart when I return. I have no need of rest. I need only to leave this cursed place."

Medusa stilled her impatience, standing straight to let Elpis wrap the linen peplos about her. Her restlessness increased as Elpis fussed over the bronze clasps and the drape of the fabric. By the time Elpis started to brush through her hair, she shrugged away.

"Leave it, Elpis." Medusa clasped Elpis' hand in hers, stilling the brush and holding her companion away from her. She reached for her sister's grey epiblema, covering her head with the shawl.

"How long will you be gone?" Elpis asked.

"Not long," Medusa hugged Elpis and left quickly.

The walk to the temple stretched before her, though she knew it was no further than on any other day. Yet this day, Ariston's broad back did not lead the way. His golden curls did not catch the wind and dance in its currents.

Her eyes burned.

She was alone. She must be strong a little longer. Then she would go with her sisters, eagerly.

But first, Athena would know the truth. The Goddess must know all of it.

Ariston could see nothing but flat black water, covered here and there by milky white fog.

His eyes scanned the distant shore. He breathed deeply, pushing against his instincts, his wariness. There was nothing left to fear now that he was crossing the River Acheron, the River of Woe, to Hades' realm.

Life, his life, was over now – for now.

He leaned over the railing, watching as the boat skimmed the surface of the water. The ship made no sound and left no ripple in its wake. The fog shifted, separating into wispy feathers as the ship cut through it to cross the river. He stood, staring ahead. There was no sign of shore.

A single flickering flame cast jumping shadows upon the deck, serving to heighten the nerves of his ship mates. He pitied them, those souls who wondered at their fate in the afterlife. But he had no plans to accept his fate.

He glared at the ferryman, knowing Charon was nothing more than Hades' servant. But the speed at which they traveled caused him to let out another impatient sigh. He supposed not all of Charon's passengers were as eager to reach their destination.

The Underworld lay before him, a promise of eternal life. A life without political dilemma, war, or heartache was his. An eternity of merriment, feasting and pleasure was his reward for dying in battle. Elysium waited.

He knew he should be thankful, or sorrowful, over his death. But he could not be.

He could only think of getting back. He would find a way back to her.

As the boat moved forward, the fog began to thin. Before him rose a fortress, bleak and dreary to the eye. Hades' house.

The fortress waited on the far side of this blue-black lake, fed by all of Hades' rivers. It dangled from the edge of a sheer cliff face, a jutting outcrop above the lake's barren shore. There were no trees, no grass, and no animals. But here, nothing lived. Its desolation did little to improve his mood.

"You'll find favor with the Judges," a man spoke, shaking Ariston from his reverie.

Ariston glanced at him, uninterested in passing the time with conversation – especially here. He knew he was not alone on Charon's boat, but he'd taken care not to note his fellow passengers.

"We'll have to plead our case to them." The man pointed to the woman and three children huddled together in the boat. "I am ... was but a fisherman."

"My father is a fisherman," Ariston said. True, his father was more than that. But his father had taught him how to fish. And he felt the need to offer comfort to this man and his family. "It is honorable work."

The man nodded. "We shall see. All will be well if we stay together."

Ariston looked at the man's family again. The youngest, a small girl, clung to her mother. Her eyes were squeezed tightly shut. The other children looked no more at ease. The boy, the eldest, held his head up. Only the slight tremor of his lower lip revealed his struggle.

"What happened?" Ariston asked.

"We were caught in the storm." The man shook his head. "A storm like none I've ever seen. Too powerful for my fishing boat, too powerful for some of Athens' ships as well, I'd wager?"

Ariston's hands tightened on the railing of the ship. The wood splintered under his grip, burying aged needles into his fingertips. "It was."

"It came on us quickly, without warning." The man shrugged. "It was the will of the Gods, the will of Poseidon."

Ariston clenched his jaw. Poseidon's will, indeed.

The will of the Gods was no longer something he revered. But he would bide his time carefully. As long as he was here, in the Underworld, he would play the part of Olympus' loyal servant – so he might find a way back to her.

"His tributes were many," the man continued, gesturing to the ship.

Ariston turned reluctant eyes in the direction indicated. He did not want to see the full extent of the suffering he'd helped birth. These people, people who had done him no wrong, faced Hades' judges because of his marriage. No, because his wife attempted fidelity.

"All from the storm?" Ariston asked.

"Most. There are some soldiers, like you, and another too old to have been at sea or in battle." The man smiled. "It was simply his time."

Ariston let his eyes wander over the faces of those with him. Most were fearful. Some were resigned. One or two were angry. And then...

"Leandros?" Ariston moved to the young soldier.

"My lord." He grasped hands with Ariston.

"Did you fall by the sword?" He regarded Leandros, little more than a boy, and felt sadness. He had been an eager recruit. Only he and Ektor had shown true skill in training.

Was Ektor safe? He had left him in Athens, to protect the temple...

"No," Leandros' voice was tight as he added, "Our ship was swallowed by the waves. Will that keep me from Elysium?"

Ariston forced the words to come. "You died fighting for Athena, Leandros. Surely Hades will see the glory in that." His stretched his hands, his frustration barely contained.

Leandros' brow furrowed. "I am sorry for you, Ariston."

Ariston looked at the boy, confused.

"My ship left last, as we were no more than a supply vessel." He paused. "Your lady's companion? The letter? Ektor found me and bid me find you. I found a sailor on your ship... Did the missive reach you?"

Ariston nodded. "It did."

Leandros' eyes were upon him. "Ektor suspected it brought troubling news?" He waited, but Ariston could not deny the truth of his words. "Would that we crossed at Lethe, and let the River of Forgetfulness have you. There can be no peace for you here."

"There is none," Ariston agreed.

"What will you do?"

"I will offer my services to Hades," Ariston paused, "if he will let me go back to my lady."

"Your services?" Leandros' face paled.

"I would lend Hades my sword and keep guard at the gates of Tartarus."

Leandros shook his head. "Your lady would have you find your peace, in Elysium, where you may wait for her."

Ariston said nothing, knowing the boy was right. Medusa would grieve, but she would honor him and his memory. She would want him to find peace.

But his dreams... He swallowed back the fear that clawed within his chest. Something terrifying would befall Medusa. He knew this, just as he knew he had to return to her.

The young priestess turned and smiled, her eyes crinkling pleasantly above the trim of her embroidered veil. "Good afternoon, lady. Have you come to pray or to leave offerings?" She spoke with such sweetness that Medusa simply stared at her.

Had she been so naïve and young? She prayed this girl might remain innocent to the ways of the Gods. There had been true fulfillment in it, when she'd thought her work was meaningful.

A cry went up, Thea's cry. She had not seen her precious pet since the night...since she'd paid Poseidon's price. Her little owl was distressed, Medusa could tell. She turned, searching the dimly lit interior for her friend.

"Thea?" she called.

The priestess' eyes widened. "Is it your owl?"

Medusa spun, turning desperate eyes on the girl. "Where is she?"

"Athena has her..." The priestess backed up, startled.

"Where?" Medusa asked, her voice rising. "Where is she?"

"Leave us." Athena's order brooked no disagreement. She stood, bearing her shield and helmet, glowering at Medusa.

The priestess bowed to the Goddess, then ran from the antechamber.

"You're forbidden from my temple." Athena's face reflected nothing but disdain for Medusa. "I assume you have come to beg for forgiveness?" The Goddess' brows elevated as she waited for Medusa's response.

Try as she might, she could not stop the words that tumbled from her lips. "Forgiveness? I need forgiveness, from you?"

"If you've not come to beg my favor, you should not be here. Unless you seek punishment for the crimes you've committed? To appease your soul?"

"What crimes do you speak of Athena? Faithful servant or faithful wife?" Her voice twisted, her pain challenging her resolve. "There is nothing more that could punish me."

Athena's face hardened. "You dare speak to me like this?"

Medusa continued. "When have I failed you? In all the years I've served you with my whole heart. And when you freed me I gave it as I chose..."

"You prattle on about your dead man." Athena shook her head.

"And the hundreds of others who died on the sea, for you, Athena – and for Athens," she cried.

"You cared little for them when they lived. If you'd taken Poseidon's offer, none would have suffered," Athena turned to leave.

"I did, Athena," Medusa shrieked. "I did. I endured all – to save them and my husband. I had his word it would be so."

"What?" Athena turned wide eyes to her, coming to stand before her. "When?"

"The storm... I called upon him to stop the storm..." Sorrow silenced her briefly, but she pushed on. "In exchange for the lives of those at sea – all for naught."

Athena stepped forward, rage upon her face. "Where, Medusa?"

Medusa looked at her. She knew the face of the Goddess. It was a face she'd loved dearly for half of her life. But this look was unrecognizable to her. Burning with violent hatred, her Goddess was... frightening.

"I know not. Nor does it matter."

"Does it not?"Athena's eyebrow arched. Her face was taut with tension. "I have something of yours, I think."

"Thea?" Medusa searched the temple, Thea's call faint but audible. "Your gift, and my dearest companion."

"Not Thea, though I have her too. She is caged."

"Why?" Medusa shared Thea's betrayal, then. Athena had loved the owl first, before she'd caged her.

"She attacked one of the guards." Athena continued to watch at her, with critical eyes. "She blinded him in one eye."

Medusa shook her head, stunned. Thea would never attack unwarranted. "She would not..."

"Yet she did." Athena held her hand forward, "For this." The Goddess opened her hand.

The leather cord was wrapped about the Goddess' fingers, but the carved owl swung freely. Medusa reached for it, her heart swelling. But Athena pulled her hand away.

"It is mine," Medusa heard the pleading of her voice and hated it. It was all she had left of him. "Thea knew it meant a great deal to me. She would have brought it to me..."

"Do you know where she found it, Medusa?" Athena shook her head. "On the night of that cursed storm my temple was struck dark. My priestess fled, hiding in the robes room as its lamp stayed bright. Once the storm ended, she returned to the antechamber to light the candles." Her eyes narrowed as she sneered at Medusa. "And on the dais of my temple she saw a man bent over a woman. At first she feared he'd brought someone injured by the storm, for the sounds of groaning and carrying on. Until it became clear that the pair were otherwise occupied. She waited in the shadows, but he would not finish with the woman. And when the sun rose, the man carried the woman out of the temple, leaving this necklace and a plain brown cloak upon the floor. The floor of my temple," She pointed at Medusa. "My temple, Medusa. The Temple of Athena Polias – chaste and wise."

Medusa could not speak.

She'd not seen anything, a kindness she'd not expected from Poseidon. But she knew now Poseidon had done more than use her body. He had used her as an offense against Athena – an unforgivable offense. "I did not know." How could she have known? "Why would he do such a thing?"

Athena laughed, clearly astounded. "Truly, Medusa, your pretense is too much. A man can satiate his lust with you and you remember none of it?"

"If only that were true," Medusa pushed her sadness aside, favoring the warmth of her anger. "Dismiss my words as lies. But ask Poseidon. He will preen proudly."

Athena's lip curled in disdain. "Your faithless dalliances are abominable enough. Do not speak my uncle's name or link him to such perfidy. Even Poseidon would not to do the things you suggest."

"Why else would the storm stop?" Medusa asked.

"Because Zeus willed it so." She shook her head. "My father sent him to see it done."

Medusa mulled this over. "Did your priestess not see Poseidon?"

"Do you think my priestess would not know Poseidon? That Poseidon would pass unrecognized by anyone? A prouder peacock I know not." She paused, a look of distaste coloring her cheeks. "He is well rid of you. As is your husband, no doubt well honored by Hades. You are a faithless deceiver, the likes of which I have never known."

Medusa's heart, what little there was left, crumbled.

She had been another attempt to prod at his niece. Poseidon's ill use of her, in Athena's temple, gave him pleasure for his body and fed his feud with Athena. All while keeping him without fault... If he denied it was he, as she suspected, her words meant nothing.

It was her word against that of a God. Albeit a faithless, lying, and manipulative deity, but still an Olympian.

She swallowed against the rising anger – and defeat.

"I've done nothing but love, Athena." Whether Zeus had instructed Poseidon to come, whether her entreaty, her sacrifice, had been unnecessary, she no longer cared – nothing mattered now.

"I will take Thea and leave this place. I will go to my father's house, beyond the Sea River, far from Athens." She would leave this place.

"Your father is hard at work on your next marriage contract. Or so it seems."

Marriage? Now? More bartering, more humiliation. She was once more a pawn. "May I take Thea with me, Athena?"

"No," Athena shook her head. "She will stay here with me, where she belongs."

Medusa swallowed this. "May I have my necklace? It is all I have left of my husband."

"No. You do not deserve it." Athena slipped the necklace into the folds of her peplos. "You have shamed him."

Ariston's words filled her heart. *The love I have for you gives me breath and strength. You will always hold my heart. Let it give you the strength to do what must be done. For you will be my lady, forever.*

"No, Athena. You have shamed me, and Athens. Your pride has robbed you of compassion or reason. Or you would see the truth of my words. Your power has turned your selfish heart to stone." She looked upon the Goddess. "I pity you. And the Gods, too. You've forgotten those who love you most – those who sacrifice all for your favor."

Athena's face darkened. Her eyes raged, burning a brilliant and fiery red. "You pity me? You have scorned the Gods. You have spoken blasphemy, loudly, in my temple. You will suffer, Medusa."

"There is nothing more to suffer." Medusa felt no fear, she felt nothing. "You've taken everything from me."

"Have I? We shall see." Athena shook her head, a hateful smile contorting her elegant features. She touched Medusa's head, caressing a long lock of her hair. "Wisdom will rule you from this day on, your constant lullaby their serpent's song. Only those with an innocent heart, women and children, are set safely apart. A heart of stone is your curse to bear as they turn man to stone with their ruby stare. Keep them safe and keep them whole, or to Hades you will send their hardened soul. Your disloyalty brings man's life to an end, but through your death they live again."

A blinding pain crushed Medusa's head. A thousand tiny daggers gouged into her scalp and neck, needling deeply into her. She shivered, withdrawing from Athena's touch, but there was no escaping the sensation. Her scalp seemed to split, pulling apart and separating to make room for the pressure that surely crushed her skull.

"What have you done to me?" she gasped.

"You will learn in time." Athena leaned close to Medusa. "But I caution you to avoid those you know and love. Your very presence will bring nothing but pain and suffering." Athena touched her cheek. "But they will keep you company in your pain and suffering."

Medusa flinched, frightened by the way Athena's words seemed to echo. She swayed where she stood, her head and shoulders sagging beneath an invisible burden.

She blinked, catching a last glance of Athena. Why did the Goddess look so pained? Her anguish was plain to see…

And then Athena was gone.

Medusa gasped as pain lanced her head.

Her eyes pressed against their lids, as if they were being forced from their sockets. Her vision was distorted, tinged with red and faded in its details.

A ripple of pain coursed down her neck, then shot up the back of her head again. Her suffering intensified as some invisible coil wrapped about her temples, pressing unmercifully against her tormented skull.

She bit her lip, catching her cry, as she crept from the temple. Another ripple spilled over her, sharper and hotter than the first. She stumbled down the steps.

The sun was blinding, each agonizing ray of light searing her eyelids. Her hands came up to shade herself, but she could not stop the pricks of fire that scorched her eyes.

She could not steady herself. With each step, the throbbing in her head grew heavier -- crippling. The sun was high, punishing her with its brilliance. How then could she feel no heat upon her skin? An uncontrollable shivering began, jarring the ache in her neck and head enough to make her cry out. The shivering intensified, forcing her to pause. The pain churned her stomach until she retched upon the ground. She drew in breath and set off, slowly.

The path was too unsteady to scale without careful attention.

But she could not bear to open her eyes.

As her foot slipped on the shale stones of the path, she pitched forward. Her hands flailed, but there was no foot or handhold to use to catch herself. She did not see the pointed outcrop of rock, and felt little else once her head struck its corner.

Her pain and worries were lost in darkness.

Chapter Ten

It was dark. But then, no sunlight reached Hades' house.

It had taken all of Ariston's persuasion, and patience, to gain audience. The Judges of the Dead thought him foolish and told him so.

"You would trade eternal paradise for eternal servitude? For a woman?" Aeacus had shaken his head. "Go forth, stay in Elysium for a few days. This woman will pale."

"You are more foolish than most, soldier, to offer such a bargain. Few who shared your journey on Charon's ship will go to Elysium. You are honored, yet you cast it aside?" Minos sneered, sparing him only the briefest glance. "Hades will laugh at you."

"Does Hades laugh?" Rhadamanthys asked, with wide eyes. "That is a sight I've yet to see in my time here."

"No, he does not laugh," Aeacus said quickly.

"I would ask him myself," Ariston said. "I must try."

Minos snorted.

Rhadamanthys sighed. "Hades' mood is bleak as of late, soldier. I fear your request will fall on deaf ears."

They continued in such a manner until Ariston feared the loss of his temper. But Minos saved him, waving Ariston away with a muttered, "Follow the road."

Now he stood in Hades' dark house, waiting once more.

Shadows filled each corner, while whispers of things unseen made Ariston tighten defensively.

He had no time for this. He had to get back to her – he had to get back to his lady.

The man who entered the room was not what he expected. Hades was tall and well muscled. His face was youthful, with a close cropped beard and smooth, pale skin.

"You asked for an audience, you have it. Now tell me, where do you belong?" Hades' voice was deep, emotionless.

Ariston swallowed. "Athens." He met Hades' gaze, but the God revealed nothing to him.

"Why? You died with honor and glory. Is that not what every soldier wants?"

"My wife…" His voice wavered.

Hades brow lifted slightly. "Lives. You do not."

"She is in danger."

"Earthly danger. She is no longer your concern, Ariston."

"The danger she faces is not earthly, but far from it…" Ariston's voice was hoarse, his desperation mounting. He took a wavering breath before he began again. "She is everything to me. I am proud of my death, but it means nothing if she is in peril. I must know." Ariston kneeled. "I beg you. I beg you to return me to Athens."

Ariston waited, willing himself to be strong.

"Who is this wife?" Hades asked.

"Medusa of Athens." He paused. "Now of Rhodes."

Hades was silent, his dark blue eyes regarding him steadily.

"When I die—" Ariston began.

"You are dead," Hades assured him.

"When I return…die again, I would serve as guardian to Tartarus. I am a skilled warrior, a skill I might offer you." He spoke with confidence.

"You vex me," Hades muttered, the slightest crease appearing between his eyes. "You offer this to me for a woman?"

Ariston nodded. "She is worthy."

Hades was silent again, his eyes shifting to the blue-white flames in the massive
fireplace.

"My words do not…adequately express the love I have for this woman. But I cannot leave her. She is at risk. I must return." The words came without thought. How could he justify such emotion to a God who reviled affection or companionship? "As Olympus has my arm and sword, she has my heart – a mortal, and perhaps weak, heart."

The room was silent for too long. He would have to fight his way out...

"It is a weakness not reserved for mortals alone, Ariston of Rhodes." Hades' words were so soft Ariston feared they'd not been spoken. But Hades continued, strong and clear. "I will return you to your ship so that you may lead your men to victory. Too many have fallen from this war and I would see it end. When that is done, you may go to your wife." He paused then added, "When you return to my realm, I will have your fealty."

The God of the Underworld, Lord of Death, gave him mercy? Mayhap there was one God he might serve with honor.

Ariston vowed, "You have it."

"It was a wise choice. He is an Ekdromoi. His skill will be needed at Salamis," Ares said with a nod. "If more could be returned, our odds would be greater."

Zeus agreed. "A leader can make a great difference amongst men."

"Then we must pray that Ariston is such a leader," Poseidon said, daring to look at his niece with a smile.

"Did he show such initiative while serving in the temple?" Hera asked.

But Athena had not heard Hera's question, Poseidon could tell. She was staring at him, her face flushed with unspoken fury. She was uncharacteristically quiet, he noted. For one known to love the sound of her voice, her absolute silence was unsettling.

"He had little chance to prove his prowess while playing caretaker," Ares snorted. "But I've seen him fight. His death was glorious. He will bring down the Persians."

"Apparently he has the incentive to do just that." Hera smiled. "A rare husband indeed."

"It is, I think, rare to find such loyalty. Be it mortal or immortal," Aphrodite agreed.

"I, too, have seen this Ariston in battle," Apollo said. "He resembles our Ares – only slightly less immortal."

"You've done well, Hades." Zeus praised his younger brother before all.

Poseidon watched Hades with interest. But no flick of pride or flash of embarrassment colored Hades' cheek or widened his eyes. His expression remained the same.

"Then I shall leave you," Hades said.

Poseidon rolled his eyes. "You rarely venture to Olympus, brother. Why do you feel the need to quit it already?"

Hades regarded him. Poseidon eyed his younger brother in return. Had he always hated the perfection of Hades' face, the mask of aloofness he'd mastered? He was too handsome to be such a sullen creature, and his brother at that. It was the austere set of Hades' mouth, the clear and disdainful look of his eyes – everything about his brother stirred mischief within him. Provoking some outburst or reaction from Hades would be quite a coup. But it had been years since he'd managed to torment Hades so. And then little other than frustration and irritation had resulted. It had not gone as he'd planned.

"Have you captured some nymph and stolen her away to the Underworld?" Ares teased.

"Not that I have seen," Apollo shrugged.

Poseidon found it hard not to laugh at such an idea.

"If the rays of your sun were as well-reaching as the cast of your eye, then Athens' crops might fare better." Demeter patted Apollo's hand. As gentle a rebuff as it was, Poseidon knew her point was made.

"Can my brother be tempted with sins of the flesh?" Zeus asked, inspecting Hades.

"You tease him," Athena snapped. "Is that not excuse enough to leave?"

All eyes settled on Athena, Poseidon noted. Indeed, she looked greatly troubled.

"May he prove himself worthy of your bargain," Ares said. "Ariston, that is. I thank you for returning him to the living, Hades."

Hades nodded. "He was most persuasive."

"Love can be – most persuasive indeed." Aphrodite smiled.

"Or distracting," Demeter countered.

Hera shook her head. "Love can be dangerous, too."

"I have heard," Hades murmured.

Poseidon turned, his gaze sweeping the Council Chamber. This group knew nothing of love.

The Goddess of Love would champion Ariston. She had a weakness for husbands, especially those who cared for their wives. Perhaps it was because her own husband, Hephaestus, openly disdained her.

Ares was more likely to bed and eat a woman than love her. He smiled at the thought, wondering if Ares had committed anything so heinous. As the God of War, brutality ruled first, raging cock second.

Hera and Zeus – was there love there? Or a series of relentless challenges and small victories that left neither truly satisfied?

Of all, Demeter might know. But the love she bore was to her daughter, familial in nature. Such affection was hardly comparable to that of this supposed bond between a man and a woman.

He suspected he knew the truth. Love was an ideal, a gentler name for a baser need. He'd tasted it, briefly, through Medusa and her husband. He rubbed a hand over his mouth, rolling his neck to ease the sudden tightening of his shoulders.

Foolish mortals – to entertain such feelings.

Hades' gaze fell upon him, his features blank. Poseidon smiled at him, but Hades only blinked and turned away. It was enough. Poseidon was distracted once more.

Why had Hades freed Ariston from the Underworld? He had never returned a mortal to the land of the living before. Never. Love would be the last reason to return a mortal, for Hades had been injured most gravely at love's expense. More likely Hades would banish Ariston to Tartarus at the mere mention of such folly.

Unless something had changed?

Athena's fingers drummed forcefully on the arm of her chair, a rhythmic irritation. Poseidon smiled slightly at yet another puzzle to solve.

Something had upset his petulant niece to the point of silence. He had yet to decide if this was a winning development or not. But he looked forward to finding the reason.

He was done with this Medusa debacle; he wanted it over. It was a relief to find so many questions in need of answering.

The skies over Salamis thundered.

Ariston's eyes searched the horizon as he lay on the sand, his head propped on his elbow. He was pleased to see the storms rolling away from them – towards their incoming foe. Tonight they would enjoy clear skies, warm fires and good company. Tomorrow they would fight.

How he wished it were morning.

One day closer to honoring his word to Hades, of fighting for Athens.

Themistocles' plan would succeed. It had to.

The Athenians had lured the Persian king Xerxes and his battered fleet to the mouth of the straits of Salamis. Tomorrow their enemy would venture in, to confront the reportedly divided Greek troops. There the Persians would move into the straits, forcing the warships and their battle into close quarters.

Xerxes had no idea that the Greeks' disharmony was a farce, industriously circulated to entice the Persians into Themistocles' carefully laid trap.

Once the Persians were in the straits, there was no escape.

And while the Persians had proved themselves skilled in battle, the constant battles and irregular supplies had diminished their numbers greatly. With three hundred triremes, the Greeks were still outnumbered by the Persians, but not at unbeatable odds.

Ariston and his troops were eager and ready.

News of the loss of Thermopylae had struck morale low.

But the stories of brave King Leonidas and his fearsome Spartiates as they staved off Xerxes had rallied all. With no more than fifteen hundred men, the unflappable Spartans had held their own against both the Medes' attacks and the Persian Immortals. Indeed, to hear his men speak of the battle, Leonidas and his Spartiates had earned the respect and glory of all of Greece.

If Xerxes' gold had not purchased a Spartan traitor to guide Xerxes into Leonidas' camp, Ariston wondered if the warrior king and his troops might not have found a way to victory.

Alas, treachery had won out.

Treachery often does.

The men sat about their fire, sharing stories and wine.

"Morning will decide our fate," Pamphilos was saying. "The Gods have made our commander immortal, or so it would seem. Surely that bodes well for the rest of us?"

The men laughed.

"The Gods honor us with such a leader," Ophion, one of Ariston's most ferocious soldiers, spoke loud enough for those nearby to hear. "Ariston serves them proudly. He cannot fall, Olympus forbids it."

"Any man might lead as I do," Ariston called back, "if they have the warriors I have."

A cheer went up from the men, eliciting a smile from him.

"However, your flattery will not keep you from your time on the oars, Ophion," Ariston added. The men laughed heartily, and Ophion shrugged.

He was proud of them, these valiant soldiers who'd fought for him.

When he had fallen at Athens, Chariton had proclaimed his death imminent. But Pamphilos and his crew would not desert him to the sea. His second had bound him, in his mats, to the deck and had Chariton ply him with tinctures, herbs and broths while they sailed to Salamis.

When he'd entered Hades' realm, he did not know.

But returning to the living was more painful than leaving it. He woke, tied to the deck with festering wounds. When Chariton had come to the tent for supplies, he'd cried out at the sight of Ariston regarding him with clear eyes.

"You were dead," Chariton had whispered.

"Was I?" His voice was hoarse.

Chariton had offered him the water skin. "Yes. I placed the coin under your tongue myself..."

Ariston felt it in his hand, and lifted it. "Here is your coin, Chariton. I will have no need of it...for now."

Even when fever had taken hold of his wound, laying him low, his men hadn't given up.

When he'd risen, the crew called him favored by the Gods. Wagers were placed on the outcome of their next battle, the number of fatalities and ships lost. With Ariston as their leader, they were assured a most glorious victory.

That he lived without care or thought as to the Gods' will, he kept to himself. He would honor his pact with Hades. If Olympus were to fall into Tartarus, he cared not.

He would honor these men and lead them to victory here, for they'd helped him back from Hades. Tomorrow would see a bloody battle that needed all able bodies, and he would fight at their side. He owed them his fealty.

But when this battle was done, he would leave them.

In the months since he'd returned, his every action had been mindful of one goal – returning to her. As his wounds healed and his fever left him, he trained. He would fight anyone and everything that stood in his way.

Athens had been evacuated after the brave Spartans fell at Thermopylae, and all of Athens' citizens had sailed to Aegina. It had been the only way to save Athens' citizens from certain death. She would not have left Athens before the evacuation. He had to believe that she'd made the journey to safety. She would be on Aegina – he would join her soon.

The Persians had decimated Athens. News had reached them that even the Temple of Athena Polias had been burned and looted. The Goddess' priests and priestess, and those who refused to leave Athens, had been slaughtered. This affront to the Gods had inspired outrage from Athens, her allies and the Gods alike.

It gave him hope. If the Gods were distracted by such offenses, Medusa might escape further persecution.

His hands clenched and the sand sifted through his fingers. While he'd been tied in his sickbed, his lady had sailed past him on the sea to safety. This hope ate at his heart and haunted his dreams.

Every moment of the day was marked with her absence.

Pamphilos leaned back, offering Ariston the water skin, smiling. "Drink?"

Ariston took the skin, swallowing the sweet wine to wash the bitterness from his mouth. He handed the skin back, nodding his thanks.

"Will your uncle's plan work? Will we crush their fleet?" Pamphilos stared out over the darkening sea with yearning.

"He's not led us astray yet. But I've no ability for divination, nor am I an oracle." His eyes strayed to the Aegean with longing as well.

"Morning cannot come soon enough," Pamphilos sighed.

Ariston nodded his agreement.

One of the men began strumming his lyre, his nimble fingers plucking the chords with ease. Ophion searched out his aulos, the melody of the long double reed pipe rousing the audience. The men's voices rose, carrying the worries of the following morning away.

Pamphilos smiled and turned back to the men, his voice loud and strong as he joined them about the fire.

Ariston's eyes wandered to the black velvet night sky. The stars, flashing brilliants in the dark, told him more than he wanted to know. Autumn storms would find them soon. This battle, this war, must end before then.

He made his way to the shoreline, searching out some peace and quiet. The water was calm, reflecting the glorious night upon its gently rolling surface. The beauty of the night stirred the vision of another, one he treasured dearly.

"Is the night sky over Rhodes very different?" The memory of her voice caused the hair on his neck to rise.

"No, my lady," he'd replied. "But the company here is far superior to any I shared there." He'd gazed at her in the moonlight. They'd loved and had lain under the moon on the sand of their beach, still tangled up in one another.

She'd turned to him, a bright smile on her face. "Oh?"

He'd rolled onto his side, propping himself on his elbow. "I believe your smile dims the stars." He smoothed her hair from her forehead, relishing the feel of her. "Be careful, wife, for you might offend Selene if you shine too brightly."

She shook her head, her eyes as deep as sapphires as they met his. "I shine only for you."

His fingers tightened convulsively now, the lingering feel of her locks a whisper on his skin.

"You are the greatest gift I've been given," he'd murmured against the column of her throat, his nose burying itself in her hair.

Her scent stirred his nostrils as if she was within his reach. He closed his eyes to savor it.

She'd said, "You are the only gift I've been given – to me, for me."

"How can that be? You're too loved to have been given nothing." How naïve his answer had been.

"You are right. Thea is mine, too. And she loves me almost as dearly as you do, I think." She touched his cheek as she continued. "But I've never been free to receive a gift that wasn't given for the priestess. Or offered in trade for some duty or service I must fulfill."

Her words were uttered without wistfulness or regret, as was her way. She spoke plainly, acknowledging her status.

"When did you leave your parents?" They'd much to discover about one another. But they hoped to have years of sharing before them.

"My father became indebted to Galenus during one of the Titans' revolts. I know little in the way of particulars, but whatever Galenus did, I was payment. Xenia had many babes, though none lived long and she grieved so. I was given as a slave, but treated as a daughter. Xenia knows I cannot stay with them forever, yet she's given me a tiny piece of her heart. Loving me too dearly would only lead to more heartache, and the poor lady has had too much in her time."

"When did you come to serve Athena?" He traced the lines of her face in the moonlight.

"I was a small thing – barely in full robes." She smiled. "My father was blamed for flooding one of Athena's olive orchards. He swore it was Poseidon, but who would believe a Titan over a God? Even I have my doubts, and he is my father."

"And so you became Athena's arrephoroi to pay his offense? Were you frightened to serve the Goddess?"

"I was terrified when I entered the temple. I'd seen her statue, of course...but the sight of her armed in her helmet and bearing her shield made me forget what I was to do. I froze, staring up at her, without kneeling or bowing. She must have found me amusing because she smiled at me."

"What did you do?" He could imagine it. Medusa's wide blue eyes would have been even more enormous when she was a child – a lovely, guileless child.

"I smiled back." Medusa shook her head. "And then I remembered myself and dropped to my knees. I've seen Athena many times over the years. And each time, she's given me nothing but kind smiles and sweet words of praise."

"Because you honor her so." He quivered as her fingers traced his lower lip.

"I would honor Selene this night and ask the Lady Moon to linger. So that I may stay at your side for whatever time she will give to us."

"My prayers join yours, wife," he murmured against her lips.

His hands had trailed over her, leisurely caressing every silken slope and curve. His lips clung to hers, parting as her smooth arms wound about his neck.

A cold wind startled Ariston, pulling him firmly back to the present.

He flexed his hands, relaxing the tight fists. He must find his bed and sleep. He would have her in his arms then, he knew. She was with him every night.

He hoped for a happy dream or a pleasant memory. But his nightmares visited more frequently of late. At least, even in his blackest dream, she was with him.

Medusa pushed herself up, swaying as her head throbbed mercilessly.

"Sister?" Stheno's voice was soft.

"What happened?" Medusa asked.

"Athens has been destroyed. All have fled, days ago, spirited across the sea to safety," Euryale voice joined them.

Medusa stared into the darkness, blinking rapidly. Two shadows huddled together. "Where are we?" she asked.

"In a cave," Stheno answered, "not far from Galenus' house."

Galenus. Her head swam.

A flash of her uncle appeared, his face lined with concern. He'd called to her, leading her to her chambers. And then...his face changed. There had been shock, then horror on his face. And his features faded.

Medusa shook her head, clasping her forehead to shake the strange images from her mind. "My head..."

"You fell, Medusa, on your way back from the temple," Euryale explained.

"And injured your head," Stheno added. "Do you remember what happened there – in the temple?" Images and words swirled about, but she could make sense of none of them. Only one image was clear.

Athena's face as she'd cursed her, Athena's rage.

The Goddess had cursed her.

"Athena..." Medusa gasped. "We quarreled."

"You challenged Athena?" Euryale laughed. "At least now there is a reason." She added the last harshly.

"I did not challenge her," Medusa argued.

"You did something to displease her," Euryale bit back. "Greatly."

"Sleep, sisters. We've delayed our journey long enough. If Medusa is well, we must leave tomorrow," Stheno interrupted.

The sound of her sisters' voices was muffled, as if something covered her ears. Her hands searched the dark. Her head was wrapped, bound by layers of fabric and tied tightly. It ached unbearably, and her neck and shoulders felt bruised as well.

She lay still in the dark, weary beyond measure. But her mind refused to cooperate. Images, flashes of brief recollections – or dreams, of words and sounds, overwhelmed her. Some were disturbing and painful, glimpses into some sort of nightmare.

She opened her eyes, but she could see only the faintest hint of what was inside. Her sisters leaned together, one hump against the cave wall. They slept, the low rumble of one's snores reaching her muted ears.

There was no fire or lantern.

Were they in danger then? Had those who attacked Athens posed enough threat to make even her fearless sisters hide?

She sat up slowly.

What was left of the city? Had Galenus and Xenia made it safely away?

And Elpis? Her heart twisted. Had her beloved companion made it from the city before it fell?

It took effort to stand, bracing herself against the wall of the cave. She would see for herself.

She followed along the cavern wall, shuffling, her hand pressed flat against its cool surface. Her head was too heavy, forcing her to lean against the wall and rest. It took so long to find the cave's entrance she wondered that her sisters did not wake, refreshed and alert.

It was not night as she'd believed. The mouth of the cave, at the end of yet another long tunnel, glowed brilliantly with Apollo's sun.

Why sleep now?

Perhaps the Persians lingered. It might make more sense to travel at night. Stheno was right. Even as hidden as they were, they would eventually be discovered. While Euryale and Stheno might be able to defend themselves against men, she knew she was not so well equipped.

Sunlight spilled into the tunnel, forcing her to wince, illuminating its sudden narrowing and the downward slope overhead. She stooped, moving forward on unsteady feet. The bindings of her head brushed the tunnel's curved ceiling.

The sun blinded her. She paused, bracing herself against the wall to cover her eyes. Still they burned from the light, soothed by the tears that sprang forth. She shielded her eyes and moved closer, leaning against the cave opening to steady herself.

A soft gasp escaped her. Athens was gone.

The Temple of Athena Polias, or what was left of it, smoked in the distance. The wall that surrounded the base of the Acropolis smoked too.

Medusa could not look for long. The glare of the sun forced her back into the dimness of the cave – a relief to her vision.

But she had to see, and risked looking out once more. She shifted, catching the bandages of her head on the roof above. Pain lanced through her, forcing her to lean heavily against the rock wall until she could bear to move.

She turned her face into the caves interior. The light was dim, more tolerable for her. Blinking again, her eyes adjusted in the diffused light.

Something stirred, a quick and sinuous movement. She jumped, startled by the suddenness, its nearness, for something hovered over her shoulder.

She turned her head, wincing in pain. She waited until her eyes found the source of movement.

It was a serpent.

A ruby-eyed, sleek bodied asp, suspended somehow over her

shoulder.

Her lungs tightened.

She could not escape it if it decided to strike her. She could not move. It was too close. Any movement might aggravate the creature.

It bobbed, smoothly rolling itself closer to her face.

It was not alone, she saw this now. There were more than five others, some closer, some further – but all within a hand's length from her face. They must be hanging from the wall arching directly over her head. This cave must be their home, one her sisters had unwittingly trespassed into.

A slow, heavy weight of undulating muscle slid down the length of her neck to rest upon her shoulder.

Every muscle in her body grew taut, yet fear bound her in place. She had a choice, one she must make quickly. Only one rested upon her. She might step back and fling the one from her shoulders. But she must move swiftly.

The snake on her shoulder slithered forward, cupping her neck as its head pressed against her jaw, weaving back and forth.

She swallowed, waiting for it to shift again. If it wrapped around her throat, she would not succeed.

The sounds of them filled her ears, a chorus of hisses and whispers as their serpentine bodies rubbed against one another. More eyes regarded her with interest.

It was unnerving, to be so surrounded by these creatures.

They, it appeared, were not so troubled by her.

The large snake moved, leisurely situating itself upon her. It seemed to be draped across her head. The greenish-gold creature lay, its length running down her neck, across her shoulder, to dangle its head off of her shoulder, at ease.

She took a deep breath and closed her eyes. It would be a cruel means to die. But, with the number of vipers so fascinated by her, mayhap the poison would work quickly.

She cried out as she pushed herself from the wall, knocking the snake from her shoulders as she fell out of the cave opening and into the sunlight.

The sun blinded her, and she flung her arm up to cover her eyes.

It bit her then.

She jerked away, but it bit her again.

"Bite me, then," she yelled, grabbing the snake about the neck and pulling it with all of her strength. "Then leave me be."

The snake coiled about her arm, anchoring itself firmly to her. She continued to pull, growing frantic as she realized she could not disentangle herself. Her freedom was slipping away as the others found her.

Her cheek tingled beneath the sting of another bite, then her ear, her jaw. They continued, wrapping around her head and neck, forcing her to release the serpent as she fought to defend her face.

A sob escaped her as she swatted the snakes away. Her fear overwhelmed her, making her frantic as she twisted and thrashed on the ground. But she could not evade them. They were too great in number.

She closed her eyes tightly and cried out, releasing her anguish and despair in that instant.

There was no use in fighting them. She had no reason to live. It was fitting that these creatures, one of Athena's favored animals, would be the end of her.

Her cry twisted. The sound grew, bouncing off of the hillside and rolling away from her as her sobs overtook her.

Would she be cast into Tartarus? She knew better than to hope she might see Ariston.

A shout rose, a man's voice, carried to her on the winds.

Persians? Did it matter now?

Her head throbbed, her eyes burned and the grief in her heart consumed her. Whether at the sword of a Persian or the poison of these snakes, this life was almost over. She was ready... No, she was eager for death to find her.

But she did not fade. The sun continued to torture her with its luster, and her head felt as if it was being pulled every which way. She hugged herself, lying still on the dirt and rocks that littered the mouth of the cave. She could not move, the pain in her head would not allow it.

The snakes did not leave her, though they ceased their assault. Instead they coiled about her head and shoulders, filling her ears with their whispers.

She stiffened, but had no will to fight or move.

A breeze blew over her, lifting her robes and cooling her scorched skin. Her heart, pounding in her ears, did not still. Her lungs ached, but did not falter. Those wounds the asps had inflicted throbbed in time with her heart. Each bite sealed a molten needle under her skin, skewering her muscle with fiery intent.

But still she lived.

A voice, a man, was close by. He was coming. She could hear him. The ground seemed to reverberate around her. He was not alone. No, two...maybe more.

The serpents stirred, filling her ears with their whispers. She swallowed, relaxing as one slippery tongue touched her neck, flicking the skin. Apparently satisfied, the serpent moved forward, sliding atop her neck towards the sound of the approaching men.

As their footsteps grew closer, the vibration of their steps shook her. The men's words made no sense to her. She knew nothing of the Persians' language, but the man sounded angry, speaking harshly to those accompanying him.

She must try to move. She must, for her sisters' sake.

She forced her eyes open, ignoring the searing white heat that sliced through them. She lifted her arm, wary of the snake that sat upon her. It stared at her face, angling its head to regard her with interest. Its head bobbed while its tongue flicked out to touch her chin. She winced.

The voice was closer, almost to the top of the hill, where she still lay.

The serpent turned towards the voice, hissing and undulating.

It seemed eager – almost as if it were waiting for them, these men.

She moved ever so slowly, shielding her eyes with one raised arm while rolling onto her side. They could only bite her again, and she was beginning to suspect they weren't fatal, but the pain in her head prevented her from moving quickly.

The wrappings her sisters had tied about her head lay beside her, but she would not bother with them now. If the wound opened, there was little she could do. Her death was imminent.

As she rose, the snake moved too, lifting from her neck with sudden fluidity. She shivered, startled by its speed.

She forced herself into a sitting position, closing her eyes long enough to gain her balance.

Surprisingly her head felt lighter now, as if some great weight had been lifted.

The voices were almost upon her, so she opened her eyes...to discover a most peculiar sight. Her shadow.

The snakes had not been suspended from the caves walls, or its ceiling. They had not been hanging off exposed roots or out of crevices her eyes could not discern. These serpents, they clung to her.

All about her their bodies and heads weaved in constant motion. Their sounds muted all else, their number was so great. She stared at them, though their attention remained unwavering as they peered at the cliff's edge.

They *were* waiting for something.

Her head swayed in time with them, she realized, though she felt steady for the first time.

One dipped down, sliding across her cheek to dangle by her chin. The hand that shielded her eyes wavered, but the snake seemed not to notice.

Athena's words ripped through her.

"Wisdom will rule you from this day on, your constant lullaby their serpent's song. Only those with an innocent heart, women and children, are set safely apart. A heart of stone is your curse to bear as they turn man to stone with their ruby stare. Keep them safe and keep them whole, or to Hades you will send their soul. Your disloyalty causes man's life to end, but through your death they live again."

Medusa's hands slipped across her forehead, sliding towards her hair with trembling fingers.

Athena looked to the owl and the serpent for wisdom. They acted upon instinct and thought, not emotion. And Athena found that virtuous.

Her hand touched a sleek coil of serpent. It moved, flicking its tongue against her fingers before shifting. There were more, varying in size and texture -- so many. Long and short, thick and thin, they acknowledged her touch and parted for her. Tongues and heads, necks and bodies...but no tails were found – because they had none.

Their bodies ended where hers began, joined as firmly to

her head as her arm or leg was to her body. They moved with her because they were a part of her.

Panic receded, fear vanished. Only horror remained.

Her lungs constricted.

What had Athena done to her?

Her stomach roiled, forcing bile up. She swallowed, hoping to gain control, but fear and disgust won. She vomited, gasping for air as her stomach convulsed and twisted repeatedly.

Why?

A man shouted, too close to escape now... And then they were upon her.

There were eight men, armed heavily. She'd unknowingly alerted them with her scream.

Surely they would kill her and this nightmare would at last be over.

But the serpents quieted suddenly, becoming utterly still – forcing her to do the same.

Her vision blurred slowly. A haze clouded her sight, obscuring the details of life as the world around her turned an eerie shade of red. She blinked, but the redness remained.

As her eyes met the first man, obviously their leader, he froze. His eyes, deep brown and intelligent, widened. Whatever words he uttered ended sharply, choked with an unseen force from his chest.

It happened quickly.

The sun was behind them, making it impossible for her to focus against its blinding glare. But she could see that it was not just this man, but all of them, gasping for air.

She stood, wavering on unsteady legs, as the men grew rigid.

A sudden snapping filled the air, followed by cracking. The man's eyes seemed to widen further, bulging as his neck convulsed and went rigid. The skin of his neck discolored, a sinister darkness creeping up his thick neck to his rigid jaw. The darkness, a strange coating like grey chalk, moved steadily, covering his cheeks and mouth. His nostrils seemed to pinch, as if he was gasping for breath, before the grey covered his nose. His eyes rolled, staring about him blindly until his eyes locked with hers.

He was in pain, horrible pain. His eyes clouded, blinking furiously until the ridge of grey overtook them. She watched, stunned, as all of him hardened, turning lifeless and brittle.

The man was stone.

She gasped and pressed her eyes closed, but it did not erase their suffering... Her chest was heavy with grief and her head felt heavy once again.

When she opened her eyes, more than two dozen ruby eyes waited for her.

It was not yet dawn. Ariston pulled his blanket up, rolling onto his side and squeezing his eyes shut. But she was gone, tearing his heart open as sleep left him.

It was cold.

The stars hadn't yet faded, but a thin band of light laced the horizon.

He stretched, stifling a groan as his stitches pulled. He was lucky, doubly so, he knew. His wounds at Salamis were minor, mere scratches compared to those he'd suffered before. He could endure them knowing that today he would have his lady in his arms.

Today they would sail to Aegina and help those Athenians return home before winter set in.

Xerxes had fled after the defeat at Salamis. And though much of Greece had battles still to be fought, he knew the tide had turned. Whatever hold Xerxes had upon them, the Panhellenic League – Athens and her allies – would make certain to crush it soon.

Now Athens needed its people, to rebuild and restore its grandeur. It needed to rally and stoke the fires of victory before another campaign began. A campaign he would gladly learn about when such news found its way to his father's home, on sunny Rhodes.

"Pamphilos." Ariston shook his second's shoulder, rousing him. "Let us be gone with the sun."

Pamphilos peered at him from between swollen lids. "Your lady inspires a great deal of enthusiasm, Ariston. She must be beautiful... or fearsome," he teased, laughing.

Ariston held his hand out, pulling his second to his feet. "She is fearsomely beautiful. With a heart more lovely still."

Pamphilos arched an eyebrow. "You've not been married long?"

Ariston laughed. "No, friend, I had two nights with my wife

before our battle off Athens' shore."

"And then we sailed on to Salamis?" Pamphilos smiled. "I envy you your homecoming."

Ariston nodded. "As well you should."

"I'll pray to the Gods your stitches hold." Pamphilos laughed.

Ariston laughed too.

Would she run to him?

He shook his head as he climbed aboard the trireme, a smile upon his face. Even readying the ship did little to dampen his joy. Once they were at sea, he relaxed. He wasn't the only husband on this ship, for many had left a wife or family when they'd set off to fight. He watched the men, wondering if any felt anticipation as sweetly as he did.

There was no shame in it, this need for her.

Fear would not rule him, though it crept upon him in moments of weakness. He could not help but worry. Had Poseidon changed her?

They need never speak of it, nor would he ask her what happened. If she needed to tell him, he would listen – and hoped he could offer her the support she might need. But he would never ask her to relive it.

His hands fisted and he pulled the sails' lashing tight, ignoring the burn of the ropes across his palms.

Would she still want him or set him aside from shame?

Or had she gone with Poseidon? He swallowed. If she'd gone, she had no choice in the matter.

No. He would not let his mind twist his heart with such thoughts.

She was waiting for him on Aegina. She would welcome him with open arms, he knew this.

And he loved her more deeply. Whatever she'd endured or submitted to, she'd done it for him. He would do the same for her. He would do whatever he had to for her safety. Nothing mattered more to him.

As long as he had her love, there was nothing more he needed or wanted.

They had time to live and love. He prayed his face was well-lined and his hair all but gone before he found himself kneeling before Hades again.

Whatever time he had with her, he would be thankful for it.

The voyage was tiresome. The crew chafed to get there, as did Ariston. But choppy seas and blustering winds tossed them about, setting them on Aegina's coast at dusk.

The docks and shore were covered in the tents of Athens' refugees. People, hundreds of women and children, came out to greet the returning heroes with cries of joy and pride. Ariston's heart grew unsteady and his gaze searched the crowd for one glimpse of flashing blue eyes or honey locks.

As the crew tossed ropes down from the trireme, the dock master clambered up to the deck.

He clasped forearms with Ariston. "Welcome home, heroes of Athens. I am Kallistratos of Aegina, and I am at your service."

"We thank you for your welcome, Kallistratos. I am Ariston of Rhodes, an Ekdromos for Athens. How fare our Athenians?" Ariston noted the slight twitch of the man's mouth and waited.

"As well as such a sizable group may be, so far from home and with little in the way of comfort." He appeared to have something more to say, but reconsidered. He smiled tightly.

"We've been tasked with taking them home on the morn," Ariston said. "Xerxes is far gone now. And Athens needs to fortify its walls before winter comes."

"Sir, some of the men are anxious to find their families." Pamphilos spoke softly at Ariston's elbow.

Ariston nodded. "As am I, Pamphilos."

"A word of caution, soldiers. There has been talk of illness amongst some in the tents." Kallistratos' face was wary, his voice dropping.

Ariston froze, raising a hand to still his men. "A fever?"

"Perhaps...of the mind, it seems." Kallistratos shook his head.

"How many have died?" Pamphilos asked.

Ariston continued to watch the man. There was something more. Something Kallistratos was not telling them.

"No... none dead, brave hoplite." He paused. "It is nothing fatal, it seems. It does nothing more than confuse memories. A few women have said things that make no sense – as if they've witnessed a creature or spirit from Hades." He looked at them and shrugged.

"It may be nothing more than poor conditions or lack of water..."

Ariston nodded. "But none have died?"

"None dead." Kallistratos repeated. "Now, I will leave you to greet the other ships soon arriving. But find me if you've need of me."

He smiled brightly before crossing the plank the crew had lowered.

Ariston watched him go. The man wanted the Athenians gone, it was plain to see.

"It would be hard to leave one's home and temple, not knowing when it would be safe to return," Pamphilos murmured to Ariston. "Such nervous fits are understandable from the fairer sex?"

"Be wary, Pamphilos. Speak plainly to the men. If there is illness, we would be wise to leave it here. Now Athens needs only the strong," Ariston answered.

Pamphilos nodded and returned to the men, looking grave.

Ariston made his way to the plank, fighting the desire to run. He would find her.

There were hundreds of people in the tent town of Athens. Faces he knew, but more he did not. After walking aimlessly up and down the rows of tents, he turned back to the dock to find Kallistratos.

"I seek news of the councilman Galenus and his wife, Xenia of Athens?" Ariston asked. "My wife is in their household. Which tent is his?"

Kallistratos face stiffened. "Sir, Xenia and some of her household have taken the tent farthest from the settlement." He took Ariston's elbow, leaning in to speak softly. "The lady Xenia is stricken with the...illness, I fear."

Ariston assessed the man's face. "Is she mad?"

Kallistratos cleared his throat. "So it would seem."

"Who accompanied her?"

"Several serving girls—" Kallistratos began.

"Galenus?" Something was not right. As spirited as Galenus was, he would not have stayed behind. He was a statesman, not a warrior.

The older man shook his head. "He did not make the journey, though I know not what happened. And his wife, Xenia, she grows dangerously agitated when asked."

Ariston turned from the man, his pace quickening as he moved along the shore. Something had happened in Galenus' house, something to distress Xenia gravely. Try as he might to avoid it, his unease increased with each step.

The tent was placed aside. A fire burned inside, but the flaps were closed.

All about him sounds of family and life, of reunion and joy. But here, the stillness of Xenia's tent warned him.

"Lady Xenia?" he called out. "Xenia of Athens?"

He heard the gasp of a woman, startled, then a ragged sob. He froze, unsure of how to proceed. There was another voice. He could hear it faintly, another woman speaking, soothingly, in hushed gentle tones.

He waited, fearful of calling out again. But he would not leave without news.

"A moment, please." The voice was close, as if the woman were standing on the other side of the tent wall. "Let me calm her."

"I will wait," he assured her.

The wind blew, threatening the flame of his lantern. He paced, his ears straining to make out the interior's happenings. But the words were whispered, too muted to make out.

He stared at the tent, willing someone to come out.

And Elpis did.

"Elpis?" His relief was instantaneous. He moved forward, clasping her shoulders. "You are here. And well?"

"My lord?" she choked out. "Ariston? But you...you cannot be here." She seemed to droop in his hold, so he steadied her. "You are dead," she whispered.

Chapter Eleven

"I am here, Elpis." His tone offered little comfort, he knew. But his wife may yet wait for him in Xenia's tent.

"You died," she insisted. "You were struck down..."

"I was struck down but, as you see, I live."

She shook her head, "But you... It's because you died." Her voice wavered and she pulled herself from his hold.

"Is my lady wife well and within?" His patience was wearing thin. "What has happened?"

Elpis shook her head, faster and faster. "No. She is not within... She was left in Athens."

He froze, staring at her in surprise. Anger, pure and unfiltered, spilled from his lips. "Left behind?"

Elpis raised her hands. "Do not wake Xenia, I beg of you." She glanced over her shoulder towards the tent.

"You may well beg, Elpis, for I will beat you soundly if you do not speak plainly." He felt the tightening of his jaw, the curl of his lip.

He cared little for Elpis' fear or Xenia's nerves. He would know everything – now.

"She was ill." Elpis looked away, her eyes avoiding his. "But she was not alone. Her sisters kept her. She could not make the journey to Aegina. She could not..." She shook her head again. "Her sisters were to care for her until she... until she...."

Ariston stared at her, his throat tightening. "Until?"

"Her head... She fell, coming back from the temple and... cleaved her skull." She was shaking her head again, her arms wrapped about herself. "I'd been with my family, readying them for our departure. When I took them to the docks, I saw that neither Galenus and Xenia, nor your lady were there. I ran back to his home, to help if they had need of me."

He turned from her, listening to her words with growing alarm.

"Galenus was gone...as was Nikolaos. Xenia was...screaming uncontrollably. She could not speak, but wailed and cried for Medusa."

Ariston spoke, unable to control the anguish in his voice. "For Medusa?"

"She wept and cried out. Stheno said the sight of Medusa was too great, for her wound was violent to behold – or so Stheno said. In truth I did not ask to see our lady... Xenia's wails stirred such fear..." Tears streamed down her face. "I could not bear to see her so, not after everything she has endured."

She was not dead. If she was...he would know it somehow, he would feel it. She was alive. "You did not see her? You did not see her wound with your own eyes?"

Elpis' lowered her gaze in shame. "No. I am not brave, my lord."

"But Xenia did?" he asked, his voice low and lethal.

She pleaded, "You cannot trouble her with this, my lord. She will be of no help, of that I can promise you. She does little but mutter nonsense, often too softly to be understood. When I do hear her, I wish I had not. Her mind...has twisted."

"She was the last to see my wife, Elpis. I will speak with her in the morning. Once we set sail to Athens, I will speak with her."

He would hold on to hope. Medusa had taught him that, above all things. He would find out what happened, and he would find her.

Poseidon drew in a deep breath, stunned by Athena's announcement. In truth the Council Chamber was silent. Even Ares' quick tongue was silent.

"What have you done?" Zeus thundered, with good reason, his voice reverberating amongst the clouds.

At least Athena had the decency not to challenge her father's wrath. Her subdued response showed no sign of challenge, only regret. "She was in need of a punishment."

Poseidon leaned back in his throne. He did not take kindly to the twist in his stomach or the flicker of conscience that worried the back of his mind.

This matter had nothing to do with him.

Medusa had dared to challenge a Goddess. Yes, Athena was the Goddess of Wisdom, but she was also the Goddess of Strategy. When challenged, Athena was quick to react – as evidenced by her reaction to Medusa.

"This is your idea of a just punishment, daughter? For whom?" Zeus bellowed. "How did she come to excite such a punishment from you?"

"She has... she has known a man – in my temple," Athena declared.

"The temple now smoldering in ruins?" Ares asked, a scornful look upon his face. "If this mortal woman elicits such a response for coupling with a man in your temple, I look forward to the justice you will serve upon the Persians that destroyed your city – and your temple."

"And burned every crop in the fields," Demeter mourned. "Even if Persephone and I work as one, Greece's people will suffer hunger."

Zeus held up his hand. "The Persians will be dealt with by us all." He leveled an angry glare upon his daughter. "Athena, you must see the error in this?"

Poseidon tensed, in anticipation and apprehension. Athena did not take kindly to being chided, especially in front of the others.

"I see nothing of the sort." Her voice grew stronger. "To have used my temple thusly is low enough, but she dared to blaspheme the Gods, myself and Poseidon, too."

Zeus looked at his brother sharply, but said nothing.

Poseidon held his tongue. This was not the time to confess his part in this tragedy. He was sorely tempted, but Athena's lack of discipline made him quiet. This was what he wanted, to thwart his self-righteous niece, to outwit her in her own home. And he had.

He'd never considered that Medusa might speak out so. They had made a bargain, nothing more. He had underestimated her grief...and her love.

Damn her.

Yet she had no right to question Athena, to demand explanations. She was a mortal. She had been a mortal.

Now she was a monster.

"You will put an end to this." Zeus stood, towering over Athena and trembling with rage.

"Father!" Athena's face grew red and her lower lip quivered. "She has wronged me after I loved her so dearly. She has betrayed me. And...and she has made a mockery of her marriage and the man she calls husband."

"The hero from Salamis," Ares noted.

"The man Hades freed?" Aphrodite asked.

Apollo frowned at Athena in disapproval. "A man who deserves honor and respect from Olympus and his wife."

"He may have returned for his wife," Aphrodite said, "but they cannot be together now."

Poseidon's pleasure paled again. Medusa had been true in all. She'd been maligned, cursed, and injured because of him. How could he reveal the truth? To slake his lust he'd promised Medusa safety for her husband, a man he'd done nothing for. To further his enjoyment, he'd pricked his niece and taken Medusa in the temple.

She'd given herself because of the love she had for her husband. A man who loved her so dearly, he gave up Elysium to return. But he'd never hold her in his arms again or look upon her adoring face – not now.

He'd not seen the wrong in it until now. He would look a villain before all, if he confessed his part. Zeus might demand justice – Athena most certainly would.

And he did not enjoy the sorrow that gripped his stomach.

"He is a hero to all of Greece and Athens," Athena said, nodding. "He was my guard, a cunning fighter, an Ekdromos of the finest skills."

"A hero with no wife to come home to." Aphrodite looked at Zeus pointedly.

"What of this man..." Zeus looked at Athena in question.

"Ariston. Ariston of Rhodes," Athena said, her voice low. "He is deserving of more from a wife, a better wife than Medusa. I did him a favor..."

"Surely he will find another willing woman to wife?" Apollo

was unconcerned.

"Aphrodite, find him someone – someone pleasing to honor his heroism," Zeus ordered.

"Brother," Poseidon interjected. "He loved his wife. He will look for her."

"He will give up," Ares snorted. "Husbands tire of wives, not women."

But Zeus watched him, his eyebrow arching in question. "Speak Poseidon, if you have something to add to this matter."

Poseidon spoke with confidence. "Ariston will seek his wife until he finds her. The man bargained with Hades for that very purpose. He may give her up – but it will take time. Time he will spend searching."

Athena's eyes narrowed. "Then his fate is sealed."

Hera rose, outraged. "You cannot condemn this man! Not after all he has done for Olympus. Husband, I implore you. There must be another solution."

Quiet filled the chamber once more. Even Poseidon mulled over this dilemma. But then, Zeus would decide the matter.

When Zeus finally spoke, there was a gleam in his eyes. "Whatever happens, no more harm must come to either of them. Until this matter is settled, I demand it."

"How can I trust you?" Medusa asked Euryale in despair. "How can I?"

Euryale shook her head, shrugging. "You have no choice, Medusa."

"It will not happen again, sister. I promise," Stheno intervened, ever the peace-maker.

"It will not," Medusa agreed. "I cannot bear it!" Whether Euryale had meant for Medusa to discover the man in the last village, she could not be certain. But his face, those of the fishermen, and the messenger, along with those Persians who'd fallen victim, haunted her. "I will not bear it!"

Euryale smiled. "Idle threats, to be sure."

"Why do you torment me?" Medusa whispered.

"It brings me pleasure. Something I have very little of in this life."

"Peace," Stheno said. "I will go, Medusa, I will go with Euryale to scout our way."

Medusa drew in a steadying breath, her head aching unbearably. She nodded.

"We need food," Euryale said as they left the hut. "I tire of berries and nuts."

"If she would eat," Stheno replied.

"I will eat it." Euryale laughed.

Medusa listened to the sounds of their fading bickering, ceasing long after they'd disappeared from sight.

They would not leave her be. They forced her on, to sleep and move and dress and talk. When she would lie still and do nothing.

She removed the wrap from her head, lightening some of her burden. They fell about her instantly, stretching and writhing in pleasure at being set free. Whispers, tongues – they slithered amongst themselves and assessed their surroundings with mesmerizing ruby eyes.

She refused to look at them, though they tried to capture her attention.

That they were joined to her, she could not deny. But she would not acknowledge them. She could not.

They were evil.

She stood, moving to the small window set in the crudely built wall of their latest home. It was sunset. She had no reason to fear the pain of the sun, time had healed that much. Yet she shaded her eyes anyway, a habit now.

The sun stained the sky rose and pink, painting the clouds with gilded edges and feather-like whimsy. She stared, unable to appreciate the picturesque view or the soothing sounds of evening. The ache was there, gnawing on her stomach with unrelenting torment.

She missed him. How she wished she could join him, if only for an instant.

"I will not think on him," she whispered. It was an oath she repeated daily but could not keep.

Her mind resurrected every moment they'd spent together. Yet, when such memories faded, her agony was greater still.

In the early hours of dawn, she recalled his features as he'd lain beside her.

In sleep, his face was both peaceful and relaxed. His lips parted. His breath had brushed across her shoulder, warm and heavy.

This was not the careful, ready man of the day. This was her lover, gentle and sweet.

She'd moved closer to him, letting his heat seep into her.

His lips had pressed against her temple. "Are you awake?" he'd whispered.

She turned to him, pressing a soft, lingering kiss upon his lips. This was the only answer he needed from her. His hands had been warm as they'd moved over her.

She shivered now. Even the sun could not warm her. In the heat of the day, when the sun made the air crackle with its heat, she shivered still – another part of her punishment.

How she missed warmth.

One serpent pressed against her jaw, slithering up her cheek and across her forehead. It was cold on her skin.

As cold as my heart.

She would not push it away, no matter how much she wanted to. She'd learned her lesson. While their poison did not kill her, she'd been struck by a fever that lingered for two days, the wounds swollen and aflame. She was mindful of anything that slowed their travel. She feared discovery, knowing her curse would bring suffering to others.

That she had no control over them was without doubt, it had been part of Athena's curse. Strangely, they had no interest in hurting her – as long as she was careful of them. At times they seemed to woo her, bobbing in front of her to stare expectantly at her. She would close her eyes until they'd gone.

Another serpent moved, resting along her shoulder to peer out at the hills and mountains stretching out before them.

She missed the sea. She missed the sound of the waves and the smell of the salt air. Though even those sounds would likely sound different now. It took great concentration to hear beyond the incessant hiss of the serpents. When she bound her head it helped, but the ache from the added weight was heavy and they, the serpents, did not like to be stifled so. They snapped and dodged, twisting about her arms and pulling at her fingers in an attempt to evade the trap.

For now, she would leave them be. When her sisters returned, she would cover them.

Euryale was unnerved by their constant motion. Stheno said little about them. Medusa suspected Stheno hoped that ignoring their presence might erase them from being. A hope that made Medusa smile – sadly.

They would need to move on soon.

Athena's curse had done more than turn her locks from silken to serpentine. She had truly brought the wrath of Olympus against her. Apollo's sun blinded her, burning her eyes and slicing exquisite pain across the scar marring her forehead. Demeter's crops, those left untouched by the Persian troops, had begun to shrivel and die when they'd tarried too long.

They'd stayed hidden in the last herder's hut for less than a week before the village wheat began to grey and fall.

She would not cause the suffering of others if she could avoid it.

This cabin, a crumbling pile of wood and stone, sat atop a rocky hill. She prayed that her visit would do no harm to the good folk who worked this land. If any remained.

So many dead, so much destroyed. Without her curse to blame.

Since she – the serpents – had killed the Persians, Medusa hid. She followed her sisters while the moon was high. They traveled in the shadows, preferring a deer path to that of the goat paths – man tended goats. She vowed to keep innocents safe. It was the only thing she could do.

It ate at her, the guilt of those men's deaths. While Persia was their foe, she had no desire to hurt another human. But the others had been Greeks, survivors of the Persians brought low by her carelessness. That she'd cause the suffering of another, a slow excruciating death, turned her stomach sour.

She could not eat – her stomach would revolt. She could not sleep. Too many memories found her – memories more nightmare than not. While fragmented and dim, she could recall making her way to Galenus' house after her fall. It had taken all day, for her head bled and throbbed with such agony that she collapsed from it. She'd stumbled through Galenus' gate and staggered towards the olive trees.

Leaning heavily against the trunk of the tree, she'd stared up into their branches to rest. They swayed and danced in the evening sun, doing little to help her gain her bearings. Her eyes had troubled her, blurring in and out of focus in the fading light.

It had been this spot where he waited for her. Where he would wait for her no more. She'd swallowed back her cry and turned towards the house.

There was great activity in Galenus' house, though she'd not understood what. Nikolaos was loading the donkey cart, while two of the housemaids ran back and forth carrying linens, boxes and sacks. What was happening?

Nikolaos peered towards the gate, his rheumy eyes narrowing as he saw her under the trees.

"Mistress?" he called out in his crackling aged voice. "Mistress, you must come quickly. The Persians are headed for Athens' shore. We must sail to Aegina."

She would have moved towards him, but her legs trembled with exertion. The pain in her temples and neck subsided, but her head had begun to sway. She tried to push herself from the tree, but her stomach churned. She'd no choice but to cling to the tree. She pressed her cheek against the bark and hoped for strength.

"I need Elpis... Please fetch her to me," she called out, shaking from the effort.

"She's gone to her father's house, mistress." He hurried to her. "Let me help you, if you are hurt...."

He'd said no more.

She had not seen it happen, for she'd closed her eyes to rest against the tree. She'd nodded, her words quivering. "I thank you for your kindness, Nikolaos. I fear I'm dearly injured..." She opened her eyes.

He'd stood before her with wide eyes and open mouth. His sparse, wiry hair had not lifted wildly in the wind, as it normally did. It had stood up in disarray, hardened grey and rigid. His wrinkled face and the gentle droop of his jaw were fixed, immovable. His hand remained outstretched, gnarled fingers extended to offer her assistance.

"Nikolaos?" she'd sputtered, unable to believe what was before her eyes. "Nikolaos?"

But only silence had greeted her.

He'd frozen, a stooped grey statue, silently regarding her in horror.

"Medusa?" Stheno's voice pulled her to the present.

She turned from the window, greeting her sisters with weak smile.

"You warn us from drawing attention, yet you stand in the window with those...those wee beasties keeping watch?" Euryale shook her head.

One of the serpents turned towards her, bobbing its head in agitation.

"Does that mean it likes me? Or it wants to turn me to stone, too?" Euryale asked.

Medusa shrugged. "I know little about them."

Stheno dropped a large bag on the table, smiling. "There were only a few villagers left and they were most generous."

"Of course they were," Euryale laughed. "You told them we would leave. They could not give us enough food."

"It is more than enough to make the journey to Delphi," Medusa said softly.

Stheno nodded. "We shall eat well."

"Tis troubling to see so many women and children alone in the country, though." Euryale pulled the veils from her head. "Most of the men must have sailed off on the triremes. Or found peace at the end of a Persian sword." She draped the veils over the single aged stool that sat beside a teetering table.

Medusa did not stare, though her serpents did. They were fascinated by her sisters, bobbing and weaving about when they first removed their veils.

"Your beasties think we are men," Euryale snapped. "Come now, monsters, we are not so ugly as that."

Stheno laughed, her eyes casting the slightest glance upon the serpents before turning back to their food.

Medusa laughed too, a little, for Euryale had startled her. Every serpent head turned towards her, every red eye widened and gaped. They swarmed about her, rubbing and caressing her cheeks and neck, her shoulders and forehead, with heightened hissing.

Stheno and Euryale gaped, startled by the sight.

Medusa closed her eyes, shivering in disgust at the affection they bestowed upon her.

"It's as if..." Euryale gasped.

"They love you," Stheno finished, her words strangled.

"She would not yield to him, not willingly, my lord. This you must know." Elpis told Ariston, swaying in time with the waves. "Even Athena turned from her pleas... When she knew your life was in danger...only then did she seek out Poseidon. She had no choice in the matter."

"I cherish her, Elpis," his words rasped out. "Nothing could change that."

"I fear you may find her changed."

He nodded. How could she not be after such an ordeal?

"I will take you to Xenia, then. She is below deck, away from the rest. Her outbursts are troublesome to the others. She's always been a fragile woman. The burden of losing Galenus, Medusa, and her home were too much for her."

Ariston followed her down the ladder. "I've no intention of alarming her."

"Then you must not press her for answers she does not have," Elpis cautioned him. "She is not capable of sense, Ariston. Be mindful of that when she tells you things."

He nodded before brushing past her to the lady Xenia.

Xenia sat, regarding him with steady blue eyes. She looked tired certainly, and distraught. But not mad. "You are Ariston? You are husband to my...Medusa?" Her voice possessed the dignity of a councilman's wife. "I remember you."

He bowed. "I am."

"Elpis says you have questions for me? About my husband?" Her voice sharpened slightly, but her eyes held his.

Her pulse, he noted, beat steadily in her throat. She did not seem greatly agitated. As yet. "Was he taken by the Persians?"

"He was not taken. Go, see for yourself. You will find him there."

Ariston paused, careful with his words. "Is he living?"

"Is he living?" She stared at him. "By the Gods, I know not."

He knelt before her, speaking in soft tones. "Can you tell me what happened, lady?"

She glanced about, her eyes scouring the darkness. "I can. But you will think I am mad, as the others do. But I am not, I assure you." She met his gaze. "The Gods have cursed us, Ariston. They cursed my home and my family."

Ariston swallowed, uncertain which was greater – his irritation or his apprehension. "What curse do you speak of?"

She shook her head, her words coming out in a rapid flow. "I know only what I saw. Whether at Medusa's hands or those of her Gorgon sisters, the Gods have unleashed something terrible upon those sisters." She swallowed. "Medusa, so lost in her grief, went to Athena against all counsel. You know this?" She waited until he nodded. "Her sisters were readying to leave, to take her to their father, or I'm certain they would have prevented her. But then the alarm was issued and the house fell into chaos...." Her eyes traveled over Ariston's face. Tears filled her eyes and she reached out to him.

He felt her sadness and took her hand in his.

"She loved you dearly...poor child." She broke off. "Her sisters found her under the olive trees. She was so broken. Blood flowed freely from the ragged gash in her head... She was pale and shivered so violently..." Xenia's eyes narrowed and she grew thoughtful, shaking her head. "There was more to it. Her head..."

"Her wound?" His voice was pinched as he forced the words around the lump in his throat.

Xenia nodded. "Euryale carried her past me. I saw the extent of her wound. She could not survive, Ariston." She squeezed his hand.

"And Galenus?"

"Was bellowing for Nikolaos, as was his way. I sent him to tend Medusa and went to find the old man. I found him, the old fool, under the trees. As I drew closer...I saw what was left." She leaned closer to him and whispered, "It was as if Zeus had struck him from Olympus, catching him up and casting him in slate. He was rock... But it was old Nikolaos. And there was fear on his grey face." Her voice hitched. "I ran to Galenus, but I was...I was too late. He stood as frozen and grey as the old man, just inside Medusa's chamber." Her hands covered her face and she drew in great gasps of air. She spoke through her hands. "Then I saw it, I saw it. An asp... It stared at me with red eyes... It stared at me from Medusa's shoulder." She shivered and began to rock back and forth.

Ariston had no response for this.

"I cried out – how could I not? I did not listen as I was greatly distracted... Euryale said something about a curse from the Gods. They would go, taking the curse with them, far from Athens. Stheno said they would take Medusa's body home to her parents for the funeral rites." Xenia continued to rock.

"Where did they take her, Xenia? Where would I find Phorcys?"

Xenia shook her head, "You cannot follow. You cannot. Ariston, she would not want you to follow her. Your lady is gone... What you know to be your lady...she is gone from this world."

Ariston said nothing more, but remained at Xenia's side.

As they drew close to the docks of Athens, he helped her climb onto the deck and gave her into Elpis' care.

"I will take her to her father's house in Athens," Elpis murmured. "I fear what fits visiting Galenus' home might cause."

Ariston nodded. "I will go to his home. If I find any of her things, I will send them to her."

Elpis nodded. "Thank you. And...and you? What will you do?"

Ariston looked at her. "I will find my Medusa."

Elpis met his gaze, then answered, "I bid you safe travels, my lord. And pray you find peace along the way."

Ariston nodded. "I will, Elpis."

Chapter Twelve

As soon as the ship touched the dock, Ariston found a mount and headed towards the Acropolis. The path was crowded, for soldiers and citizens alike worked to clear the way. He rode around them, refusing to be distracted from his purpose.

Toppled columns, fractured marble and pools of melted wax marked the site of the once regal Temple of Athena Polias. It saddened him, to see such ruination. He'd served Athena since he was a youth, her temple on Rhodes the finest on the island. And while he no longer felt devotion to the Goddess, the destruction of such a holy place still galled him.

Likely Athena would rebuild her temple, with more grandeur. She would be quick to send a message: She – and Olympus – could not be defeated. Those who challenged them or gave anything less than complete obedience would pay dearly. Ariston bit back a bitter laugh. He knew this lesson.

The Persians should be fearful indeed.

His eyes searched the site, grieved by what he found. Not for Athena, but for Athenians – they looked here, high on Acropolis, when they felt fear, or need, or joy. Seeing the temple appeased them and lifted their burdens, for the Goddess was close and – surely – she would hear them.

"This wall next." Ariston heard Ektor's voice and followed it.

Ektor stood, his arms and chest blackened with soot, giving orders with confidence. He had changed, to Ariston's eyes. In place of the eager youth he'd left stood a man.

"Ektor?" Ariston slid from the horse to clasp his forearm.

Ektor's eyes grew round, though he took his arm eagerly. "Ariston," he answered. "It's good to know some stories are true. I'm glad you're well and returned to Athens. You deserve a hero's welcome."

"I did what any man would do, in my place. We landed this morning, bringing Athens' people home from Aegina."

Ektor smiled. "It will be good to see familiar faces."

"You have things well in order here."

"Indeed." Ektor paused, his face growing taut. "I... I have something of yours, I think?" He led Ariston through the rubble, to the remnants of the temple robes room. Inside all was chaos as well. The ceremonial candles were broken, a bronze incense bowl lay dented on the floor, and several wooden trays were singed black.

"What is it?" Ariston peered into the gloom, but saw nothing.

A coo sounded, deep from within.

"Thea?" he breathed.

A questioning squawk reached him.

"She will not let anyone near her," Ektor explained. "But she is caught in a cage."

Ariston ventured into the robes room, searching for his lady's pet with narrowed eyes. He found her, the remnants of her cage twined about her talons. She was too delicate an owl to fly with such weight attached to her.

"Ektor, fetch me some meat," Ariston called out before speaking to the owl. "Brave Thea, let me help you."

The owl had wasted severely, though she cooed sweetly at his tone. His hands were quick, freeing her and lifting her against him. She cackled and cooed, leaning against him with no restraint.

"You're well now, little one."

She stared up at him, listening attentively.

"Here you are, Ariston." Ektor handed Ariston a chicken wing, pulling his hand back when Thea lunged at him.

"That's no way to thank Ektor, Thea." But he laughed, holding the bone as the owl devoured the meat. "Has she been here the whole time?"

Ektor shrugged. "I know not. From the sight of her, it's likely."

Thea continued to eat, undisturbed by the men.

"What's she holding?" Ektor asked, pointing towards Thea's talon.

Thea lunged again, slicing Ektor's finger with the tip of her beak.

"By the Gods, you are a wicked creature," Ektor swore, shaking his hand as a thin line of blood welled.

Ariston held the owl up, regarding her with steady eyes. "She is the truest friend and ally."

Thea ruffled her chest feathers and shook her wings, with none of her normal sturdiness. Ariston stifled the urge to steady her. Thea was a hunter. She would not appreciate being coddled. She was weak from being so long without food, water or light, but she was strong and would recover... Like her mistress.

His heart tightened.

"She likes you well enough." Ektor wrapped his finger as he spoke. "*You* see what treasure she's protecting so vigorously."

"What have you there, Thea?" Ariston asked softly, his hand moving closer to the owl's right talon. It was small, he could not see it clearly between the bird's talons. A leather cord looped about one of Thea's legs, its ends dangling. His fingers stroked her foot and Thea opened her claw, giving it to Ariston without hesitation.

The small carved owl looked up at him from his palm. He remembered the smile on her face as she'd lifted her hair for him to tie the cord.

Pain found him, cutting more deeply than the sword that sent him to Hades. His hand fisted about it as he sucked in a sharp breath. The cord had been broken. The knot was still tight, but the leather had been stretched or yanked firmly to remove it.

"What is it?" Ektor peered around Ariston's shoulder.

"A gift I gave to my lady wife before I left." Ariston's voice was low and controlled. He swallowed, meeting Thea's large yellow eyes to find his sorrow reflected there. His next words were a broken whisper, too soft for Ektor to hear. "You kept it for her, didn't you, Thea?"

Thea blinked at him.

She knew what had happened to Medusa. This mighty and loyal creature had been caged, locked away from her lady. But Thea would have fought to be free. She would have fought anyone to stay with Medusa...

Unless Medusa ordered her to stay?

Even as the thought occurred to him, he dismissed it. If that was the way of it, Thea would not have been caged.

Medusa loved Thea. She would have ensured her pet had the best care, if she'd been able.

How had they been parted then?

Whatever had happened, he knew it was not Athena's will. While he had no doubt of Poseidon's treachery, Athena would not turn away from one who'd loved and served the Goddess so completely.

He would not believe it.

"How fares those homes beyond Athens' defenses?" Ariston's eyes strayed in the direction of Galenus' house.

Ektor's eyes followed. "The Persians left a path of death and plague, Ariston. Galenus' house was not spared." His voice lowered. "Hesiodos has been instructed to burn it."

Urgency rose within him, pushing against his fragile control. "When?" He shifted the owl, bracing her against him and wrapping his cloak about her.

"This eve, if he can manage it. They set out to find any injured or displaced citizen, to bring them inside the walls that have been repaired. But they've been charged with burning out those homes touched by Persian hands, with their pestilence. It was thought best to do so before Athens' citizens returned to their country homes, but it was too great a task." Ektor regarded him, his voice pleading as he said, "Ariston, Galenus' home was infected... There is talk of some strange..."

"Have you been, Ektor?" Ariston asked with authority. "Have you ventured outside of Athens or from the temple since the Persians left?"

Ektor sighed but shook his head. "No, sir, but I fear your journey will lead you to nothing but more death."

"Well then, worry not over me. I've bested death once. I'm sure it will go easier the second time." Ariston clasped arms with the youth and swung up onto his horse. He turned the animal towards Galenus' house but glanced back at Ektor. "I would ask a favor, once more?"

Ektor's brow furrowed, but he nodded. "Ask."

Ariston pulled a sack of coin from his cloak, tossing it to Ektor. "My lady's companion, Elpis, and the lady Xenia have returned this day. They will stay in Athens but they have no man to care for them..."

"I will look after them. I am most relieved to know Elpis is well... the Lady Xenia as well. Will be a pleasure to serve them, though I've no need of this." He held up the sack.

"Appease me, keep it. Times will be hard for some time yet." Ariston smiled. "That it pleases you to look after Elpis pleases me more than you know. And my lady as well, I'm sure. May the Goddess bestow blessings upon you."

"Blessings to you, sir."

Ariston nodded before turning the horse towards the country.

He made the trek quickly, appreciating the speed of the horse beneath him. If he'd been forced to travel on foot, his heart and lungs would have struggled under the pace he'd have set. Instead he nudged his mount onward, surveying the countryside with mounting sadness.

The road was littered with destruction. Livestock lay dead, shacks burned and smoking, not a herder or herd animal in sight. It was a far cry from the peaceful country he'd left only months before. Even the sky seemed grey. No doubt the fires still burning lent their soot to the hovering gloom. But no birdsong or blooms greeted him. It was silent, cold and barren.

Galenus' gate was open. The donkey and goats ambled about, apparently unharmed and content to roam freely.

Thea cackled, seeking escape from his robes.

"You know where we are then?" he asked.

She cooed at him, balancing unsteadily on his forearm while she assessed the grounds of her once regal home.

The house was dark. And silent, Ariston noted. Great gaping chunks of wall had been knocked away, blackened by fires no doubt set by his enemy. Boxes and clothes spilled out of the door of the great house. Such items had obviously been intended for the cart that waited, unharnessed and empty, in the courtyard.

"Galenus?" he yelled out.

There was no answer. He had not expected one. But he had

hoped.

Thea cooed and cackled, shifting from foot to foot.

"Can you fly, little one?" he asked, for the small owl seemed determined to try. "Show me the way."

She stared at him, absorbing his words before fluffing up her chest. After a moment's hesitation she climbed up his arm and settled on his shoulder with a muffled screech.

He moved towards the door.

Poseidon leaned against the column, listening to Hera and Aphrodite with increasing interest.

"I thought today was a reprieve from the council. We sit in the gardens, not the Council Chamber," Ares sighed. "No more prattling on about these affairs, I beg of you."

"Then stop interrupting us." Aphrodite smiled at him, the kind of smile a lover bestows. Aphrodite could smile at a man no other way, it was her nature. But the Goddess of Love would be wise not to flaunt her charms in front of Hera.

"Speak plainly so the feasting can begin in earnest," Ares returned Aphrodite's smile with narrowed eyes.

"While Aphrodite and I have little in common, we are both wise to the ways of the world." Hera shot a dark glance at Ares as she said, "We are women, in every sense. It is easier for us to discern this Medusa's nature."

"Are you questioning me?" Athena spat.

Poseidon regarded the women, shaking his head at how quickly they were distracted by their own egos.

"I do not doubt your wisdom, Athena. But I know what it is to have love in my heart," Hera spoke softly.

"Love? Again with love." Athena shook her head. "If Medusa had loved me more, we would not be speaking of her now."

"How can you say such a thing?" Aphrodite laughed, astonished. "She loved you with more devotion than you know. A woman so in love can rarely control her passion. And yet Medusa did. Your priestess remained pure, chaste and devout while love, womanly love, enflamed her whole heart. It was only when you gave her freedom that she gave in to the longing she'd denied..."

"She wasted little time," Athena bit back.

"There was little time to waste on the eve of war," Hera continued clearly. "And even then, she did not give in to cravings of the flesh. She honored me, honored my husband and the marriage rites with a proper ceremony and offerings."

"She is wise. You instructed her well. Even after she'd been released from the temple, she honored us all. Marriage to a soldier who has proven worthy of your selection was wise as well, don't you see? They would not go against you while she was yours, but when she had the choice she chose to align herself with someone who serves you still. And he fought bravely for Athens, your fair city." Aphrodite's voice faded. "She did all with honor."

Poseidon was impressed with such flattery and word-play. But he tired of these matters, too. "I fail to see the point of this discussion. You do have a point, surely?"

"You believe Medusa has been misjudged?" Zeus eyes sparkled, a broad and magnanimous smile spreading across his handsome face. "And you've devised a resolution that will benefit all?"

"We do," Aphrodite agreed. "We have."

"She has been dealt with." Athena glared, lifting her chin. "She deserves no more of my time."

"We will not trouble you." Hera smiled sweetly. "We will be responsible for this...test. And, if she accepts our challenge, we will reward or punish her accordingly."

Poseidon shifted, sitting forward on the thick pelt. His words were muttered, but audible to the rest. "Has she not been punished enough?"

"Is that a flash of conscience?" Aphrodite's lips pursed playfully.

Zeus reclined lazily, turning his head to smile at Poseidon. He arched an eyebrow, echoing Aphrodite's question.

Poseidon shook his head, lying back once more.

"And the affront she paid me?" Athena asked.

"Your pride was wounded by the desecration of your temple." Ares' voice was hard.

Aphrodite spoke, before Athena could respond to Ares' barb. "And while that is an offense, did Medusa choose the place of her ravishment? Something tells me she would not have done such a thing. She was too loyal to you. She is loyal still..."

Poseidon spoke quickly, before he could change his mind. "She did not. Truth be told, she wanted to see none of it – so I blinded her until it was done."

"It *was* you?" Athena looked at him with disgust.

Apollo groaned and Ares laughed. "You owe me a chariot, Apollo," Ares' voice was merry.

"You wagered?" Hera shook her head.

"It was sport." Apollo waved her irritation aside.

"She could not bear to look at you, and yet you could still use her thusly?" Athena continued to glare at him.

Laughter overpowered the melody of Hermes' lyre.

"If the girl is comely enough," Hermes spoke for the first time, "little will stop a man in rut."

"You speak from vast experience?" Apollo poked.

"You pity me for vowing to remain pure?" Athena asked Hera and Aphrodite before turning back to Poseidon. "Is the rest also true, Poseidon? Did she give herself to you in exchange for the well-being of her husband? My guard, my soldier?"

He felt heat wash over him, angered by the flush of guilt Athena's words stirred within him.

"What's done is done," Hera said, shaking her head. "She did insult you, Athena, but not through actions. That she questioned you is worthy of punishment."

"She did so out of her desperation," Aphrodite explained.

"No," Athena said softly. "She did so because she was scared."

"She may have been, a bit." Hera nodded. "But desperate, too, with grief. The loss of her husband..." Hera shuddered, then asked, "Does she yet know that he lives?"

Ares shook his head. "He is only just returned to Athens. The battle at Salamis and carting all of Athens to and from Aegina has kept news slow at best."

"But she is no longer in Athens..." Apollo said.

"Where is she?" Zeus asked.

"The Gorgons hid her in a cave," Aphrodite said. "She fell, you see, injuring herself. Her sisters took her with them, to return to Phorcys across the sea, I suppose."

Aphrodite looked at Apollo, who agreed.

"So it would seem. I saw her stumbling from the mouth of this cave. Perhaps she was confused, perhaps she hadn't yet grasped the magnitude of her...condition, for she seemed to war with the serpents in earnest. Persians came upon her, those that had been looting and burning out the country as they retreated beyond reach of the Hoplites." Apollo met Hera's gaze before addressing Zeus. "I saw her grief as these men, her enemy, turned to stone. And I pitied her." Apollo turned to Athena. "Truly, you would have felt the weight of it."

Poseidon could envision it all. Her fear, coupled with her sorrow.

"Since then I've seen little of her," Apollo finished with a shrug. "She hides while I am in the sky and travels with her sisters at night. I've rarely found her the same place from one day to the next."

"Selene said she travels at night to keep others safe," Aphrodite sounded forlorn.

"She cannot bear it, I think." Hera spoke this time, staring pointedly at her husband. "She cannot bear to cause suffering. She hides herself away to prevent it."

"Even now, she puts others before herself." Poseidon's voice was faint.

"She wronged you, Athena. None here deny that. And she has paid dearly for that. I would give her the chance to prove herself to you. To free herself and those good men who live and serve you, and Olympus. And return a beloved wife to her heroic husband. Ariston of Rhodes deserves to have his wife with him," Aphrodite pleaded.

"How can she prove herself to me?" Athena asked. "She is no longer my priestess."

"Nor is she chaste," Ares laughed.

"She may no longer be able to serve as a priestess, but she can still yet show her devotion to you and Olympus," Aphrodite assured her.

"And if she does, you would free her from her curse?" Athena asked.

"She cannot know," Zeus stroked his beard, contemplating. "If she knew she might be released, she would say anything to find Athena's favor again."

"If she proves herself without any hope of forgiveness I would have her returned to her husband and safe from further meddling."

Hera's huge brown eyes shot daggers at Poseidon. "I would have the word of all Olympians."

Poseidon nodded. "You have it."All eyes shifted to him, so he smiled unabashedly.

"Do you agree, Athena?" Zeus asked.

A lingering silence fell, but Poseidon knew what would happen.

"I do," Athena consented. "But I will have a part in this scheme, Hera. Medusa was my priestess – my favorite at that."

Aphrodite clapped her hands, laughing. "This promises a happy ending."

"We shall see." Zeus pulled his wife into his arms.

Warm hands clasped her. The roughened pads of his fingers trailed exquisite heat over her bare flesh. His mouth traveled across her lips, kissing her cheek, her jaw and her ear. His breath seemed to echo his caress, fanning across her brow as he moved.

"Don't wake up, my love," he soothed. "Let me keep you warm and safe."

She sighed, leaning against him. No, no she would not wake up...

"I've no interest in greeting the day when you are here, with me now." His words, ever more bittersweet, haunted her.

"Medusa." It was the faintest sound.

No. Not yet. Let me stay...

She burrowed into his side, though he felt much softer now. His warmth was fading too.

"Medusa." The voice was louder this time.

"Ariston?" she murmured, pleading for him to stay.

She heard a sigh, followed by Euryale's whispered, "She dreams of nothing else. It grieves me to wake her."

She was loath to open her eyes, but her sisters' hushed conversation effectively chased away her dreams.

"Because her sadness is so pitiful, sister, that even a heart as jaded as yours aches for her. I would take her curse if I could, to free her," Stheno said. "But, as I cannot, we must help her avoid any more unpleasantness on our journey."

"Medusa," Euryale tried again, sounding more than a little

annoyed.

"I hear you," Medusa answered, though she lay still.

In the first moments of waking, her head did not ache. It was the only respite from her pain. She opened her eyes slowly, finding her sisters situated comfortably in the small hut where they'd spent the night.

"We have bread and cheese." Stheno held a plate before her.

"And grapes, too." Euryale sat across from her, popping a grape into her mouth.

Medusa looked at the plate and tasted bile in her mouth. "No. But I thank you."

"It must be part of the curse." Euryale shook her head. "How else can you have survived so long without a bite of food?"

The moon had come and gone more than once since her sisters had helped her from Galenus' house. In that time, they'd made little progress towards their destination. She tired easily, her stomach churned, and the stabbing pain in her head forced her to rest for part of every day. Each day she hoped she might grow stronger, hoped they might reach Delphi and ask the oracle for guidance.

But nothing changed.

It was more than that, Medusa knew. She was a coward. She longed to reach her father's home to escape the devastation that littered Greece. Each village, each farm or homestead they'd come upon had been the same. The Persians had been thorough in their retreat. They had cut down all those in their path, leaving no survivors.

"A heartless tactic," Stheno had observed at one gruesome discovery.

"They think to remove those who would stand against them upon their next invasion," Euryale muttered.

The three of them had spent the evening performing the funeral rites for the family, careful to place a coin under the tongues of the eight they laid to rest. It was the children, one still in swaddling, that tore at the remaining shards of Medusa's heart.

"Would that my...companions and I could look upon the savages that performed such monstrous deeds," she had whispered. For a brief moment, she would have embraced her curse, to reap vengeance for this family and the others they'd found.

Now the hissing of her serpents only served to irritate her.

She would ignore them, as always, and concentrate on her sisters. In the time she'd spent with them, they'd taken to removing their scarves and shawls. They had no need of them when it was just the three of them. While they did stand two heads taller than any mortal man she had met, their appearance was far less gruesome than their carved masks on the temple. Broad of forehead and long in the chin, their bones were more pronounced and angular. Their eyes were sunken and black, set beneath thick brows set in a permanent furrow. Their thick, pale lips pulled into a downward slope, giving the impression they were constantly displeased or angry.

It was their posturing that made them frightening.

Under such dark and forbidding garments, mortal man had little choice. To feel terror, the need to flee, was a logical response to creatures of such overwhelming presence.

But Medusa had learned much about her sisters. Namely, that they were loyal and proud women. They honored their family dearly – especially, it seemed, their little sister.

Euryale scowled at one of Medusa's companions, giggling as it slithered away.

"Are you trying to scare them or me?" Medusa asked drily.

"Why else would the Gods have made us so," Euryale asked, "If not to strike fear upon all that look upon us – your wee beasties included?"

"We are to remind man not to take their fortunes for granted, sister. We are a reminder of the beauty of life and the blessings they have through the mercy of the Gods," Stheno offered with great patience, as if she'd had to explain this to her sister over and over again.

"By being the most loathsome of creatures to look upon?" Euryale laughed.

Stheno shrugged. "It would seem."

"The Gods are most peculiar," the amusement was still evident in Euryale's voice.

Medusa's head began to throb. "Indeed." She rolled onto her back, hearing the tell-tale hiss and slither of her bed partners. It took hours for them to calm and settle down to sleep, filling her ears with their twitches and shifting as they did so. She'd taken to sleeping in some of Stheno's dark veils. The added darkness and weight seemed to ease the serpents.

The veils helped, but they did not rest for long or stay confined beneath them. And when they woke, she gave up any hope of sleep. So she would rise, with great care, as they did not like to be pinched or pinned beneath her.

They would bite her, as was their habit when irritated.

She sat up slowly, pressing a hand to her forehead. The serpents immediately plucked at the veils, nudging back to free themselves. She ignored them, asking, "Where are we?"

Stheno held the water skin towards her hopefully. "The tip of Attica. The sun sets shortly, if you'd like to go and see?"

Medusa shook her head. "No... I cannot risk it."

"Have no worries, sister. The Persians found everyone long before we arrived. It seems a shame to stay locked up when this time of day brings you such joy." Euryale's attention caught upon one the serpents. It stared fixedly at her until she shook her head, breaking its gaze.

Medusa felt one coiling about her neck. It took every ounce of self restraint not to try to push it from her. Each touch, each hiss or flick of their long, thin tongues ripped at the lining of her stomach. Time had not softened her feelings towards them. She hated them, hated what they could do – what they'd made her.

Yet she had no one to blame but herself.

"Come, Medusa." Stheno opened the door, tempting her with the beauty of the view before them.

They were indeed on the tip of Greece, rising above the cerulean depths of the sea beyond. The sound of the gulls, the steady roar of the surf and the tang of the salt reached her nose. She inhaled deeply, unable to tamp down the slight pleasure she felt. She rose slowly and moved towards the door.

She ignored the excited hiss and slither that commenced about her shoulders. They would not tarnish this. She wouldn't let them.

"Go on," Euryale urged.

Medusa nodded absentmindedly.

The sun was setting. And they were on the sea. The warmth of the evening caressed her shoulders, attempting to cut through the cold that clung to her insides since she'd stumbled from Athena's temple.

It felt as if years had passed.

But when she thought of him, it was only moments. How the sea wind would have tossed his curls and kissed the bronze of his skin.

She drew in a shuddering breath and closed her eyes against the brilliant rays of the sun. But the throbbing began anyway, causing pain to cleave her head and scalding heat to sear along length of her scar.

The faint jingle of a bell reached Medusa, its merry tinkling a familiar sound. It stirred memories of home, of Elpis and Xenia, and her beloved Thea. It, coupled with the salty sea air and the bleat of a goat, pushed her burdens aside.

Her head seemed to lighten, making her sigh with pleasure.

Relief came when she found sleep...or when the serpents spied a victim. In those moments before they found some prey or sport to destroy with their sparkling red eyes, they were one heaving mass of muscles and sound – stretching out to ensnare their prey with one fatal look. It was then, before they struck, that her head was calm and weightless...

Medusa stilled. They moved as one, swaying in anticipation of something she couldn't see. They had found something or someone to prick their interest.

The ringing bell drew closer, drowning out the sounds of her serpents.

Spare me this, I beg of you, she pleaded to whichever God might be listening.

There was nothing to be done.

They wove and bobbed, their sites fixed on their victim already.

"No," she pushed them down, frantically pulling up the thick scarf about her shoulders. One serpent snatched it, then another, and pulled it from her hold. She tried to reach it, but a breeze caught it and pushed it along the dusty ground at her feet. It blew over the rock cliff before her labored efforts could retrieve it.

She shook her head, pushing the serpents away in desperation. It was too late. They would have done their damage by now, she knew. She turned anguished eyes towards the tinkling ring of the bell.

A small boy stood there, his brown eyes wide and unblinking as he stared at her.

Chapter Thirteen

The serpents hissed and bobbed, clearly startling the boy.

She could not hold them all. She sucked in her breath sharply as one bit her forearm deeply. And still, she tried to fight them. "You must leave, boy. You must run." She could not bear to see him suffer.

But the snakes had not changed him. Even now, regardless of her futile attempts to stop them, they wove and glared at him to no avail.

The boy stayed as he was, a small and precious child. Her struggles ceased.

Athena's curse spared children...something Medusa was truly thankful for.

He stepped closer to her, wide eyed and pale. "Can I... can I help, mistress?"

She stared at the boy, surprise making her weak. Such a guileless offer squeezed the tattered air from her lungs.

"I fear you cannot," she whispered.

He continued to stare, torn between shock and fear. "Do they hurt you?"

She shook her head, letting her eyes linger on him hungrily. His was the first face she'd looked upon that wasn't her sister's – that hadn't been turned to stone.

"No."

The goats moved about them, munching grass peacefully. The ram came at her, snorting, but the boy pushed the ram away, smacking the large sheep with his crook. She felt the corner of her mouth turn up, but refused to smile at his gallant gesture.

"He has no manners, that one," the boy said, sounding wiser than his years.

"He is a fine animal."

"When he behaves." He smiled at her, his gaze only slightly less distracted by the serpents. "Are you alone too?"

She heard the sadness in his voice. "I travel with my sisters. And you? What of your family?"

"It's only me and Kore." His eyes traveled over her face.

"Where is Kore?"

He turned, pointing to the sleeping infant strapped to his back. "She's finally asleep."

Medusa stared at the red-faced babe, bound to the cradle board with mismatched knots and sagging blankets.

"But where is your mother?" she forced the words past the lump in her throat.

He turned back to her, his eyes sparkling with unshed tears. "The Persians came."

She moved closer to him, but stopped. She could not draw him into her arms, she could not comfort him. Her serpents might not turn him to stone, but she had no doubt their venom would harm this brave boy.

"Are you hungry?" she asked. "I have some cheese and grapes"

His eyes widened at her words. "If you have enough to spare?"

"I have more than enough..." she paused. "What is your name, boy?"

"Spiridion." He smiled.

She nodded. "Come with me, Spiridion. Let us find you something for that empty belly."

They walked in companionable silence, giving her time to assess him. He was thin, frail even. His face was gaunt. Even his hands seemed bony. A boy his age should still carry the roundness of a babe. If he'd survived the Persians' retreat, he must be a resourceful sort. And to care for his baby sister...he was a brave little soul indeed.

As they made their way to the cabin, she cautioned him. "Spiridion. I must warn you that my sisters..." She paused, considering her words. "Never mind. If you are brave enough to stand your ground when coming upon my monstrous presence, my sisters' scowling faces and heavy brows will give you no pause." She smiled.

"But you are not a monster."

It was her turn to stare at him with wide eyes. "Am I not?"

The boy cocked his head, examining her face and slithering locks with great curiosity. "No. Athena uses the serpent. You must be a healer...or very wise. Which are you?"

Ariston's search of Galenus' home had done little to reassure him of Medusa's well-being. He'd rummaged through every corner, overturning baskets and boxes and scouring each room with his torch held aloft.

Thea had led the way, hopping and gliding in short spurts.

The owl missed nothing. She was the best scout he'd ever known. It had been Thea who had found Medusa's mat amid the chaos, knocked into the far corner of the room. The mat was dirty, blotched unevenly with red and black. Upon closer inspection he realized it was blood that had set into its woolen fibers. So much blood.

He'd stayed, bracing himself against the silence of the house and the fear that threatened to overcome his resolve, but found nothing else.

On his way from the house, he'd stumbled over the limb of a broken statue. He'd cast only the briefest glance at it, unbothered by the Persians' looting when his lady was still lost to him. But the limb was a forearm and hand, splayed wide. The workmanship was unsurpassed and lifelike.

And on the hand was Galenus' family crest. A ring he'd been forced to swear fealty to when he'd joined Galenus' household.

"It was as if Zeus had struck him from Olympus, catching him up and casting him in slate. He was rock...he was stone," Xenia's words filled his ears and mind.

He'd stooped, examining the broken piece with care. Each tendon and knuckle was painstakingly intricate. Turning the arm, he noted the slight creases in the bend of the elbow. None was left beyond the arm, the rest had been shattered.

Thea had cackled at him, ruffling her feathers with impatience.

"We will find her, little one," he'd reassured them both as he'd made his way to his horse, tethered outside.

He'd mounted and turned, sweeping an appraising eye over Galenus' house once more. If Ektor spoke the truth it would not be here for much longer. His eyes strayed to the olive trees, those three trees he thought of so fondly.

Thea settled on his shoulder, cooing in his ear.

"We will find her," he said again.

As they approached the trees, he felt such defeat. He'd hoped that, somehow, she'd still be here. Or that there would be some sign to indicate where he should venture next. She would have known he'd come after her, surely.

But she thought him dead.

The pain in his chest threatened to overwhelm him.

He saw him then, in the deepening shadows beneath one of the olive trees. Nikolaos lay on his back.

"Nikolaos?" His voice was harsh.

Nikolaos didn't answer.

Ariston nudged his horse closer to the figure. No, it wasn't Nikolaos, but it was his likeness. Though the statue had been cut cleanly from the shaped shoulder to the figure's waist, it was as detailed as the arm he'd discovered within the house.

It was Nikolaos' face, frozen in distress, which greeted him. His stomach tightened, as did his grip upon his reins.

Perhaps there was a curse. Whatever had transpired, it left only unease within him. He would not linger here.

He camped overnight, surprised when Ektor joined him. It was Ektor who mentioned the caves, inspiring him to set off at first light.

Ariston's knees gripped his horse as he scoured the horizon for any sign of caves. The Gorgons might have come here, fleeing from Athens even when the Persians had been at their door.

He swallowed his frustration, though it choked him to do so, and turned his energies to searching the caves. He prayed they'd found shelter, for the Persians had wrought destruction well into the countryside beyond the city.

He was comforted to know Stheno and Euryale were with her. Though Elpis had described them as monstrous creatures, their devotion to Phorcys and their family was unshakable. They would guard her, tend her, and care for her as long as she had need of them, if only to return home with her.

He prayed that her wounds had healed, that she was well enough to travel. They would journey to Rhodes as soon as he found her.

Thea lifted her wings, flapping to climb into the pale blue sky.

His eyes narrowed, watching the bird's slow climb. She was still so weak. Her frailty restored his anger and gave him the energy to carry on.

The sun was high when he found the first cave entrance. It led into a series of small, shallow caverns. But there was no sign that any person had been there.

He rested in the shade of the rocks, sharing food with Thea. She could not hunt for herself yet. She gobbled the dried fish, clicking noisily before she flew off. Moments later she circled back, clicking and cawing for his attention.

"You've found something," he whispered, jumping to his feet to follow.

The entrance of the cave was small, easily missed. The ground was covered in rubble and slate, unlike the rock and walls of the surrounding caves. He nudged the stones with his feet, then bent to inspect the pieces.

It was the same stone, brittle and grey, that had made up the statues in Galenus' home.

A chill found him, but he brushed it aside.

He stood and ventured into the cave.

The passageway was narrow, forcing him to bend in order to fit. He moved swiftly, trailing a hand along the cave wall. The darkness was pitch, forcing him back out of the cave for light. Holding his torch aloft, he started again.

The tunnel went on. It was silent and cold here, deep inside the hill.

And then it stopped, turning sharply to the left and opening in to a large cavern. At first the cave offered nothing more than the rest. But the flames of his torch revealed a patch of white amidst the rocky floor. He looked closer, making out the crudely hidden remains of a fire pit, several footprints and a white cloth.

Ariston knelt, fingering the embroidered robes his lady had once worn as Athena's servant. His hands gripped the finely woven linen to his chest, pressing it to him for some sense of reassurance.

But the intricately stitched gilded owls and serpents were discolored, stained copper by the dried blood that hardened its length.

Medusa watched the boy sleeping peacefully on her mat.

Little Kore sat on Euryale's lap, reaching for the shell necklace Medusa had made the night before. The little girl squealed in delight when Euryale tipped her back playfully.

"Silly child," Euryale laughed.

Medusa shook her head. "She is precious, sister. And well you know it."

Euryale smiled at the baby. The baby smiled back.

Medusa marveled at the transformation of her sister. A week had come and gone, but Stheno had no luck finding anyone who might care for the children. And they all agreed that brave Spiridion and giggling Kore would not be left behind.

But neither could they go with them to Phorcys' house.

Stheno entered, looking ragged. She had left in the early morning hours, the quest to find the children a family or home occupying most of her waking hours. She was gasping for air as she pulled her veils from her head.

"We must leave." Her voice was urgent.

"Now?" Euryale looked at her sister with a disapproving scowl.

"What happened?" Medusa asked.

Stheno shook her head. "Someone is coming."

"Mayhap father sent someone to look for us?" Euryale asked.

"When has father ever sent someone after us, sister?" Her tone was bitter, a tone Medusa had rarely heard from Stheno. "This is a soldier, from the looks of him."

Euryale waved a hand, dismissing Stheno. "If it is a soldier, he is more likely chasing the last of the Persians from Greece. He is no concern of ours."

Medusa asked. "You think he will come here, to the cabin?"

Stheno shrugged, finally regaining her breath.

"Then let us wait." Euryale returned to the baby, her harsh face softening under Kore's happy attention. "It seems foolhardy to drag the children from shelter when we must travel at night."

Medusa glanced at the sleeping boy, then at his small sister. The time together had allowed the boy some rest. While he was thin, he seemed less fragile. He ate heartily at every meal, her sisters made sure of it. How Medusa longed to see him round and laughing... He would be a handsome boy.

But a soldier was coming, a soldier who might be able to help them.

"Did he see you?" Medusa asked.

Stheno shook her head. "I was atop a hill when I saw him. He was saddling his horse far below."

"Was he alone?" Euryale asked. "One man between the three of us is no matter. Why, Medusa could..."

"Do not suggest such a thing," Medusa stopped her.

"He is alone," Stheno said.

"Euryale is likely right, Stheno. He must be a scout. Which means other soldiers will be coming soon, if he finds something to warrant their presence." Medusa sighed.

Should they leave now? She didn't know. This soldier might pass them by.

"We must keep an eye on him," Euryale said.

"And if he does find us?" Stheno's agitation made her voice shrill.

Medusa stood, reaching out a hand to her sister. She drew back, then, wary of putting her sister within the serpents' striking range. "Maybe he would take the children to Xenia?"

Euryale startled, "A soldier? You would place their care into the hands of a man more likely to take life than—"

"Spiridion can care for Kore better than any of us," Medusa challenged. "Who better than a soldier to protect the children? Who better than Xenia to raise them? She is alone now. She will shower them with such love... Love they deserve." She watched her sisters, praying they would see the logic in her plan. "She will offer them what we cannot, a home and family."

Stheno nodded. "You are right, Medusa. If he comes upon us, I will ask for his aid."

"*If* he comes upon us," Euryale argued. "There is no need to search him out."

Medusa's heart was heavy. Her sister was loved for the first time, joyfully embraced by the eager arms of tiny Kore.

For a moment she imagined life remaining as it was. It could be a good life, watching the children grow into strong and happy youth.

But if they stayed as they were, Spiridion would not live to be a man. Her companions would make certain of that.

His young life would be cut short by the very love she now bore him.

She shivered as she spoke. "It is better if he finds them now, sister. The longer we have them, the greater their loss will finally be."

Ariston watched the old man with narrowed eyes. This was the first living person he'd found in more than a fortnight. His path had been littered with graves, more akin to Hades' domain than that of Greece.

This man, moving slowly on his aged legs, was a surprise. Had the Persians spared him because of his weakness?

"Soldier," he wheezed. "I fear you've come too late."

"Too late?"

The old man shook his head. "All who lived here are dead."

Ariston nodded, grieved by the man's words. "These are sad times, old man."

"They are," the old man agreed. He stood, regarding Ariston with startlingly clear eyes set deep beneath weathered wrinkles. "Will you eat with me? It has been too long since I've had company other than myself."

Ariston swallowed his impatience. It did no harm to visit with this man. He'd pushed on, rarely stopping to sleep or eat. He, too, had suffered loneliness of late. The stronger Thea grew, the more frequently she left him.

He nodded and slid from his horse, guiding the animal into the shade of some fig trees.

They settled, sharing their dried fish, fruit and the remains of the hard bread Ariston had scavenged from a ruined farmhouse.

"You've traveled far?" the old man asked.

Ariston nodded.

"And you fought in the wars?" The man raised a gnarled hand, indicating the jagged scar visible above Ariston's exomie.

"I did." Ariston took a deep drink.

"I was young and able once. I remember the feel of a sword in my hands."

"Do you?" Ariston smiled slightly.

"Glory, boy, is everything." The old man regarded him with raised eyebrows. "If I'd died on the battlefield, glory would have been mine. Instead I lived to see my children and grandchildren cut down."

Ariston swallowed. "I am sorry for your loss."

"Do you have a family, soldier?" The old man bit off a mouthful of fish, chewing carefully.

The bite of bread lodged in his throat, but Ariston forced the words out. "I have a wife."

The old man nodded, smiling. "Is she fair?"

He drank deeply, but the knot in his throat remained. "She is most fair to look upon and gentle of manner."

The old man studied him. "She waits for you?"

Ariston drew a deep breath to steady himself. "I am looking for her now. She was injured and carried away by her family."

The old man sighed, leaning back against the tree. "I have seen no one in these parts." He was silent. "Except for the Gorgons." The old man shivered, tossing the pit from his olive over his shoulder.

Ariston sat forward. "When? When did you see them?"

The old man turned curious eyes upon him. "You cannot be looking for them, soldier. They are cursed by the Gods."

"I care little for curses, old man." He leaned forward, meeting the rheumy eyes. "When did you see them?"

"You care little for curses? And the Gods?"

Ariston stood. "I've lived my life in service to Olympus. As did my lady wife. And yet the Gods turned from us both. So I no longer care about their curses, their will or their spite." He smiled sadly at the old man.

"Have you no fear?" the old man asked in hushed tones.

"None."

"What of honor?"

"You spoke of an honorable death? I had all but made my way to Elysium, for the will of Athena and the protection of her great city. I chose to come back to her – my wife – so that I might protect and love my lady. We would have served and honored Olympus, together, in the years ahead." He paused, swallowing his anger. "And still they took her from me."

The old man regarded him in silence.

"I ask you again, when did you see the Gorgons?"

The old man sighed, "I will tell you. But first you must answer a question."

Ariston could not stop his hands from clenching, or the tightening of his jaw. He had no patience for this. And yet, this old man had news he needed. "Ask quickly then."

"Your lady wife – would she turn her back on the Gods?"

"No," he said. "Even now, when they have used her poorly, I know she would serve them. She has a faithful and forgiving heart." He laughed, a hard mirthless sound. "And I tell you, old man, I would honor the Gods with her, for the rest of my life, if she were returned to me."

The old man stood, nodding. "They are there. On the top of the farthest hill, keeping a herd of goats it seems."

"It is rumored they have a fondness for goats." Ariston smiled in spite of himself. *Or goat herders*, she'd laughingly said. He collected his things, hurriedly strapping the sack onto his saddle.

"Is it?" the old man asked. "Be careful, soldier. You seem a good sort. And whatever it is that plagues those creatures harbors only ill will towards man."

Ariston heard the words as he mounted his horse. He was so close, so close after so very long. "I thank you for the food. And the company." He kicked his horse on, impatient for the journey to be behind him.

By this evening, she might be in his arms once more.

He turned, to wave his thanks to the old man. But the man was gone. He was no longer reclining against the tree, enjoying the shade. Nor was he hobbling along the path. There was no sign of him.

"Hera," Medusa whispered again. Her knees ached from kneeling on the cold rocks beneath her. "Hear my prayers, I implore you."

The morning sun was rising, signaling the end of her day. The serpents hated the sun almost as much as she did. But she would continue to seek Hera's guidance until she was forced to retreat inside the small cabin where her sisters and the children still slept.

She must find safety for Kore and Spiridion.

"These children need your protection..." she repeated her prayer over and over. "Guide the soldier to us so that he may keep them safe."

Even if she'd lost favor with Olympus, the Goddess would not turn away from these children. Surely, she would protect them.

"I beg you for mercy, Hera – for the care of these precious children."

"And what of the soldier, Medusa?" The voice started Medusa from her prayers.

A woman stood before her, with lush round curves and curly brown hair. She was small, dainty and feminine – and regal. There was an aura about her that Medusa recognized. This woman was not a mortal.

"If he comes to the aid of these children, you put him at risk." The woman spoke again, her voice warm and soothing.

"I... I will hide," she stammered.

"He might try to find you," the woman returned. "He might try to kill you. News of the Gorgon curse travels, and men are fools in their need for conquests."

"Would that he could kill me, lady," Medusa whispered.

"You seek death?"

Medusa nodded slowly. "I am a danger to others."

The woman said nothing.

Medusa was silent too. What should she say?

The whisper of the gently blowing breeze brushed her ear, fanning the sounds of evening about her. The faint hoot of an owl, the soft sounds of the surf far below, even the call of a gull reached her.

And still the woman watched her in silence.

At first, Medusa dismissed the owl's calls. It was only as

they grew louder and more insistent that she turned towards the approaching bird. A coo, sweet and pleading, reached her.

And Medusa saw her.

"Thea?" her anguish was audible.

The owl circled her, obviously distressed by her mistress' companions. Medusa shook her head, wrapping her arms around herself so Thea would find no place to grasp her. She curled inward, desperate.

"Are you a messenger from Olympus – from Athena?" she gasped, unable to stop the waiver from her plea. "Keep her from me, I beg of you. Let no harm come to her."

"I am not Athena, Medusa. I am Hera. Did you not call for me?" The woman's voice was sad.

"Forgive me, Goddess. Thea..." Medusa's words trailed off. How happy she was to see her beloved Thea. And how desperately she wished her pet had not found her.

"Your pet did not come with me," Hera said.

Thea landed on the ground, staring at Medusa with her huge yellow eyes as she cooed plaintively.

"Dear Thea." Medusa smiled at her. "Stay where you are, little one. They would not take kindly to your affection."

Indeed the snakes were stretching towards the owl with uninhibited aggression. Medusa pushed them back, ignoring the burning stab of their fangs as she did so.

"They bite you?" the Goddess asked with unrepressed horror.

"It's a small thing – no more than a passing irritation. I am at their mercy too. Though the suffering they cause their victims is far more...cruel." She paused. "If there were a way, if I had some warning to prevent their whims, I would control them."

"But you cannot." Hera regarded her with huge brown eyes. "So how will you protect this soldier?"

She drew a deep breath, knowing she had only one choice to guarantee this man's safety. "I will leave. My sisters will give the children into his safe keeping."

Hera moved forward, standing over Medusa. "If I agree, what do you offer me?"

"What would you have me do?"

Hera cocked her head. "You would you serve me? No matter

what I ask of you?"

"I would," she answered.

"Set thoughts of death aside. Your death, that is. I would have your companions punish those in need of punishment."

Medusa shivered. "Who?"

"You will start here. There is a camp of Persians in the cove below. They wait for a ship that will not come." Hera watched her closely. "These are the same men who left this path of death you've traveled with your sisters. The men who made these children you care for, and many more like them, into orphans. These men will set upon the warrior coming this way, and most assuredly kill him. Unless you unleash the power Athena has cursed you with."

Medusa nodded once. Her curse had a purpose – justice. These men deserved death. "I will visit them this eve."

The Goddess smiled. "Then you shall make your way to the caves on Crete. There you shall stay to deal with those sent to you. I give you my word both children will live long and healthy lives."

"I thank you Hera, for your mercy. They are sweet and gentle children, deserving of love and protection."

Hera continued, "Yes, yes. I have news that might lighten your heart."

She asked, "Is there such news?"

"Your owl is not alone. She travels with the soldier, a hero of Salamis on a most desperate quest. He is looking for his wife."

"A sad quest for a favored soldier." Her words were soft. If Ariston had lived... No. Hera's words could do nothing but bring her more sorrow. She did not want to hear of this man or his quest, she could not. Too much pain lived in her heart already.

"You would be surprised, I think, to know the rest of this man's story." Hera walked closer, watching the owl as it circled its mistress again and again. "He was injured on the seas, at Athens, struck dead by an infidel's blade. But he would not rest, he bargained with Hades to come back."

Medusa stared at Hera. "Why would he do such a thing? Surely rest in Elysium and glory on the battlefield are all any man desires?"

Hera nodded, "I agree, your words are wise. This soldier, however, does not agree. He left matters unfinished, matters he valued more than glory or rest, so it seems. His wife was seriously injured at Athens, her household cursed, and destroyed. He believed her in more danger still – and would protect her once more, if he could find her. But she was carted away by her sisters, before he could send any word to her of his return… Now he searches for his wife, knowing she believes him dead. For more than two moons now he has traveled across the countryside so that he might bring her home with him to Rhodes."

Hera's words filled her ears.

Her chest began to spasm unbearably.

Her heart, so broken she knew it would never beat properly, throbbed to life with sudden force.

"He will not give up, Medusa. I have never seen a man more determined than yours."

Whatever pain she felt fled at the realization that he lived. Some faint recollection of joy found her. "He… He is well?" Her voice broke.

"He is."

Medusa nodded, covering her mouth to catch the laughter that escaped. He lived, and loved her still. Even though he must know of her betrayal… Did he know of her curse, as well?

Nothing else mattered. "My… my heart is full." She looked up at the Goddess, smiling through her tears.

Sadness shadowed Hera's eyes. "I thought as much. But what will you do?"

She had little time to come to terms with Hera's revelation. Later she might linger over this news, but not now. "He must be kept safe… I have given you my word and I will honor our bargain. Nothing changes. But knowing…knowing he lives makes all bearable."

"Does it?"

Thea cooed at her, stepping forward, then dodging back as the serpents moved to reach her. Medusa grabbed one, forcing it behind her and wincing at the bite it gave her in response.

"Almost…" She nodded. "Yes."

Chapter Fourteen

It was past midday when Ariston reached the cabin. His horse was covered in a layer of sweat, exhausted from the climb. He slumped in the saddle, his body aching from the relentless jarring. As they entered the clearing, his mood lightened.

A herd of goats scattered before him, bleating as they went. His eyes surveyed the scene with care.

The small rock cottage looked deserted, and no smoke rose from the dilapidated chimney. There were no horses, or carts, no guards or dogs to alert those inside the cabin they had been found. It was peculiar, this lack of regard for discovery.

A sudden movement caught his eye, and he turned to find a young boy.

The boy froze. The bucket the boy carried sloshed, spattering his thin chest with what appeared to be goat milk. Large brown eyes stared back at him.

Ariston stopped, regarding the boy in surprise.

"Are you the soldier?" the boy asked.

"I am a soldier," he answered. "Are you expecting one?"

"I think it's you, sir." The boy grasped the bucket with two hands, and moved towards him. He shrugged, smiling up at him. "Maybe."

Ariston smiled back.

"They're in the cabin. Kore is hungry, that's why I was milking."

Ariston looked at the boy, understanding nothing the child

said. "Who is in the cabin?"

"Stheno and Euryale." The boy tilted his head towards the cabin. "It's too hot to bring the baby outside."

Ariston followed, confused yet exhilarated. "Is it only Stheno and Euryale?"

The boy's eyes grew round and he opened his mouth. But he seemed to change his mind and nodded vigorously in answer. The child was nervous about something.

"Boy..." Ariston began.

The shrill sound of a baby reached them.

The boy laughed. "I told you she was hungry."

"She is, Spiridion, so run. The soldier can find his way inside, surely?" a woman's rough voice called from the recesses of the cabin.

"Don't stare," the boy whispered before he ran ahead, into the cabin.

Tread carefully. He would find the truth.

"For a soldier, you lack both speed and stealth," the voice goaded.

"I wasn't aware I needed speed or stealth, lady," he answered. "Should I retreat and start again?"

Laughter, hoarse and grating, "You do have an excellent sense of humor."

His first impression was one of height. The woman, a Gorgon to be sure, stood in the doorway staring down at him. She shifted, exposing her features to him. And he understood why the boy had warned him about staring.

"You are Ariston?" she asked.

"You know me?"

"Of course," another said, stepping forward. This one wasn't smiling. "Our sister dreamed of little else and we were forced to sleep under one roof... In the time we had with her."

"Where is she?" he asked.

The unsmiling Gorgon answered quickly, "She is no longer with us..."

"She joined Hades this very morn," the other added.

Ariston surged forward, staring about the dimly lit cabin.

They were wrong, they had to be. She could not be dead. If she were dead he could no longer look for her – hope for her.

He fought the urge to run. But six prying eyes watched him with various expressions, and he would find what answers he could.

"She suffers no more. That is more than she'd dare hope for." The Gorgon continued, "I will take you to her grave after we eat."

"Come in and sit," the other suggested. "Let us cool our tempers and our tongues before we exchange tales, shall we? Leave him be, Euryale. Spiridion, fetch him some water."

The boy did as he was told, handing the water skin to him with tear-filled eyes. "Here you are," the boy whispered.

Ariston stared at the boy, at the pain on his young face. He said nothing as he took the water skin from him.

Medusa crept onto the beach, keeping to the shadows that leapt and danced about the crackling fire.

Her heart, thumping wildly, rebelled against what she was about to do. She knew these men were monsters, she had seen the torturous handwork of their retreating swords and spears. She and her sisters had buried their victims, praying that their souls might still find entry to Hades' realm – and peace.

If she could but think on those faces, those beaten and murdered by these men, then she might find some satisfaction in this task.

The men talked amongst themselves, laughing and jesting as comrades often do. To look upon them, as she did now, she would never have suspected them of such treachery. They were men, no different in appearance than those who visited the temple in Athens or Galenus' house.

Was it possible that the men she knew, men she loved, could be capable of such heinous acts?

Images of Ektor's young face, Galenus' fiery temperament, and Ariston rose unbidden. Could their hands have struck down women and children under the guise of war? Violated them with such ruthless abandon?

The serpents writhed, pulling upon her head wrap with deliberate intent. They could hear the men. She knew it by their rhythmic motions – and their absolute silence.

The Persians' words rose and fell. She understood none of

them, though they seemed at ease and jovial.

Little did they know that death had found them.

She pulled the wrap from her head, freeing the creatures with one sure movement. It slipped from her hands, falling to the sand with no sound. Her feet crept forward as the red haze descended over her eyes. The serpents had taken over and led her nimbly, eagerly, towards their prey.

As she made her way into the light of their campfires, the men began to react. One stood suddenly, his face a mask of horror. But he turned, crackling to a brittle shell before the other men had time to react.

A shout went up, and one man threw a spear. It sailed past her, cleaving a serpent from her head and igniting a fire in her temple. The man was caught that way, his hand aloft as he'd released his missile.

There were more than she'd thought, too many to count. The snakes turned a handful quickly, turning five more before the pain in her head, her wound, forced her to withdraw into the shadows.

She fell, praying the soldiers would follow her and end this chore for her. As she lay on her back, the serpents moved about her head and neck. Blood, hot and thick, flowed down her temple, marking the loss of her companion.

She felt no sorrow at the loss, only pain and frustration that she had not completed her task. She must, in order to gain Hera's protection for the children.

She sat up, watching the men as they gaped at their stone comrades. Some were fearful, speaking in hushed tones. One began to chant, falling to his knees. She rested on one elbow, willing the pain to recede and her strength return.

Even her companions were distracted from their prey. They seemed to recoil, twining into themselves – grieving over the loss of one of their own.

She waited until the throb in her head was bearable before venturing back onto the beach. She'd made Hera a bargain and she would see it through. She had not finished with these men, not yet.

When the beach was quiet, she walked amongst them. Contorted faces, defensive arms, wide eyes and pleading mouths fell still and silent. She touched one, flinching against the smooth hardness of the statue. How cold they were, how empty...

She had done this.

There was no time to grieve for them or for her. Hera had sent a boat. It would carry her to Crete – far from Athens and Ariston.

Peace was hers now. She would gladly go, gladly serve, knowing the children were safe – with Ariston.

"Is Polydectes such a tyrant?" Ares scoffed.

Poseidon knew the name, but cared little. Then he heard Aphrodite mutter, "It has nothing to do with Polydectes. This is about Perseus."

Perseus? The boy was another of Zeus' bastards.

Poseidon glanced at his brother. Why would Zeus risk angering Hera, his wife, by speaking of his bastard at council? There had been peace between them for some time now. Long enough for his brother to forget the wrath of his jealous wife? Surely not.

"We are speaking of Polydectes, sweet Aphrodite," he answered.

She turned to him, a knowing smile on her perfect face as she whispered, "Are we? We shall see."

Zeus was speaking loudly. "... shown troubling leadership. He is demanding every man in Seriphos give him a tribute, a horse."

Poseidon laughed. "Every man? He demands a steep tribute, this king. What warrants such an extravagance?"

"Yes, husband, what is his purpose?" Hera's eyes narrowed.

"Polydectes? Have we not discussed him before?" Demeter asked. "Is he not the same king who denied me tribute at Harvest?"

"He is," Zeus nodded, relaxing ever so slightly – or so it seemed to Poseidon.

"The same king who misused sweet Chara. A beast of a man," Aphrodite said.

Poseidon watched his brother closely, curious.

"He has long since forgotten his offerings to us," Apollo said. "He has claimed that Seriphos suffers poor harvests and famine."

"He would have better harvests if he remembered to honor the Harvest," Demeter affirmed.

"He claims Seriphos is unable to offer tribute?" Athena stared at Zeus in surprise. "But demands his people offer him horses?"

"Why have we done nothing to punish this man, then?" Ares asked.

"Why indeed?" Hera agreed.

Poseidon enjoyed watching his brother at work. Truly, Zeus was a master at such games. Whatever his intent this time, his brother was taking pains to ensure Olympus would rally behind him.

"There was no one fit to take his place, wife," Zeus' words were layered, spoken with care.

Hera's lips pursed, but she said nothing.

"What does he want? Why is Polydectes calling for such tributes?" Hermes asked, his young face inquisitive as he searched the faces of his fellow Gods.

"He's offered marriage to Hippodameia," Zeus continued.

"He would use the vows of marriage to gain his fortune?" Hera asked.

"Is that not why mortals marry?" Ares argued.

"It is," Hermes agreed.

"But not at the cost of their kingdom," Athena said. "Seriphos' people cannot manage such tributes without leading to their ruination. He is a fool."

Poseidon had heard his brother's answer and knew there was more to it. "You said there was no one to take his place, to rule Seriphos. There is now?" Poseidon asked.

"Mayhap Apollo has found one," Zeus suggested softly.

Poseidon's gaze narrowed, noting Zeus's posture. *He can scarce contain his excitement.*

Apollo nodded. "While the king has been quick to silence those who would question his demands, one has dared to speak out against Polydectes. He has great courage, a certain charm that the people admire. His name is Perseus."

Aphrodite turned to Poseidon, a brilliant smile upon her triumphant face. He covered his mouth, catching his laughter quickly.

"Perseus?" Hera asked without rancor.

So Hera did not know who this Perseus was. She would have been quick to react if she had. It was apparent that Zeus had no intention of telling her Perseus was his son. Not just yet, anyway.

Poseidon bit back a grin, catching Aphrodite's gaze once more. She, too, was waiting expectantly.

"Perseus told Polydectes it would be smarter to expect Medusa's head than a horse as he was better able to take her head than find a horse. He is without property, adopted son of Dyktes, a simple fisherman." Apollo finished, clearly amused.

Poseidon shook his head. The boy must be Zeus' son, to have such rash overconfidence.

"What was Polydectes response to Perseus impudence?" Ares asked, greatly amused.

"Polydectes accepted his offer." Zeus said.

Silence fell upon the Council Chamber.

Poseidon froze. No...this was not what had been decided.

Would Hera intercede again? Mayhap Aphrodite would champion Medusa's plight, as she was greatly fascinated with the husband, Ariston. That she'd turned herself into an old man to gauge the man's devotion boggled Poseidon. What had it accomplished? Nothing save more dissatisfaction with the cretin she was sadly wed to. He supposed he might seek out other husbands if saddled with one as dreadful and morose as hers.

As the silence held, his stomach clenched.

"What of the promise you gave Medusa?" Poseidon asked Hera.

Would no one honor their word to this woman? His eyes traveled about the chamber and knew none would defend Medusa. Why did it trouble him?

"The children will be kept safe," Hera answered. "Medusa has made peace with her life. She has some happiness knowing her man lives."

"Tis past time for Polydectes to meet Hades' judges," Apollo said.

"What of her test? Did she not do everything you asked of her? Has she not proven herself loyal to us all still?" Poseidon's voice was flat, his anger barely under check.

Would they all forget her now?

"She has proven useful, yes. But I am not so sentimental as you think. She cannot be spared if it means others, all of Seriphos, will suffer under tyranny, Poseidon." Hera shook her head.

"It is a great sadness..." Aphrodite said, her lovely face somber.

"Her husband?" Poseidon asked.

"Brother," Zeus smiled his most lascivious smile. "He is a man, after all. He will find solace soon enough."

"She wants death, she said as much to Hera," Athena said. "And with her death comes freedom to those she's turned."

Ares snorted, amused. "The Persians broke some, the Gorgons more still. I fear Medusa's death will release no one as the Gorgons have sent them on to Hades' realm. Once their statue is broken, they cannot be freed?" he asked. When Athena nodded, he continued, "Oh, to have an army made up of the likes of them. What a fearsome regiment they would lead."

"We must assist Perseus, I think," Hera mused. "Athena, Hermes, you must help this young man defeat Medusa. He must put this Polydectes in his place."

Poseidon sat back, unsettled by the twinge of guilt that twisted his gut.

"You are displeased?" Aphrodite asked, her huge blue eyes warm upon him.

"What, me? Why would I care what happens to the girl and her besotted husband?"

"And yet you do, I think." Aphrodite smiled slightly. "Is this not a sort of justice for her? For them both? There is some sort of freedom in death."

Poseidon shook his head, his mocking words meant for her ears alone. "This has naught to do with justice. Zeus seeks to gain Hera's favor for his bastard. A quest, a noble quest to be sure, might aid my brother in this."

Aphrodite's eyes never wavered. "Do you care for her?"

Poseidon swallowed, considering his words. He had no answer.

"I know too well the sting of unrequited love." Aphrodite smiled brightly. "There is little help for it. Medusa will fall, it is Zeus' will. You need distraction, I think… Under this night's full moon, I will send one of my eager Nereids to you. Find some solace in her arms; your heart will heal in time." The Goddess studied him at length, her glistening blue eyes and plump red lips tempting him greatly. "I must admit, Poseidon, finding you've a heart at all is a pleasing surprise to me."

"Is it?" His chest tightened as his lust rose. "If this nymph does not please me, I may yet visit with you to see what other pleasures you might bestow upon me."

He smiled at the instant flush of her skin, the subtle tremor of her chest as she drew in breath. He had no doubt that he would visit her very soon, but he would enjoy this Nereid first.

In the time Ariston had spent searching, Athens had rallied. Gone were the smoldering remains, harried citizens and falling temple on the Acropolis. Its walls had yet to be completed, more than half of its homes still needed repairs, yet its people seemed focused, full of hope and determination.

The docks were no exception. Finding a ship for Stheno and Euryale had been an easy task. And they were eager to return to their parents, to share the news of Medusa and grieve together.

"Listen to Xenia," Stheno said to Spiridion, her tone soft and coaxing.

"In the years Medusa lived with her, the lady showed her only love," Euryale continued. "Make her love you, boy, and little Kore."

"She will miss you." The tell-tale quiver in Spiridion's voice was unmistakable. "Kore, I mean. She will miss you."

"She'd better," Euryale teased.

"But you will be too busy in your new life, child, to linger on memories best forgotten," Stheno chided. "Let all that has happened fade. Your life, a good one to be sure, begins again this day."

Ariston listened quietly, waiting to help them from the wagon he'd found on their way. One horse amongst five people did little good. And since most of the villages were deserted or destroyed, taking their horses was hardly stealing. His actions saved them from starving in their untended pastures and stalls. Finding the wagon had been a greater blessing still.

Euryale took his hand, stepping down from the wagon with care. "If any harm comes to the boy or the babe, I will find Xenia and—"

"No harm will come upon them," Ariston assured her. "They will have a home, food, and love. What more does a child need?"

"I know your heart is heavy at leaving them, sister, but it is the only way," Stheno said as she joined Euryale on the dock.

"Shall we stay and wave you off?" Spiridion asked from the wagon.

Euryale shook her head quickly. "No."

"On your way, boy. Serve Xenia well, serve the Gods," Stheno added.

Ariston studied them, their long dark veils covering their faces. "I thank you for the care you gave Medusa. I would repay you..."

Stheno moved forward. "She was our sister, Ariston. And we loved her too."

Euryale said nothing.

Ariston nodded, then climbed into the wagon. He said nothing more as he urged the wagon forward.

Spiridion climbed up onto the seat beside him, leaving the sleeping baby carefully arranged upon mats in the wagon bed.

"Will they like us, Ariston?" Spiridion asked.

"I know little of Xenia, except what my lady told me." He took a deep breath. "Lady Xenia chose to love her as a daughter, even though she was a slave. Xenia's heart, I think, will welcome you and Kore. Her husband was lost during the invasion. I imagine she is lonely."

"Stheno told me," Spiridion said.

Ariston nodded, feeling sympathy for the woman.

"She must miss him. As you miss Medusa." The boy's words were soft. "I loved your wife, too, Ariston. She was so beautiful, even with the scars. But she was so sad. Was she missing you?"

Ariston could think of nothing to say. That she'd been sad, that her injuries had scarred her, and yet this boy had offered her love when she needed it most – he could say nothing. He smiled at the boy, thankful he'd found her.

"I think Euryale will miss Kore the most," the boy continued.

"Why is that?"

"Kore would cry," Spiridion explained. "And since Medusa could not hold her, she begged Euryale to comfort her. Medusa pleaded and wept until Euryale picked Kore up. As soon as Euryale held Kore, she stopped crying. Kore made Euryale forget to be fearsome." He paused. "I think Medusa knew that and wanted her sister to have joy."

"She was a wise and loving lady." Ariston felt the lump in his throat.

"She is...was." Spiridion stuttered, then mumbled, "She was."

They fell into silence as they navigated the newly packed streets. Some stopped and watched with interest, others waved or nodded in general greeting.

He felt trapped, the rising walls of the houses sealing him inside. He missed the open roads and blooming hillsides. He missed the open air and the view of the sea, its blue-green depths sparkling in the sun.

He missed a great deal.

At the gates to Xenia's home, Ariston left the wagon and horses with Xenia's servant and led Spiridion through the gates. The boy hefted his sleeping sister with ease, refusing to relinquish her in this time of uncertainty.

Ariston watched him, admiring the boy silently.

"Ariston, you are most welcome," Elpis greeted him with a warm smile.

"How fares the Lady Xenia?" Ariston asked.

"Recovered." Elpis stood aside. "And happy, I think. She has had quite a time making plans for the children's arrival. No sooner had Thea delivered your note than she set to work on making room for them."

Ariston was pleased that Xenia was improved. He glanced at the boy, who was staring wide-eyed about the courtyard. Ariston followed the boy's gaze.

While in the heart of Athens proper, the home and gardens were shielded from the city's gaze by the tall courtyard walls. Time had fractured the walls plaster, and blooms of violet and honeysuckle colored the air and filled it with their sweet scents.

It was a different kind of home than the one this boy had known in the hills. But it would be a good home, one that would never want.

"These are the children you sent word of?" Elpis smiled down at them. "What a handsome boy you are."

Spiridion stared at her, shifting his sleeping sister with ease.

"Spiridion, this is Elpis – Medusa's dearest friend," Ariston said, hoping to comfort the child. Though he'd not known Spiridion long, he knew the boy must be overwhelmed with the changes taking place.

So much heartache for one so young, Ariston thought. To lose his parents to the Persians was enough. He had no knowledge if the boy had been present when the attack happened. He prayed the child had not been.

But then the boy had found solace with the Gorgons and Medusa. Stheno had told Ariston the whole, how Medusa had played and teased and smiled at last, when she'd found this boy and his baby sister. Losing Medusa to fever had upset the boy so he refused to speak of it.

And then, the Gorgons had bid farewell to them at the docks.

"You are not alone here, Spiridion. And you will grow, strong and tall, within these

Walls," Ariston attempted to comfort the child.

"You must be very brave," Elpis said. "My husband is eager to meet the boy who can care for an infant and befriend Gorgons."

"Euryale and Stheno were good to me, mistress. They showed nothing but kindness to me and my sister. I shall miss them, even if they weren't as lovely to look upon as you ...or Medusa." Spiridion spoke quickly.

"I've never seen a maid as lovely as my mistress," Elpis agreed.

She was beauty. Ariston nodded.

Her laughing eyes and joyful laugh warmed his dreams and made waking the nightmare. Each day the weight of his loss grew heavier.

In the weeks they'd traveled back to Athens, hearing her name had become no easier. Speaking of her...

"Handsome or not, I thank the Gorgons for keeping you safe." Elpis knelt before him. "This is little Kore? She is sweet."

Spiridion looked at his sleeping sister. "She is asleep now. You may find her otherwise when she wakes."

Ariston smiled, ruffling the boy's hair with affection before looking at Elpis. "And here is your fine husband, or so I was told at the docks? Happy news indeed, Ektor. Spiridion, this is Ektor. He will foster you, teach you how to be a capable Greek and Athenian – if you wish it?"

Ektor clasped arms with Ariston, his youthful face no less open and pleasing than before the wars.

Ariston wondered at it. Was it only his world that had changed so greatly, while all else seemed to be as it should?

"I will be a healer," Spiridion said, "like Medusa."

Elpis took his hand, casting a questioning glance at Ariston. "Would you? It would seem you are quite capable at caring for others."

Ariston and Ektor watched Elpis lead the children into the house, her sweet voice praising and encouraging as they went.

"You married well." Ariston smiled at Ektor.

Ektor nodded. "Xenia has been most generous to us. If she had not asked us to stay with her, I'd have nothing to offer Elpis' father. As it is, this home, this property, will be mine – Xenia declares it will be so."

"She is a compassionate woman," Ariston said.

"Will you stay with us, Ariston?" Ektor implored. "Athens is in need of leaders. People follow you."

Ariston could not meet the younger man's eyes. "I'm in no mind for leading. But I would rest awhile, if you will have me?"

He had delivered the children.

He had no purpose now.

"You are always welcome," Ektor nodded, though Ariston saw the concern that crossed his young friend's face.

Chapter Fifteen

The boat bobbed at the end of the dock, rising and falling with the gentle rhythm of the waves beneath. The water was darker here, at the edge of Greece and its borders, but it beckoned to Medusa all the same. And it gave her, in some small way, pleasure.

She sat on the dock, dangling her feet in the warmth of the water. She closed her eyes and let her mind wander, her memories filling her. Somehow her memories no longer pained her, knowing he lived. With endless days before her, she sought him out more and more – each memory revisited aplenty.

She remembered the day he'd come to Galenus' house fresh from the training field, his shirt darkened with sweat and his arm bleeding from a wound he'd sustained. Why he'd been sent to them so quickly, where her old guard had gone, were mysteries she'd never lingered on.

She'd stood, covered in her veils, beside her scowling uncle as Galenus read the note.

"Well, soldier," Galenus had sounded most aggrieved, "you've been ordered to reside here, under my basileus, by Athena's order. You are to serve as the priestess' guard, and accompany her to and from the temple daily."

"Yes, sir," he'd said, barely glancing her way.

But his tone had caught her attention. He was not pleased to be there, nor any more pleased by his assignment than her uncle. And for some reason, she'd found his barely repressed irritation heartbreaking – and comforting. She knew what it was to chafe against one's lot in life, and she ached for him.

She had known even then, in some small way, this man would change her.

She sighed, the salty air burning her throat and dragging her from her thoughts. The sea view that greeted her offered little to appreciate.

A crumbling temple, the only remains of the island that lay mostly below the water's surface, was her home. It was a small island, set far off the northern coast of Crete, beyond the range of travelers. Only those lost would find this place.

Or those sent by the Gods.

There had been several. Aloeus of Thrace, Phocus of Aegina, Molus and Tityus of Delphi, and more – more than twenty slate grey statues littered the mouth of her cave. Hera had seen fit to send her a guard. The creature, said to be the son of Cerberus, Hades' hound, had arrived with her sisters. A gift from Hera, they told her.

He had no fondness for her, and kept to himself. But his howl set the hair along her arms on end, for he only bayed when someone approached. His call meant her companions had work to do.

Heavy footfalls set the ancient dock swaying. "Will you eat?" Stheno asked.

Medusa glanced up at her. "You still ask?"

"I will continue to, though I know your answer. You're as frail as a wraith, almost a shade of yourself." Stheno sat heavily beside her.

"Do not trouble yourself over me," Medusa murmured.

"I will," Stheno argued.

"What of father?" Medusa asked. They had returned only this morning, after traveling to their father to share her fate.

"He wishes you would come home." Stheno shrugged. "I told him your bargain, but he cared little for it."

Medusa stared out over the darkening waters. "He cares little for bargains that give nothing to him." She sighed. "Why would he have me home now? I am of no use to him as I am?"

"That I cannot answer, sister." Stheno bit into an apple, chewing heartily.

Medusa glanced up as her other sister joined them on the dock.

"Did you tell her the news?" Euryale asked.

Stheno glared at Euryale, "Not as yet."

"What news?" Medusa asked.

"Spiridion has learned to throw the discus." Euryale smiled.

"He was seen at the games," Stheno explained. "He and Kore grow strong and healthy. Elpis' marriage to Ektor blooms as well, for I was told she is with child."

"And Xenia?" Medusa asked. Memories of her beloved aunt, her terrified face, woke her nights.

"She dotes on Kore and preens over Spiridion," Euryale sighed.

"You were right to have Ariston take them to her," Stheno agreed.

His name...

"Will you not ask about him?" Euryale asked softly.

She was silent, desperately trying to staunch the throbbing pain she felt. "He is well?"

"He is. He stays in Athens, helping them assemble a new council," Stheno said.

Medusa nodded, pushing herself to her feet. She said nothing as she left the dock. The sand stuck to the wet soles of her feet as she ventured down to the water's edge. Mercifully her sisters did not follow.

She'd tried to assure them that she was well, that they should go home without her. But they refused.

"Worrying over you has become Stheno's favorite past time," Euryale had teased. "Would you deprive her of one of her pleasures? She has so few."

And Medusa had let it be.

Silently she knew their presence was all that kept her from desperate despair or madness. They served as a balm to her troubles, but she couldn't bring herself to tell them so. If they decided to leave, she would not stop them.

Sometimes, though, she wished they would leave.

It was not enough to prod her about eating or force her out of the temple at sunset, Euryale had found some poor soul she'd terrified into keeping up with Spiridion and Kore. And, somehow, there was always news of Ariston too.

It hurt to hear of him, but it was worse not to. He was a good man, strong and able, tender and loyal. She could not imagine what he'd suffered, what he'd endured, to earn his freedom from Hades.

Each night she prayed he would find happiness and love again. She would not have him suffer an empty, lonely life.

And then she cried until her tears were spent.

The full moon was high overhead, pale and round. It seemed to be within Ariston's reach, if he had any desire to try to capture it.

He didn't.

His eyes burned, but he would not succumb to sleep. Not yet. When he slept, she was waiting, her very presence bidding him stay. Waking was torture, too much to bear willingly. How he longed to stay with her...

So he held himself rigid, carrying out the tasks set before him each day.

He could find no satisfaction in Athens, though the new council had asked him to stay. He'd given all he could. He needed to return to Rhodes. Mayhap his home, his family, could soothe him.

He closed his eyes, leaning against the base of the tree. The crackling of the fire, the rustle of the wind in the trees, lulled him into an uneasy doze.

Some nights he longed for her fiercely.

His fingers clasped the owl pendant he wore about his neck. It was all that was left, all that was real. He'd found his gift, draped with care atop her grave. Thea must have left it for him, before leaving him.

He was alone now, with nothing but his memories.

He stood, walking without purpose.

Flashes of her, her scent, the feel of her under his fingertips, pulled upon his patience until he began to run. His feet fell in an even, rapid rhythm. He ran, faster and faster, until he came to a break in the trees.

A small cove greeted him, the silver-tipped waters rolling under the night sky.

He moved towards the inky waves, scooping handfuls of its bracing saltiness over his face. He shivered before he rubbed his face with raw impatience.

He heard a sound to his right, a slight breathy giggle, and turned to find its source. In the shadows was a woman, a nymph, mayhap, for she glowed faintly in the moonlight. She was unaware of him, distracted by her companion. Her companion, his broad back white and well formed, faced away from him.

He turned, eager to leave this couple, when the nymph ran towards him, laughing.

Seeing him, she froze. Her amusement shifted swiftly, fading to irritation.

The man drew up behind her, unaware of Ariston's presence – or uncaring. One great hand reached about her, cupping one of her exposed breasts.

"No more games," the man's voice rolled over Ariston. "Come now."

That voice... That voice haunted his dreams.

This man had said "I will have you," to his lady.

This man had tormented and used his wife.

He knew this voice – for it haunted his dreams and chased his lady into the mist. His blood began to throb, growing hotter and hotter until it seemed aflame.

"I grow tired of playing." The cajoling tones unleashed Ariston's anger.

"He knows a great deal of games, lady," Ariston said, the words helping to tamp down his rage. "But I caution you against this choice in bedfellows." The fury that stole over him was powerful. He'd been caught in the throes of battle many times. Had he hated his enemy? He thought so. He'd been willing enough to take their lives. But this was nothing like that.

Hate did not encompass the violence that tightened every muscle of his body. He wanted blood, and suffering. He wanted death and revenge.

His mouth flooded with bile as Poseidon's eyes met his.

Poseidon's pale blue eyes regarded him with disinterest, raking him insolently as his hand slipped slowly from the nymph.

"Be careful, soldier," Poseidon warned. "You'd be wise to leave this place."

Ariston smiled, the harsh twist releasing some of his wrath. "Then I shall stay."

The nymph, forgotten, cast a wary glance between the two before dashing into the woods.

"You cost me my prey." Poseidon's eyes sparkled, more amused than offended. "But you've made me curious. What is it you want?" He walked into the water, dousing his long dark locks with water. He sighed, turning back to Ariston. "Or do you know?"

"Your death."

"You cannot kill a God," Poseidon laughed. "You do know who I am?"

"I do," Ariston bit out. "You are the great Poseidon. Your death is the only thing I want. But since I cannot kill you, I will have to be satisfied with your suffering."Ariston pulled his xiphos from his belt, savoring the weight of the blade's hilt in his hand. His blood continued to roar within him, tensing his body and heightening his senses. He noticed the slight quiver of Poseidon's nostrils, the tightening of the God's mouth, and then, in a flicker of understanding, the God's eyes narrowed.

Poseidon's pale gaze fixed upon her necklace, the wooden owl resting against the Ariston's chest.

Poseidon's voice was low and harsh. "You are her husband?"

Ariston felt the laugh, one he'd hope would prove his virility, stick in his throat. He swallowed. "I am Medusa's husband, yes."

Poseidon eyed the sword. "You seek revenge?"

"What else can you give me?" Ariston taunted.

Poseidon said nothing.

Ariston charged, embracing the fire in his chest.

A wall of water rose high above him, dropping down upon him and forcing the air from his lungs as it slammed him into the beach.

"Peace," Poseidon said.

Ariston stood, wiping the water from his eyes. "I have none. I shall give none." He ran at Poseidon again, so close he was almost upon him. He swung his sword, stretching to ensure the blade would strike true.

But the water rose up beneath his feet and lifted him, once again throwing him back to the sandy beach. His sword fell from his grip, but he was too enraged to notice.

"You accomplish nothing," Poseidon said, shaking his head.

Ariston glared at him, breathing heavily. The water was

Poseidon's domain, it was a futile strategy. On land, he might manage one cut… If he could lure him from the water, bait him.

"You fight like a God," Ariston laughed, "hiding behind your tricks and deceit. Are you too weak to fight as a man? Or too afraid?"

Poseidon's mouth formed a small smile. "Afraid? Of you?" He turned to go, the water rippling in his wake.

"So it would seem," Ariston retorted.

Poseidon turned back to him with narrowed eyes.

Ariston sneered back, fighting the urge to rush forth, to storm into the water once more.

The water shifted, carrying Poseidon quickly to the sand before Ariston. "I will fight you, then, Ariston of Rhodes."

Ariston nodded, clenching his hands.

"But this fight cannot give you what you seek. Tell me, do you rage against me for using your wife? Or because she hides from you, even knowing you search for her?" Poseidon paused, watching his face closely.

"She is dead…"

"So say the Gorgons. Mayhap she wants nothing of you now."

Ariston's arm whipped forward, meeting the cold flesh of Poseidon's stomach with uninhibited fury. He savored the warm burn of his knuckles, sending his other fist into his Poseidon's side with a roar.

He drew his arm back and released his fist, crazed with bloodlust. He struck Poseidon's haughty chin squarely, a gratifying smack filling the air.

Poseidon reacted then, throwing his elbow into Ariston's chest and robbing him of breath.

Ariston threw his fist forward, hitting the God in the neck and swiping his leg. Poseidon fell onto the sand, lying at his feet.

He offered his hand to Poseidon. "I am not so easily satisfied."

Poseidon stared at his hand, then stood.

Ariston stooped and rammed into Poseidon, his shoulder smashing into Poseidon's stomach and lifting him before letting him fall to the sand again.

Poseidon stood once more, his face no longer distant and haughty.

Ariston laughed. "Come at me then."

And he did, forcing Ariston back against one of the large boulders that dotted the beach. His hands closed about Ariston's throat, his intent obvious. Still Ariston managed to break free, knocking the God off guard by kneeing him forcefully in the groin.

Poseidon crumpled on the beach, kneeling as he fought to regain his breath.

Ariston stood over him, wanting this over.

"Is my suffering akin to yours? When you learned...that I had her. Were you crippled so?" Poseidon's words were muttered in choking breaths.

"Your suffering cannot be compared to mine," Ariston assured him. "I would put an end to it for you."

Poseidon rose quickly, Ariston's sword clasped in his hand. "No, Ariston, I think not." He lifted the blade, pressing it against Ariston's neck.

Ariston smiled again, lifting his chin and exposing his neck. Was it wrong that he wanted this?

Poseidon's brow rose. "You doubt my intent? You have no fear of death?"

"None." He meant it. "Kill me." *End my pain.*

Poseidon's face twisted. "You seek death?"

"It is better than what waits for me now." He cursed himself, cursed his words and the desperation that filled them.

"For a woman? All for a woman?" Poseidon tossed the sword aside. "You are no man to let a woman rule you so. No woman alive is worth..."

"But she is not alive. She is dead!" Ariston's words ripped from him with such anguish that even he was surprised.

Poseidon shook his head wearily. "If you are so eager for death, let me help you on your way. Your lady wife lives, hiding amongst the caves off Crete."

Ariston froze, stunned by Poseidon's statement, but Poseidon only watched him.

"You lie," he raged, moving to strike Poseidon again, but the God grabbed his fist.

"I have nothing to gain, Ariston of Rhodes. I am done with... this. I would help you on your way, if this is truly what you want?"

Ariston stared at him, ripping his fist from Poseidon's grip.

"I warn you, Perseus of Seriphos has been sent to kill her," Poseidon added.

"Why?" Why would she be sentenced to death?

"To end the curse. With her death, those cast in stone are free."

Ariston was shaking his head. "The Gorgons' curse?"

"It is Medusa's curse."

"Medusa?" Ariston could hardly speak the words, his mind was so addled. "It matters not, I will find her."

Poseidon fell silent, his pale eyes traveling over the sea before he said, "If you go, you will find her. And no good will come of it." He paused, turning back to Ariston with something akin to sympathy on his face. "Hear me, soldier. She will not thank you for going after her. And you will not live through the reunion."

Ariston pushed himself away from the boulder, his ire forgotten. "I would rather face death at her side tomorrow than live without her."

Poseidon's look of surprise almost made Ariston pity him. He was immortal, ruler of the sea, but he knew nothing of love.

Ariston picked up the sword and set off. He had a long journey ahead of him. But this time he knew where was going and what he would find.

Poseidon slammed his cup onto the table. No wine eased his irritation.

If he'd killed the man would he feel better?

His dinner companions quieted somewhat, casting curious glances and whispers his way. Athena seemed most pleased with his foul mood.

He smiled brightly at her, her instant scowl lightening his spirits. But not enough.

"You're vexed?" Ares regarded him over the rim of his goblet.

Poseidon sighed, leaning against the back of his chair with practiced insolence. He shrugged but said nothing.

Aphrodite watched him too, he knew. And he was aware of her, the sway of her hips, as she made her way towards them. His loins tightened instantly.

"You found no pleasure with Sappho?" Aphrodite's voice

rippled over him.

He stared at her, not bothering to disguise his hunger for her. "I did not."

Ares chuckled. "From the gash on your brow and the bruise on your throat, I'd like to meet this Sappho."

"No Nereid would behave such a way." Aphrodite leaned forward, inspecting Poseidon's face with concern. "Who dared to cross swords with you?"

Ares snorted. "Poseidon has no use for a sword. I've never seen one in your hand." Ares shook his head. "These wounds are from fists, I think. I've given enough in my time."

Aphrodite's luminous eyes turned on Ares. "Your boasts of brutality are tiresome."

Ares' nostrils flared as he rose from his seat. He towered over Aphrodite, his body a solid wall of muscle. "I will bore you no longer."

Poseidon watched the hulking God of War storm from the dining chamber. "You've upset Ares, my dear. Is that a wise move?"

Aphrodite sighed, her eyes searching his. "You mistake me, Poseidon. I am the Goddess of Love, not wisdom." Her cheeks flushed and her lips parted beneath the heat of his gaze.

His eyes lingered on those lips, eager to sample them, before they strayed to the swell of her breasts. Her nipples grew taut, hardening beneath the fabric and issuing him an invitation he would not ignore.

He stood, the blood pulsing hotly in his ears. "Walk with me, then. I have matters to discuss which might interest you."

He led her to the gardens. Need raged, engulfing him as he reached for her.

The silken rush of her lips against his made him moan. He'd been too long without a woman.

She wrapped her arms about him, her lips parting beneath his. She seemed just as desperate, just as hungry.

His hands gripped her hips, lifting her as he bore her back against a column. She groaned, pushing his chiton out of the way to grasp his bare buttocks. He was eager to accommodate her, thrusting her skirts above her hips before settling himself between her legs.

Her hands tangled in his hair and her legs wrapped tightly about him as he drove into her. Again and again he filled her, exulting in the sounds of pleasure she made as he did so. It took no time for him to find his release, moaning against her neck before sagging limply against her.

She pushed him away from her, her soft face yet flushed. "And that is why you are the God of the Sea, Poseidon, selfish and fleeting. You've no gift for pleasing a woman."

Poseidon cupped her cheek. "And yet, I am greatly pleased."

She slapped his hand away, straightening her tunic with trembling hands and smoothing her tresses. "While I am left wanting. I will not keep you from…your schemes."

Poseidon watched her retreating figure, his mood restored. He called out, teasing her. "What? Will your husband not assist you in the matter?"

She glanced back, making him flinch beneath the pain he saw. "He would more eagerly assist you, Poseidon. As well you know." She swept from the gardens.

Poseidon sat on a nearby bench, shaking his head.

He would never love, he vowed. It brought too fleeting a pleasure for too many trials. He'd be wise to remember his cock was just as satisfied by a Goddess, a nymph, or a mortal maid. There was no purpose in sharing any more than that with any woman.

Ariston blinked against the rain. He wiped his eyes, the sting of the ocean water cleansed by that of the rain.

The island, a patch of solid black atop the storm-tossed sea, was small and exposed. No one could approach it without being seen long before they reached land. He'd known he could not risk such a journey by day.

As strong a swimmer as he was, he grew weary. He'd had to anchor his ship far out at sea, along the reef. The rest he would have to do on his own. And while the storm only aided in providing him cover, it churned the waters and made his journey a greater challenge yet.

But he had cause to keep going.

She was here.

He'd learned a great deal about the happenings of this island.

"Three Gorgons live on that rock." The old man had leaned

forward, whispering through sun-baked lips and almost toothless gums. "I've seen only two of them, but I know of the third, Medusa. It's her magic that takes me to the island. It's her curse that punishes those who've broken the law."

Ariston had sipped his wine with care, the tightening of his hand about the cup the only evidence of his discomfort. "Who sends these men to be punished?"

"The Gods." The man peered about the room before he continued. His whisper was so soft that Ariston leaned closer. "I take them to the island, and my son lives in Asphodel instead of Tartarus." The old man shook his head. "It is a bargain of sorts."

Another bargain offered by the Gods.

"And these witches," his voice was harsh. "Why do they do this?"

The old man waited for Ariston to refill his cup before he shrugged and continued, "I've heard stories. Some say the witches want immortality. Others say they have some of Hades' gold in the temple, protecting it." The old man shrugged again, finishing off his drink once more. "Mayhap they enjoy the suffering of others? No one speaks of them too loudly, for fear of bringing the curse to shore."

Ariston took another sip of his wine. "But no man named Perseus has traveled through these parts?"

"Perseus of Seriphos?" The old man smiled. "Not yet. But we know of his boast, we know he will come for Medusa's head. And all know the Gods favor him. Maybe I will be the one to take him to her? What an honor that would be."

Ariston had left quickly, pleased he was not too late. It had taken time to make his journey, time to find her refuge, and time to track this fisherman – the only man who'd ever visited the Gorgons' island.

He feared he had little time to reach her.

He'd purchased a small fishing boat and set sail in the direction the old man had mentioned. It took him the better part of the day, and then only the faintest break in the horizon showed Ariston where the island was.

He'd circled, remaining too far to be seen clearly, and waited until darkness fell. Now he swam in the rolling sea, battered by a thundering storm.

When his feet at last touched the sand, he crawled onto the beach and lay still beneath the storm. He did not think on the rain or thunder or lightening. He did not care that his limbs shook with fatigue or his heart raced with anticipation...

"It is Medusa's curse," Poseidon had said.

What had happened to her? Why would any magical being, Olympian or no, cast such a curse?

He rubbed the water from his eyes. He did not know what waited for him, what had happened to his love. But he did not fear her or her curse. How could he?

A flash of memory rose, warming him.

"Like this?" she'd called to him as she'd hefted the fishing net.

Her smile had pleased him so.

She was too tender, her heart gentle. Whatever had happened, he knew she had suffered dearly. He would do whatever he could to end her suffering.

But first he would hold her. How he ached for the feel of her arms about him – her silken hair slipping between his fingers.

Chapter Sixteen

She lay, lost in her dreams.

She dreamed she was on their beach, with the sun warm on her face and the sand beneath her bare skin. She could feel his large hand enclosing her ankle. His touch surrounded her, causing her to shiver. How she missed his warmth. His hand lifted, though he pressed a kiss to her knee. She could hear him shifting to lie beside her.

She turned slightly, pressing her face into his shoulder with a sigh.

He spoke, "My lady. How I love you so."

She felt her heart twist, for his words seemed to stir the air beside her ear.

His lips brushed her forehead, her cheek, her chin and her throat. His head dipped down to rest on her chest. "You sleep so deeply, love. But your heart beats so I will not fear. Only wake up to me now."

Medusa felt the tears in her eyes. What a wicked dream this was.

She could smell his scent, of sea water and fresh air, beneath her nostrils. His curls were soft and pliant, damp, beneath her grasping fingers.

Such sweet torture, that her lips could remember the feel of his lips on hers so well.

Maybe this dream, so painfully real, would finish her now. For she knew she couldn't bear to wake.

"Medusa," he whispered against her lips. "Wake up, love."

And, with a shuddering sigh, she did.

The floor beneath her was hard and cold. There was no sun, no distant sound of waves or gulls. She could not bear to open her eyes for fear he would fade away...

But his lips...his lips were against hers and his breath stirred her face as he sighed.

No...no...

"Speak not, Ariston," she begged softly.

There was silence.

It was a dream. He was not here.

Her eyes opened to the sweetest sight she had ever seen.

He lay at her side, smiling at her with unconcealed pleasure. "I will speak, my lady. For I have been too long without you and I would have you know how I have missed you."

He was no dream.

His curls, wet from the rain, clung to his forehead. His grey eyes regarded her, an ever constant warmth. His hands clutched her cheeks, his thumbs caressing her...

Her heart filled with love, such love.

"For I have missed you, wife."

The veil moved. She felt them, heard them, as they responded to his voice.

Her breath tore from her, but she bit back the sob. She had to hurry.

Tears poured from her eyes as she shook her head. She placed her hand to his mouth, covering it and whispering fiercely, "Peace, husband, I beg you, speak not. For I would have you leave this place, at once, of your free will..."

His lips pressed to her palm and he whispered, "I will not leave you. Not again."

They moved, stirring the veil. They were hissing, ever so softly, in her ears.

"If you love me, you will go now. I would have you live. Please. For once they wake, I cannot stop them..." She pulled her hands free and covered the veil, pinning it in place. They began to bite, viciously, but Medusa held them tightly. "I beg you..."

"I cannot." He spoke quickly, desperately. He searched the lines of her face, his joy and anguish tearing a whole in her heart. "I cannot."

His lips descended on hers swiftly, silencing her pleas and breaking her heart.

"I will not part with you again, love..." His lips grew so cold upon her.

No... She pressed her lips against his. They did not yield to her.

His hand was hard, rough, upon her cheek.

No.

"No." She could not breathe.

The curls she'd stroked only moments before were as solid as the slate floor beneath her. His grey eyes, closed in a kiss, would not open.

"No... No!" Her words were an angry cry, torn from her throat. "Ariston."

She clung to him, cupping his face with trembling hands. She kissed him, wrapping herself around him as if she might warm him with her touch. Ragged sobs ripped from her chest, yet she pressed herself closer to him, as close as she was able.

He lingered there, all around her.

The floor beneath her still held his heat. The air was scented, flooding her nostrils and constricting her throat as she choked to draw him in. "Ariston..." she sobbed, pressing her lips to his ear. "I love you, my love. I love you."

"Medusa?" Stheno called out as she ran into the temple.

"What has happened?" Euryale followed.

She pressed her cheek to his, nuzzling his ear as her tears flowed freely.

"Medusa?"

She would not look at them. She could not open her eyes. She could not look upon what she had done to him. "Leave me."

Euryale hand touched her ankle, seeming to steal his warmth with her very touch. She shook her sister's hand off, fitting against him so that the hard stone scraped against her skin.

"Leave me!" she cried. "Go!"

There was a moment's silence.

"What can we do?" Stheno asked.

Euryale's voice wavered, "Let us help you, sister, please."

"Kill me. Kill me," she pleaded, "so that he might be free."

Silence hung in the cave, broken only by the sound of weeping. Whether it was her or her sisters, she cared not.

She had turned him. She had done this. And she could not bear it.

A serpent moved, slithering across her cheek – towards Ariston.

It would not touch him. She would not let it touch him.

They will never touch him.

She reached up, grabbing the serpent with all of her strength. Never had she felt such rage, never had she felt hate. Yet it consumed her, empowering her with the strength she needed to tear the snake free from her head.

The pain was blinding, robbing her of breath and sapping the fury that drove her.

The serpents were on her then, biting and twisting and twining about her. She did not fight them, but fell back on the marble floor. They writhed, slipping and tightening about her neck. She prayed they would finish this.

But they grew slower, sluggish in their movements – becoming as weak as she was.

Her head, throbbing mercilessly, was too heavy to lift or move. And the pain...pain meant she still lived. The knowledge filled her with such anguish.

Her face felt hot and sticky, but she had no will to wipe the blood that flowed from her wound. Her hand still clutched the serpent, hanging limp and lifeless. From the weight and girth of it, it was a large serpent. She could not close her hand around the creature...surely it would leave a gaping wound – one that would bleed her heavily.

If she had the strength, she would pull them all from her... And ensure the end of this. She lifted her hand, reaching up slowly, but they were on her.

The serpents wrapped their bodies about her arm, pinning her down. A rain of fangs and venom showered the side of her face and arms. Yet, she made no move to protect herself. It didn't matter, not really.

She lay still.

"Medusa," Euryale was sobbing in earnest now. "Please stop."

"Let us tend your injury," Stheno cried, too.

"No," she whispered. "They would bite you...hurt you... I can take no more." She turned her head, away from them.

She opened her eyes.

He was beautiful.

Her tears and blood blurred his face, but she'd no strength to wipe them away. She drew in breath and raised her trembling hand. The effort was great, for there was none of her that did not hurt. But she reached for him, touching his cheek. "I can take no more."

Her feet had been so cold.

The bones in her ankle had been prominent, fragile. Clearly traceable beneath his seeking fingers.

"You are not dead, Ariston." Hades voice stirred him from his thoughts. The God sat in his chair, before a roaring fire. "But you are not alive either."

He cared little for Hades' words.

Gone was the sun-kissed gold he remembered, the soft lush curves he'd caressed. She was too thin, her curves replaced with sharp angles. Her skin was so pale it was almost translucent. But her pulse had throbbed steadily in her throat, giving him some sense of ease.

Hades cleared his throat. "I would have you stay in my home until this farce is finally over."

Ariston inclined his head, absently, his mind racing.

She was still his love. In those moments of waking, she had leaned into his touch and sighed in pleasure. Until she'd opened her eyes and discovered he was not a dream.

"If you love me, you will go now. I would have you live. Please. For once they wake, I cannot stop them..." she'd pleaded.

"Wine?" Hades offered, holding a goblet towards him.

Ariston stared at the cup, taking it when Hades pressed it into his hand. "Thank you."

He had been too long without her. He could not look away from her or hear the warning she'd tried repeatedly to give him. His eyes had feasted on her face, noting the long scar that ran across her forehead and the dozens of small punctures, bites of some sort, dotting her temples and jaw.

The blue of her eyes had not dimmed and the curve of her lips had been too great a temptation to resist. As his lips had found hers, her scent assailed him.

His fingers contracted about the goblet, cracking the stoneware. "She has suffered more than *any* should suffer," he ground out.

Hades' heavy-lidded eyes met his, though his face revealed nothing. "You both have."

Red eyes.

They'd risen from the dark veils she wore, bobbing and swaying together as they fastened their attention on him. And coldness had seeped into his bones, binding him in place. His feet and legs, his body and arms, his chest grew heavy and prevented him from drawing in breath.

She was weeping beneath him, her sobs pure agony. He'd closed his eyes against her torture. And then, he could not open them.

He'd heard her scream. "No…"

And then he'd opened his eyes and found himself here, with Hades.

"What offense did she commit to…to warrant such a punishment?"

Hades sat back in his chair, "I avoid Olympus, Ariston. I find it taxing more often than not. I know Medusa lay with Poseidon to protect you. When she learned of your death she went to Athena. She quarreled with the Goddess, something few have dared before. And in doing so she let loose Athena's wrath." Hades took a sip of his drink.

"Is there no reprieve?" Ariston asked.

"There is nothing you can do," Hades shook his head. "Perseus comes soon. He will leave a hero and she will be free at last."

He swallowed. "I cannot stand by and let her die…"

Hades stared at him. "You have no choice."

"You cannot…"

Hades rose, his face devoid of any expression. "You would set her free. And soon she shall be. What life would she have, even if the curse was broken? Mayhap Olympus will favor her for all she has endured. She has a part to play in Perseus' tale."

Ariston tried to draw in breath, but his lungs felt tight.

"And with her death, you are free," Hades added.

He turned to the God of the Underworld. "Let me stay."

"The Land of the Dead is for the dead, Ariston." Hades crossed to the fireplace. His brow furrowed as he peered at a wilting bloom pinned on a white satin pillow. He stroked the stem with a hesitant finger and then drew back. "As you want her freedom, she would give you yours."

Ariston's eyes lingered on the flower, recalling the flash of tenderness he'd seen on Hades' face. He had to try once more. "Life and freedom mean nothing without her."

Poseidon watched, anxious for this to be behind him. As was Athena, he thought, and Zeus. Each of them had their own design for the day's impending events.

"He has *some* skill with a sword," Ares sounded skeptical.

"Enough?" Zeus asked.

Ares' brow lifted and he shrugged.

"Have Hermes take this to him." Athena held forth her golden aspis. "To keep him safe and give us eyes. We will see what he sees, hear what he hears."

If Athena grieved for her favorite priestess, Poseidon saw no evidence of it. Perhaps Athena longed to forget Medusa – as he did. Her death would speed the forgetting.

Zeus took the shield, nodding at his daughter. "My thanks, Athena."

"He will have your helmet?" Hera asked. "If he is invisible to her serpents, he will have the advantage."

Hermes nodded. "He will. My helmet and Athena's shield..."

"And this." Zeus handed Hermes a sword, sheathed in a scabbard of gold. "Hephaestus made quick work of it. It will cut clean and true."

Hera smiled. "He will not fail."

So Hera had yet to learn of Perseus' sire? If she had, Poseidon knew she would throw his gifts from Olympus and champion

Medusa.

"And Ariston?" Aphrodite asked.

"He is In-Between," Apollo answered. "Hades has him, for safe keeping I think."

Poseidon wondered at this announcement. Hades vowed never to meddle in the mortal realm. Hades came to Olympus so infrequently because he despised the sport his brethren made of mortals.

"Hades is sheltering Ariston?" Poseidon voiced.

"It astounds you that your brother would find some mercy for the man?" Aphrodite asked. "Have you all forgotten what this man has done? For Greece? And for his wife?"

Hera sighed. "No one has forgotten."

Athena grew still. "He is a hero to Greece. And for that alone do I honor him."

"A true warrior," Ares agreed, "with a warrior's heart."

Poseidon nodded. "He was." He knew so more than any other here. He could find no fault with the man. Though he'd never admit to it.

"How will we honor him?" Aphrodite asked.

Poseidon watched his fellow Olympians.

Zeus spoke, "Go to him, Aphrodite. Give him whatever he wishes."

"One gift?" Aphrodite asked. "One gift for a champion of Greece? One who's given his life twice for his country?"

Ares laughed. "What would you give him?"

Zeus' voice boomed, expressing his irritation. "We have no time for this. Go, Aphrodite, give him two gifts, but nothing more. Hermes, you go to Perseus. His ship will reach the island soon."

Finally, Perseus of Seriphos was here. It was his ship that was tied to the dock, she was sure.

He'd come for her head, though she knew little else about him.

This man, this would-be treasure hunter, was no different from the mighty Heliodoros or wild-eyed Nereus. And yet her companions had seen Heliodoros harden before he'd freed his giant hammer from the strap on his back.

Euryale had great fun smashing his towering figure into sand.

Nereus had given her pause. He moved with predatory grace, smiling as he saw her. She could admire his form, and his confidence. His statue had pitched forward and shattered, unbalanced as he'd been turned mid-run.

But when this ship appeared on the horizon, she'd sent her sisters to Crete, none the wiser. One plea for figs and cheese had so delighted them that they'd been almost giddy when they left.

She'd watched them go, bidding them silent good-byes.

She was glad she was alone. Whatever happened, she would have her sisters free from harm. After all they had done for her, she loved them too dearly to have them harmed.

The candle she lit flickered. A gentle sea breeze teased the flame higher, then near to sputtering out.

She felt strangely calm, even though the air about her pulsed with energy. The Gods had a hand in this, she could feel it.

Every creature on the island must have sensed it as well. The only sound to be heard was the wind.

The dog, Cerberus' spawn, had begun to whimper at midday, when the ship was almost upon them. Now he paced back and forth before the temple's crumbling entrance. His bay, hollow and deep, rose steadily again and again.

"Let him come for me," she whispered.

She rested her hand upon Ariston's head, caressing the angle of his jaw with trembling fingers. He'd been with her, like this, for more than a fortnight now. She would release him, now. "I pray for you, my love, for your freedom. Be happy. Be at peace."

The growls deepened to barking. She stilled, listening.

A man's curses filled the air, followed by the sound of something hitting metal, solidly.

The dog snarled, breaking into a long howl.

Then it whimpered sharply, and fell silent.

Her hand slid from Ariston's face and she backed away, slipping into the shadows that filled her lonely home. She would not make this easy for him, even if the Gods had sent him to kill her.

She pressed herself against the wall. The urge to run gripped her, but the tell-tale rhythmic sway of her companions and the sudden lightness of her head told her running would do no good.

He was inside. The scattering of pebbles upon the flagstones told her as much.

Another sound, faint but audible, caught her ear.

Some steady tapping, rhythmic and wet, pricked the hair along her neck. He must have shifted, she thought, for the sound stopped suddenly.

A stone slid free, rolling towards her across the floor with a resounding racket.

Enough of this, she would see this finished.

"Perseus? Are you Perseus, then?" she asked lightly, testing his nerve. "Are you the boy come to set me free?"

Silence fell.

"I am." His voice was strong, but unsteady.

She laughed, a bittersweet sound. He thought he was brave, did he? "What is it you want with my head? Gold? Power? Or do you wish to be a hero, celebrated by the Gods?"

"No," he mumbled, but his words were lost amongst the clang of metal and stone.

He was nervous, moving without the stealth or skill of a proven warrior.

"No?" She laughed again. "You've made me curious now, brave Perseus. What brings you to hunt such a dangerous trophy?"

She heard his indrawn breath and smiled. He was more than nervous, he was afraid.

"Something you know nothing of, Gorgon. I come in the name of love. For the love of my lady." His voice rang out, echoing off the walls.

His words pierced her calm. She had no words, no witty retort or set-down for this impertinent whelp.

No, she thought, perhaps not so impertinent as naïve and foolish. She would know the truth of the matter. It was fitting that love would end this, for it was the cause of it all.

"Love?" Her voice broke. "Well, then, Perseus, you must heed my directions if you are to take my head without turning yourself into stone. I will have you succeed on your quest...for love."

Silence greeted her announcement. She understood. She would be wary as well.

"And, if the Gods are finally done with me, I might at last find peace in Tartarus...or Hades before this day is through." She laughed sadly, praying she spoke the truth. "Listen closely, boy."

She heard him shift, heard his harsh breathing.

"You come with the Gods' favor?" she asked softly.

He was silent.

"Tell me of your love," she coaxed.

His hesitation was brief. "Andromeda... She will be sacrificed to Poseidon's beast for her mother's treachery."

Medusa's heart was not stone. His voice was full of fear and yearning. She understood. "How will you defeat this monster?"

He cleared his throat, "Your...your head..."

"Will turn the beast to stone?" She encouraged. "And your mother? There is more to your story?"

"How do you know such things?" He was clearly astounded.

"I may be trapped on this island, but I have sisters who love me, boy. They listen and learn all they can – to keep me safe," she explained. "Your mother is being pressured to submit to this Polydectes?"

"She is." His voice was low. "He used this quest to be rid of me, so it seems. My mother, Danae, has fled the city to hide in the temple. And still he tries to press his suit with her."

Anger filled her stomach. "You are an honorable son -- and a devoted lover."

There was not much he could say to her praise.

"Then I ask you again, Perseus, do you have the Gods' favor?"

"I do."

"And have they equipped you with the tools to complete your task?" Her calm amazed her. But she was resigned to her fate – and would hurry it on its way now.

"Zeus' sword, Hades' helmet and Athena's aspis." His words were tight.

She smiled. "Athena's shield? Use it to aim and strike, brave Perseus, for my companions' reflections wield no power. You will be safe...and successful."

His words spilled out in a rush, "Why do you help me?"

"Because I know what it is to lose your love." The anguish in her voice stopped her. She drew in a deep breath and continued with more reserve, "I would not wish such misery on you, not when

I have the power to give you what was taken from me." She paused. "I am done with this life... It is the will of the Gods."

She ignored the slip of the snakes as they stretched forward. They would find the prey they heard, unless she succeeded.

"Set the shield, Perseus, and I will go to it. You will have but a moment, while they are distracted. Be quick, I beg you."

She heard him moving rapidly, no longer worried about stealth or grace.

"It's done." His voice was agitated.

She followed his voice and found the shield, resting at the broken base of one of the temple's columns.

She stared at the shield, fighting a flash of memory. She'd been a child when she'd first looked upon this shield. Athena had stood straight and tall, smiling down at her. And Medusa had been overwhelmed with love for the Goddess.

She shook her head and closed her eyes, kneeling before the shield. Her hands searched the floor, grasping several rocks. She stood and took aim, but paused.

Beyond Perseus shield lay Ariston's statue. His face, forever hardened in a tender admiration, stole her breath. But it was the gentle line of his right arm, still reaching out to cup her cheek, that captured her attention. It ended abruptly.

His arm lay on the ground, separated from the rest.

He was broken.

She swallowed her sob, and tore her eyes from the statue.

She heaved the stone at the shield, the metallic ping reverberating throughout the temple. Her companions twisted, all eyes fixed upon the shield.

Her vision went red, her neck steadied as the serpents readied for the kill.

Had they failed then? Her breath escaped, the sob slipping from her lips.

The cold kiss of steel struck the back of her neck, followed by a searing cut.

Darkness claimed her.

"She cannot cross, Ariston. She will fall," Hades said calmly.

Ariston shook his head. "Fall?" Was there no end to the God's meddling?

"It is the will of the Fates," Hades explained. "Those cursed cannot travel with Charon. No funeral rites are given, so no penance can be made. Even as a shade, their curse follows them. They're to be cursed in the Underworld too. They fall, from grace and favor, into Tartarus."

"Then I will meet her there."

"Are you so eager for eternal pain and suffering?" Hades asked.

"No," he assured him. "But I can find no purpose in any existence without her. I tried and failed."

Hades inclined his head.

"Mayhap I can help," a woman spoke softly, moving from the shadows. "I am Aphrodite, Ariston of Rhodes. Olympus would give you two gifts."

"Let me share Elysium with my wife," he said at once.

Hades regarded Aphrodite. "And the other?"

"That is all I wish." There was nothing else, he knew.

Hades regarded him intently, then beckoned him to the balcony overlooking all of the Underworld. "It can be done, but your trials are not yet over. She will still fall. You will have to catch her. Go to the fields there, and look up. You will see the eye of a storm cloud, churning above. Fire, ice, rain, wind – all will rail against you. Look for the flash, a rift that splits the sky. It is then she falls. If you do not catch her, Ariston, she is lost to you. Even I cannot overrule the Fates."

Ariston nodded, his eyes fixed upon the darkening skies.

Hades urged, "Go now."

Ariston spoke quickly. "Thank you, Goddess. And you, my lord, Hades..."

"You've no time for pretty speeches." Hades waved him away.

But Aphrodite smiled brightly at him.

Ariston nodded and made his way from the hall, Hades' home, and across the bridge separating the massive black castle from the fields. His legs flew, moving towards the darkening clouds overhead. When he reached the field, his eyes turned towards the sky.

The clouds rolled, caught up and twisted by the strong pull of the wind. A clap of thunder shook the field, and the air crackled about him, pulling his hair straight up.

The wind roared hotly about him, scorching his neck and cheeks. His cloak twisted up, choking him. But then it lifted, burned or blown away. And still the heat scoured the inside of his nose and throat as he breathed.

Lightning struck the grass at his feet, splitting the ground wide and singeing the grass before him. He peered over into the dark place beneath, but turned quickly from the sight.

He would catch her. She would spend no time in that wicked place.

The clouds overhead spun, churning at an ever faster speed as a sudden rain fell upon him. Shards of ice followed, pummeling him with such force that he widened his legs to maintain his balance.

His eyes turned back to the skies, and he waited.

Then he saw her.

Her hair was a streak of gold, hurtling from the rift in the clouds straight towards the jagged hole at his feet. He braced himself against the edge, tensing his arms. The frozen rain beat on, and still he waited.

He blinked the rain from his eyes and reached for her.

The wind shifted, pushing against him when he would reach her. Her body, carried by the wind, landed in his arms with a mighty force – knocking them away from the hole and across the field.

He gasped, sucking in breath as the air fell still about him.

Ariston's arms were heavy, full.

His hands formed against the curve of her back, clasping her softness with trembling hands. He sat forward, cradling her in his lap and pressing his face into her hair. The silken softness of her honeyed locks slipped against his cheek. Her scent tickled his nose, making him press her to him fiercely.

He was shaking, overcome.

He opened his eyes.

Her eyes were closed as she lay in his arms.

His hand moved over her face, brushing her hair – her glorious hair – back. Her cheeks were pink, her skin perfect. No scars or marks of the serpents remained.

He pulled her close again, nuzzling her neck with his nose.

He pressed a kiss to her forehead, her nose and then her lips.

They were soft, velvet, beneath his. And they parted, her breath mingling with his as his hold tightened upon her.

"Ariston?" Her voice filled his ears.

"I'm here," he whispered against her lips.

She returned his kisses, eagerly. Her hands twined about his neck as she clung to him. Then she sighed, sounding pleased, and burrowed against his chest.

He pulled back, soaking in the sight of her.

Her huge blue eyes fluttered open, dismayed. She stared at him, disoriented. "Am I dreaming?" she asked as her eyes traveled over his face. She raised a hand, her delicate white hand, and placed it upon his cheek.

He shook his head.

"You feel warm and solid beneath my touch," she murmured, caressing his mouth with her thumb.

Her brow furrowed then, and her hand fell to her hair. She tensed in his arms, turning wide eyes upon him.

"This is no dream." His hands cupped her face gently, his words soft. "You've come back to me."

Her hand lifted slowly, stroking her neck with trembling fingers. She blinked, then took his right wrist and pressed it to her chest. She kissed his wrist, her breath hitching as she asked, "Are we..." Her eyes filled with tears, but she smiled as she looked at him. "Are we in Hades' realm?"

His hand stroked over her face again, tracing her lips. "We go to Elysium, wife. We are home."

"Forgive me," she murmured, her words a plea that seared his heart.

He shook his head, pressing his lips to her. "There is nothing to forgive, lady. I beg you leave it behind."

He felt her arms slip about him as she pressed herself against him. He could not fit her close enough to him, could not stop himself from crushing her against him.

But she seemed little bothered by his unyielding hold.

"Let us stay this way," she whispered against his throat, "until I know you are real. I cannot let you go."

He inhaled at her temple, pressing a kiss to her brow. "I will hold you until you are done."

She laughed, a sweet, free sound that surprised them both. "Then you will never let me go, husband."

He laughed too, his hand cupping her cheek with tenderness. "No, wife, I will never let you go."

Epilogue

Poseidon tore his eyes from Aphrodite. All were held captive by her tale, for her telling of Ariston and Medusa's reunion was magical. He cursed the pull he felt upon his heart.

"She is reunited with her husband." Hera wiped tears from her cheeks.

"She has found peace," Aphrodite murmured. "And all are satisfied."

"What of Hades? His mood of late is most perplexing. Is he content to lose Ariston in such a way?" Zeus asked.

Aphrodite nodded, but said nothing.

Poseidon felt less than satisfied. In fact, he felt an emptiness closing in on him.

"The Gorgons wail yet." Apollo shook his head.

"Let them wail," Athena spoke finally, her face ashen from Aphrodite's tale. "I would have a satyr pipe made to mimic their cries. I can think of no better way to remind us to act with care." She turned angry eyes upon Poseidon, speaking to him as if they were the only ones in the Council Chamber. "Mortals are fragile creatures and we must treat them as such."

Poseidon lifted an eyebrow. Did she think to chastise him? Even now? He smiled.

"It shall be done," Zeus agreed. "And I would place Perseus and Medusa in the stars."

Hera's brow arched. "Truly?"

"Is it not enough that her image is now etched onto Athena's shield?" Ares groaned, impatience written upon his hard face.

"Must we see her in the stars as well?" Poseidon seconded Ares' irritation.

"You sound like a jealous child," Hera laughed.

Athena goaded, "What, Poseidon, has losing Medusa left you without sport?"

"I've no doubt you'll find some poor maid to tempt your appetites soon enough," Apollo smiled.

"Why am I blamed for all mischief?" he asked innocently.

"Because you have a hand in most," Zeus said.

Poseidon laughed.

He glanced at Aphrodite. How she turned from him with downcast eyes. Mischief had been made already, in the gardens of Olympus. Though Hephaestus could not bed his wife, he would hardly be pleased when his wife bore Poseidon a son.

The thought brought a slow smile to his face.

"Zeus!" Demeter burst into the Council Chamber, her face lined with tears. Never had Poseidon seen the Goddess so undone, so shaken. He rose, waiting to hear what Demeter had to say. "Persephone is gone...taken I fear."

Zeus rose swiftly. "Taken? When?"

"She was in Sicily, collecting her flowers...white lilies." Demeter took the hand Hera offered, her voice shaking with fear. "And then she was gone... I was not with her, but the nymphs told me they heard her scream."

Zeus' brow furrowed, a dangerous sign, Poseidon knew.

"Apollo," Zeus said quickly, "Hermes, find her."

The women crowded about Demeter, offering words of comfort.

Poseidon stood, offering, "I will search as well."

But Zeus was distracted, lost in thought.

"Brother, I will ..."

Zeus shook his head stiffly. "Leave matters be," he whispered.

Poseidon turned a questioning gaze upon his brother.

"Fair Persephone will return to us, in time," Zeus said, turning from the women and leading Poseidon from the Council Chamber.

"You know where she is then?"

Zeus smiled, shrugging. "Perhaps Aphrodite will have another tale to spin before the moon is full. We shall see, brother, we shall see."

Sasha Summers

Sasha is part gypsy. Her passions have always been storytelling, romance, history, and travel. Her first play was written for her Girl Scout troupe. She's been writing ever since. She loves getting lost in the worlds and characters she creates; even if she frequently forgets to run the dishwasher or wash socks when she's doing so. Luckily, her four brilliant children and hero-inspiring hubby are super understanding and supportive.

Sasha can be found online at sashasummers.com.

Acknowledgements

Thanks to Angelyn Schmid, Sandy Williams, Carolyn Williamson, Deidra Alexander, Suzanne Collins and Allison Burke-Collins (aka Shakers) for your tireless support, zeal with a red pen, and ability to talk me out of giving up. Thanks to D.A.R.A. and S.A.R.A for turning dreamers into writers. Gretchen Craig, your input was invaluable. To Donna O'Brien for loving my novel and Candice Lindstrom for your seamless edits. And to Liliana Hart and Club Indie for inspiring me to go Indie with my Olympus books! Here goes nothing...

Very special thanks to Summer, Emma, Jakob and Kaleb for nurturing my imagination and stories every single day. Your patience and love means more to me than you can ever know.

Glossary Terms & Reference Index

Anestheria – a Greek Festival celebrating Dionysus. In the book, aspects were modified to help the storyline.

Arrephoroi – young girls (7-11 yrs) selected to serve as acolytes in the temples.

Aspis – circular shield carried by infantryman. Weighing 17-30lbs and one meter across, this shield could protect a soldier from chin to knee. It was typically made from wood and covered in metal/bronze. Held by a handle in its center, the shields could be placed together in an overlapping scale-like pattern (a phalanx) to hold off attackers.

Athena Polias, the Temple of – Athena's temple on Acropolis that preceded the Parthenon.

Basileus – leader of chieftain of a family, the head of the household

Chiton – men's tunic of lightweight fabric

Chlamys – a short cloak, worn by men and women, made from one seamless piece of material

Doru – a spear, 7-9 feet long, used by the Greek infantrymen

Ekdromos/Ekdromoi – skilled infantrymen used for special missions or close combat

Epiblema – a woman's shawl

Hedna – gifts given to a girl's family by her suitor or betrothed

Himation – thick cloak. Large enough to be used as a blanket or folded into a pillow

Hoplite – Greek infantrymen

Kleros – a plot of land passed down through the family. A man cannot marry without having a kleros.

Linothorax – armor worn by more military leaders or affluent soldiers. Made of thick padded leather, fabric covered in metal scales of metal – depending upon the soldier's ability to pay. Not all soldiers could afford armor.

Oikos – the household – not the house itself but the property, livestock, family and slaves

Peplos – a full length tunic worn by women, usually made from one large piece of fabric to be pinned, sewn or draped.

Peltasts & *Psiloi* – foot soldiers without extensive training

Salamis, the Battle of –The straits of Salamis are a narrow water channel. The Greeks did lure the Persians here, trap them and defeat them.

Shades – souls or ghosts

Strategoi – ten generals chosen from ten Greek tribes

Themistocles – Athenian statesman responsible for creating Athens' fleet of triremes.

Thermopylae, the Battle of – the battle fought by King Leonidas and his soldiers (Spartans/Spartiates) against the invading Persians. While there is much conjecture as to how many Leonidas had with him (300, 1000, 3000?), he and his troops were significantly outnumbered and still managed to last days against their Persian foe. This battle caused outrage across Greece, building strong anti-Persian sentiment and prompting them to take evasive measures.

Trireme – a ship, propelled by three rows of oars, possibly 25 or more oars, on each side.

Xiphos – soldier's short sword used as a secondary weapon to the spear/doru.

Levels of the Underworld:

Elysium or Elysian Fields – reserved for heroes or special mortals, this was 'Heaven' to the Greeks.

Asphodel Fields – Most occupied level of the Underworld, it was neutral – shades that came here had neither good nor bad

Tartarus – Feared by all, this was 'Hell' to the Greeks.

Rivers into the Underworld:

River Acheron – River of Woe

Lethe River – River of Forgetfulness

The River Styx – River of Hate

Pyriphlegethon – River of Fire

Cocytus River – River of Wailing

Sneak Peek: For the Love of Hades

The Loves of Olympus, 2

Hades glanced at the lily propped atop the mantle. The blossom was bright white against the black silk to which it was pinned, light against the darkness. He reached up, tracing one petal with an unsteady finger. He saw the tremor, cursed it, and clenched his hand, drawing back from the flower as if it had burned him.

Turning abruptly from the fire, he made his way to his chair and sat heavily. There was a sweetness to his burden, but it was no less a burden.

He leaned forward, rested his elbows on his knees and covered his face with his hands.

What had he done? How could he make amends now that his heinous act had been hidden so long? Using his powers to aid a mortal would seem trivial in comparison with the offense he'd committed against Demeter. Against Olympus.

And yet, he felt whole.

The raw emptiness that he'd held at bay, for nigh on an eternity, no longer threatened to consume him. Having her here, with her constant laughter and endless conversation, had changed his world irrevocably.

If not for her, he would have remained bitter and angry. He would not have interfered at Cypress. He would never have thought to champion the mortal, Ariston...

"My lord." Her soft voice interrupted his thoughts.

He lifted his head from his hands, surprised.

Persephone stood, beauty to behold, watching him with wide green eyes. In the blazing firelight her hair glowed copper, warm and rich. Her face, normally alight with smiles and laughter, was drawn. Was she not fully recovered? Or did the tension between them tire her as well?

His voice revealed nothing. "Persephone."

Her steps were cautious, but she made her way to him. "Aphrodite?"

So she had seen Aphrodite. "Has gone." And she should have gone with her fellow Olympian. He should have insisted she do so. He swallowed against the lump in his throat, ignoring the tightening in his chest.

"I thought as much." She stood so close he could see the front of her tunic. The fabric trembled, thundering in time with the rapid beat of her heart.

Was she disappointed? Was she ready to leave him… his realm?

She should go. She should have gone weeks ago. He knew it was right. Yet knowing it did nothing to soothe his agitation. He clutched the arms of his throne, clinging to control.

"I've not asked you for anything in my time here." She paused. "Have I?"

He shook his head once. No, she'd seemed happy, though he had little knowledge of true happiness, he supposed. His gaze found shadows beneath her eyes and a tightness about her mouth. He was a blind fool.

Have you been miserable? He could not ask the words aloud, fearing her answer.

Her voice was no steadier than her pulse. "Nor would I trouble you now, if my need were not so great."

"What is it?" he asked. His voice sounded harsh to his own ears.

She sank to her knees, glancing at him with an almost timid gaze. Her hands lifted, wavered, and covered his hands. He stiffened, stunned by her actions. She touched him… He swallowed. The feel of her hands upon him squeezed the air from his lungs.

"Show me mercy. Show me the same mercy you've bestowed upon the mortal… the soldier Ariston." Her hands clasped his tightly.

He would not reach for her, he could not. No matter how he might want to.

"Have I been cruel, that you feel the need to beg for anything from me?" His words were a harsh whisper. She shook her head and he continued, "Then why do you kneel before me?"

"It is a selfish request, one that may turn you from solicitous to," she paused, her cheeks growing red, "... sickened."

Was it possible for him to feel so towards her?

He stared at her hands, wrapped about his. He would not meet her gaze. He would not reveal his damnable weakness to her. He could not risk losing himself in the fathomless depths of her green eyes. "Ask me," he murmured as his traitorous eyes sought hers.

She drew in a wavering breath, ragged and labored. Her whispered words were thick. "My lover... Release him. Release the man who loves me, please." Her eyes sparkled, mesmerizing him while his heart, so newly discovered, seemed to shudder to a stop once more.

CPSIA information can be obtained at www.ICGtesting.com
Printed in the USA
BVOW06s1918200116

433666BV00013B/172/P

9 781515 011897